LOST WORLD II

THE END OF THE THIRD WORLD

Other Avon Books by
Marcio Souza

DEATH SQUEEZE
MAD MARIA

Avon Books are available at special quantity discounts for bulk purchases for sales promotions, premiums, fund raising or educational use. Special books, or book excerpts, can also be created to fit specific needs.

For details write or telephone the office of the Director of Special Markets, Avon Books, Dept. FP, 1350 Avenue of the Americas, New York, New York 10019, 1-800-238-0658.

LOST WORLD II

THE END OF THE THIRD WORLD

MÁRCIO SOUZA

Translated by Lana Santamaria

AVON BOOKS • NEW YORK

If you purchased this book without a cover, you should be aware that this book is stolen property. It was reported as "unsold and destroyed" to the publisher, and neither the author nor the publisher has received any payment for this "stripped book."

LOST WORLD II: THE END OF THE THIRD WORLD is an original publication of Avon Books. This work is a novel. Any similarity to actual persons or events is purely coincidental.

Originally published as *O Fim Do Terceiro Mundo* by Marco Zero Ltda., São Paulo, Brazil.

AVON BOOKS
A division of
The Hearst Corporation
1350 Avenue of the Americas
New York, New York 10019

Copyright © 1990 by Marcio Souza
Cover illustration by Richard Bober
Published by arrangement with the author
Library of Congress Catalog Card Number: 92-97476
ISBN: 0-380-89829-2

All rights reserved, which includes the right to reproduce this book or portions thereof in any form whatsoever except as provided by the U.S. Copyright Law. For information address Thomas Colchie Associates, 324 85th Street, New York, New York 11209.

First Avon Books Trade Printing: July 1993

AVON TRADEMARK REG. U.S. PAT. OFF. AND IN OTHER COUNTRIES, MARCA REGISTRADA, HECHO EN U.S.A.

Printed in the U.S.A.

OPM 10 9 8 7 6 5 4 3 2 1

Contents

Book One: One Hundred Degrees in the Shade

On the Unusual Habits of Writers	3
Where Is Maple White?	17
Is It Still Possible To Be a Hero in Today's World?	33
Never Risk Your Neck for an Economic Anachronism	45
The Most Amazing Thing in the World	69

Book Two: Between the Gotha and Erfurt Train Stations

What Is Left to Prove?	93
Tomorrow We Will Disappear into the Unknown	111

Book Three: Endangered Species

The Remote Frontiers of the New World	147
Who Could Have Known?	170

CONTENTS

The Most Marvelous Things Happened   183
A Sometime Hero   204
It Was Horrible in the Forest   224
An Unforgettable Vision   250
It Was Horrible in the Forest (Repeat)   270

Book Four: Cucarachopitecus Tragicus

On the Unusual Habits of Writers (Repeat)   277
Take a Chance on Miss Challenger   294

Book Five: Megathere Country

Elementary, My Dear Sir Delamare   303
What Was That?   322
What Was That Again?   329
The Jihad Jívaros Effect   342

Book One

One Hundred Degrees in the Shade

On the Unusual Habits of Writers

It all began when a journalist wanted to know what I was writing. To ask a writer what he is working on is almost as common as asking a politician what he is not working on. I accept this curiosity as a perfectly natural manifestation, even complimentary. These days, wanting to know about a particular writer's new book beforehand is still one of the few inoffensive things that remain for us in this troubled world. For this reason, when I find myself in front of a curious reader, I never get upset or even become sarcastic.

But I hasten to say that my attitude is quite personal and ought not to be generalized, since there are writers, some of them well known, who react in very diverse ways. Certain daring readers have already paid bitterly for their audacity. In the past, great writers became notable for the manner in which they confronted this question. Petronio, of *Satiricon* fame, would grab the curious one by the arm and relate his project with so many details and so completely that the intrepid fellow would immediately regret his boldness. Petronio's halitosis was well known in Rome. Balzac, who experienced so many financial difficulties that he very well could have been born in Brazil, when queried on his next book, would ask right off for an advance of money in order to describe his forthcoming work. Dostoyevski, with a financial situation no less complicated, when he didn't react with an epileptic fit, would remain silent.

LOST WORLD II

Among all of them, the most pitiful case is that of Juan Sender. Sender is a Chilean author whom I met in a literary conference in Bulgaria. He lives in exile in Barcelona, and on a day-to-day basis he is a good and sensible man. But no one should dare ask him about his next book. The timid and quiet Juan goes berserk; he literally becomes a wild beast. And he bites. It is obvious that this irrepressible attitude has caused him much vexation. As if it weren't enough to bear a bitter and long exile, Sender has his meager authorial earnings constantly consumed by huge legal fees, sizable court costs, and startling hospital bills.

Since, as a matter of professional etiquette, I avoid asking my colleagues questions of this nature, our friendship prospered in the midst of the festive Bulgarian Conference, overflowing with red wine, yogurt, and real socialism. I heard his sad story in his own words, and the list of bold interrogators was not a short one, an evident demonstration that human curiosity is in itself as extravagant as the idiosyncrasies of a writer. Without counting the outbursts that preceded his exile, in a little less than an hour, he enumerated a succession of lacerations of ears, cheeks, fingers, ankles, knees, etc., not without elaborate statistics—since he is a methodical man—in which his victims were grouped in percentages of round figures according to their profession, sex, and nationality.

It's a pity that I can't reproduce here the complexity of his statistics, but some details jump right out, so to speak. For example, the largest group seemed to be television interviewers; in second place were professors of Latin American literature, and in third, Chilean tourists. Juan Sender's worldwide fame was assured after his disastrous participation in the 1984 Frankfurt Book Fair, when he nearly won the dubious

THE END OF THE THIRD WORLD

honor of a listing in the *Guinness Books of Records*.

Sender is a tall, slender man, a figure out of an El Greco painting. In a photo taken in the party that brought to a close the Bulgarian Conference, he stands out easily from the rest of the group because he is between a Vietnamese poet and an Afghani literary critic. That night, after a few glasses of wine, he confessed to me his greatest bitterness. It wasn't so much the monetary cost of his problem that vexed him but the fact that it limited his contact with editors. Indeed, because one of the peculiarities of editors is exactly that they are always asking their authors, almost as a duty of their calling, about their next book. This is why only one of Sender's books had been published in his mother tongue. The others—and this isn't exactly easy to understand—had appeared only in Serbo-Croatian and Urdu. Beautiful editions, let it be said in passing, and quite successful, even though Sender's novels always deal with extremely nebulous regional matters and are constructed with torturous passages similar to those of the sixteenth-century Spanish poet Luis Gongora, if you know what I mean.

"Do you know why this happens to me?" he asked me with a rather sad smile that revealed his perfect teeth.

"No, I don't know," I responded, keeping a prudent distance.

"It's just that a novel that an author can summarize in a simple conversation isn't worth writing."

As a matter of fact, my poor friend could never summarize one of his complicated stories without first reaching a paroxysm. This isn't exactly my case. My books, in general, not only can be summarized in a simple and rapid interview, but they have often been rearranged and slaughtered in twenty lines by certain individuals as candidly enthusiastic as the victims of my illustrious Chilean colleague.

LOST WORLD II

And so, without so much as a quiver of a psychological nature, when asked about my next book, I didn't frustrate the journalist's curiosity. I lied, of course, but this is part of the rules of the game. I wasn't writing anything at the time, but to tell the truth would have been just as aggressive as sinking my teeth into the tender ear of that young man who had so recently finished his course in communications and landed a job in the arts section of the local newspaper.

"Right now," I said, with the jovial tone I use to speak with reporters of the arts section, "I'm working on a novel that will be entitled *The Lost World, Part II*."

"Part II?"

"Yes, the first part was published in 1912."

"In 1912!" he exclaimed, puzzled and making a nervous search on the photocopied sheet supplied to him by the paper's research department, a futile effort since the unexpected title had apparently been omitted from the bibliography.

"But I wasn't the one who wrote the first part," I hastened to confess. The young man couldn't have been more than twenty-five years old, and right away he regained his composure, abandoning the frightened way he looked at me, as if I were a gerontological miracle. "In fact, it was Conan Doyle who wrote it."

"? . . ." There was no irony in his reaction, only innocence and anticipation.

"Sir Arthur Conan Doyle."

"Huh?"

"The creator of Sherlock Holmes."

"Ah, sure!" he exclaimed with the ardor of one who recognizes something familiar in a strange landscape.

"It seems that Conan Doyle wrote the book in order to play a joke on his evolutionist friends, like H. G.

THE END OF THE THIRD WORLD

Wells and Huxley," I said, "but I don't have the same intentions with the sequel that I am planning to do of his book. After all, the only evolutionist I ever knew was my professor Gioconda Mussolini, at the University of Sao Paulo, who has already disappeared, victimized by the natural selection put to practice here in Brazil by the military. My book is going to be much simpler."

The reporter was now listening to me with a studied neutrality; interviews are never really dialogues, rather a stage where we dabble about in the half-light, a simulation of conversation, evasive like an echo that drifts away. Out of the corner of my eye, I observed him, wielding the pen with which he intended to capture my words, zealous in this deceptive chain of power to which he believed he belonged. As for me, like a silhouette more somber than darkness itself, I was little by little able to get my idea across.

"In Conan Doyle's novel," I went on, "Professor Challenger, a short, muscular English zoologist, who loved to sock journalists, makes a trip to the Amazon. There on the upper Negro River, he finds a plateau where evolution has remained stationary since the Jurassic period. The place is rather inaccessible, and on his return, the few concrete proofs that he had are lost in an accident. The only two things that he has left are his notebook and a dried wing of a pterodactyl.

"Of course, in London no one takes him seriously; the press begins to ridicule his claims, the scientists say that the wing is nothing more than a falsification (the English are experts in fossil falsification), and the professor shuts himself up in his mansion. Finally he is challenged by a colleague, Professor Summerless, and as a result, an expedition is organized. They leave from Southampton for Manaus, on the Transatlantic Booth Line, and from

LOST WORLD II

Manaus, they go up the Negro River to the so-called plateau. In brief, everything that the professor claimed was really there. Dinosaurs, brontosaurus, diplodocus, iguanodons, even a herd of hominids, all for the purpose of saving British face.

"All right, in my sequel, Professor Challenger's granddaughter appears, a short and petulant Englishwoman who works for a financial magazine designed for yuppies. After covering the closing session of a meeting of the wealthy nations in Geneva, bored to death, she enters a travel agency and buys a ticket for the furthermost spot she can get to for a weekend trip. She winds up in Manaus, lodged in the Tropical Hotel, where she has three days of unusual adventures.

"Returning to London, she takes advantage of the staff meeting to make a tremendous revelation. She announces that in South America, in Brazil, in the city of Manaus, she discovered that there still exist—and reasonably healthy and well fed—species of capitalists considered extinct in England since the eighteenth century. Her colleagues burst out laughing, and her closest friend, being of a Marxist orientation, explains to her that this is impossible, that Brazil, with all of its problems, has had significant advances in its means of production and in its production relations.

"But she isn't the kind of person to become discouraged; she insists, fights, even manages to convince the magazine's editor of the importance of her discovery. A team of reporters is sent to Manaus, and once again the Britannic skepticism is forced to bow when confronted with the eccentricities of an exotic region and Challenger's testimony. Naturally they are not pursued by hungry dinosaurs or aggressive pterodactyls, but there is a collection of live fossils of another kind just as ferocious as the former species.

THE END OF THE THIRD WORLD

"She discovered that there still exist—reasonably healthy and well fed, species of capitalists considered extinct in England since the eighteenth century."

You can imagine, there I was, trying to please a reporter, irresponsibly throwing a young Brit to the Amazonian rigors, which reminds me of a friend of mine, also an Englishwoman, who spent a few months in Manaus. Her name was Ellen; she was an anthropologist and supposedly should have been prepared to face conditions much more precarious than the heat of that city. When we met she was confined to a bed in the Tropical Diseases Hospital, confined under the suspicion of having malaria. It wasn't malaria, only a virus contracted while still in the airport.

Sweet Ellen, as a less than subtle parasitologist would observe later, had a metabolism that was irresistible to the local viruses. She was transformed into a major attraction of the Tropical Diseases Hospital, where she remained during her entire stay in Manaus, visited ceremoniously by the Honorary Consul of England, Mr. Varney, an orchid exporter, and by the fifth-year medical students who used her as a live compendium of parasitology.

Because of this experience, and understandably so, she would be a different person when she left the hospital. She left Manaus forever, abandoned anthropology, and resolved—in her own words—"to find her niche." She is currently playing the trumpet and performing in a naturalist restaurant in the West End; however, the viruses didn't entirely corrode her combative spirit. Once a month she joins a group picketing in front of the Brazilian Embassy, protesting the reduction of the ozone layer prompted by the burning of the Amazon forest.

Ellen is living proof of the transcendental experience that the Amazon region can be.

LOST WORLD II

And so, how could one predict Miss Challenger's destiny?

My dear friend Peter Schneider, a writer from Berlin, made the foolish mistake of visiting Manaus in the middle of August. I happened to find him overcome by the heat, leaning against a wall in the shade of one of the last fig trees remaining of the old city arbor. Peter was panting like a Germanic barbarian after a fight with Roman centurions in the garrison of Reno. There is an Amazonian saying that says that at noon in the streets of Manaus, one only finds dogs and Germans. I confess that I never understood this saying, as enigmatic as the rest of the local folk wisdom. The truth is that at noon not even the lowliest mutt would dare set foot out of the shade where it found asylum; nor, for that matter, would a German from Stuttgart risk abandoning the comfort of air-conditioning in order to roast in the sun.

My friend Peter, who isn't from Stuttgart, never managed to walk more than a few meters in any direction in Manaus without his body protesting with dizziness and torrents of sweat. His image of the city was blurry at the least. The violent light hardly left space in his mind for contrasts, and the impression that he had, as a result, was of a wavy landscape, most likely an effect of the constant evaporation and the sensation of lassitude which he had never before experienced, where every movement was a physical effort and even the act of thinking was painful.

When, some time later, we met again in his house in Berlin, he insisted that I explain how someone could write in Manaus, since the brain, seemingly struggling to keep from boiling in the intense heat, appeared to have difficulties achieving even the most elementary synapses. In order to pacify him, I explained that the natives were perfectly adapted to the climate. The mysteries of natural

THE END OF THE THIRD WORLD

selection, I argued. But he couldn't contain his horror when he heard me describe how every day I would sit down at the typewriter, wearing only a pair of Bermuda shorts, and in the same proportion that my body would dehydrate, I would produce my novels. Since that day he began to regard me with the same respect that we tend to give to lunatics and eccentrics.

And Peter had every right to do so, because Manaus is an eccentric city, fruit of an eccentric project and inhabited by an eccentric people. The heat, to be sure, is a fundamental ingredient of this eccentricity, because as it cooks our brains, it makes each inhabitant of Manaus a peculiar character, one who never wastes energy reasoning and is happy with the low voltage of the most primitive instinctive reflexes, a rather reptilian attitude in a city that has the atmosphere of a great and decadent saurian creature near extinction.

In fact, the heat is terrible. It's not that the city experiences high temperatures, like the summers in Rio de Janeiro where 120 degrees Fahrenheit in the shade is commonplace in the months of February and March. The problem isn't the unusually high temperature; it is its persistence combined with the high humidity. It is ninety degrees almost all day long and throughout the whole year. At dawn there's not so much as a fresh morning breeze; we wake up sweating because it's already ninety degrees and holding. In the early hours of the morning, the town sleeps and the Bohemians drink—and how they drink there—without a trace of the sweet vagabond breezes of sleepless nights because the ninety degrees won't let up, not even for a little Bohemianism.

For people like Miss Challenger, who live in temperate climates, with wide and well-defined temperature variations, the effects of this persistent heat are usually devastating. Now, add to this constant condition the

LOST WORLD II

high humidity count. In the equatorial zone this count reaches almost ninety-five percent. It's like breathing underwater. The humidity in the air and the recalcitrant heat create a strange consortium, to say the least, and the city of Manaus, for this reason, has a certain Devonian atmosphere more appropriate for the metabolism of the great reptiles than the warm blood of the higher primates. Many times this stove effect has made me imagine that the planet Venus will one day be colonized by Amazonian astronauts, the only beings suited for such an adventure.

The problem is that the effect of the heat on certain metabolism isn't exactly temporary. Euclides da Cunha, for example, the celebrated nineteenth-century author, an ultrasensitive man, immediately realized that the heat of Manaus was an ideal ecosystem for palm trees. But as far as human beings are concerned, well, allowing themselves to be exposed to the heat of Manaus could have unexpected results. The author himself, even though he was comfortably lodged in a beautiful house in Adrianópolis, a pleasant neighborhood, apparently suffered irreparable harm. Upon his return to Rio, his behavior never again appeared to be guided by a brain in perfect running order, which eventually led him to the homicide attempt that cost him his life.

That was some time after he had noted the extravagant reality of Manaus, its surprising urban contrasts, the mansions and small art nouveau palaces beside shacks built on unsteady stilts, the human parade in the streets that placed haughty Englishmen and hurried Yanks beside Indians in rags and coarse Northeasterners. Whatever it was that he wanted to say with all that, Euclides da Cunha's rapid brushstrokes described a city that exalted ambition at every street corner and sought fast wealth, a city of nervous rhythm whose inhabitants

THE END OF THE THIRD WORLD

seemed to lead a provisionary life that left them little time for reflection on their own municipality. Much of what this tragic and celebrated author wrote about Manaus is still entirely pertinent.

Almost twenty years later, another visitor wandered through the streets of Manaus and confronted the heat with a good dose of sarcasm, which apparently saved him from any aftereffects upon his departure. The visitor was the poet Mario de Andrade, a cool character by nature, who, going from one banquet to another, still found time to converse with the local intellectuals and make note of a certain lack of coordination between the urban planning project, which was typical of the turn of the century, and the stingy proportions of the same project.

He wasn't bothered much by the heat; it certainly didn't stop him from constantly taking jabs at the city's "backward" intellectuals. Mario de Andrade was offended by Manaus's architecture, with its pretentiously art nouveau solemnity that in reality was merely ostentation, without the grandiosity of the European originals that they had wanted to imitate; as if those avenues, plazas, and palaces had been flattened, miniaturized, squashed, by some perverse equatorial timidity or, he didn't know exactly, by some Turkish bath syndrome that shrinks and diminishes everything. But if the poet didn't suffer from the torridity, the trip wasn't without its consequences, since it was there in the Manaus heat that he conceived of the synthesis of the Brazilian: the total absence of character.

It is true that these were very different men, but each of them experienced something of importance there. Da Cunha suffered from the climate, as only he could suffer; on the other hand, there is the chuckle and the ironic point of view of the poet Mario de Andrade. But just

LOST WORLD II

between us, while no one else is around, I believe that in Manaus the suffocating heat and the lack of character, so nouveau riche in its own way, are two virtues that only an Amazonian could detect. I doubt that a little Englishwoman with her turned-up nose could comprehend these things.

With its disagreeable climate, Manaus is far from being a healthy city. Quite to the contrary, the Amazonian capital is much more apt to corrupt. And this is its attraction, because nothing is more placid and dreadful than the hygienic atmosphere of certain cities with their clean air and temperate climate, with their consumptive and pale tourists bathing in sulfurous and medicinal waters. Manaus is exactly the opposite of this; it is a city where one contracts a disease rather than gets cured of one. And although the heat, along with inviting inelegance, requires bathing, a lot of bathing, one is not going to find crystalline waters, rather the cool foam of the narrow straits or the dark waters of the Negro River, warm like placenta. They are waters that cure nothing; instead they awaken a primeval euphoria that must have been felt at the dawn of time by the first creature that abandoned the sea and tested land millions of years ago.

I have the impression that as soon as Miss Challenger arrived in the city, she concluded that the heat was responsible for the manic-depressive and insipid eccentricity of its inhabitants; though this isn't entirely true, the heat has weight, thickness, and volume, making time flow with a maddening slowness, as if one were swimming in a primal soup that constantly synthesized the humidity, over a constant and unabated temperature. I know that there was one Englishman who didn't find this the case. It was the naturalist Wallace, a man so extravagantly peculiar that he called that

THE END OF THE THIRD WORLD

furnace a romantic country. Which just proves that no one has a patent on eccentricity. But eccentricity aside, my heroine Miss Challenger wasn't a descendant of Wallace but of Professor Challenger, a man who would have thought it as absurd to call the Amazon romantic as it was to find intelligence in the average Londoner.

But now that I think about it, none of this has anything to do with the story. These unlucky gentlemen were there a long time ago, before chartered flights and five-star hotels. More than likely, my heroine hardly feels the climate, going from one air-conditioned establishment to another. Taking care to avoid any possible prolonged exposure to the hostile atmosphere. In addition, it is almost certain that Miss Challenger would not at all like, shall we say, the informality of the place, and would have limited herself to those observations of an objective reporter. Moreover, if she detested the city, it wouldn't be the first time, because Manaus, as we have seen, isn't exactly the kind of place that is capable of leaving a good impression. Even I, if I weren't a native with a great deal of acclimatizing fortitude, really would have preferred that my ancestors had been impervious to the fascination of America, or at least with a certain criterion when it came to latitudes. Yes, because writers have the uncommon habit of being born in any kind of city, including Manaus.

As far as I'm concerned, it is merely my birthplace, even though I write this line with certain hesitation, because although there are only three kinds of relationships between people and their birthplaces—love, hatred, and indifference—Manaus isn't exactly a city that fits any one of these three emotions, or all three of them at once for that matter, much less in the self-serving explanation that it is my birthplace. Especially this Manaus of today that

LOST WORLD II

seems like a symbiosis of Miami and an open-air market in Calcutta.

This Manaus only interests those simpletons who go there to enjoy the delights of consumerism, in search of the latest electronic gadgets. This isn't the case with Miss Challenger, because she would soon realize that this is the exotic side of the city; nothing is more exotic than a shop filled with electronic items in the middle of the magnificent Amazon forest, a privileged atmosphere for the preservation of all kinds of economic fossils. But if this city—which was born under the sign of the second industrial revolution, just to see itself transformed by decree into a platform for exportation—seems to have lost its direction, swollen by internal migration and scorned by successive mediocre and plundering public administrations; it is still like a melting pot of strange social alchemies. Anyone visiting Manaus, searching for something more than a simple videocassette recorder, will find it's a city that can be used for one's own ends.

When it was a great city, in the bygone years of the rubber boom, Manaus was known as the most remote capital of Christendom. Not anymore; one can arrive and escape from the city on any of the numerous daily flights that tie it to the four corners of the world. For its inhabitants, perhaps a certain psychological isolation remains, which is actually more a dread of confronting the role that it came to occupy in the national context than a real problem. But for the visitors, the sense of isolation turns out to be something unexpectedly revealing, because Manaus is like a microcosm of the nation, a variation of its future that is stagnating in the past.

Who knows if this won't be the Amazonia that interests Miss Challenger after all?

Where Is Maple White?

The truth is that I didn't pay much attention to the consequences of that interview. And I had almost forgotten about Miss Challenger when one day, still living in my home in the endless lands, I was sought out by an English reporter. To be sought out by foreign reporters wasn't a novelty. Whoever dares live in Manaus knows that these things happen. There is always some adventurer snooping around there for some reason.

These international crews, be they from TV networks, newspapers, or universities, continually came through Manaus. And they always wound up at my house. They arrived as if they were under the influence of . . . of what? Of the smell of the place? The heat? Perhaps the whiskey that some of them carried in quarter-liter flasks. But also the effects of the garish colors, blazing out from the poor neighborhoods, the sinuous rhythm of the loud music, and the languor of the brown-skinned people, guardians of the latest mysteries. Without any apparent reason, feeling a sensation of abrupt alienation, I saw myself as a foreigner as well. I wanted to lose myself in the streets of Manaus, to observe the city with the same foreignness that those green or blue eyes do, with the beards of the old explorers, handmade sandals and leather bags, contrasting with their expensive photographic equipment.

But there must be something decidedly elusive in the act of living in Manaus. It is almost like submitting oneself to constant doses of depressant drugs; there is an unreality, probably activated by the high temperature, that compels the imagination to sleep, to transform itself into flashes of lucidity, fleeting spasms that grow faint in the labyrinths of tropical isolation, an aquatic voyage that invites oblivion. Nothing seems real, misery fuses with simplicity, the garish colors merge with the opaqueness of the people, the calmness of their gestures blends with the turbulence of a consciousness that is drowning. But it is all in subtones, like a plaintive melody inspired by submerged trees. And I ceased to ask what I was doing there, because questioning was futile in Manaus.

Then I got lost. Not like a foreigner, rather like a native in the midst of a collapse of familiarity. Just like the legend of Theodore Mommsen.

Mommsen, one of the great historians of the classic era, was born and lived in the old Wilhelmian Berlin. His lectures were famous for their erudition and literary sharpness; he was able to describe hour after hour the geography of Athens in the time of Socrates, pointing out the streets, the squares, the fountains, reconstructing the very spots where so many dialogues transpired, going so far as to place certain homes, such as that of Lisias, who lived with Epicrates, according to a passage of the Phedro. At the same time, Mommsen needed an assistant in order to get around the streets of Berlin. He was capable of identifying the temple of Olympic Zeus of Athens in the fifth century, but he couldn't find his way around in the trivial route between the zoo and the Unter den Linden.

However, returning to the Amazon, that visitor to my home wasn't just any English journalist. Her name was Virginia Challenger. Exactly: Challenger! According to her business card.

THE END OF THE THIRD WORLD

And she was making a documentary for the BBC.

It was somewhat of a rebellious interview. I didn't want to talk about Amazonia. Could it be because I was just as disoriented in Manaus as Mommsen had been in Berlin? I remember a time when to come to a place like the Amazon River region was to experience the realm of adventure and the unknown. Lands like Amazonia were challenges, but challenges with human stature, not statistics of catastrophes. In that epoch, each travel account could be an amazement, a collection of marvels that celebrated the diversity of civilizations, the whim and the force of an indomitable nature, the living face of tenacity. These adventurers risked everything because they offered up their very lives, and upon their return, safe and worn-out by the difficulties of their trips, they communicated to us their deep-rooted belief in the daily enchantment of city life. The West was a slate roof, a good and well-served table, breakfast eaten without a care to the sound of wind in the beefwood trees. Now it all comes down to a moral crisis.

"I would say that we are made of moral crises, Sr. Souza."

It was an ironic remark, of course. The BBC reporter was sweating from every pore; aside from the dark circles under her eyes, the only color in her pallid face was that of her thin lips, which still preserved some reddish hue, a faint memory of blood flowing in a metabolism made insipid by the oppressive heat.

"Our raw material is something else," I responded.

"Something else?" she asked.

"We are made of resentments."

"That's what I had heard about the Third World. Resentment as a propellant. But could it actually work? Won't it be too explosive a combustible?" She stopped and dried her face with a Kleenex, quickly hiding the tissue in her purse, as if she were ashamed of that industrial convenience.

She is one of those who still feels shame, I thought. Cynicism degrades much more.

"What I mean," she went on, panting, "is that resentment is too unstable to build anything out of it."

"We live in an unstable world; that's why resentment functions as a link in our chain of events. The Third World is an oddity; of that I am convinced more and more every day. It is an enormous social and economic black hole, swallowing up everything that gets close. Even good intentions."

The reporter observed me with a jovial severity. Very English, I would say, if it weren't a dangerous cliché. Her oval face, thin, slightly sunburned, displayed its intensity in her gray eyes, charmingly slanted like those of a Eurasian. What a pity that she hid herself in that kind of chic proletarian clothing, a sign that the powerful forces of the black hole were already dragging her in. In fact, along with sweat, she was exhaling commiseration from all her pores.

"This must be the tenth European TV crew that comes through here this year," I observed in a neutral tone.

They were all alike because the forces of attraction of the oddity were always the same. That's why I couldn't expect anything different from those avidly sympathetic people, distinguished by their feelings of solidarity that were more equivalent to ingenuousness, feelings that had the consistency of soap bubbles, beautiful for a while and hypnotically inconsequential, an improbable coalescence that hardly simulated determination, effectiveness. And she came to discuss the instability of our resentment; but our resentment was only the reverse of their remorse, symmetrically placed as matter and antimatter, polarized differently and always ready to

THE END OF THE THIRD WORLD

annihilate each other in an incandescent liberation of useless energy, the gamma ray of the century's political conflicts.

"Just look," I said, "the Minister of Culture only recently discovered that he was speaking in prose all the time. But I guess this isn't of any interest for your project."

She smiled, trying to be understanding with this creature who seemed to her to be an anachronism, who insisted on clouding the conversation. Seeing myself through her eyes, bored and weary witnesses of the affluence of the times, I was incarnate in the skin of some emblematic figure, somewhat Dostoyevskian in the sense of convulsions of backwardness, or something of the kind, because they were always expecting from us hailstorms of accusations and a few prophecies.

"Here in Manaus, there isn't much to do," I said. "Aside from plugging your nose when the folklore index gets too high. Actually, we're on the fringe of the black hole's maelstrom. In some ways, we are a part of it, and in others, not a part of it. We are being swallowed up, and at the same time some currents of matter are still allowed to escape, some photons. We Brazilians occupy such a large expanse of land that all kinds of frauds can effectively get established. Thus the generalized disbelief and despondency. We are the first tired Americans, trying to preserve, with the airs of progressive politics, the worn-out practice of rural lobotomy that reduces the country to a pathetic plantation producing twine and clay figurines."

She didn't understand me; she wasn't there for this sort of thing. She needed information that would help the crew to film the program, places to visit, people to see, facts, local color, rags, diseases, injustices, ethnic cataclysms. How could one make her understand that generally the most interesting story was gathered by listening attentively to what "people" say? There was nothing more characteristically exotic than the figures of speech, or, if you please, the Freudian slips, like one made by a recent Minister of Justice who classified the government that he worked under as in the "vanguard of backwardness"? But not always does the Portuguese language, converted to an instrument of power, allow itself to sting with the generosity of the loquacious minister, a barrister from the Northeast who had eaten too much protein and went about lost in the rarefied stratosphere of Brasília.

At any rate, our situation as an oddity doesn't favor us in any way because we are losing more than we gain. It's a part of the entropy that is our lot.

"Sometimes I think that our very language was partially devoured by that insane voracity. I have the impression that, for those who are imprisoned in that anomaly, even the language is no longer a reliable means of communication. You who are English, what do you say about an English speaker from Kenya?"

"I'm not French," she responded, raising her shoulders and reaffirming the well-publicized Anglo-Saxon linguistic tolerance.

"Perhaps so," I said grudgingly, "but don't go so far as to tell me that you left India in defeat, brought down by passive resistance. I'm sure that Lord Mountbatten could no longer stand that horrible accent, not to mention the smell of Gandhi's urine. He preferred to hand over the country rather than give one more audience to that hateful figure, the emblem of the Third World."

The journalist looked straight at me with an air of your-version-of-history-seems-altered-by-your-Brazilian-sarcasm. I know she must have been thinking that behind our rough exterior, we probably are lined on

THE END OF THE THIRD WORLD

the inside with silk, velvet, or raw leather. But on second thought, why would she think this?

It so happened that every time the vortex of oddity that is devouring us seemed more real than the heat, I would remember a conversation I had with Heinrich Boll in a pizzeria in Cologne. It was cold, of course. A mild and wonderful cold autumnal day on the Rhine. And Boll, smoking his filterless cigarettes, was speaking of his arm-to-arm combat with the German language.

"I imagine that the Brazilians, after a military dictatorship, ought to be facing the same problem," he said.

Just consider that Boll grew up seeing the Nazis little by little gain control of the streets, with their parades and their provocations; he wrote a touching book full of compassion for this part of his life, and he spent his youth fighting as a soldier in the war. He saw his country be literally reduced to shambles by the hysterical rhetoric of the Nazis. After the war, he decided to be a writer. And what a surprise it was to find that not only the cities were in ruins, but the German language itself was frayed and contaminated by the Nazi lunacy. For a writer like him, trained in the Catholic Rhine tradition, it was disheartening to acknowledge that his language had been transformed into a stinking quagmire and that his generation of writers had their work cut out for them. In order to realize their dreams as artists, they would have to do nothing less than reinvent the German language. Once again words needed to be weighed, each expression purified, cleansed, treated so that the distortions left by Nazism could be retracted. Hundreds of words had suffered abominable alterations in their semantics; various apparently trivial expressions had taken on terrible connotations. For example, if today someone were to use the expression "degenerate art" here in Brazil, at the most, people are going to think about television programming. But in Germany, to say such a thing is scandalous. "Degenerate art" is one of the expressions that was not recyclable; it became a historical concept, marked forever by Nazi intolerance.

I realized this quite clearly when I participated in a debate on television in Cologne, where hours later we would be conversing around a pizza. In the debate, aside from Boll, there had also been a Soviet dissident. The topic of our conversation was exiled writers. The Soviet, whose name escapes me, was a bootlicker. He was there looking for money, speaking ill of the Stalinist bureaucracy and demonstrating the most complete political ignorance. Suddenly a question came up for Boll; citing a right-wing minister of the government by the name of Strauss, who had come out in the press saying that Boll's writings ought to have been sanitized by the West German government because it was "degenerate art." Strauss's observations must have been ill timed; the Bavarian minister went so far as to call Boll the "grandfather of terrorists" and other such pearls, which goes to prove that even certain German politicians suffer from verbal intemperance once in a while. I noticed the uncomfortable atmosphere, a kind of bitter and unpleasant feeling in the TV studio; but Boll wasn't a man to be intimidated. He refreshed the television viewers' memory as to the meaning of the expression "degenerate art," without raising his voice a single time.

The next day, Strauss, who has recently died, was pictured in the newspapers, as gentle as a lamb, saying that it had all been a misunderstanding, and that he would never use such an expression, etc. As a good German of the postwar era, even belonging to the right, Strauss knew that after the Nazis, the question of the use of words was a very serious matter. He was conscious of the fact that using language as an instrument

THE END OF THE THIRD WORLD

in a political discussion, even as a representative of the right, didn't give him much space for retreat. Much less in a debate with Heinrich Böll, a man whose life was intertwined with the democratic reconstruction of Germany. Böll's generation, obliged to answer for everything, had drained the swamp left by the Nazis; they had reinvented the old language. Strauss's retraction was proof of this.

But Böll turned the question to Brazil. What was it like there in the postdictatorship period? Well, we hadn't experienced any world war, in spite of the fact that the results weren't any less devastating. But not many writers considered language to be a political issue. Brazil is a country of shock waves, of experiments in the language, of anxious expectations of modernity that can only be achieved when blended with the primitive and rural—just look at our literary masterpieces *Macunaima* and *The Devil to Pay in the Backlands*. But in these two cases, the language was an invention, an illusion, as in poetry. As far as the part that wasn't primitive or rural, it remained reflective, personal, exclusory. That's why it was not enough to deal with the question only as a phenomenon of the last twenty years; it was necessary to dig deeper, to do some archaeology, in order to get to the root of the problem, which was the baccalaureate tradition, like a neurotic atavism to be backward, a strange destiny manifested in reverse.

That country, so far from Cologne, that the Russian dissident identified with heat, beaches, and Creoles in white jackets, was a country where the language was a thing for jurists, shyster lawyers of the ilk of Ruy Barbosa. Curiously, these were the real masters of the language. No one remembered the great writers like Machado de Assis or Graciliano Ramos. Thus, it was just a hop, skip, and a jump from the pandering jurist to the swindling

LOST WORLD II

technocrat. After all, between Ruy's retorts and rejoinders and the current institutional decrees, what is the difference? The vigilant belletrist horror of the institutional decrees could only generate the humorous cruelty of the technocrats' discourse. The language of the jurists seemed to be vulgar Latin; that of the technocrats is the supposedly sophisticated English of the university campus. Both were created by a horrible natural selection, appropriating hundreds of words, semantics, in the manner of spoken Brazilian Portuguese.

Having normal hearing and a sound mind is enough to cause one to feel nauseous at the mention of such words and expressions as "revolution," "national integration," "corruption," "national objectives," "national memory," "security," "sluggish inflation," "distribution of revenue," "development," "external debt," "national identity," "anarchy," "freedom with responsibility," "national leader," and all of the syntactic crudeness of the ethics of "to get the upper hand." But there were certain similarities with Heinrich Boll's experience. Here, as there, the language has been degraded by ignorant people, by a refuse of politicians and military men incapable of applying the most elementary rule of agreement, except as a nostalgic cultural model of the plantation owners, the slave owners, put in practice by its jurists and technocrats. What can be done? Subvert the use of pronouns? Revolt against the inflection of verbs? Yes, but at the same time avoid the traps of "writing well," because there is no amnesty in matters of language.

The Englishwoman must have had a good heart, because she was still there, perspiring without letup, hoping that my silence would eventually produce something useful for her work. Her training enabled her to put up with the peculiarities of Latins; every once in a while

THE END OF THE THIRD WORLD

she would glance outside, where the evaporation was reaching the consistency of a light voile curtain blown by a wind that didn't exist, that didn't even have the strength to push the few lazy clouds that were stuck in the scandalously blue sky.

"Do you want to know something? I think it's a good thing that you all come to do these things here."

She smiled, shaking her head.

"No, it's true," I insisted. "What we've got here seems less absurd when seen on a foreign television program."

"It is an extraordinary place, Sr. Souza."

But then everything is extraordinary. When we left the pizzeria in Cologne, I didn't know that it would be the last time I would see Heinrich Boll. He said good-bye, smiling, walking with a firm step toward the network car that would take him home. But our conversation echoed in my mind, an astute gentleness emitting radiance, persuasive in the responsibility that it contained.

Language and idiom. In the sixties, one writer impressed me greatly in the manner that he wrote. It was Kurt Vonnegut, Jr.; initially I read him in translation. In Portuguese he had a strange flavor, sarcasm poorly disguised by an idiotic style, or an idiotic style poorly disguising sarcasm. That's what made me distrust the translation, and I began to read him in English. The translations were faithful, because Vonnegut sounded exactly the same in the original. It was fascinating how he articulated his phrases using a basic English vocabulary, achieving an unexpected humor and at the same time saying the most defamatory things. I know now that Vonnegut pointed the way to another approach for a writer to deal with his language.

While Boll worked with a German contaminated by the Nazi gang, Vonnegut wrote in the sandy terrain of the mass media in which the English language had been

27

transformed. It couldn't have been easy; Vonnegut wasn't a simpleton, nor was he writing solely from intuition. He had an academic background in anthropology, and what he was doing, rather than spontaneous, was deliberate and sophisticated. In the United States, the manipulation of language is a product of an elaborate system that utilizes a powerful communications machine, the fruit of a society that is liberal, complex, and mass-oriented, but that needs to maintain and reproduce itself, appropriating generous portions of freedom of expression.

Kurt Vonnegut's English bewildered me. It was so apparently simple that initially it gave the impression of the work of an imbecile. But that was his strategy, his trap for careless readers. Many critics were fooled by this, not recognizing his cleverness, or they felt insulted because the sarcasm and virulence were derived from the structuring of the sentences, and the choice of words, as if the discourse of an imbecile were capable of capturing the society of postwar America. A writer such as this, writing at such close range, was bound to be influential. During the sixties, he was the author most read by the young people; they realized that he had taken their tame English and turned it inside out, that Puritan English, smelling of the sixteenth century, full of pious interjections. He set about equipping it with the language of the millions of voiceless people. And he did it with an ingenious alchemy, becoming at the same time a highly intelligent and concise writer.

One of Vonnegut's novels is worth ten of those diluted Marxist pamphlets of the Latin American writers. That's why I wasn't surprised when I read in the paper that they were burning his books in the Midwest and banning his novels from high school reading lists, and even withdrawing them from school libraries in the Bible belt.

THE END OF THE THIRD WORLD

Vonnegut is "dangerous," he shows imbecility, and the fundamentalists and bonfire advocates knew what they were doing. And Vonnegut was never a sweet-smelling flower; he appeared on the scene in the most despicable form, in paperback, with all the critics turning their noses up at his work. He became a legend amongst contentious university students of the sixties. Then he appeared on the best-seller lists, selling thousands of copies. But he didn't sell out, he continued writing in the same vein, exposing the senility of his country with a precision that is nonexistent amongst certain pompous cretins who pretend they are denouncing American imperialism. So he went to the bonfire.

What is odd is that before leaving Cologne, the specter of Conan Doyle suddenly appeared.

"Did you know that he was here, in Cologne?"

I was with a Portuguese language professor at the university.

"Conan Doyle, here? Don't tell me."

"In 1911. Cologne was a part of the route of the famous rally organized that year by Prince Henry. It began in Hamburg, passed through here, and continued on to Münster, Southampton, Edinburgh, and finally London. Sir Arthur Conan Doyle, what an atypical man of letters! He loved action. He drove a beautiful car, of which he was very proud, a twenty CV Dietrich Lorrain."

"Are you writing a paper on Conan Doyle?"

"Of course not. I like car races. As he did."

"I detest automobiles, racing or standing still."

"How strange!"

"I believe the automobile was a technological folly of the industrial revolution. An individualizing error in an epoch that aspired to collectivism."

"Ah! There is another thing that you would like to know," she said without paying attention to my attack

LOST WORLD II

on automobiles. "In that same year, Conan Doyle made his first airplane trip."

"One could say that 1911 was a full year for him."

"And in the fall he wrote *The Lost World*, the first adventure of Professor Challenger."

In 1911, in the fall. And now we're at the end of the twentieth century. Professor Challenger would recognize little of that dense, dark forest that so impressed him. That forest that Conan Doyle knew only through the stories of his friend Alfred Russell Wallace, a man of a delicate and meticulous demeanor who traveled up the Negro River in a large canoe, carrying frugal supplies like manioc flour and rum, but who could also be eccentric and include a live turkey to be roasted at an opportune time. A temperament so different from Professor Challenger's creator.

"What do the residents of Amazonia want?" the journalist asked.

"Just to live," I said.

But perhaps that wasn't enough. The cassette tape, silently running in the small tape recorder, seemed to contain more than what was being said. No, it was not a matter of paranoia. I didn't believe that the TV crew was there gathering material for some undisclosed strategy. Far from that. My impression was that those tapes arrived prerecorded; there was an extra track on them, unbeknownst even to the crew, where an idyllic primitive tribal component was registered, a component that was thought extinct in Europe but that ought to be compared to that idyllic primitive tribal world supposedly still alive in the Amazon. At the bottom of all this was some kind of reencounter, because those Europeans secretly seemed to lament that the asphalt of their superhighways had covered over the old fields of the long-gone Burgundians, Suevians, Kachubians,

THE END OF THE THIRD WORLD

Goths, Welshmen, Iberians, and so many other tribes.

Of course, the Amazon demands to live, but isn't there some deeper truth within the region that is facing the risk of being lost forever, as a result of these exchanges, as pleasant as they are, these previously arranged, charming ruses, whose components never seem to change? On the one hand, there is the desire to experience a thrill, a fascinating place, because primitivism, in these times of environmental concerns and doubts concerning the concept of progress, is regarded as almost sacred, a negation and a mystery, an invitation to a zeal far removed from the age-old attraction of adventure. And on the other hand, where we, the ones who are observed, find ourselves, our role is to recognize their efforts to show solidarity, attesting, in our poor man's way, to the fragility of the poor.

For a long time, we tasted in our imagination a sample of life's experiences. We're Amazonians, and therefore we know what it's like here. A grasp of life's experiences is a kind of universal understanding arrived at through local practice; that is what established us as Amazonian beings. For those who came visiting, we had a right to the Amazon because our life experiences had granted us the ownership.

In fact, our life experiences paralyzed us. But we didn't even suspect it.

And do you know why?

Because even though we didn't have profound dreams, the reality of our inquiries invaded the emptiness. From this came our impression that no one really perceived our real stature even as a broader interest in the region was returning.

We were invisible, phonies. Even the most humble jobs would have filled us with joy. But seeing the level of development of the travelers, we lost our aptitude, the

LOST WORLD II

framework in which our life experiences were relevant; our own particular intelligence was reduced to ash and marginated us.

The truth is that we had always hoped that these travelers would take us seriously, but not just for what we could offer them. We aspired to find our own alchemy that would transform our disparity of privilege.

That was it! The look of those foreigners, those affable visitors of so many nationalities, astonished us; it disconcerted us to the core that they sized us up, scrutinized us, and gave in to the temptation to point out solutions, because situations like ours always seem to be so simple and easy to handle: destruction or conservation.

Then, I thought.

Rather than feigning displeasure, why not have Miss Challenger understand our pride in another way? Through a new kind of contact, far from anything she had yet experienced, in order to free us from the role of supplicant, something that we've already had our fill of, something that causes our exclusion and reduces us to resentment and a desire for revenge, when it doesn't bring us to the pure and simple acceptance of our supposed destiny of backwardness.

"Have you read *Lost World*, by Conan Doyle?" I asked.

She looked at me perplexed, visibly tense and nervous. She was pretty, but not in a conventional way, as there was something strange about her, something that detracted from her attractive features, perhaps her nose or her cheeks.

"When I was a child, I believe," she responded, slowly. "Why?"

"Nothing. It's just that perhaps we are quite complacent with our own weaknesses."

Is It Still Possible To Be a Hero in Today's World?

The following night the BBC crew invited me to a bouillabaisse made of tucunaré. Even in Manaus, life has its compensations, and bouillabaisse of tucunaré is one of them. And the most delicious, if you can't eat it in the home of an Amazonian, is the one made at Sao Francisco Restaurant. The restaurant couldn't be in a better location; it's in Educando district, in the only place where the city doesn't turn its head from fear of the river. One can see the glossy immensity of the Negro River as it flows towards its encounter with the Amazon River.

"Do you know that this is the second time I come to Manaus?" Virginia said.

"And we're here at her insistence," Lester, a member of the crew, revealed. "If you knew what she did in order to convince our bosses, you would take her for a lunatic."

I know, I thought. I am certain of one thing: In the novel that I'm going to write, Miss Challenger won't be very different from this other Miss Challenger.

"What happened is that a new chief took over in our department just when Virginia was out of the country."

A new department chief. Only it wasn't in the BBC, rather in the business magazine. And because he took over during a bad week, few people felt the impact. Spender, the new editor, came from the documents department, and his appointment must have seemed as surprising for him as it was for the editorial staff. But that week was full of unusual occurrences. The Dow Jones index in the New York stock market signaled disaster, and a tremendous gale hit the city, uprooting old trees in Hyde Park. The fall rains arrived with much the same intense perversity of the plummeting dollar, and Jane Challenger, yes, she would be called Jane, had mysteriously disappeared in Geneva, leaving behind in the editorial room a trail of diverse and malicious speculations.

"The fellow isn't exactly a first-class TV journalist," Virginia was saying with a smile, "but he seems to have the confidence of the board of directors, which is perhaps the most important thing in such a sensitive time as this with Mrs. Thatcher in the government."

"So you can get an idea of what he's like," said Lester, "I'll say that he is one of those types that wear round tortoiseshell glasses, a glazed expression of complete puzzlement at any of life's surprises, wool tweed sport coats and gray flannel trousers even in the summer; one of those men who is so sheltered that he would have remained celibate if he had not found a woman who asked for as little in a mate as he did."

"For God's sake, Lester," Virginia protested.

"That's all right. I understand," I said, laughing, since in my novel the fellow was married to the oldest daughter of the third vice president of the parent company that controlled the magazine. He was the new editor of the *New Economist*.

Everyone in the editorial room knew Spender, who had worked on the magazine since the sixties, and they knew he wasn't a bad person, quite to the contrary. He was conservative with an absentminded liberal inclination; he could even be a charming character if he maintained a certain distance and moderation in his contacts. His charm came from the fact that he seemed to be at peace with himself, a peace very recently acquired after a bellicose adolescence filled with inadequacies. On the other hand, he was a boring person, accepting his total unsuitability to the positions that he had held with irritating stoicism.

"Our friend," Lester went on, "is one of those chaps who is born knowing that when he travels, his luggage will never get lost, but it will always be the last one to come along on the conveyer belt."

Virginia let out a belly laugh and finished up, "The kind who draws the name of the company president in a secret-friend party and has to buy him a present worth fifty pounds."

"And if there is someone whose existence seems to have been made in order to put our good friend to the test," Lester said, "that someone is Virginia Challenger."

Or Jane Challenger, the red-haired journalist who had become legendary covering the last gasps of the present worldwide economic order, without displaying the slightest sign of disgust as she passed through the halls of those five-star hotels in Geneva.

"Virginia had disappeared," Lester continued, "and when we returned on Monday, we expected just another chaotic week. But the new chief was upset. I wondered if the problem had something to do with her, and I was right."

At the end of the day, Spender left with one of them, a young, athletic fellow with dull blond hair, who, in spite of his age, was a member of one of the oldest editorial teams. His name was Billy Lester, and the magazine's readership associated him with the most conscientious and critical texts. But that afternoon he was visibly uncomfortable with Spender, who had been following him as an abandoned dog follows someone in the street.

A little later, over the din of the pub crowd, he listened to Spender's public school accent as he whiningly detailed something about a problem that Jane Challenger was creating. Even though a journalist rarely wanted to go in to the same pub as his editor, that afternoon it was impossible to avoid it. He had hardly loosened his tie and turned off his terminal when Spender leaned over his desk with the obvious air of a cabinet member exposed in flagrante delicto in the headlines of *The Sun*. It was his gravest expression, used when all other escape routes had apparently been blocked.

"Yes, she returned," he was saying with a large dose of masochism that made him repugnant. "And she wants an additional sum of money, a supplement. Who knows what she means by that? I had hoped that the trip would do her some good, but she returned worse than ever. God knows I never thought she would put me in such a situation. What do you think I ought to do?"

Lester now began to feel pity for the editor, but right away he tried to rid himself of such a feeling. If tradition dictates that a good journalist never feel sorry for his editor, he wasn't going to be the one to start now, much less with Spender looking at him with those bleary, anxious eyes.

"I don't think I can help you, Spender. I still haven't had the chance to talk with Jane since she returned. I didn't even know that she had shown up at the office this afternoon."

"She showed up," he said resentfully. "She went directly to my office."

Little by little the pub was getting livelier, with almost the whole editorial staff of the magazine fraternizing, as it usually did, with the personnel of a nearby advertising

THE END OF THE THIRD WORLD

agency. Hiding his uneasiness, Lester glanced around, looking for a head of red hair, but he was only able to see the punk hairdos of the secretaries from the advertising agency and the short blond hair of the girls from the editorial room. Not a sign of the radioactive crimson cloud that was contaminating Spender's life.

"So where was she after all?" Lester asked, overcome by curiosity.

Spender passed his fingertips along the inside of his collar and winked. "Ah, so you don't know?"

"No. Our relationship hasn't been good since the last miners' strike."

"But that was a year ago. What happened?"

"Differing interpretations of what a journalist's role should be."

"I understand," said Spender, obviously not understanding anything, posing for a few seconds as a hard-boiled professional who's seen it all, but quickly returning to his anxious state.

"You haven't told me where she was," Lester insisted.

Spender leaned over the table and whispered very near the journalist's face. Even his breath was odorless.

"She was in South America," he said, choosing his words with disgust as if they were immodest.

Lester gathered whatever he still had of irony and, simulating horror, he recoiled. Spender, who never was especially subtle, felt comforted.

"No!" the journalist exclaimed.

"Yes!" Spender replied, furiously, blinking his eyes.

"But—but—" the journalist stuttered, in an attempt to find some logic in that conversation.

"South America! Really!" Spender reiterated.

"It's a vast region," Lester commented.

"How so?" Spender asked, surprised.

"I said that South America is a vast region."

LOST WORLD II

"And she wants to go back," he added, with visible discomfort, as if going there once was reproachable, let alone returning.

Lester took a slow sip of his beer and seemed to have momentarily forgotten Spender. What could Jane Challenger have seen of such importance in that troubled part of the world to want to return? After all, he thought, Jane wasn't one to be impressed by small children dying of hunger, or violations of human rights. What would there be there, aside from a monumental external debt, for someone like Jane, who considered herself to be the perfect incarnation of professional objectivity and enemy of sentimentalism, to come back so moved? For someone who knew her so well, who was accustomed to seeing her move so haughtily in the midst of so much misery, certain that the only thing worse than underdevelopment was the pity of the rich, all that conversation made no sense.

Lester could remember a hot, dark night in Madras; it was like a live nightmare for him as he watched Jane impassively traverse the streets near the harbor of that Indian city, her bright red hair radiating in the darkness of the sea of the Bay of Bengala. Without the slightest ceremony, she passed by beggars who were dying of starvation and whose cadavers would be collected by the sanitation workers in the morning. The conference of nonaligned nations, which they were covering, had ended the day before, full of good proposals, but the unbelievable vision of degradation cried out for something more than political rhetoric.

Upon their return to England, and still under the impact of that night, he was appalled to hear Jane comment that she had been happy to leave behind that country that smelled of shit the whole time, even in the executive bar of the Hilton, where they had stayed. And to his surprise, in the next edition he humbly compared his article with hers, in which her concise and even brutal analysis portrayed the useless loquacity of the nonaligned meeting and tore to bits the compassionate vision that permeated his text.

"South America, you say?" he asked Spender one more time.

"That's what you heard," he responded with a sigh.

"But what in the devil did she find there?" Lester exclaimed.

Spender shrugged, his favorite gesture for affirming his editorial authority and which almost always brought his subordinates to the verge of murdering him. It certainly wasn't pleasant to receive a gesture so charged with disdain from someone expected to give a clear definition. But Spender was like that; if you went to him and asked if you could examine the Buckingham Palace urinals for an article on the devaluation of the dollar, he would respond with a solemn shrug. He expected to show his subordinates with this nonchalant gesture that there was not the slightest difference between being experienced, as he hoped everyone believed he was, and being bored to death, his usual attitude in any situation where he sensed risk. Of course, everyone knew that Spender wasn't bored to death, because behind his snobbish mask was a man afraid of assuming responsibility.

"She is crazy, I dare to say," Spender stated.

"Are you sure?"

"Well, I'm a journalist, not a psychiatrist," he said, coming forth with a series of little chuckles that soon turned into a convulsive belly laugh, while his eyes blinked as if they were flashing red lights, announcing that he had just come out with a magnificent demonstration of Britannic humor.

LOST WORLD II

Lester faked a complacent smile and wondered if Spender couldn't set a new world's record for psychosomatic ailments, as even his manifestations of humor seemed to drain inward rather than sparkle forth as was normal.

"She said she was going to speak with Lord Delamare," Spender concluded, laughing hysterically and totally collapsing over the swivel barstool.

People began to look down toward his end of the bar, commiserating with him, and some colleagues shot expressions of pity and solidarity for their hapless coworker. Lester's throat was dry, and his curiosity slowly began to replace his initial lack of interest. He did something then that would never have entered his head in any other circumstance: He asked for another round of beer. Spender quickly pulled himself together and downed the rest of his tankard of beer before the next one was served.

"You have to talk to her, Lester," he pleaded.

"Me? You're completely out of your head, Spender," Lester responded.

"But you two are friends, I presume."

"Friends! What does that mean?"

"Don't pretend otherwise, Lester. I know that she was a childhood friend of yours. You even have nicknames for each other."

Lester picked up the tankard of beer that was just served and he drank it down in one long gulp. He wiped his mouth with the back of his hand and got up. But his rude gesture didn't have the expected effect over the impressionable editor. He realized that Spender was terrified, so terrified, in fact, that he managed to surmount the horror he normally experienced when coming into physical contact with one of his subordinates, and he took Lester by the arm.

"You have to help me, Lester. She can't talk with Lord Delamare."

Lester looked with shock at Spender's hand on his arm, and he saw his yellowed fingers loosen and pull away like an indolent mollusk.

"That's impossible, Spender. Nothing would be gained; she won't listen to me anyway."

Spender's head dropped and his shoulders sagged like a broken jack-in-the-box. He seemed like a snowman in the process of melting, reluctantly accepting Lester's attempts to dodge the matter and consider it already settled.

"Aside from that," Lester added, "I don't even know exactly what's going on. All of this is very vague."

"It's not my fault," he complained. "She refuses to go into it with me. She asked for a staff meeting for tomorrow morning."

"And are you going to call one?"

"Absolutely not. What kind of an editor would I be if I called a staff meeting without knowing what was on the agenda?"

Technically, Spender was entirely right, even though he never had an iota of influence over the makeup of the agenda of the *New Economist*.

"When I said that I wasn't going to call an impromptu staff meeting," Spender went on, "she became just furious. She almost jumped on top of me; you know how she is. And she left my office saying that she was going to see Lord Delamare."

"I'll see what I can do," Lester promised, without much conviction, putting an end to the conversation.

He left Spender sadly leaning over the bar like a dead dolphin washed up on a polluted beach. Out on the street, he considered what Jane might be up to at that moment, probably bothering the butler of

LOST WORLD II

Pembroke Square, insisting that Lord Delamare see her.

He was now in a hurry, uneasy, sensing that something was about to happen, and it couldn't be anything good. He ran to Aldwych and descended into the subway in the middle of a silent crowd of office workers. With a little bit of luck, he could still arrive at home before nine o'clock. But the cosmopolitan fauna of the London streets continually carried him back to Jane Challenger's mysterious trip, for the Third World also existed there, in the African chords played on an exotic instrument by a black man in dreadlocks, in the sounds of the bamboo flutes played by four young men in colorful ponchos, or in the face of a pale young girl in a sari who sold incense sticks. The subway car that he entered was full of festive Pakistanis, or were they Indians? That doubt, he knew as the good Londoner that he was, could be fatal. He decided to leave aside the subtleties of the Asiatic nations, so visible in the streets of London, and instead to make an effort to understand the strange conversation that he had just had with Spender.

Could Jane really have said she was going to go see Sir Delamare? After all, one of the things taken for granted amongst the editorial staff was that no one was to bother Sir Delamare, no matter how serious a crisis might become. Sir Delamare, at the age of ninety, was still in good form, with the exception of a convenient deafness and the habit of playing a kind of senile golf wherever he was; he was one of those men whose accounts with life were now completely closed. His title had been granted in the 1950s, apparently by mistake, or so gossips say. And as a matter of fact, his enemies' perfidy is probably not far from the truth. Until his elevation to Knight of the British Empire, his only accomplishments were having participated in the last war in an obscure intelligence

THE END OF THE THIRD WORLD

network in Liberia and having married the daughter of a newspaper magnate, a Mr. Wilbur. He survived the two of them and came out of it as the owner of a newspaper empire, for which he demonstrated an enviable impresario instinct.

Today the influence of the Wilbur group extended into many other communications and information sectors. But Sir Delamare hadn't directed his enterprises for at least a decade, even though he went to his office daily to sign congratulatory letters and, on certain occasions, to send telegrams of condolence. Delamare was able to enjoy the eternal bliss that was awaiting him, for the golden rule of the company was never to disturb him with minor matters, a category that was so broad as to include practically everything. To break that rule, in short, meant unleashing something so sinister that until that time, no one had dared to even consider it. Spender had good reason for being in a dither. And Jane; where could she be? Was she in Pembroke Square, in the magnificent Tudor mansion that Delamare maintained in good condition in Kensington?

He got off the subway in Hampstead and went on foot through the fine mist, trying to imagine himself in the middle of that mess. He couldn't risk his neck now. He had just bought that damn co-op apartment, with immense windows and built-in armoires, that cost a small fortune to heat in the winter. Jane was a rich woman; she had inherited a yearly income of almost 150,000 pounds; she worked because she wanted to, and for this reason she could risk such a challenge. Lester's family was ruined in the postwar era, and his father, when he died, left so many debts that they were almost reduced to begging in the street. He still remembered quite clearly the occasions when he let himself get involved in the hassles that Jane caused. She was objective, and many times glacial, professionally speaking, retaining a contradictory and anachronistic heroic spirit that was typically Challenger. This had always fascinated him, because it was the opposite of the parsimonious bourgeois mentality of his own family; however, Jane's excesses of heroism always ended up knocking him out in the last round.

He entered his apartment. A pile of magazines, a sink full of dishes waiting to be washed, and the greasy used pizza packages invariably depressed him, but that was what he had: a co-op apartment in a neighborhood made up of intellectuals and liberal journalists and writers, those affable and well-educated people who displayed their political concerns by sticking discreet adhesive messages on their automobile windshields. That apartment was exactly the image he sought, an image that was different in every way from Jane Challenger's world.

Never Risk Your Neck for an Economic Anachronism

Some days after the tucunaré bouillabaisse, Lester, the one from the BBC crew, was hospitalized in the Hospital of Tropical Diseases. I went to see him, but he wasn't receiving guests. Virginia was worriedly pacing the hospital lobby. I thought that there must be more than just professional camaraderie between them, but it wasn't any of my business. She was wearing a blue summer dress, and she didn't seem much like that journalist on a tropical excursion with whom I had dined just a few day before. She seemed tense, with visible concern on her clean, sunburned face. I told her what a doctor friend of mine had told me: Lester was under observation, but there was no indication that the fever was a symptom of anything serious. She listened to me intently, but it was obvious that she had no confidence in our medicine. I felt like telling her that there was no reason to worry, because in my novel Lester doesn't get sick; at that moment he would be waking up to find a dreary and damp Tuesday.

He awoke later than usual—around noon—because his sleep had been disrupted by nightmares, short-lived and soon forgotten. Living alone for so many years, he had lost the capacity to share his emotions with other people. Although he was in his early thirties and companionless, he wasn't lonely or self-centered; rather he had constructed for himself an ideal, a worldview of solidarity with others that he believed would be his

LOST WORLD II

anchor no matter where his emotions carried him. And it was precisely that belief that frequently got him into trouble.

Recently he had been unhappy in his work at the magazine. And it was in this state of mind, along with the exhaustion of a sleepless night, that he showed up at the office, flaunting a lack of enthusiasm for whatever he would have to face in one more unpleasant day. The weather didn't help either; the persistent autumn fog and the constant fine drizzle put him in a mood to react negatively to what he judged to be a lair of social climbers, a silly little magazine full of trite expressions created by the city's young financial elite, yuppies, as the Americans called them, those who were always the first to note the appearance of new trends in this end-of-the-century epoch. The truth is that he had reached the point where he was incapable of collaborating anymore with that editorial staff.

The *New Economist* began to be published five years before. It went through an initial phase when it was labeled irreverent. But today, thanks to the performance of its editorial staff, a team that created its own style—a prose that seems more to have been vomited out rather than properly written—the magazine has won the preference of the well-heeled young men and women, who are paid well and fed poorly, due to their expensive naturalist diets, and who dedicate their high-tech existence to making new blood flow through the sclerotic veins of the economy of the former Empire. These readers, more than his colleagues of the editorial staff, for whom he was obligated to produce weekly articles of six to ten thousand words, left him with his conscience smarting. But who, if not he, poor Lester, as Jane sometimes called him, still had a conscience to smart?

The editorial staff occupied a whole floor of the Wilbur

THE END OF THE THIRD WORLD

Building. It was covered with light green carpet, and the work space was divided by white fireproof partitions, a nightmarish synthetic ivory. The office furniture was quite contemporary, like in those television commercials for jeans, and the whole staff was hooked up to the main computer. In this atmosphere of the maximization of human output and the advanced Taylorian philosophy, everyone tried to personalize his or her own corner as much as possible. The secretaries and receptionists were the most creative, covering their terminals, monitors, and PBXs with dolls, vases of flowers, pop stars, and pictures of Princess Di. From time to time, when they went overboard, they were the objects of memoranda from the head of personnel, who on certain occasions had gone so far as to limit the presence of what he called "objects of personal affection" to two items per individual. The girls' efforts to humanize their spaces served as a means to gauge the discreetness of the rest of the office.

Haynes Williams, who occupied the same cubicle as Lester, a taciturn character who was never seen in anything but solemn black clothing, hung an indecent caricature of Margaret Thatcher on his monitor. Even Spender wasn't above this human weakness; he decorated his neatly kept desk with a small, silver-framed portrait of the Queen Mother, which he locked in the desk at the end of each day. Beneath the glass desktop of Jane's desk there was a black-and-white photo of former Minister Profumo, an unforgettable name since the sixties. According to her, this unfortunate gentleman inaugurated the paranoiac state of the domestic political scene, something known as the Profumo Syndrome, a condition that provoked an enormous expenditure of energy and large doses of sexual frustration for the cabinet members since his time. Lester's "object of personal affection"

LOST WORLD II

was, of course, a framed picture of Engels, which sometimes stood near the phone, but that was only sometimes because when his conscience reached the consistency of burning ash, the picture disappeared from view, only to return in its Victorian glory when the atmosphere appeared less polluted by resentments or in the moments when he wanted to offend the sensibilities of the new right who contaminated the place like a miasma.

What Lester could not predict was that on that particular Tuesday, old Engels was going to witness the exact instant that his life would be turned upside down.

As soon as he arrived at the office, he went to find Jane at her desk, but there was no sign of her. And in Spender's office, with its glass walls and bamboo blinds, the distinctive touch that reflected his position, there was no sign of its occupant. He vaguely pondered the whereabouts of the two of them as he glanced around the still calm editorial room with its terminals and fax machines humming discreetly.

Haynes was absorbed in entering something into his terminal. He was twenty-five years old and frequented a fitness gym; if there was anyone of the staff who personified the readers of the magazine, it was he.

Lester took off his leather jacket, wondering again where Jane and Spender might be. He sat down in the chair cautiously, grimacing because the supposed ergonomic design of the chair hurt his spine, which was accustomed to seats that were less functional, and as a result, each time he sat down, he couldn't help moaning, which bothered Haynes, who nearly always stopped what he was doing and waited with a sarcastic expression for Lester to open the desk drawer and pull out the picture of Engels. That afternoon he didn't even open the drawer.

He turned on the terminal and pulled a notepad from

THE END OF THE THIRD WORLD

his pocket. He was writing the first draft of a piece on the repression of the leadership of the miners' labor unions throughout the twentieth century; it was what he did on Tuesdays The piece would also be published in the United States by *The Nation*, for whom he regularly submitted articles of this type.

The heating system, like everything else there, worked with studied subtlety, and Lester's fingertips began to feel cold. Winter was still a few months away, but the editorial room normally was cold. He tried to concentrate on his work, though his mind wouldn't cooperate. His thoughts were constantly drifting away from the miners; Lester got up and stretched his neck over the partition to see if Jane had arrived yet.

"So you don't know?" Haynes bothered himself to say to Lester after the tenth neck-stretch.

"Don't know what?" Lester asked worried.

"She was fired. I guess no one told you."

Lester dragged his chair closer to Haynes's desk.

"What did you say?"

"She tried to speak with Sir Delamare, yesterday evening."

"And she managed to do it?"

"No, of course not. His secretary, that Irish bitch, you know her, intercepted Challenger in the foyer of Eastmoore."

"So she really did go there; just like I thought."

"She did. She left here after speaking with Spender, and she went directly to Pembroke Square. She's driving a white Ferrari; did you know that?"

"What about Spender? I don't see him around."

Haynes smiled his usual neo-gothic smile and pointed upwards.

"He's catching hell up on the twenty-fifth floor."

Lester looked up at the ceiling covered in opaque

acrylic and imagined, with the slightest bit of cruel pleasure, what might be happening to Spender in the higher circles.

"It seems that Spender's head is going to roll as well," Haynes said with his nasal voice that seemed to imitate perfectly the last gasps of a sick terminal. "According to the executives, Spender ought to have been firmer with Challenger."

Lester chuckled condescendingly, and Haynes made a face. They both knew that to ask Spender to be firm was like asking a mouse to be brave in a confrontation with a cat. And to believe that someone could be firm enough to prevent Jane Challenger from doing what she wanted to do was about as ingenuous as expecting a fundamentalist Muslim to accept Boy George as a philosophic alternative.

Haynes was the best-informed person in the office on the meteorological variations of the administrative hierarchy of the house, with the exception of the head telephone operator, who happened to be the lover of the assistant comptroller. Unlike the head telephone operator, who was absolutely discreet, Haynes used his bits of knowledge with the same care as a skunk spraying his odor. And sensing that Lester's interest in the matter transcended the simple morbid curiosity of a subordinate in his superior's fall from grace, he stopped typing, and after slowly wiping his gaunt and permanently damp face with a handkerchief, he continued.

"She was somewhere in the Third World," he said, carefully observing Lester's reactions with an oblique glance. "She was a different person when she returned. I would say that the tropical sun made her sick, or the water, or she was attacked by some exotic virus."

"What do you mean?"

THE END OF THE THIRD WORLD

"She came back strange, refusing even to say where she had been. It must be something in her family," Haynes insinuated. "First the grandfather, then the father, now the daughter. What a heritage."

"She was in South America, as far as I know."

"Yes, but where? It's such an immense steaming region."

"And there is nothing wrong with going to South America."

Haynes pursed his lips, showing his doubt. "Perhaps," he retorted slowly, attempting to provoke him. He knew of Lester's sympathies for those distant and tragic lands. "There wouldn't be anything wrong if our impetuous redhead hadn't returned saying she had found incredible things there."

"What incredible things?"

Haynes exaggerated his perpetual air of boredom, playing with an expensive Mont Blanc fountain pen.

"She went around talking in whispers, showing some old papers, making some absurd statements."

"Did you have a chance to talk to her?"

"Of course not; all that I know is what she was saying at Pembroke Square. The Irish bitch who takes care of the old man almost called the sanatorium."

"Was it that serious?"

"She is crazy; believe it. This time the old bitch was completely right, even though I hate to admit it. Just think about it. If someone came up to you saying that he had found the entrepreneurs Mallet and Ottley alive and well, what would you think? That the person was mad, right?"

"Mallet? Ottley? What are you talking about?"

Haynes attempted to smile slightly, but it seemed more like a grimace of pain.

"I suppose that you have read *Das Kapital*?"

"*Das Kapital*? What in the devil does *Das Kapital* have to do with Miss Challenger?"

"If you really have read *Das Kapital*, a work that is a little excessive in my opinion, then you ought to remember that in volume one there is a moving chapter entitled 'The Production of the Absolute Surplus Value'?"

"Yes, of course."

"It isn't my favorite chapter. Actually, I prefer Charles Dickens in terms of misery, but there are a few impressive characters. It makes one consider the limitless nature of human ambition."

Lester's tiredness caused his thoughts to come slowly, without much agility. Haynes words were meaningless to him. Naturally he knew *Das Kapital*, but at that moment, such a frivolous reference left him blank. It was like an intentional sarcasm made solely to irritate him. After all, what in the devil did *Das Kapital* have to do with South America? Then he remembered. Of course! They were some seventy pages in which Marx traces the situation of the former English factory workers who were forced to work brutal shifts in the factories. And he gave many examples, as was his style, citing names and figures.

Chapter XIII was full of stories that would always be associated in his mind with the word *Dantesque*. Forced to face shifts of twelve hours without any break for meals or physiological needs—which was illegal—those workers rapidly lost their human characteristics. And when the owners were required to give some sort of explanation to the newspapers, they maintained that the workers themselves were against any interruptions in their work day. In a textile mill in Dewsbury, Yorkshire, five boys between the ages of twelve and fifteen were forced to work thirty consecutive hours without any protection, in alcoves where the wool was processed to take out discolorations amidst clouds of dust and residue that gravely affected their lungs. When they were brought before the magistrate, the factory owners, pious members of the Quaker sect, informed him that although they would have allowed the youngsters to sleep four hours a night, the boys didn't want to go to bed. These weren't employees of Mallet or Ottley, two other owners cited by Marx who also got rich from unlimited exploitation, but they represent, along with their owners, the antediluvian epoch of capitalism.

"She didn't have to go so far away," Haynes argued with a certain brutality. "If one wants to find these kinds of gentlemen, all one has to do is take a stroll through the streets of the West End, or in the squalid dwellings of Handsworth, and take by surprise some of the illegal immigrants who are going through the same kinds of problems."

Lester acquiesced, moving nervously in his chair.

"As a matter of fact, that was the topic of your article last winter," Haynes recalled. "The whole editorial staff was shocked by the Dickensean tone of the text. My God, what a stage you chose to portray: tubercular Asians toiling day and night in noxious Chinese laundry cubicles, malnourished Jamaicans wasting away day by day in the pork slaughterhouses of Manningham, wretched Pakistanis slowly starving in the illegal candy factories of Bradford. It was quite a success, Lester. You gave all of us a beating. Graham Greene's letter acknowledging the piece was just one indication of the success that the article had."

The article, which had been published in November, created quite a debate in the editorial room. Less for its content than for its style. Originally it had been written for *The Nation*, but it wound up coming out in the *New Economist* without any modifications since the editor, a liberal of the old school, wanted something "poignant" for the beginning of the season. Lester's position in the magazine had been a bit matchless; his texts were published without having to pass through the purification process at the copydesk. This privilege arose from the fact that he had published two books of journalism that had gained relative success in sales and much critical acclaim.

The first, published in 1972, was an exposition of the British pharmaceutical industry, and the publisher had to fight off twelve libel suits. The second, published in 1985, won a press prize from the Bertrand Russell Foundation; it dissected the relationship between the conservatives and the European neofascists. When this book was published, *New Economist* was in its irreverent phase, and it brought in Lester to do investigative journalism. For two years he prepared material on alcoholism, drugs, teenage unemployment, the proletarianization of the middle class, and the crisis in the labor union movement, until the irreverence was substituted for the current enlightened cynicism, which had as its days of glory the Falklands war coverage.

As far as the terrible things that Lester saw while he was gathering material for the article on the illegal immigrant workers, Haynes was entirely correct in interjecting so much irony. Jane didn't need to make a twelve-hour transatlantic flight in order to find out that the extraction of surplus value hadn't changed in four generations.

Feeling even more upset, though grateful for the information, Lester returned to his desk; there he remained immobile for quite some time. Finally he opened the drawer and pulled out the picture of Engels, setting it beside the terminal. The picture had been taken when

THE END OF THE THIRD WORLD

Engels was forty, a decade older than Lester; he seemed to view the world with a serenity worthy of envy, especially for one who had seen so many bitter blows and had passed into history as the loyal friend, but lesser man, of the great master.

Slowly he returned to his work on the article at hand, reviewing a tape of an interview he had made with a leader of the miners' union from Wales. Listening to the archaic accent of the subject through the earphones, he didn't notice that Spender had approached with a demoralized demeanor.

"Lester!"

He took off the earphones, and, somewhat surprised, looked up at Spender.

"You don't know what's going on," he said, complaining.

"What's happened now?" Lester's nerves began to show signs of collapse.

"I just came down from up there," Spender said, pointing reverently to the floor above them.

"I already know. She lost her job. But don't worry, Spender. Miss Challenger certainly isn't going to die of hunger."

Spender adjusted his Italian silk tie and brought his hand to his chest as if he were about to have a heart attack. "It's a little more complicated than that, Lester."

"It always is!"

"Exactly. Sir Delamare was still awake last night when Miss Challenger was at Pembroke Square. He heard the altercation that she had with Miss O'Henry, and he wanted to know what had happened."

"But she was fired, wasn't she?"

"Of course, just as soon as the directors were informed. That's the rule, isn't it? But Sir Delamare reacted, as always, in an unpredictable manner. The poor old fellow!

Upon discovering that someone from the magazine had sought him out, he was elated. He said that she was the first person in ten years who hadn't considered him to be just a impertinent old coot, a corpse that refused to lie down and die. Sir Delamare demanded to see Miss Challenger immediately."

"Excellent."

"But now she's the one who doesn't want to talk with him. She told the vice president to go you-know-where! I was called upstairs and given twenty-four hours to convince her to meet with him or I'll be transferred to Africa! Oh, God!"

"You're going to like Africa, Spender."

"I hope that you also like it, Lester. Because you're in the same boat as I am. I told them that you were the only person capable of changing her mind."

Lester smiled, a jovial smile, his first display of good humor on that miserable Tuesday afternoon. "At least we are going to be far away from Jane Challenger," he said, because a post in Africa didn't frighten him in the least. To be perfectly honest, it would be wonderful. To get out of this editorial room, even if it was to a branch office in hell, would be something of an unexpected miracle.

"You don't understand," Spender shouted.

Off to the side, Haynes looked at the editor with an ironic mask of fright, and turning to Lester, he cleared his throat. Lester shook his head, in disapproval.

"Excuse me, Lester," Spender said, trying to make amends. "Perhaps you don't mind being sent to God-knows-where, but I can't leave here. My wife just wouldn't adjust. She barely manages to spend the summer in Spain."

"White women ought not to be taken to the tropics,

THE END OF THE THIRD WORLD

Spender," Haynes said sardonically, with the timing of an actor, "unless one wants to be rid of one."

"Come on, Haynes, have a heart," Spender protested, his hands pressed together as an old woman at prayer.

"All right, Spender," Lester complied, "I'll give her a call, but I don't believe it will do any good."

Lester sat down at his desk and asked for a telephone line. He dialed the number by heart as Spender looked on. Despite the cool temperature of the editorial room, beads of sweat slipped down the face of the anguished editor. Even Haynes, for reasons totally opposite of Spender's, kept quiet.

"She doesn't answer," Lester said after various attempts. "Just a damn answering machine, and it isn't even her voice. She must have ordered Henry to make the recording."

"Henry? Who is Henry?" Spender wanted to know.

"Her butler," Lester explained.

"Ah! Certainly she has a butler," Spender commented almost to himself, wondering whether or not this was too great of a problem for just a mere editor like himself. Jane Challenger, after all, was not exactly a simple journalist whom he could keep under his thumb. She was much more. She had a name, a silver spoon, so to speak. She had a butler. Exactly like Sir Delamare.

"Spender! I have an idea," Lester said, jerking the editor out of his sudden apathy. "We'll send a letter."

"You send it, Lester. You sign it. I'll see to it that it gets delivered."

"I'm going to see if she will receive us this evening," Lester explained. "But I really would prefer going to Africa."

A half hour later the letter went out with one of the young men from a special delivery service. Spender withdrew to his office, and pouring one cup of tea after another, he awaited an answer. Unable to do any more work on his article on the miners' leadership, Lester opened an issue of the *New Economist* and began to leaf through it, much to Haynes's surprise.

The suspense was over around five o'clock in the afternoon, when a messenger from a private courier service entered the office, looking for Lester. If there was one thing that Lester admired in Jane, it was the shrewdness with which she could execute a dare. The arrival of the messenger, an Asian boy dressed in clothing reminiscent of an operatic cavalry officer, had the effect of raising Spender's blood pressure to pinnacles worthy of registry in the *Guinness Book of Records*, if this book kept such records for hypertension. Maliciously ignoring Spender's name, in spite of the fact his name was mentioned in Lester's letter, Jane's response didn't surprise Lester.

It was an example of beautiful style. And it said the following:

Enmore Park, W.

Lester,

I was taken by surprise this afternoon by your letter. As I know that the post office, if it had to depend upon you, would go broke, I confess that the letter caused me to feel great curiosity. I hurried to read its contents, in order that I could dissipate the expectations of its deliverer, a charming fellow whose raucous motorcycle contrasted with his mute servility. And just as silence reigned again, I was able to ascertain that you are no longer the Lester that I once knew. Leaving aside our political differences, which many times soured our relationship but never were able to terminate our friendship, this letter reveals a character flaw that I consider inexcusable. No doubt you have

THE END OF THE THIRD WORLD

good reasons for justifying such an attitude, but I hope you use them solely to placate your own conscience, sparing me the necessity of hearing them.

With respect to the concern you express for my future, I want to tell you that I was profoundly insulted by your reducing my professional perspectives to the destiny of a magazine that presents itself as the paradigm of the economic stability of the Empire and doesn't hesitate to provide suspicious little parties in the suites of the Clarence Hotel, in order to grub double-page colored ads from obese princes from the Persian Gulf. Contrary to these desert emirs, who arrive here intent upon transgressing their medieval ethics in the London fog, I am not willing to give free reign to my principles.

Someone once stated that we English are specialists in inventing strange traditions. I agree even though I have my doubts concerning the quaintness of such a custom. And the most recent tradition cultivated amongst us seems to be the transformation of rich old men into cadavers in suspended animation. We have reinvented the character of Mary Shelley with the addition of a senility controlled by gerontologists and a contest of administrative committees. It was Bernard Shaw who said that one doesn't grow old in this country anymore, once simply goes to the grave at the age of ninety, with a golf club in hand. That English perversion of taxidermy has even managed to improve upon the mummifiers of ancient Egypt. It has created those prodigious infants of Tanatos, protected by priestesses with enormous breasts and scribes in wool suits.

What I can't imagine, dear Lester, is that after so many speeches justly taken from the ideology of the sixties, you would fall in with those mummifiers.

Please, consider yourself freed from any obligation to me. And don't waste your time coming here, alone or accompanied by someone else.

Cordially,
Jane Amazon Challenger

The letter, which Lester read aloud, had the effect of a not so subtle dose of arsenic in Spender's sparse hopes. And it was like a sock in the stomach for the addressee. Haynes, who had been listening to the reading with an expression that might call to mind a savage cannibal observing his victim cook in a steaming pot, choked at the letter's end. Standing to the right of Lester's desk, Spender gasped in what seemed to be a series of hysterical spasms, while not far away, seated at his desk, Haynes coughed, desperately in need of air, choking on his own saliva that had been secreted initially out of pure joy. Amidst these two hysterical displays, Lester felt like a veritable fool. He deliberated between giving the two of them a few slaps in their pretentious, pale faces or leaving them gasping for air, as they were, until they suffocated. He was saved by the little bit of self-respect that he had left.

"Stop the clowning around," he shouted.

The two stopped short and looked at him amazed. No one raised his voice in the editorial office, as serious as a disagreement might become. For a few seconds, no one moved. The secretaries stopped typing at their terminals, the telephone operators halted their compulsive gestures of tightening switches, and the office boys who distributed papers froze their peripatetic impulses. The only audible sound was the distant buzz of the heating unit.

"Let's go to my office, Lester," Spender offered, rather embarrassed, but assuming once again the role of editor. "And you, Haynes, not a word about what you have just heard," he warned somewhat futilely, retreating to his refuge.

Still trembling with rage, Lester stored Engels's picture in his desk drawer before following Spender.

In his office, after having requested more tea, Spender waited for Lester to reveal himself. He assumed he was in the presence of an intractable individual who detested hierarchies and would refuse to cooperate, and that caused him to lose heart. But he knew that his future wasn't in Lester's hands, but in the niggardly hands of chance.

"We have no way out, do we, Lester?" Spender wanted to know, seeing that the other insisted on drinking his tea in total silence.

Lester finished his tea and sat back in the easy chair of synthetic leather that smelled vaguely of disinfectant, the perfect odor for the occupant of that office.

"I think that we should clean out our offices, Spender," Lester responded coldly.

He shrugged his shoulders and glanced nostalgically round the office.

"We could go there once and for all, Lester. Who knows..."

"It would be useless. We would be wasting our time."

"Perhaps not. If we were to get in," Spender said, thoughtfully, the beads of sweat descending into his soaked collar. He remained silent for a few seconds, and then began to speak in a whisper. "If we got in, she would be obligated to hear us out."

"What are you saying, Spender?"

"Nothing, nothing. I just want a little more time, until the end of the day. Don't leave yet, Lester; let's go to West Enmore Park," he responded, rising impetuously and leaving Lester alone in the office.

A fine mist covered the city as the Morris left the company parking lot. The traffic was at a standstill and

LOST WORLD II

Spender was quiet, ruminating his rancor, while Lester, more than a little despondent, sought a way to convince Jane to speak with them.

Lester knew the Enmore Park mansion very well, in spite of the fact that he no longer went there with the same frequency as he once did. His entire childhood he had spent in that neighborhood, in the house built by his grandfather and sold by his father to a contracting firm. The house no longer existed, and on the lot a dreadful sixties-style condominium had been built. As a matter of fact, nearly the whole area around Enmore Park was changed. The imposing residence of the Challengers was one of the few left, with its majestic Greek revival portico, its white marble stairway, its doors of carved oak, and bronze knockers that shine in the evening lights.

When the car stopped, Lester noticed that the two wide windows, draped in heavy velvet curtains, didn't give any indication of light within.

Almost as if he were following an old custom, he sprinted up the stairs and rang the doorbell while Spender hid himself at his side. The door was opened by the person Lester expected.

"Hello, Henry." Lester greeted the man familiarly; at the same time Spender seemed to withdraw in fear at the sight.

"Good evening, Mr. Lester," Henry responded. The butler, a rather peculiar fellow, had been associated with the house as long as the Challengers; for one thing, he had been born in the house, where his parents had lived, and before them, his grandparents. He was a short man, with Malayan features and a muscular body that didn't quite fit into the suit and tie that he always wore. The impression the Henry invariably conveyed was that he didn't feel comfortable in his clothes, most likely for some ancestral reason.

THE END OF THE THIRD WORLD

"I would like to speak with Miss Challenger."

Henry remained impassive, but his voice betrayed him. He and Lester were friends, and for that reason the orders that he had received were not easy to deliver.

"I'm very sorry, Mr. Lester, but . . ."

"What is it, Henry? Is Jane not at home?" Lester purposely used the familiar tone in order to make him even more embarrassed.

"Yes, she is, sir. But I am sorry to say that she gave me explicit orders . . ."

"Come on, Henry. Don't tell me that she won't receive me?"

Henry apparently couldn't be shaken, but Lester knew him sufficiently well to know that he was ill at ease.

"Hell, she must really be mad at me, Henry," he said, trying to be jovial in order to hide his disappointment but deciding not to insist further. "All right, I'll come back another day. Good night, Henry."

He turned around and walked back to the car, but Spender didn't follow him. Lester stopped, waiting for him, but then he witnessed something unusual. Spender surprisingly had put his arm over the butler's shoulders and was whispering something in his ear. Astonished, Lester saw Henry's inexpressive face light up and, as if from the touch of a magic wand, he beamed.

"Mr. Lester, please, listen," Henry said, eagerly.

"What is it, Henry?" Lester asked in a jealous and defensive tone.

"My orders are not to receive anyone through this door." Henry spoke in his unmistakable accent. "But there is nothing to stop me from allowing friends to enter through the back door."

"Good for you, Henry!" exclaimed Spender, patting the butler on the shoulder.

Stupefied, Lester stared at Spender's display. Something was amiss, he thought, worriedly, and it wasn't only this surprising demonstration of casuistry on Henry's part.

"Don't worry, my dear Henry," Spender said, maliciously winking at me, "we won't let you down."

Henry, in the meantime, had returned to his normal state, protected by the impenetrable and simulated screen that he had cultivated as part of his character. He bowed, excusing himself, and closed the door, leaving them on the sidewalk.

"Let's go," Spender invited. "Where is the back door? You must know."

In silence, Lester in the lead, they walked around to the back of the house. Enmore Park occupied an entire block, its enormous fig trees with their puckered trunks and magnificent crowns casting shade throughout. Behind the high walls, there was grass that smelled of dew, hedges artistically trimmed in the forms of exotic animals, a lake stocked with catfish that swam in slow motion through the murmuring water. And the labyrinth. The small labyrinth of brambles where, as children, he and Jane lost themselves in their fantasies. He and Jane. What a hassle, he thought. Could that damn labyrinth catch him again?

"My God, what an estate, and so huge," Spender commented, panting as they arrived at the back door.

"The owner of Enmore Park doesn't need the *New Economist*," Lester said.

Spender shrugged.

Henry, as if he were seeing them for the first time that night, opened the door.

"My dear Lester, what a surprise!"

Lester mumbled something and went on in. The maids bent over giggling as they passed by. He knew where Jane would be; no one needed to tell him. Like a hound

THE END OF THE THIRD WORLD

dog, Spender tried to follow him, but Henry pulled him rudely by the arm.

"It's all right, good fellow, don't get nervous," Spender said, hurriedly handing over to the butler a yellowed package that he drew from his coat pocket. "A promise made is a promise paid."

Leaving for later a probe of Spender's more than suspicious behavior, Lester walked toward the library, where he believed Jane would have sought seclusion. There, among the shelves of books sumptuously bound in leather and the collections of antique tomes on zoology and natural science, inherited from her grandfather, Jane commonly retreated when her life became complicated.

But before Lester was able to get halfway down the hall, the library doors were flung open and in the threshold stood the svelte and petulant figure of a small woman, dressed in brown serge pants and a loose blouse full of pockets. Framing her face was fiery red hair; her green eyes flashed with rage.

It was Jane. And she wasn't there to play games.

"I never thought that you would sink so low," she shouted.

"Jane!"

"Don't dare speak to me, Billy Lester."

She advanced toward her friend, forcing him to retreat. He had never seen her use physical violence, but there were precedents in the family. Her grandfather was famous, among other things, for striking journalists. Her father had the habit of shooting a shotgun filled with salt at photographers who tried to surprise him during his morning walks through the gardens around the house.

Disregarding Lester, she passed through the room with the single-minded brutality of a hurricane. Her red hair seemed to leave the trace of an incandescent reflection, and as Lester knew so well, she was ready, willing, and able to repel that invasion at all costs. Spender could not have been more imprudent.

Having no choice, Lester followed her as if he were dragged along by the vacuum left by her abrupt and determined dislocation.

"Henry!" she screamed.

She had a potent contralto voice. A scream of hers was enough to dislodge the whole household staff.

Henry appeared. Lester noticed how pale he was, if that cocoa-colored face can be said to achieve pallor.

"Miss Challenger," the butler mumbled.

Jane extended her hand.

"Hand it over," she ordered harshly.

Henry's Malayan eyes contracted; a look of stupor came over him.

"Come on, Henry," she insisted, moving her hand. "I don't have all night."

Henry pulled the package that Spender had given him out of his pocket and gave it to her in one rapid movement.

"Where is that swine?" she asked.

"In the kitchen," Henry informed her shamefacedly.

"Kick him out."

"But . . ."

"Do as I say."

Henry hesitated; then he decided to obey the order, and turned on his heels.

"He doesn't need to literally kick him out," Lester stammered.

"It is better that you not get involved, Lester," Jane responded, deigning to expend part of her wrath on him.

"If Henry hurts Spender, you'll be hit with a lawsuit," Lester warned her.

"And the worm will be hit with one of his own," she

THE END OF THE THIRD WORLD

said, showing him the package that Spender had quickly passed to Henry.

"What in the devil is this?" Lester wanted to know, genuinely curious, ignoring the expression of anger and deception that she was radiating.

"Hashish," she said with disgust. "That scoundrel Spender must have investigated everything about us and discovered this . . . weakness of Henry's."

"Hey, I didn't have anything to do with this," Lester stuttered, astonished. "You know that I would be the last person to intimate these things to Spender."

She rewarded him with the same disdain with which she had referred to Spender's little scheme. The disdain was a bit too much, and he thought that he didn't need to put up with it anymore. Jane might mean many things to him, the best part of his life, a parameter of boldness in an aimless epoch, a precious friendship that was perhaps beginning to unravel, but she certainly didn't mean that much.

Lester shook his head, turned his back on her, and began to leave.

At the end of the hall the maids were peeking curiously.

"Lester!" he heard.

He almost stopped, but he thought he was delirious, because it was the warm voice that she used in her moments of good humor.

"Lester, wait."

Lester hesitated.

At the end of the hall, Henry appeared, blushing.

"Miss Challenger, it wasn't possible to kick him out on his rear; he ran out before I could do it."

"And you, you scamp, selling yourself for nothing!"

Henry tried to explain himself, but he was cut short by the melodious laughter of his mistress.

It was a warm, frank laughter, typical of Jane in a good mood.

That laughter didn't make any sense.

Lester decided to turn around.

Jane was standing with the package of hashish in her hand; she had stopped laughing. And without losing the luminosity that her victory over Spender had given her, she looked at him with an unexpected tenderness.

"If you had not come, in spite of everything," she said, continuing to smile, "I never would have forgiven you."

The Most Amazing Thing in the World

Lester examined some papers. They seemed to be some pages from a rudimentary cashbook, the typical ledger used by a careless accountant. Lester looked at the totals, glancing over the annotations without being able to understand the language in which it was written.

"What do you think?" Jane wanted to know.

Without saying a word, Lester returned the mysterious papers to her.

A flash of lightning lit up the night, followed by a powerful thunderbolt. A violent storm was breaking over London, but there in the sparsely lit library, it was peaceful and comfortable.

"Is this all that you've got?" he said finally.

"That's it. I had some problems..." Jane responded laconically.

"I don't understand the language."

"It's Portuguese," Jane explained.

That didn't seem to get through to him, and she persisted.

"It is written in Portuguese language."

"And do you understand Portuguese?" he asked, surprised.

"You know I don't," she responded, somewhat abruptly. "But that doesn't matter," she replied quickly. "I had someone translate it. Just as I expected, it is part of what could be called a second set of books."

LOST WORLD II

Lester showed his lack of interest by diverting his attention to the enormous portrait of Professor Challenger. The painting, enthroned between elegantly bound book spines, revealed a pudgy gentleman with disheveled hair, a black beard, and fleshy eyelids that nearly covered his eyes. A real bullfrog, as his detractors described him.

"And what of it?" said Lester, indifferently, still examining the contrast between the figure in the painting, close to a Neanderthal man, and the perfection of his descendant. "A second set of books is a venerable institution in the capitalist system."

"For that very reason, it is revealing," Jane argued, beginning to get impatient with the lack of interest that her reluctant friend demonstrated in the subject.

"Naturally, every set of second books is like a secret original of a work of art which we know only in its miniature, duplicate form," he said ironically.

Jane grabbed another stack of papers and nearly threw them in Lester's lap.

"Now examine these papers," she ordered.

They were photocopies of microfilms. They all bore the mark of the British Museum stamp. Lester looked through them, little by little acquiring an interest. Each page documented the official bookkeeping of a British firm from the first industrial revolution. Old records in faint cursive, written in the peculiar spelling of the eighteenth century.

"Interesting, isn't it?" she commented excitedly.

"Very," he responded vaguely.

"And if, just by chance, you were to find one of these entrepreneurs in the flesh?"

"What entrepreneurs?"

"For example, the owner of this woolen mill in Warwick." She pointed at one of the pages.

THE END OF THE THIRD WORLD

"This one? But the woolen mill is from . . . from 1798!"

"Exactly, Lester. And if you were to find an entrepreneur from 1798 alive?"

"I would have good reason to doubt my sanity."

"Well, I found one of these specimens."

"Oh, please, Jane," he protested.

"And not only one, I found a good number of them. A whole economy. A lost world."

From the wall, Professor Challenger observed the conversation in silence—something he had never done while alive—and with an air of complicity.

"I know what you are thinking," she said, imagining the terrible things that could be going through Lester's head.

"So you went there . . ."

"Purely by chance."

"I can't believe it."

"I swear, Lester. And now I think there is some truth to the legend."

Perhaps, he reflected. After all, legends are a poetic transformation of something that really took place. And in the Challengers' case, what had happened involved such detail, one could hardly call them familial legends. They more closely resembled a curse. Professor Challenger came back from there speaking of dinosaurs. Jane's father, Dr. Challenger, Jr., returned from those wild lands swearing to have pacified authentic Amazons, tribal precursors of today's feminists. Now the granddaughter is talking about capitalists who have been extinct since 1800.

"I hadn't intended on going there, believe me," Jane affirmed, somewhat disconcerted to see that he was genuinely shocked.

"You used to swear that you would never go near that place, Jane."

LOST WORLD II

"I know, I did. But everything happened by chance."

Lester shook his head and started to get up.

"No, wait. At least you should hear the story. To understand how it happened."

"Thanks, Jane, but I'm not interested."

"Do you want some brandy?" she suggested, with an irresistible tone of command.

She served the drinks and began speaking, happy with her victory.

"Well, last week, as the job at Geneva was drawing to an end, I realized that I was exhausted."

Lester could empathize with that; he knew only too well what was involved in covering one of those economic conferences, especially when the topic was Third World debt. A swarm of sixty-year-old men and their younger advisers, sitting around a large conference table, all of them in the good physical condition of morning joggers. For the reporters hovering around them, they always reserved their most serious expressions, full of grave concern. Inside, away from the press, "off the record," they all were quite happy with themselves, and why not, since they were earning high interest, spreading out the loans, which were always paid with incredible diligence by the sly bureaucrats of those hot, miserable countries. It was disgusting. Lester understood that, but what he didn't understand is how it could have affected Jane since she wasn't one to be impressed with the ostentatious show of power, with the insensitivity that penetrated every word, with the arrogance of every last one of them, from the most secondary executive to the great financiers.

"These conferences are really exhausting."

"Stupefying is more like it," she said with a certain restraint. "When it was all over, without any conclusive resolution, of course, I felt so drained that I returned to the hotel and slept for twenty-four hours straight."

Jane paused and fixed her green eyes on Lester, as if she were trying to detect in him some sign of condescension. But Lester had never patronized her, even when he had been indulgent with her haughtiness or ironic with her fits of temper. He knew that for Jane to reveal the smallest sign of weakness was as inconceivable as renouncing her principles.

Feeling somehow disturbed, she got up and silently walked around the library, which was lit up from time to time by lightning flashes. She wasn't able to overcome her own uneasiness, nor was she able to explain the impulse that led her to go into the first travel agency she happened across. It was a Thursday, she remembered, a pleasant afternoon, and the travel agent was attentive and patient. She wanted to spend a weekend in the most distant place possible. Some place that was really far away, on another continent.

She assumed the salesperson took her for an eccentric, because one usually doesn't spend only a weekend in some really distant place. But the travel agent didn't appear surprised; it appeared she was accustomed to all types of eccentricities. She consulted her list of packages, and after verifying with Jane that there were no price limitations, she showed her what seemed to be the only option for that weekend. It was a chartered flight that left that very night and returned to Geneva the next Monday. And of course, it seemed difficult to believe, but for some reason she didn't pay attention to the name of the place when the agent presented the plan to her. She simply paid the price, which included the cost of lodging, and since it wasn't necessary to visit the consulate for a visa, she returned to the hotel, packed her bags, and went directly to the airport.

LOST WORLD II

That same night she was on a jet, crossing the Atlantic Ocean, without knowing exactly what she was doing. She fell into a deep sleep, and when she woke up, she saw that they were flying over a carpet of forest that lost itself in the horizon. She began to feel uneasy when the airplane made a long and smooth turn over the dark waters of an enormous river and came down for a landing. That landscape below terrified her because it brought old images to her mind. She was seated near the window, in an uncomfortable and meager tourist-class seat in the unpleasant vicinity of an older couple whose longevity apparently had given them a dispensation from all basic bodily functions; at least that is how it appeared to her. Since the takeoff and during the rainy night spent on the plane, the two elderly people had not moved from their places; they remained belted into their seats, rigid in the stoic wait of those who fear airplanes.

The symptoms, she knew well enough; frequent travelers are quick to perceive those types of individuals who enter the airplane with an ancient and profound disbelief in man's scientific capability. The old man, who was still hale and hearty, was red in the face upon boarding; later he appeared relieved, and his skin took on more of an earthy tone. The man was wearing a wool suit and wine-colored silk tie; overall he appeared to be one of the city's veteran banking bureaucrats, perhaps a bookkeeper for some financier, on his first vacation in many years, taking his wife on a long-awaited dream trip. The old lady wore a small, colorful hat, pinned in her hair by a hatpin; she dressed in sober gray tones. Her facial expression as well as her skin color rivaled her husband's in its cheerlessness and anxiety. Jane herself was dressed as inappropriately as the couple, and in addition, she felt horrible.

THE END OF THE THIRD WORLD

Twelve hours later, they were disembarking in an airport that differed little from any other airport of the world. It was early morning, yet it was already hot, very hot. Right away it was evident that their clothing was poorly suited for that stifling climate, reminiscent of the hothouses of Kew Gardens. Deep inside her it evoked an even older memory, one that had accompanied her since childhood and always seemed present in Pembroke Square, a memory so strong that she wasn't able to avoid it, as if it were a part of her own soul.

But perhaps Lester understood her; after all, he had also spent his childhood in the middle of that nebulous, remote atmosphere that evoked a scalding and mysterious land, the custodian of primeval secrets hidden by the equatorial nights.

"You were in Manaus!" Lester exclaimed excitedly.

"Yes, Manaus." She repeated the strange sounds of this name as if reciting some sort of primitive incantation.

"So then what did you do, when you realized where you were?"

"I felt an enormous panic. I tried to return, but it was impossible; one can't change the schedule of a charter flight with three hundred Europeans, wrinkled by the crossing and suffering from jet lag. Fortunately I restrained myself, or they certainly would have thought me crazy."

"I'm the one you're making crazy," Lester protested. "Tell me what happened next!"

"Everything seemed turned upside down. It was six hours earlier than Europe; I was feeling hungry at the wrong time of the day and cursing the moment that I had entered that travel agency in Geneva. My grandfather had visited Manaus in 1910, my father in 1947. But I felt little comfort knowing this."

LOST WORLD II

A strong electrical discharge fell near the house, and the lights went out. The thunderbolt made Jane instinctively draw closer to her friend. When the lights came back on—and it didn't take long—she had stood up and was breathing heavily, as if she were out of breath. The storm continued in its intensity, almost in a tropical fury, and Jane tried one more time to overcome the feeling of futility in explaining to her friend what she was feeling as she disembarked from the plane in that city. Indeed, it had been idiotic, the way in which she blended in with the tourists. The heat made her sleepy and disturbed her sight. The day began with a very strong, glimmering horizon of light that hardly enabled her to see as she was led to the tour bus by solicitous and smiling native guides. And curiously enough, those guides, with their white teeth, olive skin, and slightly Asiatic features, had a calming effect on her. There was a pure happiness about them, as rough and unpolished as a natural crystal.

Once on the bus, she stayed at the window, watching the distant strip of undulating jungle that freed itself from the blue blanket of morning mist. Some distance from the road, in ugly cleared areas, groups of houses and miserable huts could be seen; from them natives waved at the bus with a timid cheerfulness. Jane had read quite a bit about the destruction of the Amazon jungle by deforestation, but she had not been seriously concerned. She had assumed that the jungle would always be greater that the depredators, having listened as a child to the profuse descriptions of those forests, in the summer gatherings in that same library, when her father and her grandfather would vie with each other to see who could impress the children more with their stories. She often went to bed overly excited and had upsetting dreams of gigantic trees and mushrooms that

THE END OF THE THIRD WORLD

could serve as hiding places for little girls who got lost in the forest.

"How about another brandy?" Lester suggested, breaking the silence. He was going to need more than just another shot of brandy to hear her out to the end of the story.

"I think that I am boring you," she said.

"No, please. I want to hear everything. I really am interested," he assured her.

Jane seemed convinced, and after serving the brandy, she resumed the narrative.

"When I arrived at the hotel, I was beginning to feel a little calmer. Even the fact that I was among a group of tired tourists ceased to irritate me. It had its advantages; if I gave myself over completely to the program organized by the travel agency, I would have my time entirely occupied, and there would be no possibility of my becoming involved in any unpleasantness. The hotel seemed to maintain a high level of service, considering that it had been built in the middle of a huge tropical forest, on the edge of a wide, dark river. Nearly all of the guests were Europeans or North Americans; the only Brits were the old couple and I."

"But naturally you did more than just follow the program," Lester commented.

She looked at him, offended. "I did all of the damn tourist program," she retorted, annoyed.

"But—"

"I think that I was the only one in the group who did all of it, from the boat trip to the lunch on a floating restaurant full of hysterical parrots."

"You're saying that you didn't go out on your own?"

"Not once. Whenever I went out, it was to take a bus somewhere or make a boat trip, and I was always accompanied by the members of the group and our guides.

LOST WORLD II

Also, the hotel was far from the center of the city, which I visited only once, for three hours, when we toured the famous Amazon Theater."

"And what about that figure from the past, the so-called eighteenth-century entrepreneur? Was he selling arts and crafts in front of the Theater? Singing Rigoletto, or who knows what?"

She smiled, shaking her head. "You really are bored, aren't you?"

"Please, Jane," he said, wanting to prolong the conversation, "I am very interested, but you could be a little more objective."

At that point, Jane walked over to the window and gazed out for a time. "You're right. I was just trying to review the strange sequence of circumstances in which everything happened," she said after a few seconds.

"You were talking about the opera . . ."

"Yes, but it happened in the hotel itself."

"What happened?"

"You're going to find out soon enough," she said, with some perplexity remaining in her face.

But Lester was impatient with her. All of this seemed very mysterious, and not at all like the Jane that he knew.

"It was our next to last night in the city," Jane said, "and there was some sort of social gathering given by the hotel management. However, I was not exactly in a sociable mood, so I decided to stay in the bar near the swimming pool, have a few drinks, and retire early. I think that all the hotel guests were at the party and having a wild time, because the bar was empty except for an old, dull waiter. I was drinking a fruit drink, feeling rather good for the first time in a long while. It wasn't hot; the night was subtly perfumed by the fragrances of the forest. Scents that brought back strange

THE END OF THE THIRD WORLD

recollections of my childhood, especially the visits that my father and I would make to Ireland in the years right after the war. In the summer the Irish countryside had similar fragrances.

"About that time, a man walked into the bar. At first I didn't pay much attention to him, but having nothing else to do, I started to study him carefully while he chose a table. He was an older man, medium build, immaculately combed white hair; judging from his European features and impeccably tailored jacket, he could have been an entrepreneur from any Mediterranean country. He chose to sit at a table near the pool, and seemed to be contemplating the surface of the blue water, which was illuminated by underwater lights. It appeared to me that he was unaware of my presence since he hadn't once looked my way."

"What happened then?" Lester asked, getting more impatient every minute.

"It was all very strange. The man obviously waited until the waiter had moved away from the tables; then, finally looking in my direction, he got up, gave me an elegant bow, and said: 'Are you by any chance Miss Challenger?'

" 'What did you say?' I responded, disbelieving what I just heard and glancing around the empty bar, a little worried.

" 'Are you by any chance Miss Challenger?' he repeated. His pronunciation was that of a person who spoke English well, but the question itself contained a hint of anxiety.

"I looked around the bar again, searching for some indication of what that remark meant, but there was only the old waiter, hanging on to the bar, half-asleep.

" 'Challenger, yes,' I responded. 'Is there something wrong with that?'

" 'No, not at all,' the man responded. 'I knew that you were staying here; I just happened to be consulting the registry of hotel guests today. Don't be alarmed. I wasn't deliberately looking for you. I was trying to find the name of a friend who should have arrived in the city today. Apparently he didn't come. Manaus is as distant from everything as one can get.'

"I purposely took a large swallow of the tropical drink and responded, without actually knowing why: 'Very distant. Do you know me, perchance?'

" 'Not exactly,' he responded, reluctantly. 'But I was curious. It is an uncommon name, even in England. Are you possibly a relative of Dr. Alfred Challenger?'

"I almost fell out of the chair upon hearing my father's name. 'I am his daughter.'

" 'My God, I could have guessed!' he exclaimed. 'I studied with your father at Eton. The graduating class of 1944. Difficult times, those. War, rationing . . . But you don't know anything of this, miss; you were not even born yet.'

" 'Are you Brazilian?'

" 'Amazonian,' he responded with an expression of involuntary nonconformity. 'The son of Portuguese immigrants. I was born in a city in the interior of Amazonia. But I went to England at the age of seventeen.'

"I don't quite know what I responded. It was really such an unexpected situation, finding someone who had studied at Eton now living in the jungle. I looked at the pool again, the deserted bar, and the domesticated jungle in the form of a park that surrounded us. Some lanterns gave a hint of pale light in the darkness of the jungle. The noise of the crickets and a concert of insects completed the image of the tropics. The jungle.

THE END OF THE THIRD WORLD

" 'Father talked a lot of this city. And my grandfather, as well,' I confessed, breaking the strained silence and trying to make conversation, but the man limited himself to looking at me with an uncomfortable enchantment.

"He nodded his head, solicitous and attentive. 'They were here, like many Englishmen. But they were unique. My father helped Professor Challenger in his second trip, the one of 1912; they became friends, and that was decisive in my going to England. Normally the young men from this area were sent to study in Paris.'

" 'I would like you to know something. The fact that my grandfather was here, and my father as well, was not decisive in my coming here. It was pure chance. I only realized where I was as I was disembarking in the airport.'

" 'I understand,' he responded, solicitously. 'Can I sit down for a moment?' I offered him an empty chair, and he extended his hand.

" 'But allow me to introduce myself. I am Danilo Ariel Duarte.'

" 'Jane Challenger,' I also introduced myself, shaking the fine, white hand of my father's unexpected friend.

" 'Manaus,' I said, murmuring the strange syllables of that word. The man was startled upon hearing the word, with its nasalized sounds which I pronounced accentuating only the consonants; it was as if he were hearing it for the first time, or only in that instant the mysteries of those phonemes were finally revealing themselves to him.

" 'Manaus.'

"And we sat there in the silence. Crickets in the night, toads. The tropics. The smell of decaying fruit. Chlorophyllous sleep. Nocturnal mugginess. Fireflies.

"Suddenly a glass shattered on the ground. It had fallen from the man's hand; he sat staring at the pieces of glass and the pool of liquid that had spilled on the marble floor. He didn't seem well; he was quite pale, and drops of sweat were running down his face. The old waiter, abruptly awakened, came quickly to clean the floor, mumbling something. The familiar noise of breaking glass brought me back to reality. And I realized that my father's friend was retiring without saying another word.

"I immediately got up and decided to leave the empty bar, where images of palm trees swayed in the pool's blue water, and the heavy smell of chlorine was everywhere."

"And then what happened? What had he wanted?" Lester asked uneasily.

"I don't know exactly. When the glass fell, it was as if I were being rescued from some sort of vertigo. He left the papers you saw here tonight on top of the table."

"On top of the table?" he tried to verify.

"I hadn't even noticed them, but the waiter ran after me with the papers in hand."

"How strange!"

"I went to my room, but I wasn't able to sleep. I tried to read the papers, but none of it made any sense. The whole thing left me rather apprehensive. You know that I'm not the type of person who gets paranoid, yet I began to feel a little afraid. I feared that it might have been some sort of conspiracy, and I wasn't the least bit interested in involving myself in the internal matters of that country."

"In what year was your grandfather there?"

"He went two times, in 1910 and again in 1912. And my father, in 1947."

"It must have been very different then."

"More uncivilized, you mean?"

"Perhaps not. It must be an extraordinary city."

THE END OF THE THIRD WORLD

"Indeed it is. Out there surrounded by a huge tropical jungle," she said with a sigh.

Lester looked at his watch; it was three in the morning. He was tired. Considering the distance to his apartment and the time that it would take him to get there, he decided that if he left right then, he would be arriving home around four in the morning. He could call a taxi; it would be rather expensive, but there was no other way. Jane went over to a leather easy chair and curled up as if she were cold. She observed her friend's movements with twinkling eyes, understanding his fretting.

"If you want, you can sleep here tonight," she suggested, resuming an old custom abandoned many years ago.

"Nah, I don't want to inconvenience you."

"No, it's no inconvenience; you can sleep in the guest room."

He agreed, surprising himself with the little resistance he put up before accepting the invitation.

"You're going to like the guest room. I had the wallpaper changed," she said, revealing her pleasure at his acceptance.

"I would like to hear the rest of the story, before going to sleep," he asked, stretching out on the couch in a more comfortable position. "Or do you think that I'll be able to go to sleep without hearing the epilogue?"

"I thought that I was boring you."

"And you are, but that's all right," Lester teased.

"The truth is that even now I'm still mystified by what happened," she said.

"What do you mean?"

"The plane was leaving the following night," Jane proceeded. "There wasn't much time left if I wanted to find out anything about the papers and my father's supposed friend. It was impossible to get any information about him from the hotel reception desk. They were very reticent and not too bright, or so they deliberately pretended to be, something that really tests my nerves. The next day, after a tedious outing by boat through a flooded forest, I found a message from the mysterious Mr. Duarte. He invited me to meet him at his place of business at five in the afternoon, to continue our conversation."

"And you went! I just knew that you didn't limit yourself strictly to the tourist program."

Jane motioned to Lester so he wouldn't interfere. She was completely serious, looking at him soberly, as if she were finally reaching the crucial moment of her narrative.

"Naturally I was there at the right time. Mr. Duarte received me courteously, thanking me for my interest."

" 'Do you have enough time to hear a fable?' he asked me as soon as his office door was closed.

" 'A fable?' I was prepared for any eventuality. I had not even excluded the possibility of being in the middle of a political conspiracy, but the question took me by surprise.

" 'It is an old custom of mine, miss, now anachronistic. I am one of the last practitioners of the art of fable-telling, the re-creation of parables. And, just like the fables themselves, I am an extinct animal. People like myself ought to figure in those ecological lists, along with the capuchin monkey and the gray whale.'

" 'You forgot these papers,' I said, showing him the envelope that he had left on the table in the bar.

" 'Keep them,' he answered back. " 'They are just old fossil remains. But you still haven't answered me. Would you like to hear a fable?'

" 'Why, yes,' I responded, trying to hide the irritation that had begun to build within me. The idiosyncrasies

THE END OF THE THIRD WORLD

of men in the Third World have never been something I could tolerate.

" 'The fable is called "Fly off the handle, and your fortune will fly out the door." '

"I had a coughing attack, which was calmed by a glass of water hastily brought to me by his secretary. And as there was no other alternative, I sat back in an easy chair and prepared myself to suffer the effects of Mr. Duarte's literary estrus.

"Once upon a time there was a poor rubber plantation owner who had three sons: Joao, Joaquim, and Manoel. Feeling death was approaching, he called his sons to his side and spoke: 'The end is near, and I'm almost ruined. All that is left is the profit from this last harvest. Divide it in equal parts, and each one of you do your best to make your part multiply.' Saying that, he laid his head down and gave his last breath. Mourning their father, the grieving sons went to the London Bank of Manaus in order to make their fraternal partition.

"Each one received five hundred pounds. Joao, the oldest brother, pondered their situation. 'Brothers, our shares are so small; if we do nothing, we will be in the poorhouse in no time at all.' To which the second son, Joaquim, replied, 'One of us ought to take the initiative. Since I am a graduate in business administration, I would like to be the first one to try.' The next day he put on his best suit, his best Italian tie, and saying good-bye to his brothers, he left.

"Right away he realized that it wasn't going to be easy. The economy was in a deep recession, the country was going through a difficult political phase, and the banks were charging extremely high interest rates. Toward the end of the afternoon, tired of looking for a good investment opportunity, he went to have a little nip during happy hour at Mandy's Bar. Seated at a table near him was a young entrepreneur, the nephew of a general who at that moment was a minister in the government.

" 'Good afternoon,' Joaquim said, greeting the general's nephew.

" 'Good afternoon, Dr. Joaquim. How's it going?' the general's nephew said with interest.

" 'So-so, just taking it as it comes, looking for an investment.'

" 'So let's start a business,' the general's nephew said. 'I also have a little capital; we can become partners in a savings and loan business. My uncle can get us a business permit as a lending institution; we'll attract the savings of the little people and finance low-income housing.'

" 'It seems like a good business,' Joaquim concurred, knowing that with the housing shortage for the masses, the deal could yield millions. Not a bad investment for someone who had only five hundred pounds.

" 'But there's one condition; the first one who gets his dander up and flies off the handle will lose his part in the partnership,' the general's nephew warned.

" 'I'm in,' Joaquim said enthusiastically. 'That will obligate us to act in a civil manner toward each other.'

"In just a few months, the partnership prospered. Thousands of savers deposited their savings, and the new partners financed housing projects for the poor. The work sites multiplied, and nothing seemed capable of shaking the stability of that investment. Until one day a bureaucrat from the Treasury Department appeared and presented Joaquim with a lien on the business, also indicating that he had been installed as temporary administrator of the business.

" 'How is that possible?' Joaquim said, perplexed.

THE END OF THE THIRD WORLD

" 'The two-hundred-thousand-dollar check that you cashed on the Recife office has bounced.'

" 'But I didn't sign that check. It was my partner, the general's nephew.'

" 'As the president of the firm, you are responsible,' the temporary administrator said, sitting down in Joaquim's chair.

"The young man lost his patience, and grabbing the bureaucrat by the lily white collar, he threw him out of his office, saying, 'Get out of here. Before I let this business go under, I'll skin the scoundrel who cheated me.'

"Joaquim was furious as he searched for his partner. He found him in Mandy's Bar in the middle of happy hour, where he was enjoying an amaretto sour.

" 'I'm going to bust your sneering face open,' he shouted, seeing the general's nephew calm and sure of himself.

" 'Ah! Could you have forgotten our agreement?'

" 'Go to hell, then,' Joaquim shouted, very near apoplexy, beating a retreat with a huge emotional trauma.

"Exhausted and humiliated, Joaquim returned home. After a strong dose of tranquilizers, he told his brothers what had happened. Joao, the oldest, after hearing his brother's drama, said, 'Let me take care of it. I'm going to find that fellow, and I'll get out of him not only the money you lost, but also all of the money that swindler has earned up to now.'

"Having said that, he left the next day, dressed in his most elegant Saville Row suit, to find the general's nephew in Mandy's Bar. It just so happens that the general's nephew had a magnificent business, which was an exclusive contract for the logging of hardwood from an area that was slated to be flooded by a government hydroelectric project. The business seemed fabulous; not only was the government paying to have the precious lumber removed from that area, but it also was extending a generous line of credit to facilitate the exportation of the lumber. But just about the time Joao was waking up to the fact that the business wasn't quite as good as it had seemed, the general's nephew had absconded with the government's money, depositing it in a bank in the Bahamas and forgetting to tell Joao that he had only six months to log the hardwood from the sixty-five thousand hectares of forest. The business, of course, went broke, and Joao flew off the handle, consequently losing his part of the partnership.

"Manoel, the youngest, being of reserved temperament, said, 'My turn has arrived, brothers. It is high time someone settle accounts with the general's nephew, and I'm just the one.' Of course, the two older brothers were afraid for the youngest and for the little that was left of the family inheritance as well. But they finally agreed, and Manoel set forth.

"Right away Manoel entered into an agreement with the general's nephew, and they built a distillery to produce alcohol and rum, using money from fiscal incentives. Some time later, when the business appeared to be prospering, Manoel found out that there was an accusation against the distillery stockholders with the Federal Police, which accused them of administrative fraud, fraudulent sales, ideological falsification, misappropriation of funds, the use of false documents, simulation of duplicates, and crimes against the popular economy. Manoel at this time was married to the daughter of a powerful general, an influential member of the information community, and due to this association, the accusations were shelved. The distillery was acquired by the Ministry of Industry and Commerce and was turned over to the son of another general, who was also

THE END OF THE THIRD WORLD

quite powerful, and who transformed it into an ethanol production plant.

"When the general's nephew realized that his latest partner had not flown off the handle, he felt proud to have come across a representative of the pinnacles of the modern national economy in that backward society. He invited him to be a partner in a new contract, this time in the political arena. Today the two of them are leaders of a moderately liberal party that preaches the politics of deregulation and a free market economy.

"Duarte brought his fable to a conclusion with a broad and dramatic gesture. As he did so, the study door opened and a flamboyant and energetic man entered."

At this point in her narrative, Jane's expression changed completely; she became tense, impatient. And as if to shake off the troubled thoughts that plagued her, she began to gesture emphatically as she spoke, something she commonly did—as Lester knew so well—when confronted with unpleasant situations. This habit is not at all uncommon among professional journalists, but by the extent of Jane's agitation, it was easy to see that the annoyance she must have suffered went beyond a question of mere rudeness. Caught up in the story, Lester realized that he was sitting on the edge of the couch.

"That despicable bandit," she muttered to herself.

"Who are you talking about?"

"About Mr. Duarte's partner. Someone named Pietro Pietra, Jr."

"Well, what about him?"

"He tried to end our meeting; he practically threw Mr. Duarte out of his own office, and he said he would take me to the hotel. He is one of those types of people who won't take no for an answer, Lester. He wanted to find out what we were up to."

"And what did you do?" Lester asked her nervously.

LOST WORLD II

"I pretended to be innocent, the daughter of an old friend of Mr. Duarte's, that type of thing," Jane said, her lips trembling and a flash of anger on her freckled face. "But he wasn't anyone's fool."

"What do you mean by that?"

"What I mean is that he ended up with the papers. Not all of them, but he grabbed those that interested him and left only those that you have seen."

"But hadn't you put them away?"

"Yes, I had. But he went with me to my hotel room. We talked for a while; I began to feel a strange drowsiness, as if I had been drugged, or something of the sort. I fell asleep and had a very strange dream. When I woke up, he wasn't in the room anymore, and my things had all been ransacked."

"You had the authorities look into it, didn't you?" he asked indignantly.

"What authorities?" she said, returning the inappropriate question back to Lester angrily. "You know how those grotesque societies are run, don't you? I was only sorry that the papers were missing. What could they have contained? I still cannot get over having lost them!"

Lester started pacing around the library impatiently, not knowing what to say, attempting to assimilate the story that Jane had just told. She herself seemed insecure and a little frightened, as if there were something she hadn't told her friend in order to save him from an even greater shock.

"All you want to do now is retrieve the papers, isn't it?" he wanted to know.

"Exactly, Lester. I can't think about anything else. I want you to help me."

Book Two

Between the Gotha and Erfurt Train Stations

What Is Left to Prove?

Jane Challenger's intriguing narrative remained hanging on the phosphorus green monitor. I stored the diskettes, stopped working on the novel for several months, and for some reason, felt the temptation to back out of it. After all, declaring some intention in an interview doesn't obligate the author to do what he declared. The history of journalism is replete with contradicted and false declarations. And when you think about it, who really pays attention to what a writer declares anyway?

It just so happened, however, that some months later the author of these improbable lines was on a train.

The train was crossing a highly industrialized region of Prussia. Colors had been banished forever from that region, and the melancholy of the place was like the soot that had impregnated the plants, the rooftops, and the austere and crumbling buildings that passed by our window. The Germans in the Federal Republic had warned us that the railroad line between Frankfurt and East Berlin was obsolete, the wagons were uncomfortable, and the attitude of the personnel on board was frankly paranoiac. We took these warnings as symptoms of the rivalry between the two sides of the German coin. But there really was a difference between the two sides; even the countrysides were different. It's just that it's Prussia, I thought. This area was always like this, gray, polluted, grimy, and oil-stained. Industry was never clean. But I didn't want to think about these differences, nor find reasons for the old Prussian spirit to have been transmuted into socialism.

The military patrols at the border really made us uncomfortable; not so much for the arms that they carried but rather the disarming look in their eyes. No one likes to be scrutinized in that way. They asked for our passports politely enough, which they rested on a curious little pad, full of ink pads and rubber stamps, that was attached to their belts, and then the uncomfortable ceremony would begin. They opened the passport to the photograph page and started to move their eyes mechanically from the photo to the face, from the document to its holder, repeating the action for several minutes, without a single change in expression or facial tick, apparently until the person being observed was emptied of any content. Or was that just what I felt at each of these encounters?

"Perhaps readers do the same thing when they are reading our books, and we just don't know it," said the writer Joao Ubaldo Ribeiro.

"It makes no difference to me," said the writer Lygia Fagundes Telles. "They can do whatever they want, since we don't have to have them looking at us."

There happened to be a group of Brazilian writers traveling in the cabin where the border guards were examining documents and issuing transit visas, which they did with the blank stare of a Victorian doll. And as everyone knows, writers, when they get together, only talk about serious things, such as incredibly complicated literary theories and extremely intricate projects. It isn't a good idea for readers to travel with writers, unless they want to die of boredom.

THE END OF THE THIRD WORLD

"I adore my readers, principally my female readers," said the writer Ignacio de Loyola Brandao.

The only one who didn't actively take part in the conversation, keeping somewhat apart from the group since our departure from Frankfurt, was the poet Haroldo de Campos. He was completely engrossed in the reading of a translation by an Occidental bard of the epic poem "Gilgamesh," recently discovered in a Polish abbey. Once in a while he would give some sign of life, saying things like "A plot that revolves around the hero's misery is presumptuous," or "Sometimes the translator treats the mythical plot as nonsense." And that was all.

"There is an ancient and endless discussion within literature," the novelist Loyola Brandao went on, "concerning the relationship between the writer and his reader. I would go so far as to say that it is a crucial but little-researched issue. I have thought about publishing some of my field studies on the topic."

"That would be a good idea," I retorted. "I, for one, aside from being a writer, have always been an inveterate reader who reads every sort of thing. If I don't have something to read, I'll read the label on a medicine bottle. I'll read anything that I can get my hands on. Just so you can have an idea of this compulsion of mine, every time there is a lull in our conversation, I try to read this pamphlet that I found in the bathroom."

"What is the pamphlet about?" asked Lygia, always curious.

"I don't know. I can't read a word of German!"

"I don't read so much anymore," Joao Ubaldo confessed. "Lately all I can manage to read are the Odes of Anacreon."

Loyola Brandao didn't seem to agree with his Bahian colleague.

"As a reader, I learned that literature only serves a purpose when it is pleasurable," the author from Sao Paulo said.

"You're right," I added. "I also only like to read when what I'm reading gives me pleasure. If I don't like it, I immediately ask myself if the absence of pleasure enriches me in some way."

"You must be some masochistic deviant," Loyola teased. "You had better be careful or you'll end up writing newspaper articles for a living."

"What the hell," exclaimed Joao Ubaldo. "Sometimes I ask myself that same question. Especially if it is a theoretical book, or a so-called nonfiction, as those works are now classified. In theory, one can't always demand a pleasurable experience, but that doesn't mean, nevertheless, that theoretical texts can't be pleasurable."

"But in the case of fiction," Lygia intervened, "I would say that everything is lost if there is no pleasure. And I accept my literary hedonism."

"When I am writing my own novels," I said, "I keep in mind just one commandment, one which I learned as a reader. This commandment is 'Don't piss anyone off.' I love to read, I write so that I can be read, and what interests me in literature is the playful contact between the author and the reader."

Loyola Brandao smiled and seemed to agree.

"It is a game of subtle seduction," he said, "of involvement, of mystery, of disarmament."

"What I adore in this game is that it isn't eternal," I added. "It's something here and now, realized between persons who are engulfed in the same contingency. I say this to demonstrate my choice: I am a writer who doesn't fix his sights on eternity, who prefers to be contemporary to his contemporaries. What's more, I find it much more exciting to have a tête-à-tête with today's readers than pretend to speak to my readers who are hidden in tomorrow's shadows."

"Readers perceive this, I believe, when they read a novel," Lygia said, flashing one of her magnificent smiles. "They realize it right off when someone is writing for their particular delight."

"And not for some theoretical levitations," I added.

Lygia's smile weakened slightly, because she isn't one to get interested in such murky issues. Lygia is solar; everyone knows that.

"I recognize, nevertheless, that it isn't always easy for an author to keep his readers in sight as he is writing," I went on. "In literature total premeditation isn't possible. You don't just sit down and say that you're going to write for your French reader, or your Canadian reader, or your Bahian reader. Since the act of writing demands isolation, the reader's face doesn't hover like a phantom in front of the writer. As far as I'm concerned, such a thing would lead to writer's block."

"I have had books published in many countries," Loyola Brandao replied, "and I would run the risk of being haunted by the faces of Brazilians, North Americans, Italians, Germans, Spaniards, Swedes . . ."

"That is true," Joao Ubaldo said, "but in spite of it all, I need a face, because when we maintain a dialogue with someone, we need to look in their eyes, feel their complicity, their warmth."

"I don't know how you all will resolve this question," Lygia spoke up, "but I write for my friends."

"I like to do this, too," I said. "They read my books, some of them even before they're published, and they participate up close to the creative process. They interfere, disagree, agree, make suggestions. Many times I am writing a chapter and I think, 'Ah! So-and-so is going to love this part.' The worst thing is that sometimes they don't; they say that it's nothing special, and a discussion ensues that leaves me furious. Aside from that, I have a group of friends that is quite diverse. To begin with, my most ferocious critic is my wife, Ida, who also writes. But I have everything from the most cultured friends, who have already read 'all' the nouveau-romain without suffering a single mental insult, to friends who are working-class people."

"Don't you have any Indian friends?" Joao Ubaldo wanted to know.

"None. Indians should not read novels; it could cause them to become extinct. But to a certain extent, my friends universalize what I write. They drag me out of isolation. With their help, I arrive at my objective, which is to be read; even though there are those who believe it is possible to create literature without being read."

And *Lost World II*, I thought. What in the hell do you want to do with that book? Is it a novel? Are there still novels?

I'm not here to respond to these kinds of questions, I said to myself as the phantom of Miss Challenger came down the passageway of the car, holding a cigarette and hiding her face in her red hair. She was wearing a sober navy blue gabardine coat and carrying a crocodile-skin makeup case, ostensibly anticonservative. I am here, she seemed to say to me in her indifference, to show you what you are when you are pure emotion and let yourself be led by the creative juices, and what you are when you adhere to the theoretical problems and want to be in the vanguard of literary research. What kind of writer are you anyway? An amphibian who swims between the banks of theory and the current of fantasy?

I excused myself to my colleagues and went out to the passageway. I lit a cigarette and tried to attract the phantom's attention. But Jane Challenger didn't want to

THE END OF THE THIRD WORLD

be the slightest bit friendly. She had never been a nice person, agreeable, or gracious; and she certainly wasn't going to change there, on that dingy train. Listen, Jane! Let me explain! At the end of the sixties I was studying social sciences in the University of Sao Paulo. I was there in the last days of that university's most brilliant period. At that time, questioning ideas was still practiced. This happened, of course, before the purges of 1969, and it profoundly marked my intellectual formation. It isn't common in Brazil to establish a radical attitude as a cogitative parameter, where doubt is the initial premise of any ratiocination.

I was young, and young people learn. Well, I learned to measure all things by the parameters of doubt, and to investigate everything before taking a step in any direction. This spirit, which is typical of the USP, aside from a critical boldness, entailed other advantages such as impetuousness, the willingness to pass any contingencies through the sieve of radicalism. I, who came from Amazonia, where no one dares to venture beyond the indifference of your typical public servant, immersed myself in that perspective, which only the modernity of Sao Paulo could offer. Thus, upon becoming a novelist, I didn't abandon the practice acquired there that always makes me look for a confirmation based on research.

"That doesn't justify it!" she shouted. "That doesn't justify the fact that there are so many things intruding into my story."

"Forgive me!" I begged. "But I'm just not able to write a novel anymore without these interferences."

She put her cigarette out in the ashtray. Irritated with me, she refused to look my way.

"In the things that you write, there is always a coldness, some sort of fear of the personal side of the story. To be in this book is the most disagreeable thing that could ever happen to me. My grandfather's author never would have written 'these' things. After all, what is it that you intend to do? Exhibit me as an example of a novelistic impossibility? And what in the hell am I doing here, when I ought to be in London, trying to get that nitwit Lester to move his ass? God, what a sidekick you've arranged for me!"

"Do you think that this novel is very strange?" I asked.

"If this is in fact a novel," she responded crossly.

"Perhaps you're right."

"And why did you put me in the role of a violated woman and then forget me!"

"You don't need to get all upset."

"It almost seems that you don't have anything to say." She intensified her attack. "That's about the minimum that a character should be able to demand of her author. Don't you have plot? Have you lost your imagination?"

"I know that it looks like a lack of plot," I said, trying to calm her down. "But I don't want to start talking about a lack of plot. One of the oldest tricks used by those who must write something, and they have nothing to say, is to write precisely about the lack of plot. A dirty trick that always works because it is incantatory, like the ancient rain dances. But I swear that it isn't for a lack of plot. There is really a lot to be told."

"So why don't you tell something?" she asked ironically.

"All right; do you want to hear a story?"

She shrugged her shoulders and shook her head, as if she were once more lamenting her luck. Damn, I could have been an Edwardian writer!

There was once a writer who felt a great affinity for the eighteenth century. He thought that the so-called century of reason was enchanting because it was the last century that the great political and economic changes coexisted with a moderate technological advancement. No electricity, for example. Many revolutions occurred, but all under the light of candelabra. And terrorism? A few attempts were perpetrated, but the terrorists were content with bombs with short fuses.

Our bad luck, he used to say, is that the twentieth century had to follow the nineteenth century. And, being a coherent man, he liked to see himself as one of the last representatives of the century of reason. Not that he was a reactionary; he simply had a conflictive relationship with the products of the second industrial revolution. He hated paper napkins, psychoanalysts who had opinions on everything, vacations taken on credit, air travel, and the principle of planned obsolescence. But his greatest dispute was the automobile. He was never able to learn to drive a car with a stick shift, because the gears confused him. He used to say that the most he knew about these vehicles came from consulting the Encyclopedia Britannica entry on combustible engines. Perhaps his attachment to the eighteenth century doesn't go beyond an intellectual excuse for his inability to deal with certain practical necessities of life, inasmuch as he was born near the banks of the largest river in the world, and he didn't know how to swim.

To get around, however, the writer frequently used taxis, a practical though expensive solution considering OPEC's bad example to the Brazilian government's economists. But to ride in a taxi is always an adventure in any part of the world. In spite of paying through the nose just to get around the city, he became more and more convinced that the taxi drivers, though not exactly the equivalent of the old coachmen due to their rude speech patterns and their indiscretion, were true representatives of a new tribal structure. He saw them as nomads, restrained because they wandered through the

LOST WORLD II

delineated perimeters of the city, but lords of a new cultural apparatus and an unpublished supply of customs that made them stand out in the gallery of urban types. Their nomadism gave them a sensation of autonomy, the illusion that they could determine their own paths, and this made them different from the average mortals, masters of a special and clear vision of the world.

For this reason, the writer thought that nothing was as interesting as the opinions of these exceptional beings who traverse the tangled maze of the human agglomerate with enviable ignorance of its topography, devoting the most solid disrespect for certain natural laws, especially that geometric principle that says that a straight line is the shortest distance between two points. This is something that has caused some rather sensible people to become needlessly irritated with the atavistic ignorance that the taxi drivers seem to have of the city streets, a rather absurd requirement, because it isn't the taxi drivers' job to know the streets and thoroughfares, rather to guide the passenger from one instant of life's contingency to another. This unreasonable attitude on the part of the passenger prevents him from understanding that the principal function of a taxi driver is to have opinions on everything. After all, they are the only citizens to have opinions at a fixed rate determined by the number of miles clocked, and who, while juggling a rapid route or the atrophy of a bottleneck, delight our souls and liberate our histamine with unforgettable and dialectically profound observations on the economy, politics, sexual practices, the dilemma of particle physics, or the bubonic plague in the thirteenth century.

Anyone who is reasonably observant and has an open spirit can be a collector of the exploits of taxi cab drivers. I could write an entire book myself just using my own experiences with cab drivers because they seem

THE END OF THE THIRD WORLD

to embody human diversity and the unexpected. For example, one time when I was in a hurry to arrive at the New Jersey airport, I jumped in a cab in the Lower East Side, and the driver, a Haitian who spoke beautiful French, explained to me that the force of gravity wasn't renewable; it was spent like any other natural resource on the planet. As such, any upward movement dangerously wasted this resource, such things as elevators, planes, and fireworks. One day we won't be able to walk on the surface of the earth; we will float off into space, he predicted, as he left me off in a street in the Bronx because he didn't know how to get to New Jersey. Already a cabbie in West Berlin, in the outrageous English that we both were utilizing, showed a certain comparative inclination, telling me that Germany was created in order to drive the Latin peoples crazy. The driver was an Arab and he didn't even know my friend Ignacio de Loyola Brandao, who at that time was living through a phase of Teutonic insanity.

But let us return to our writer. The other day he took a taxi downtown, and for one of the many reasons that any Brazilian can invoke in order to explain his most bizarre attitudes, the driver, who was visibly deranged, was driving the car like a madman. The perilous trip forced the writer to grip the car seat and call out prayers to the improbable patron saint of writers. To make matters worse, it was raining and visibility was poor. Of course, the writer, wise to the ways of cabbies, thought that it was going to be the kind of race that caused coronaries. But later he changed his mind when the driver, a young mulatto with Ray Ban glasses and a thick mustache, adjusted the rearview mirror and wanted to know if by chance he didn't work in TV. The writer attempted to deny it with as much conviction as possible, but the driver didn't accept it.

LOST WORLD II

"I'm almost sure that I saw you on the TV," he insisted.

"It's possible," the writer responded, somewhat vaguely, but right away he regretted it, fearing that the driver might take him for some government technocrat, one of those fellows who appear on the tube saying that it is actually salary increases that cause inflation.

"You see, I'm a writer," he finally added.

"A writer? What do you write?"

"Stories . . ." he said, deliberately vague this time.

But it wasn't a matter of arrogance, or prejudice. The writer, aside from the rather frightening way the driver was operating the taxi, was afraid that he would prove to be one of those types who can't possibly see an author without immediately trying to impose upon him that "incredible story that would make a wonderful novel if only I were a writer, but I'm going to tell it to you, and you'll thank me for the idea." You can imagine that there is no greater torture for a writer than to have to bear that kind of generosity.

"Novels?" he demanded, observing him in the mirror with an expression that to the writer seemed ironic, although he could have been perfectly mad, having recently fled a sanatorium for the simple reason that he wanted to drive a taxi in the rain.

"Yes, I write novels."

"The novel is dead," he said, causing a cold chill to run up and down the spine of his wary passenger, if one can really experience such a thing while still alive.

The taxi was confronting the curves on the road like one of those Formula 1 race cars, which made the nervous writer regret never having signed a life insurance policy.

"To write today," he went on, "is to practice fake paleontology. It is to reinvent the Piltdown man."

THE END OF THE THIRD WORLD

In spite of the fact that it was a provocation, the writer felt calmer. He thought that the driver wasn't too far off the mark; novels in the twentieth century weren't much more than paleontology, the same absurd paleontology so full of hope that Professor Challenger engaged in, one could say.

"I know what you mean," the writer responded, looking forward to the dialogue that would ensue. "Anybody who writes novels today ought to feel like one of those fishermen on the island of Madagascar who in 1938 caught a coelacanth, swimming happily in the Indian Ocean."

The driver laughed and abruptly shifted gears, with a grinding protest from the transmission.

"The image of the coelacanth, a three-hundred-fifty-million-year-old survivor, is not bad," the driver said approvingly, "but the novel disappeared just like the dinosaurs."

"Even accepting that the novel is a species on the extinction list, or, as you insist, already totally extinct, I don't believe that its disappearance has any resemblance to the speed with which the saurians vanished from the face of the earth. This story of the death of the novel, if we take the example of certain species of its genus, is closer to the dodo bird than the cataclysm of the Cretaceous period."

"That's hardly any consolation," the driver retorted. "Right now the novel resembles that prehistoric fish caught in Asia to such an extent that many specialists were known to have been surprised by the existence of the genus in places as remote as the lost world discovered by Professor Challenger. Do you know Professor Challenger, by Conan Doyle?"

"Of course," the writer responded humbly. "That's the reason why every time I begin a new novel, I realize soon enough that I am engaged in an exotic and extemporaneous act. I sit at the keyboard, and I watch the cursor pulsate. Where is the former wonderment? Where's the pleasure of a well-written story, readings that enchanted by evoking other existences, other universes? What good were all those woven words, so fervent and resounding, metamorphosed into literature?"

"The barbaric joy of inventing stories has ended," the driver said.

It appears that all that is left is apathy, he thought, because what was worthwhile wasn't the text of adventure but the adventure of the text.

"I'm over forty years old," the author added, "I have published many books, and no one is going to convince me now that my barbaric joy was nothing more than one of the manifestations of the primitive world, a rustic product of backwardness."

"It serves a purpose," the cabbie replied. "Don't worry about that. When it is a humorous product with a lot of local color, it works like hot sauce, delighting overworked palates that have lost their sensibilities. But if it is an angry, accusatory book, it works for its prophetic tone, since there are also those readers who need to satisfy their guilty consciences. Naturally, to write these books isn't any sin. Quite to the contrary; in certain latitudes of the globe, they ought to be the only books produced."

"Gide used to say that Stendhal's great secret was to write instinctively; he didn't stop long enough to weigh what he was writing. But what is one to do in these days when everyone jogs in place so as not to have to leave the house?"

Nevertheless, I do persist, the writer thought. And he made an effort not to impose his perplexity on anyone's disillusionment. There was a time when disillusionment

THE END OF THE THIRD WORLD

was something peculiar to black-and-white European films. Who hasn't felt a mixture of astonishment and boredom while watching one of those films, where close-ups of pensive faces seem to drag on forever, without wondering if it was necessary to carry tedium to such exaggerated lengths? After all, for those Europeans who spend the night drinking and exercising their incommunicability, there isn't anything better than the healthy and simple need to earn a living to dedramatize their existence.

Almost twenty years later, here he was, just like a character from Michelangelo Antonioni's movie *A Night*, in danger of being suffocated by boredom. And without the moral alternative of having to earn a living, since he had really never stopped working or he would have starved. What's more, he knew that the problem wasn't really metaphysical, as European elegance had required in the 1960s. Quite to the contrary, his case was one of crass materialism because he wrote in order to earn a living, and he was only able to earn a living if his books were published and bought.

"I'm going to tell you a story," the writer said. "It is real, not fiction. I have a Danish friend who writes to me from time to time. His great passion—completely enigmatic to me—is Brazil. Or, better said, he has an accentuated interest in things from the so-called (and justly, I now recognize) Third World. And from all of the horrendous nations that are wallowing about in this category, he singles out Brazil.

"Now you are going to ask me what this Dane has to do with the death of the novel. And the question is quite pertinent, even though my perplexity doesn't have the slightest Scandinavian inspiration. The point is that this friend, every time that he writes to me, puts me in the worst predicaments. It's a good thing that he isn't a very frequent letter writer. Once in a while he sees something on TV about Brazil—fortunately that is a rare occurrence on the news channels over there—then he sends me a letter asking for explanations. Things such as: 'How is it possible that the president of the party that supported the military dictatorship can assume a leadership role in the new civilian government?' Things like that, you see. And I, who have abstained from giving my opinion, since here in Brazil it was neither heard nor observed, and much less never tallied, am obligated to respond with the most surrealistic explanations. But I'm beginning to suspect that this is exactly what he likes.

"My genteel friend lives comfortably in Copenhagen. He's a little over forty, he is an economist, he works in a large auditing firm, he is married to an intelligent and handsome woman whose six-foot stature exudes a kind of aurora borealis health, and he is the father of two adolescent daughters. His annual salary, about average for the standards of his country, would easily be enough to support a few dozen families from Brazil's Northeast for about five years. He is aware of this fact, but that is not why he is interested in this tropical abomination. Likewise it is not because of the samba, or the folklore, or the fear that the destruction of the Amazon forest will cause their Danish summer to occur between the hours of three and five one July afternoon.

"No, these reasons, and others that the vain Brazilian imagination couldn't even come up with, might be why other foreign friends of mine are interested in this civil catastrophe. For example, my friend Charles from New York. He is so fanatic about the samba that every year he dresses up like a woman from Bahia for the carnival party at the Waldorf Astoria. And his house in Queens is so full of Brazilian war drums, tambourines, and other artifacts that it looks more like an ethnographic room in the Smithsonian Institute, and that is not even mentioning

THE END OF THE THIRD WORLD

his record collection. Or my other friend Kazuo—in the area of eccentric friends, I am not lacking—who collects the Brazilian magazine *Manchete*; he has every issue from year one, properly bound and listed in a complete computerized file.

"Dear old Jurgen, the Dane, isn't so simple. He came to Brazil for the first time in 1978, along with a team of auditors to do an audit of a firm of theirs in Sao Paulo. He visited Rio de Janeiro and Salvador. He returned home another person. He got off the plane with a necklace given to him to keep the devil away. According to his wife, who is a psychologist and thus must be accustomed to treating the most serious maladjustments caused by the Scandinavian well-being, Jurgen was a different person. Even months later, he was still repeating, as if entranced by some form of tropical delirium, that the world was an imposture. Of course, no one understood what he meant by this. That the world is not perfect was obvious even to the most insane Danes. What they had no way of knowing was that Jurgen had discovered the only people on the planet who had invented imposture as a civil system. And you still want to talk about the death of the novel!"

I heard a scream, when I expected to hear at the very least a light chuckle indicating agreement, some sort of intellectual encouragement. But no, it was a scream of rage, of vexation, that interrupted me.

It was my character.

"Do you want to know something?" she said, almost snarling. "Screw the taxi driver, and screw the Dane, too! And you can go—"

Before I could respond, she had quickly walked to the other end of the car and disappeared into another cabin. I went after her, because I didn't want to leave my character in such a state, so frustrated and worked up. It was a Pirandellian situation. But arriving at the cabin where she had entered, I found an English couple who, upon seeing me, began to hand over their passports. I turned around and pretended to watch the sad Prussian forest pass by, parched and dying from the acid rain.

"Excuse me, do you speak English?" I heard someone ask.

I turned around. It was the young Englishman whom I had disturbed a few moments before in the cabin.

"Yes," I responded, showing my shame.

"Did you want something? Do you need anything?"

"No, thank you. It was nothing. I thought that I saw someone I knew enter your cabin. I was wrong. I beg your pardon."

"There's no reason! Are you Italian?"

"Brazilian."

"Brazilian! We will go to Brazil next year. To visit the Amazon."

"How interesting. I am from Amazonia."

"That is nice to know. My name is David Challenger, and my wife is Jane Challenger."

I felt the train rushing under my feet and I woke up in a hotel in Berlin.

I never manage to write while traveling, so I could hardly wait to return home. On every street corner, in every subway or railway station, I would glance around to see if by chance that damn Englishwoman wasn't preparing an ambush for me. Writing is paranoia!

Tomorrow We Will Disappear into the Unknown

The place was so unbelievably wretched that only out of courtesy would someone call it a bar. A shanty with poorly nailed planks, swaying on four immense logs, moored on the left bank of the Solimões River, about two hours by boat from the city of Benjamin Constant. The rare customers showed up in old canoes; they entered in silence, drank to the sound of a station precariously tuned into Brasilia, and they disappeared before nightfall. They wore old, worn-out pants and shirts, and they didn't seem to notice the woman who was seated right near the entrance. The owner of the establishment, a short, fat half-breed with protruding eyes, apparently paid her scant attention himself.

Everything there was filthy and old, rotted by the muddy river water and parched by the intense sun. Since there was no electricity, when night fell, the half-breed would light the smoky kerosene lantern that hung from the doorway like a tenuous sign of life; then he would take off his shirt and lie down in a grimy hammock that he tied with a studied slowness near the window that opened to the river.

The woman practically didn't move from her place from sunup to sundown. She seemed tired, her white skin painfully red with signs of blisters, her light hair hanging in damp locks, barely covered by a blue scarf that she wore tied on her head. After the half-breed lay down, she also extended a travel bag and tried to sleep,

LOST WORLD II

but it was impossible. Her wet boots were uncomfortable, the thick material of her jeans irritated her skin, and her beige gabardine shirt was stifling. Now and then, clouds of mosquitoes descended mercilessly on her, humming an infernal melody that didn't allow her to close her eyes the entire night. For five days she had been there on that floating dump, every night turning from one side to another on her travel bag, tormented by the uncertainty, by the helplessness, and by the immensity of the river that hid itself in the dark and impenetrable night.

In the morning, just as soon as the sun appeared, the half-breed untied the hammock, came outside, and found the woman already up and brushing her teeth. They exchanged looks for the few seconds before he dove into the water for his morning bath. Then he made breakfast. He didn't offer her any, not out of discourtesy, for like all the people along the river, he observed an age-old custom of hospitality, but the woman had refused to accept anything from him since the first day: food, drink, anything at all. And he eventually gave up because that was how she wanted it. In truth, he had no idea how she could go so long without eating or drinking something. These foreigners really were strange, and now they were beginning to show up around there more frequently, snooping around about the Indians, who were making trouble.

Some time in the middle of the day, the CONTAG boat stopped to see if it could get some ice, foolishly, of course, but it was the woman's salvation. I was on the boat, returning from a meeting with Indian leaders, having completely forgotten that I had a novel to write and of Miss Challenger's persecutions. I had not expected to run into Miss Challenger, but it was not Jane, rather Virginia Challenger, the BBC reporter from London.

THE END OF THE THIRD WORLD

I assumed that the English team had already left a long time before. It had been two months since our last meeting and Lester's hospitalization. Someone had told me that the journalist had been discharged from the hospital without any further complications and was in good health. Then I didn't hear any more of the Brits. But now Virginia, somewhat refreshed, having bathed and changed her clothes, was telling about her adventure.

She had lost contact with the team, which was still in Benjamin Constant. They were trying to film scenes of the conflict between the squatters and the Tikuna Indians. She, very audacious, perhaps believing herself safe by virtue of carrying a passport identifying her as a subject of the queen, had gone around the city asking questions. Some fellow, whom she identified as Raimundo, showed up, saying he was a Tikuna; he convinced her to board a motorboat and weighed anchor in the middle of the night, without any explanations. Realizing her mistake, initially she thought that she would be killed, but she wasn't harmed, and the mysterious Raimundo simply abandoned her on that isolated bar on the banks of the Solimões, without a telephone and without any possibility of making herself understood.

"Now I know what Amazonian isolation really means," she told me. "This place isn't for humans; it is for the gods."

She was right; that land is for the gods. Perhaps she knew that the other Challenger—the one in the novel—would come to the same conclusion. I was the only one who had still not realized the coincidence.

It was a little later, in the sluggishness of my own apprenticeship, that the connection was finally evident. It was a Saturday afternoon, and I was listening to a story. I heard it from an old classmate from the Dom

Bosco High School; he was a taciturn but hardworking fellow who was always seated in the last row. After leaving school, we saw each other only occasionally. He was from the interior, from the Negro River, I believe. Indian blood predominated in his brown facial features and short, squat body; he was modest in his clothes and reserved in his manners. He came to Manaus, and stayed. I know this because we sometimes ran into each other at social events like that one. As a vigorous forty-year-old, he seemed much changed from the schoolboy I had known.

"I recently discovered that my boss is a god. I'm serious," he said to me. "There are many gods here, if you haven't discovered the fact already. Entities, astral beings; do you understand?"

"It is a very rich region, mythologically speaking," I responded.

"But it isn't a matter of mythology, my good man."

"You mean to say that . . ."

"Yes, we are still before the myth. Much before."

I acquiesced, trying to stay near the air conditioner. It was very hot that August, and my ex-classmate, always so discreet, had discovered a god. It made sense. He graduated in economics and was working in the financial division of a manufacturing company in the Industrial District. Considering what we were living through, any economist could suffer this type of theological hallucination.

"My boss is a minor god," he went on amiably, his pitch-black Amerindian eyes shining in the night light. "An archaic, secondary, and unimportant being. That's why he's often indecisive, and almost always unconscious of his orphic mutations, if you forgive my using terminology borrowed from the Greeks. He is what you could call a peripheral, little god, far from the large gods

THE END OF THE THIRD WORLD

and from God. But he is a god from the old times of polytheism."

I never know how to act when confronted with these kinds of things, and the problem is that people have the habit of revealing their strangest dreams, their most bizarre nightmares, and their most beloved eccentricities to writers, because we are some sort of public psychoanalysts or handy sorcerers.

"I never revealed this to anyone before," he assured me. "I'm only telling you in the event you would like to use it in some story."

"How did you discover it?" I asked him.

"That he isn't human? It hasn't been too long. He himself doesn't know it yet; it takes a while for them to realize it. Especially when they achieve a new human incarnation."

"I understand! What a remarkable thing!"

"It isn't as unusual as one would think," he said.

"You're right. The unusual part, I would imagine, is to remain unpunished after discovering such a thing."

"That's true; those who discover it and dare to reveal the discovery pay dearly for it. And we're not just talking crucifixion here. The modern methods of deicide are much more subtle, but they are very resilient. My boss, for example, will find out soon enough that he is an indecisive god, somewhat inconclusive, little accustomed to logic, and near entropy. All of this is to the infinite degree, of course."

"Knowing Parmenides' conception of a superior being and the God of Saint Thomas of Aquinas, these attributes that your boss has are novel, to say the least."

My ex-classmate gave a hint of a smile and shook his head, thoughtfully.

"He has more mobility," he said, after a pause. "You ought to remember that Parmenides' being, as a result of his perfection, is absolute like a concrete block. Of course, this may have its advantages; there's no room for error. But likewise, there is nothing beyond the eternal immobility. It's a shame that there are no gods like that; in actuality, they are all fallible, speculative, and impulsive."

"And what is his mission here on earth?"

He didn't answer me; he limited himself to scrutinizing the outside view through the smoked-glass window. That silence was very significant for me. We were in one of those condominium compounds, the home of a mutual acquaintance who was hosting a lunch. The window, purposely closed so that the heat would not invade the room, revealed an abandoned lot, which had been invaded by the spreading branches of a castor-oil plant in full bloom, the flowers with their masculine globule parts dominating the feminine floral buttons beneath them, in the constant proliferation of their species. In the middle of the castor-oil plant's woody boughs grew an absurd thicket of Napoleon's caps, which was covered with faded orange flowers. An immobile, old cycad palm stood forgotten in the back of the lot, defying the sun, which seemed to reverberate off its rotting leaves.

"One afternoon," he went on, "I was on my way out of the company office, the one downtown on Joaquim Nabuco street, and I began to feel sick. I thought that I was having a heart attack. At our age, you know how it is! Joao Bosco Santoro went in just that way. I was the only one in the office; it was past six and I was putting in some overtime. I thought: 'Is it possible that I'm going to die here, alone?' I took the elevator, untying the knot in my tie and removing my jacket.

"When I reached the street, I saw my shadow projected on the sidewalk, and it occurred to me that I wasn't going to die after all. The truth is that I decided that for me to be dressed in a jacket and tie was just as improbable as the mystery of death is for all of us mortals. But there I was, my presence projecting a shadow on the sidewalk, wearing a beige linen suit and an Italian tie around my neck, dark glasses, and an executive briefcase in my right hand. And they were there in front of me on the sidewalk.

"Who?"

"My boss and an Englishwoman. A young woman; she was pretty and appeared to be delicate. She was standing on the sidewalk, arguing heatedly with him. The pain in my chest increased, and I felt like I was being sucked into the vortex that the two of them were generating. They were gods, both of them. I must have lost consciousness, and I woke up the next day in the hospital. But during the time I was unconscious, I was a prisoner of that vortex. She was wearing perfume. I could smell the fragrance even though my boss couldn't. His olfactory sense developed much later, when his intelligence became better adapted to the world. But she was there, as if she were unaware of my presence. Her skin was red from a sunburn, and she was dressed very simply.

"The last few employees were leaving the building, and they passed them indifferently, dodging the garbage cans filled with office papers, hurrying to get out as the security guards were closing the doors. But no one noticed that I was suffering cardiac arrest. From time to time she looked at her wristwatch, reluctant to get into my boss's car. She must have been around twenty-five years old, calculating the passage of time that it takes us mortals to learn the necessary skills to survive. The most unbelievable thing is that I was able to syntonize myself with my boss's feelings; he was nervous, insecure, concentrating completely on something that the Englishwoman was hiding.

"It was obvious that this wasn't the first time that this god had visited Manaus, but perhaps it hadn't exactly been a city the previous times. How many times had he come here? In what time frame had he come? I don't know what to say except that the gods don't concern themselves with the human concept of time. It is a useless and dispensable fragmentation. Even a god as minor as he can accept the grander entropy, the chaos that is subtly hidden under the material inversion. Obviously that god knew that he didn't amount to much, nor did his brothers, nor all of the pantheon of primitive polytheism that today seems to gravitate like clusters of nearly imperceptible particles about monotheism. Tachyons, neutrinos adrift in the swollen river of beliefs. Or not? What does it matter? At any rate, the Englishwoman, visibly upset, began to show signs of impatience."

"And who was she? I'll bet that she was a Celtic goddess! Or Fata Morgana herself, if she really was from Great Britain," I said, interrupting the astonishing narrative.

"To this very day, I'm still not sure. But since we are running across gods all the time, it is quite possible that she was one of the two."

"Were running across them, don't you mean?"

"No, nothing has changed. The asphalt on the streets fools us. But beneath that black layer, the gods' footsteps are still fresh. Nevertheless, no one should feel uneasy about it."

"This happens in the best of the rapidly growing urban centers of the world," I said.

"The problem is that mortals are prone to believe that the breaks in the asphalt are the result of mere erosion, having to do with matters of rainwater, or something of that sort. But they are mistaken, poor things."

THE END OF THE THIRD WORLD

"An interesting observation," I agreed. "And the Brazilian asphalt, one would agree, isn't the best in the world when it comes to stability. Once in a while, for example, the asphalt in Sao Paulo is broken up by a trio of electric guitars. And what is such a trio but a northeastern-style estate with more decibels.

BENEATH THE BLACK LAYER OF ASPHALT
THE GODS' FOOTSTEPS ARE STILL FRESH

"Asphalt is perhaps the most solid material created by the urban world," my ex-classmate continued. "Even when the indecent heat of the tropics melts it, the asphalt remains suitably consistent. That's why it is easy for one to be deceived by the city's asphalt; you see, not even the best street covers of the most expensive avenues, under which there may only be traces of primitive gods, are completely free from the great wonders."

If that is the way it is, I thought, why not accept the flexibility of asphalt, and look for what perishes under the flow of traffic? And borrowing the fantasy that my ex-classmate so kindly offered me, I took possession of the body and soul of that god.

Jane opened the car door and jumped. Pietra, Jr., hadn't counted on that, and he turned off the motor. He got out quickly and attempted to intercept her as she ran towards the building.

"What in the devil is wrong?" he growled, huffing. "Didn't I say that I'd take you to the hotel? And that's where we're going."

Jane's anxiety increased when she realized that the building was closed, the lights were out. There was no one left there, not even a straggler. In the dim light of dusk, the building seemed to dissolve into the darkness, an indistinct mass barely discernible by eyes not yet accustomed to the night. But the look in the man's eyes, primate eyes whose sight is filtered by a brain made of salty water and chains of protein, showed he would not allow the young woman to escape. A burst of air, coming from the lungs, filled his throat and caused his vocal cords to vibrate. His lips moved and he heard his human voice.

"What do you intend to do now?"

The woman seemed to pant, inhaling large gulps of warm, humid air.

"I need to speak with Mr. Duarte," she said.

Pietra, Jr., attempted to be amiable. He was aware of his own body, its sweaty dampness. He took off his dark glasses; darkness had fallen, and only a few distant lights illuminated that portion of the street.

"Please. It's important. Afterwards you can take me to the hotel."

"All right, but he has probably already gone."

"It is very important that I speak with Mr. Duarte again."

"What were you and Mr. Duarte talking about for so long?"

"Look here, Mr. Pietra. I don't even know you, who you are, or what you do. And I don't like what's going on here," Jane said, irritated and ready for a confrontation.

"I'm not doing anything," Pietra said with irony. "I'm just trying to give a pretty girl a ride."

"Go to hell. Why don't you go hit on your secretary?"

"All right, all right," he placated her. "Let's go see if Mr. Duarte is still at home. But you could talk to him tomorrow as well."

"I'm afraid that I won't have another chance," Jane replied brusquely. "I leave this evening for London."

"Let's go to my office. In the event he has left, you can call him at his home."

THE END OF THE THIRD WORLD

"Yes, please," she agreed reluctantly.

They returned to the building and took the elevator. During the long ride to his office on the top floor, Pietro Pietra, Jr., kept his distance from her, attempting to appear courteous. As the new president of the business, controlling the largest number of Brazilian stocks in the firm, he had a large office, his name on the door, a private bathroom, a team of five secretaries, and a fax terminal. The opulence of his office left no doubt as to where the company's center of power was to be found. For Jane, however, that ostentation was evidence in itself of underdevelopment, an unsophisticated indigence that was apparent in the drapes, whose expensive cloth was cut by inexperienced hands, and in the luxurious carpet, which was poorly laid, and in the furnishings, which were obviously imitations. But the window allowed the clear, limitless Amazonian sky to invade and debase the spurious modernity of the place, its swamplike air-conditioned atmosphere, its subtle moldy odor that the sweet perfume of the disinfectant couldn't disguise.

Pietro Pietra, Jr., proudly showed Jane his office, expecting that she would be impressed.

"Here we are," he said, offering her an armchair. "Wouldn't you like to sit down while I try to locate Mr. Duarte?"

"Are you from Manaus?" Jane asked, sitting down.

"No, Miss Challenger, I am from Sao Paulo. The descendant of Italian immigrants. My grandfather was a successful entrepreneur in the twenties; he lost everything in the depression."

"What did your grandfather do?"

"He bought and sold precious stones and Amerindian artifacts. He handled some very interesting things; muiraquitas, for example."

"Muiraquitas?"

LOST WORLD II

"They are small jade sculptures made by Amazon warriors. And they have magical power! But they didn't bring much good luck to my grandfather."

Jane remained silent, certain that Pietra, Jr., was enjoying himself at her expense.

"I'll try to locate Mr. Duarte now," he said as he picked up the telephone and began to dial a number. He spoke to someone for a few seconds in an authoritative voice and hung up. "Just as I imagined. Duarte left the building just as soon as his meeting with you was over. He still has not arrived home. I left a message for him to call you at your hotel."

Jane momentarily lost her self-possession; a hint of disbelief crossed her face as she addressed Pietro, Jr.

"If that is the case," she said dryly, "I had better return to the hotel. I still have many things to do before leaving for the airport."

She rose from the chair, showing her intention to leave right then.

"Perhaps I would be able to help you. Why don't you tell me what the matter is?"

She shook her head impatiently. "I don't think so," she replied coldly. "To tell the truth, I believe that someone doesn't want Mr. Duarte to speak with me."

"My goodness, what foolishness! Now, why don't you let me help you?" Pietra, Jr., implored her rather pretentiously, but his voice, which rose and fell with the same ingratiating inflections of an adolescent, contributed in no way to breaking through the glacial hostility with which Jane observed him.

The hesitancy in his voice, however, was a result of his anxiety. Pietra, Jr., knew that he could not let her simply leave, but she was proud and sufficiently astute to perceive his real intentions. On the other hand, he could not act precipitously and risk losing everything. He needed

THE END OF THE THIRD WORLD

to be cautious in spite of the fact that caution was not exactly his forte. What he actually felt like doing was grabbing that haughty female and forcing her to spill everything that old, worn-out Duarte had told her.

"I don't want to insist, but I am the new president, and if it is something relating to the company, perhaps I could help you myself. I don't want you to leave with the wrong impression," he explained anxiously. "Mr. Duarte is retiring soon; I believe he no longer has much to do with the business. In the recent take-over, he became a minor stockholder, on the sidelines, so to speak."

Jane said nothing, turning her back on him to look at the city below, dotted with flickering lights. She gave the impression that she was more interested in the illuminated buildings in the distance than in his presence. But unbeknownst to Pietra, Jr., he had already been chosen to play a part in a grander scheme. And how could he have known?

"I'll take you to the hotel now," he said.

When the elevator stopped at the ground floor, he inadvertently grazed her shoulder. Jane jerked her body away, shunning any contact with him.

"Excuse me!" he said casually.

I'm going from bad to worse, he thought. It was the innate ingenuousness of the small divinities that was manifesting itself, always vacillating between wanting to be loved and wanting to be feared, in the interminable cycle of relationships between gods and mortals. It's a shame that Pietra, Jr., didn't live in an Olympus, Valhalla, or Paradise. He wasn't adept, nor would he ever be, at plunging passionately into human emotions. He was, indeed, a god, but a very simple and even pathetic one.

"It isn't necessary for you to drive me. I'll take a taxi," she said gruffly, confronting him with her eyes.

Pietra, Jr., could no longer accept being treated with disrespect. He was a rich man, powerful, and feared by many. And on top of all that, he also considered himself to be a lady-killer, a man who appreciated beauty in a woman and knew something of seduction. And that woman, with her breasts heaving beneath her blouse, wasn't any better than other women.

"But of course I'll take you to the hotel," he insisted, for it was at the hotel that he hoped to discover the real involvement that this pretentious Englishwoman had with Duarte. And nothing would be more gratifying for him than to break down the resistance of a woman like Jane. "You are going to have trouble finding a taxi at this time."

"I don't need your help," she snapped, retreating a few steps as Pietra, Jr., stared at her with an intensity that in former times would have prompted metamorphoses, mutations, genetic changes, and morphological accidents.

Pietra, Jr., noticed that for the first time she appeared to have lost a bit of her self-confidence, although she wasn't totally disarmed. She observed him belligerently, sizing him up, scrutinizing him, and trying to discern his real intentions. But Pietra, Jr., wasn't hiding anything, he was simply following the flow of the mysterious and potent current that was the cause of that encounter.

"All right," she said without emotion, "I'll accept the ride. Perhaps you can even answer a few questions."

And so they set out on a long trip, full of surprising turns.

After a few minutes, Pietra, Jr., looked at his watch and said, "Shortly there will be a blackout in the city. Don't be alarmed; today the comet comes into full view."

Almost immediately darkness fell throughout the city. Only the headlights of the passing cars, tunnels of blind

THE END OF THE THIRD WORLD

light with nothing to illuminate, cast a glow in the blackness of the night.

Damn comet, Jane thought, averting her eyes from the headlights of approaching cars. She hadn't even realized that it was the year of the comet. What a shame the comets of the twentieth century didn't have the impact they once had. Once they flashed across the skies, touching the most paralyzing fears of the simple folk and confirming their own ephemerality to the powerful. They cut through the medieval nights, adorned in the purest Gothic style. They illuminated the darkness of those times of excessive certainties, perhaps affirming that the rusticity of the epoch was, after all, a type of sophistication that humanity would someday lose forever.

Who knows if comets, in their nocturnal splendors, weren't prophesying this: the irreparable loss of the ability to feel awe. Could there be anything more terrible? Without the power of awe, humanity would be as lost as a king without a throne, as hopeless as the populace of a medieval burg facing the plague. But, on the other hand, how can one be awestruck by these cosmic visits when they appear so much more grandiose in the mass media than they do on earth, overshadowed by the neon lights of the big cities?

Jane considered and reconsidered these absurd ideas in her mind because she didn't want to face what was actually happening to her. Pietra, Jr.'s, behavior up until that time had not gone beyond the limits of propriety, but she knew that sooner or later, she would have to be convincing in order to get rid of him.

"The appearance of Halley's comet is so frustrating," Pietra, Jr., said. "Don't you agree, Miss Challenger?"

"I have heard many stories about Halley's comet," she said evasively. "My grandfather witnessed its last appearance."

"Do you remember Kohoutek, in the nineteen sixties?"

"I remember. The manufacturers of optical instruments must have made millions of dollars selling telescopes, binoculars, and other such items," she replied, appearing affable.

"I know a Communist who says that he scanned the skies in search of the marvelous phenomenon, but he found the most amazing spectacle of the sixties was the terror going on in Brazil itself."

"Perhaps it wasn't a comet that he was actually looking for," she said.

"Perhaps you're right. But he was frustrated nonetheless."

"And now, when they look into the sky, what do the Brazilians see?"

"More frustration," Pietra, Jr., responded. "Brazilians are incorrigible; they are never content with just what is possible."

"Why should they be content? They were promised something glittering and shiny, and it all turns out to be a fiasco in the darkness," she said.

"Do you also find Brazil to be frustrating?"

"Yes, and disappointing."

"The legacy of twenty years of military regime isn't altogether as negative as some would paint it," he said. "At least our military leaders didn't do what the Argentines did, trash the country. Here at least we have some modern capitalism remaining; granted it may be somewhat caricatural, but at least it is modern."

"This kind of compensatory illusion never hurt anyone, I suppose," she commented sarcastically. "But this so-called modernity of Brazil isn't obvious in the streets, only in the statistics, in the calculations of the government's economists. Just like Halley's comet only appears in the astronomers' bulletins."

"It's not that bad," Pietra, Jr., protested.

"It's not that bad? It seems to me to be Pakistan. Hunger, superstition, and an atomic bomb."

"It was worse; at least we've been able to build a competitive industrial infrastructure, politically active and modern, which was capable of stimulating the old agrarian system. Not one country has done this without a certain amount of violence. In some ways, we are repeating here what happened in England in the eighteenth century."

"Or trying to preserve the eighteenth century indefinitely. That is the impression that I have of the place."

"Just an impression," he insisted.

"I do know other Third World countries," Jane said. "In all of them there is a kind of contradiction between the modern concepts of the economists' plans and the reality of everyday life. Here, like in all the other countries, the modernity winds up being an abyss that separates the majority from the minority, even though I have never seen such a vast and well-cultivated abyss as the Brazilian one. On the other hand, there are those who die of hunger, blacks and other wretched folks in the slums, your *favelas*. They can't even get a job as day laborers. They are perpetually captive to the culture of the stomach. Nevertheless, those who do make money are deceiving themselves. They are the ones in charge, I presume, those who eat regularly, have some education: the consumers. But in the middle, the abyss is wider every day, splitting open the asphalt, insurmountable. Yet there is something that makes this country different from the rest."

"The difference is that we are going to escape from the Third World."

"Quite to the contrary. Could it be that a perfect system has been discovered to keep the country in this situation, without causing a major explosion?"

"You mentioned Pakistan. I can't agree. Brazil isn't a country that is fragmented culturally by religious and linguistic differences like some Asian countries."

"Some streets in Kabul were also paved," Jane taunted. "And don't forget the fractured asphalt of the avenues of Managua."

Astronomers never tire of saying that they observe comets on a daily basis, just like the Brazilian economists who regularly come up with indicators of the country's modernity. These errant vagabonds of space are so common that they only provoke yawns amongst the scientists. Even now, astronomers from the United States are advancing theories that the planet Earth is supplied periodically with water by the comets that arrive from frozen regions. Can you imagine that the glass of water that you just drank came from some star? That water, tolerably treated and collected as if it were liquid gold, is an extraterrestrial substance, just as alien as the famous little green man from Mars. When considering all of this, why doubt Brazil's chances? But then perhaps Pietra, Jr., was right. Brazil is difficult to explain. How could one understand a country where a sophisticated system of telecommunications was placed under the authority of government ministers who were veritable cavemen?

"The only organization that can traverse the Brazilian abyss has experience in the field, with almost two thousand years of effectiveness."

Pietro Pietra, Jr., shifted his body; he thought she was going to bring up the Communists.

"What is that?"

"I am referring to the Catholic church," she clarified.

"I understand. But the Catholic church will never be

modern. It may traverse the abyss precisely because it is archaic, feudal, and cryptic."

"Yes, I know. The Catholic church never managed to absorb capitalism. And if it coexists with capitalism here in Latin America, it is because of its nostalgia for the thirteenth century. The most surprising thing is how well tuned it is to the rest of the society."

"The Latin spirit and Catholicism; is that what you mean?"

"Exactly. What is considered modern here, seems to me to be more like Brazilian Gothic."

"Brazilian Gothic?" he exclaimed, surprised.

"Yes, Christian base communities, feet planted in the earth, simplicity. It is the equivalent of Asiatic frugality, primitivism Western-style."

They remained silent for some time, the car's headlights levitating out ahead, opening the way in the darkness of the cometless night. Jane finally picked up the conversation, believing that it was to her advantage to do so; thus she could gain ground and raise protective ramparts about herself.

"My grandfather, Professor Challenger, believed that the epidemic of Spanish flu was brought by Halley's comet. One year after the comet's last sweep, in 1911, the world was brought to its knees in one of the last known global epidemics. Millions of people lost their lives. As you can see, there is always someone trying to find explanations for every imaginable thing. My grandfather went so far as to write a book about the matter, and he called it *Cosmic Poison*."

"Around here," Pietra, Jr., said, "no explanation really succeeds, because the wretchedness of the place causes superstitions to grow like bacteria in an organic soup."

The headlights finally revealed the entrance of the Hotel Tropical, where Jane was lodged. It was a bucolic construction, a contemporary tribute to Brazilian colonial architecture, in the middle of a well-tended forest, bordering the famous and polluted beach of Ponta Negro. The hotel was lit because it owned its own generator, and no doubt its guests were free of astronomical curiosity. Pietra, Jr., parked the car, and in a typically Latin gesture of cavalierism, he walked around the car to open the door for Jane to get out.

"I'll say good-bye here," Jane said resolutely. "Thank you for driving me here. It would have been difficult to find a taxi with this blackout."

"Good-bye, Miss Challenger. I believe that we'll meet again."

"Possibly," she responded, before turning around and walking into the hotel. She remained haughty, attempting to show her self-assurance even though she felt uncomfortable knowing that she was being observed.

When she had crossed the lobby of the hotel, she couldn't resist the temptation to see if Pietra, Jr., was still standing there, but the only people to be found in the small area lit at the entrance to the hotel were the two young porters in gray uniforms. Feeling uneasy as she sensed that her dealings with the entrepreneur might not yet be over, she opened the door of her room and turned on the light. To her own shame, she heard a scream escape from her throat as she caught sight of Pietra, Jr., seated on the bed, motionless like an enormous, hyperrealistic statue. At that very moment all the lights of the hotel went out.

Jane didn't know exactly what had happened to her in that hotel room that night. Sometimes she thought that it had all been a nightmare, some kind of hallucination or a dream that seemed very real. But whatever it was, the experience had affected her more than she wanted to admit. It had been both frightening and pleasurable.

THE END OF THE THIRD WORLD

A novelty in itself. In her confused memory, Pietra, Jr., seemed to be gleaming in bright flashes of light, and in spite of the darkness, she saw him melt like an enormous piece of hot wax, bursting into incandescent particles and reagglomerating in a scarlet brilliance. Shit, I always detested these American special effects, she thought. But, overcome by the scintillations, Jane was disarmed of her usual irony, and she began to understand what was happening.

It was the encounter of two worlds; two civilizations were colliding, strewing reverberations throughout the room, bursting through the walls and illuminating the whole area, the entire valley, the mass of vegetation that rolled and billowed beyond eyesight, off into the immense horizon, in order to reveal the scorched ruins into which everything was being transformed. Flashes of lightning illuminating destroyed lands, crimson blazes that must have lasted weeks and reached millions of hectares, rivers stopped up with mercury-soaked silt and mud, stretches of torrid, sandy land exposed to the sun by deforestation, drowned trees exuding toxic vapors, pestilence rising like clouds of insects.

And with every flash of lightning, a glance at the millions of dead people, the subjects of the kingdom of the god of desolation, Pietra, Jr., the lord of destruction, whom Jane had dared to disturb. And the cadavers opened their toothless mouths, and out of them came hundreds of tongues, sounding a tremendous deafening clamor, more strident and desperate than the crackle of the lightning coming in throbs over the translucent body of the abomination that was contorting on the hotel bed. Adventures, epics, small dramas, all these creations millennially cultivated and struck down in a single blow, now wanted to be heard in their own languages, some of which were irrevocably dead, others in their death throes, nearly all of them on the way to becoming silenced.

That chorus of voices became a crescendo causing sonorous high-intensity waves that made the walls of the room bow and all of the glass objects shatter into pieces. The mirror, glasses, windowpanes, light bulbs, they were all smashed, sending smithereens everywhere. The anxiety of those putrid throats was so great, so long had they been mute, that now they broke forth with the strength of a hurricane, a storm that swept the room, moved about the furniture and other objects. In the midst of the agonizingly shrill noise, Jane realized that she could be reduced to debris as easily as the unrecognizable and charred remains of the great forest, so poorly understood and undervalued. The kingdom belonging to Pietra, Jr., was that mangled countryside that shocked the sight, burned the retina, bewildered the mind, and punished the memory.

Then, in the middle of the maelstrom, Pietra, Jr., learned just who Jane Challenger was. She was not an offering, nor a key to the tabernacle, nor a sacrificial lamb, nor a heart still beating in the high priest's bloody hand, nor was she a votive candle in the middle of a gale. Jane Challenger was a priestess, one who had appeased gods with ancient spells, who had led the lamb to slaughter and held without repugnance the still-beating heart in one hand, while with the other she protected the weak flame of the candle. But she ought not to expect metamorphoses or wonders from the golden age, nor an exhibition of golden rods, nor incursions into the animal kingdom or mineral simulations.

If she were to accept his offering, he wasn't up to causing golden raindrops to fall into her lap, much less the sensations of a lascivious goose between her milky white thighs or a wild bull carrying her off in a rustic

THE END OF THE THIRD WORLD

sweat. No, she should know that he was the tormentor of the humid forest, and its ground carpeted with rotting leaves, a god of decaying matter, of the lichens and the fungi, of the mushrooms and the mosses, but also the terror of the small rodents, the timid reptiles and of the songbirds. And she should know that perhaps this was his first human incarnation, after millennia of existence in the acids, in the vapors of pestilences, in the exhalations that corrode the most beautiful alabaster petals of the orchid, in the dust that covers the gravel deposits on the banks of the backwaters. This was his realm.

Then Pietra, Jr., moved out of his tortured body. Everything stopped. The silence of the ages resounded like distant crickets, and he began to levitate toward the ceiling. There he remained, a sluggard with all the time in the world, drawing a faint line in the dusty plasterboard ceiling. And because observing is the thing that gods do best, it took a while before Pietra, Jr., finally felt the urge to converse. He wasn't a monotheistic god, one of those who prefer contemplation.

"Is it still possible for us to understand? Is there something left?" Jane asked herself. "How can four hundred years of progress and failures be reconciled?"

"There is no more time left," the sluggard murmured. "It is irreversible. The conductor wire is lost. It was slender and fragile like this line that I am drawing."

"How is it possible?" she went on. "So many things have disappeared with a trace. How can we recuperate these lost civilizations which for thousands of years the process of natural selection enriched, molded, and endowed with special techniques?"

"It's too late!" hissed the sluggard.

And impulses of this dead past suddenly burst forth in the room, like time's sobs.

"Geography is destiny," whispered the sluggard.

LOST WORLD II

"That's absurd!" Jane protested. "I refuse to be a fatalist, to simply state that they achieved quite an admirable operational rationality. No, they created civilizations here, after all. And they disappeared. Even the dinosaurs left more vestiges than they. Why is that?"

"Who won? Who was more primitive?" the sluggard needled her.

What a difference these last four hundred years have made. The hydroelectric dams not only drowned the animals, they also covered forever the myths, and thus set up the paradox. The greater the center of production, the greater the degradation. The more riches withdrawn from the earth, the worse the condition of mankind.

UNDER THE SIGN OF A PARADOX
THAT SEEMS MORE LIKE
A PAINFUL COMEDY OF ERRORS

"What is it like to be an Amazonian?" she asked, noticing that his body was now lying on the bed, his thighs open and his knees bent. His body was naked, and his face was serene.

"What would it be like to be born in a land where history loses itself in a labyrinth of ambiguity?"

Jane approached the bed, sitting down near him. From time to time, as they talked, her thigh lightly brushed his leg.

"The paradox of progress," she said. And she elaborated in an extended monologue even though he was hardly listening anymore.

Just how does one define a native of Amazonia, he thought, if everything is in bits and pieces? It would be like trying to reconstruct a building that collapsed in an earthquake without any blueprint. But perhaps the issue of having an identity isn't so important after all; on the other hand, it could be that the so-called Amazonian identity is the fragmentation itself. A paradox!

Paradox?

"There was a time," he said, interrupting her monologue, "in which we believed that this land was a kind of storehouse. A typical truism of people who live out on the frontier, of course."

She lay down on the bed and stared at the faint line that the sluggard had drawn on the ceiling; it encircled the broken light fixture. The light of the moon invaded the room, reflecting off the fixture. From outside, they could hear the commotion of the hotel staff as they attempted to restore the electricity and help the guests with their lanterns.

"Why do you all believe that countries have a destiny?" she asked.

"I don't know," he responded. "Here we never stop long enough to think about our destiny; things always turned out worse when we did."

Destiny! How can you think about destiny when you constantly live on the defensive, in the middle of a demolition? What in the devil did this Englishwoman mean by that? This is a land replete with obscure points, enigmatic things, complex relations. Nothing is as it seems to be here. What does she think? That she can have access to us through what she judges to be our "Occidental" side? Let her try. She won't find the pass; she'll stumble into chasms as huge as inland seas, empty spaces resembling great swamps of oblivion. And she will think that we are products of a causality, of some kind of determinism. Or that our strange nature is impervious to change.

Still lying down and with decisive movements, she began to undress, freeing herself quickly of her clothing. Wearing only her panties, she turned on her side so her back was to him, and raising her right knee, she seductively opened her thighs.

"But there is no reason to despair," she said, her voice slightly subdued as if she actually hoped he would remove her panties. "This frailty can be explained by the backwardness," she offered. "The ruling class must be quite primitive, and the local yokels incredibly incompetent."

Obedient, like all willing gods, he pulled on her panties until they were no more than a handful of nylon. His eyes were then attracted by the fascinating exposure of her sex organ, almost hairless, inviting and soft, pink and venerable. He let go of the panties and placed his head between her thighs, kissing the discreetly moist lips. The Englishwoman shivered, and he felt that she excitedly entwined her fingers in his straight hair, tilting his head back without interrupting what he was doing, but in such a way that Jane could see his eyes when they spoke.

"I keep thinking about what public administration must be like here," she said, moving about gently. "I imagine that nothing is done quite right, which would most certainly cause an enormous hardship for the entrepreneurs, let alone the people themselves."

It appears that everyone discards the waste, the poorly used remains, Jane thought, while they pursue their own personal objectives.

"Do you know something?" she went on aloud, slowly moving her body. "You are all alike; you want to stand out precisely because you are exploited, as if underdevelopment were some distinction."

Feeling offended, the god intensified his work, taking her to the point of orgasm.

"So you mean that we use our underdevelopment in order to guarantee certain special treatment?" he said, eliminating the possibility of an orgasm at the last

THE END OF THE THIRD WORLD

moment. "What effrontery! Haven't we already been exploited enough in the name of presumed privileges?"

She dug her fingers into his hair even harder and pushed his face to the spot that most interested her at that moment.

"Idiot!" she snarled. "To know that one country is exploited by another is simply to know that it is exploited. Nothing changes. There isn't any relief from it."

"I know, I know," he repeated, half-suffocated by the tuft of red hair.

"No, you don't know. Unless you are pretending, because the situation is much too advantageous. The economists of the Third World, for example, are cynicism personified. They are always preoccupied with the microphenomena, and when they attempt to fly a little higher, they become prisoners of their own daydreams, of involuntary and ridiculous philosophizing or delirious apocalyptic warnings."

"It's because most theories quiver here," the god said with a sigh.

"Theories that don't shudder? What does that mean?"

"The reality that is dogging us around is much more complex than what our vain philosophy could suppose."

"Don't stop!" she protested, holding his head firmly between her thighs. "It was so good. Go on . . . yes, like that. Just listen to me."

How could he explain to her that it was like a valley of many cultures and many visions of the world there, where not only some major European languages were spoken, like English and Spanish, but also Portuguese, French, Dutch, in addition to the more than 150 indigenous languages? Except that the latter were being pushed against the wall, and their speakers didn't have any alternative but to submit to the psychology of the colonized.

"What does it mean to be born here?" she moaned. "What kind of identity could one have when he learns Tukano at home and has to speak Portuguese with the boss at the factory?"

"Nonsense, that is nonsense," he shouted, bringing to a definite close that phase. "To be born is to have an identity. And as far as the rest is concerned, if he does, by chance, belong to the majority that wallows around in a glorious alienation, which is close to being the corollary of life of the people in this land, he can be happy and never even concern himself with these issues."

He looked at Jane. Her face was flushed, with a hint of reddish color in her checks.

"Those are of little interest to me," she said, tense and irritated. "I was referring to those who manage to raise their heads above this ominous alienation."

"Well, they will be, without a doubt, restless creatures, who at the very most will carry to the grave the heavy conscience of their own impotence."

Becoming impatient, he changed position, resting his back on the headboard of the bed, slowly caressing with one hand her smooth inner thigh. Jane, while he spoke, let her eyes rest from time to time on his firm organ, which peeked out, semierect, from the tuft of black pubic hairs.

"No, some of them will notice something more than the exotic and picturesque touch," she said on the counterattack, carefully choosing her words.

"For those who do, our congratulations. What a shame that reality itself doesn't tire of providing differentiations. And all that has been done to date is a cataloging of the differences that supposedly separate the 'primitive' world from the 'occidental' world, reenforcing in the natives the colonial mentality."

THE END OF THE THIRD WORLD

"It's enough that you cease being 'natives,' " she taunted.

"And what is left?"

"Full citizenship, which is the only way of escaping this colonial mentality and avoiding the false alternatives of the missionary, with his insulting commiseration, or the ethnographer, with his pretense of exclusivist cleanliness."

In this short four-hundred-year period, the god thought, we have seen the missionaries mark us with honorable defilements to better conquer our impenetrable souls. And with regard to the ethnographers, they came here to invite us to reconstruct our world based on its anomalies, and thus calm their consciences. With all that we have had to swallow, it's a wonder that it is still possible to be "native."

"The worst thing is," he argued, "that we never had the chance to even open our mouths. So many times we ended up being clandestine even to ourselves, hiding our things so well that nearly everything became inalienable. There is a story of a Salesian bishop who bragged that he had systematically burned all of the large collective huts of the upper Negro River. He confessed publicly, full of pious pride, that he had achieved the same policy of razing native lands as the previous Portuguese invaders, but with less expense.

"Now I understand what you meant with the term 'theoretical tremors.' And so, as the exotic jumps at our throat like a furious feline, terrorizing us with the possibility that we might be taken as an anthropological hoax, we hold fast to the belief that we are from the 'Occident,' and thus, as always happens, even with the 'Occidentals' themselves, we come to the conclusion that we are 'civilized.' "

"A sad deceit. As you live within the paradox, you will constantly run into a reality that is difficult to abandon."

"That's why, after each one of those unusual encounters, we rush back to the lap of 'civilization.' It's a pity that 'civilization' is also a strange and inhospitable place, because becoming acculturated isn't easy when the original components burst like absolutions."

Absolutions like outbreaks of malaria, thought Pietra, Jr., because throughout centuries Amazonians loved to feel that they were the target of greed; they were all puffed up with a native pride that hid the dark side of their souls, reduced to ashes the past, and made them content with bits and pieces, castoffs. A lacerated, yet a secret, memory.

Like fevers, absolutions provoke deliriums. Malignant tertian fevers infiltrating the body with agony, the exhausted mind assailed by frights. And Jane made a great effort to come to grips with so many sensations, so many ideas that filled her head, knowing all the time that it wasn't really necessary. An understanding of all this was perhaps unalterably beyond her reach, inaccessible as a result of its extreme simplicity, as prosaic in its mystery as the erection that he was now showing her, a swaying shaft that tapered from the base to the tip, gently curved toward his belly, the imposing rosy oval head dominating the rod with its indistinct blue veins. And Jane could feel just how proud he was of it because he was a very primitive god, one who still believed in the commanding power of the penis. But after that night of the comet, Jane knew, the last links between gods and mortals had been broken.

Time stopped in homage of that instant, and they were engulfed in a burning brume, where fire etched the images in their minds, raising the temperature of their bodies. Only in this way would it be possible to traverse such indomitable worlds, to cover their ears to the cries of those who shouted that it is inevitable, that everything is victimized by the picturesque, that even when a few disguise themselves as romantics, they are still unpleasantly primitive and ought to be put out of their misery.

He pulled her towards him and whispered in her ear so that those voices couldn't interfere.

"We are forced to accept our own imposture as our identity. And so as not to recognize our complete insignificance, we are content to be projected as substanceless."

"This is the primary sign of the primitive world," she said. "In which the people are willing to forget, without so much as a struggle, their original nature, urged toward the deplorable phenomenon of acculturation. This is true of the Europeans as well. They all become lost and alienated by a shock whose meaning was concealed from them. In the same way, your identity is a product of confrontation. You are Americans; you ought to be accustomed to it."

"No, we will never become accustomed to it. Under the sign of the paradox, many times the solidarity that they proclaim to have appears more like a long-awaited opportunity to rid themselves of us. Because solidarity is like the blade of a knife, making us bleed in silence, even when we come together publicly with those who come here to cry over the spilt milk. When a holocaust lasts five hundred years, the pain freezes. There is a type of vacancy that installs itself in the soul, that drives us to an insipid laziness, that feeds on possibilities, on daydreams, but that in the end only wraps our lives up in a shroud of disillusionment."

"No matter what," she replied, her green eyes glittering with impatience, "your resentment is no longer acceptable. There is no place for those who delight in insignificance when time is voracious. At this point, you don't move anyone; we are tired of those who allow themselves to be held hostage by expectations of backwardness."

"So then, the paradox is our delirium?" he asked.

"Latin America is a paradox," she responded.

He positioned himself on top of her, because there was nothing more to say. They got comfortable, and he slowly penetrated her, holding on to her thighs and watching everything his body did, following the insertion centimeter by centimeter, until he saw that he was entirely inside her, and then he rested. The priestess was a small woman, soft and damp, who moved continuously while he contemplated what he was doing, subtly trembling in perfect harmony with her, riveted to that muscular entrance that wanted to carry him off farther and farther from those sad ruins that surrounded them both.

How long did that night last? Not more than a few minutes. Or did millennia speed by while they twisted and moaned? Apparently time was very condescending with them, waiting for their bellies to contract and relax, for them to hold each other tightly, and for them to give themselves to each other as an offering: he, the god, debased and consumed; she, brought down by her own prejudices. And the two of them were carried off by the whirlwind of time; they levitated over the crowns of the gigantic trees, extraordinary chestnut trees about to succumb, traveling over storm clouds up to the snow-covered peaks, hanging over treacherous slopes where the great rivers are born as timid drops of dew. In each one of them a transcendental mask of innocence, the startled smiles of those who witness an epiphany.

Before the final flood, Pietra, Jr., had the strength to whisper, "And so, have things changed?"

THE END OF THE THIRD WORLD

"Is there still hope?" she asked.

"What can one say?" he again whispered to her, observing that she had shut her eyes and a rictus pulled her mouth open in an immense smile.

The god also showed his white pre-Columbian teeth, making short movements, because there were no more responses, only the same incoherent voices, the old cacophony whistling like the northeastern wind coming through the crown of the chestnut trees, saying that the acids of contingencies will one day corrode all of the mysteries and that, at last, when the waters recede, on the first sunny day after the flood, the ruins will have been restored and the paradox exorcised.

With a sharp shout, they fell into the abyss.

And Jane Challenger awoke.

She was alone, entirely dressed, lying on the bed. Only the light in the small foyer was on, but she could see the mess that the room was in. Frightened, she tried to pack all her things in the suitcase, and much to her surprise, she discovered that part of the papers had been carried off. She looked at her watch; in two hours she would take the return flight to Europe. Yet perhaps she might never really be able to leave that place.

Book Three

Endangered Species

The Remote Frontiers of the New World

Dom Tomasi di Lampedusa believed that Sicilia was the America of the classic era of antiquity. The Ionians and the Dorians, forerunners of another discovery some twenty centuries later, encountered in the thorny vegetation of the Sicilian mountain slopes an aromatic labyrinth. In that first venture, under a blue, cloudless sky, they were intoxicated by the myrtle and scotch broom, and the smell of thyme. What remained of those sensations in the contemporary olfaction? Apparently nothing more than a vague poetic memory, flashes of ecstasy, shreds of surprise.

Curiously this olfactory issue began to make me uneasy just as soon as I finished the previous chapter. The transformation of an act of sexual violence into a liturgy of revelation didn't seem quite right to me. Especially since I knew a number of Pietro Pietra, Jr., types in person, and I was certain that none of them possessed divine attributes, not even the most primitive kind. None of them were interested in testing odors, and if by chance they paid a little attention to nature, they wouldn't choose the smell of the pepper tree or the aggressive beauty of the amaranths, rather the phallic form of the tropical miratanga plant. Because as far as they are concerned, the only thing that matters is the prick.

Pietro Pietra, Jr., as you are beginning to imagine, was quite an eccentric fellow; in his own way he was an

LOST WORLD II

extraordinary man, combining wisdom with an enormous sense of opportunism, and capable of committing some cruel act in order to exercise his compassion. The most successful fellows I have known, some of whom have amassed large fortunes in the last twenty years, seemed to live on the defensive; they hated subtlety and lacked the most minimal entrepreneurial tact. They were successful because they were under the protective umbrella of Brasilia and didn't risk a thing. Their fortune was earned as a result of their impunity, not from daring put to a test.

The flesh-and-blood Pietro Pietra, Jr., could be seen in any of the five BBC television programs directed by Virginia Challenger, and not one of them had a knack for divinity. If it had been possible to interview Pietro Pietra, Jr., he would have said that he had been born in the city of Bauru, Sao Paulo, into a family of modest means. He didn't make it to high school, because he had to get a job. At the age of seventeen he was making deliveries and doing small jobs in a neighborhood shoe shop, which is where he first displayed his precocious talents of persuasion. He was a natural-born salesman who could convince the customers to buy old merchandise, thinking that they were getting the latest styles. He could win over the most recalcitrant buyer and tolerate with infinite patience the most torturous indecisiveness. No one came out of the shoe store empty-handed if Pietro was in the store.

And naturally his boss rolled out the red carpet for him, and on one of the corners of the carpet he found the boss's very marriageable daughter. Pietro felt that he was still too young for marriage. He had just turned eighteen and barely escaped military service by bribing an officer with a pair of German boots, but he didn't want to disappoint his benefactor, and much less the

THE END OF THE THIRD WORLD

nubile offering, who, by all indications, wasn't something to toss out. Pietro learned then and there that one cannot please everyone at the same time. Making an effort not to disappoint the eager young maiden, he wound up leading her astray. Her father, realizing that it wasn't exactly a matter of orthopedics, resorted to his .38-caliber, attempting to show the persuasive salesman that deception could be dangerous.

Pietro fled the city under the cover of night, swearing to himself that from then on he would only try to please others when he himself was pleased. He became just another face in the city of Sao Paulo, where he worked in various positions, as a factory worker in an auto parts company, as a desk clerk, and finally as a door-to-door salesman selling contraband items, or, as they are sometimes called, unofficially imported articles. His specialty was selling Japanese cameras, and he was so skilled at it that he began to be known as Pietro Pentax. Profits for middlemen like him weren't much; he made just enough to dress with a certain refinement, drive a secondhand car, and live in an area of the city that wasn't completely indigent. What Pietro liked most of all was being around people with a good income, because they didn't complain, they were avid followers of fads, and they never seemed to tire of him.

The years passed rapidly, and one day Pietro realized he was thirty years old. His life was at a standstill; he was marking time. The camera business was for a very exclusive clientele in a country that had as its principal political ideology the exclusion of the majority of the people. One day, as it happens, he found a new customer who wasn't interested only in cameras. In fact, he didn't have the slightest bit of interest in photography. He was a flighty, fickle, and unhappy young fellow, quite rich and bored to tears; he had met Pietro while the latter was making a delivery at the home of a friend. It wasn't just a Pentax the fellow was interested in: it was Pietro Pentax. What followed is now history.

In order to unravel a bit more the theological bent of my narrative, I found out right away that my ex-classmate shared his story with everyone. He told anyone who would listen that his boss was a god, which in itself isn't especially a novelty in the history of production relations. What was worse was the fact that the hardworking student of Latin from the Dom Bosco High School, and a devotee of Saint Dominic the Sage, was a member of a curious sect that had been experiencing a lot of success at that time.

The name of the sect was "Brothers of Tajá"; it had already recruited a number of television actresses and two or three of the old left-wing militants of the 1960s. The sect's main attraction was its emphasis on mysticism; in addition it had as the core of its liturgy the ingestion of a drinkable laxative known as "water vine." Its scientific nomenclature was "Dolorecorpus breviflatulenceitus Garcke," which the follower would chant slowly, and upon arriving at the word "Garcke," bang, the elixir would take effect.

The Brothers of Tajá began as a religious movement with a distinctive popular and primitive character, in an apparent attempt to promote the synthesis of the beliefs of the northern migrants, who began arriving as early as 1877, with additional and unrelated aspects of the indigenous cultures. Up to this point, there was nothing unusual. It was a phenomenon that was ripe for some serious ethnographic research undertaken to undermine the archaic Brazilian world. It offered very little that was different from the other sects that used miraculous drinkable potions that spring forth in the

THE END OF THE THIRD WORLD

Amazon with the same impetus as a McDonald's chain. What is annoying in this story involving sects is their tendency to attract a fauna of stupid vocabulary and majestic conceptual torments regarding the void, concepts better suited for the beaches of Rio de Janeiro, where various microbes, coliforms, and the hepatitis A virus are certain to restrict their proliferation.

But the sad reality was that my ex-colleague was transformed into one of those fastidious idiots of nature. And with that Indian face to boot!

Personally, I am just a little bit prejudiced. I don't have anything against those tribes of urban folklore who give themselves airs of having all the answers; they are as inoffensive as the little Mickey Mouse figures that are said to be dipped in LSD and passed out to children. On days of unabashed liberalism, I can indulge in a three-second conversation with one of those knuckleheaded alternatives. But I find it impossible to face the invasion of those heralds of liquid nirvanas around Manaus. That was all we needed! In the first place, because it is an open invitation to all kinds of meddling. We were always very reserved, and unlike the northeasterners, we didn't accept just anyone who showed up offering solidarity and demanding explanations. Especially when it had to do with the interests of a certain urban middle class that goes around like a stupid cockroach in this vermin-invested country and that already went rampaging like some Attila the Hun over the Afro-Brazilian culture, not to mention the Oriental imports and their eminently expert gurus.

That is why, before what happened to the blacks happens to what remains of the Indians, let's make everything perfectly clear. We just die of shame when we see some lovely television actress announce that she drank a few swallows of water vine, and bang, she became ecologically minded and began defending the Amazon forests. Not too long ago, one of those born-again mystics declared, after visiting the region, that he had been surprised by some such "energy that whirls in the rain forest." I found out about his declaration and I thought: What in the hell does he mean with this business about energy that whirls in the rain forest? Because I've done my share of walking in the forest, and with the heat that there is during the day, the only thing that I saw with any energy, and it wasn't exactly whirling, more like flying and crawling, was the millions of insects that infest the jungle.

That is why, when I encounter one of these fellows that thinks that metaphysics is a branch of thermodynamics, or vice versa, right away I warn him.

"Look here, the Amazon isn't Nepal, and the Indians, with their loincloths and other paraphernalia, aren't the perfect substitutes for Indian gurus."

The Brothers of Tajá sect threw together a syncretic doctrine with generous portions of the most backward and moralist spiritualism, bits and pieces of Catholic liturgy from the time of the Council of Trent, and some poorly digested elements of the indigenous beliefs. In the beginning, it was a popular movement that attempted to express its own despair, its own lacerations, until the citified middle class got ahold of it. In a region convulsed by problems of land ownership, nothing could be more convenient than a doctrine that promises nirvana attained through a digestive apparatus and preaches passivity as a major virtue. We were lucky that the Amazon never was a fertile soil for certain rustic furors. The northeasterners realized this right off; one never found in our midst the slightest trace of hired gunmen, much less religious fanatics of the ilk of Jim Jones of Jonestown fame.

THE END OF THE THIRD WORLD

Pietro Pietra, Jr. a god? Only if by the grace of poetic license, or a vulgar manifestation of urban folklore, like that story of the Doberman pinscher that choked on the finger of the burglar who was trying to rob his master's house.

And since we've lost some precious time in this digression, we'll jump directly to Sir Delamare's mansion, where Jane Challenger and Billy Lester have just arrived.

What surprised Billy Lester the most upon meeting Sir Delamare was the fact that he looked better in person than in his picture that appeared in all the newspapers, magazines, and broadcasting stations of his empire. It was interesting, in these sick times in which the media reigns supreme, to see that some people, even the most powerful ones, were somewhat more whole than a simple close-up. Sir Delamare had the body, voice, and agility of a younger man. His withdrawal from the world, the distance that he maintained from interaction with common mortals, was a deliberate attitude, a chosen option. And Lester began to understand his motives.

The Tudor mansion, located in Pembroke Square, was equipped with a sophisticated communications system, diverse types of vehicles, and a heliport that afforded him a mobility that few could even imagine. Sir Delamare was an adventurer, an old and obstinate pioneer who refused to accept the impositions of his age. At ninety, he appeared solid, as robust as one of those rare individuals who knows the secrets of longevity. A master in the almost extinct art of chivalry, without concealing a particularly spontaneous gruffness left over from his modest origins, Sir Delamare was demolishing all of the barriers of hostility and distrust that Jane Challenger felt toward him. He knew it was inevitable that she held a rather negative impression of him. After all, he was one of the richest and most mysterious men of the United Kingdom, and even worse, he was her boss. But what won her over immediately was his forthright personality, the calm awareness of his position, and the aura of power that he transmitted with familiarity.

"The rich are the greatest victims of prejudices," he said, receiving the two of them in his study, "but we aren't here to speak of the prejudices of the poor against the rich, are we?"

"You were sure that I would come," Jane said, peeved.

Sir Delamare shook his head gravely. "No, I wasn't sure. From what I know about you and your family—and I believe I know you well enough to form an opinion—nothing indicated that this meeting would come to pass. People generally believe that I am able to satisfy all of my capricious whims, but no power on earth is strong enough to make someone like you change your mind."

"Do you have any idea of what happened to me?" Jane asked, pacified by the explanation Sir Delamare had just given.

"Very little, to tell you the truth. But I couldn't help hearing when you came to see me last week. I had no idea who you were, much less that you were a member of the Challenger family, but it was obvious you were a person of strong character and determination. Everyone who works for me knows that I am not to be disturbed."

"Spender wouldn't listen to me; he's an idiot. And I no longer work for you."

"That is the rule. Spender was doing his job; he is a good fellow. He isn't the idiot you think he is."

"He must be just right for the job."

"Exactly," Sir Delamare agreed. "But this has nothing to do with why you're here."

"You're right. Nothing at all," Jane said.

"It seems that you wrote a report, some kind of proposal for a story; isn't that so?"

"It must have been filed away by Spender."

"I had the opportunity to read what you wrote, and I would like to know what really happened." Jane tried to speak, but he made a sign for her to wait. "It just so happens that I am an old friend of Sr. Danilo Ariel Duarte."

"You know him?" she exclaimed.

"It was during the last world war; you and your friend had probably not even been born yet. Duarte, a student at Eton, exported rubber for the war effort; he was in Lisbon, by chance, when the Germans tried to kidnap the Duke of Windsor from his villa in Espirito Santo. He was instrumental in unraveling the Nazi operation, colliding head-on into one of the cars used by the kidnappers and attracting the attention of the Portuguese police." Sir Delamare smiled and went on, savoring his memories. "I was under surveillance by the Germans, and Duarte, who was always a disastrous driver, crashed into their car with so much force that he put all of its occupants out of commission for the rest of the conflict. And he was only trying to park his own car in order to pay a visit to Espirito Santo. We have been friends ever since that incident."

"How long has it been since you last saw him?"

"I believe we ran into each other at the end of last year. And Duarte didn't seem well at that time; by that I mean he was all right physically, healthy enough for his age, but mentally he seemed depressed, worried."

"And justifiably so," Jane said. "Just at that time Sr. Duarte's firm was being taken over by an opportunist."

"He didn't mention anything; he always was very discreet, a very refined man with a first-rate education. He speaks exemplary English."

"His English is excellent," agreed Jane.

"However, yesterday I received this in the mail," Sir Delamare said, picking up an envelope with green and yellow borders that had been on his desk. "It is a letter from Duarte. Actually, it is an invitation."

"An invitation?"

"The Brazilian government, it seems, is organizing a meeting of international investors. Duarte is asking me to accept the invitation."

"Do you have interests there?" Lester asked.

"It is possible; I'm not sure."

"And do you intend to accept the invitation?" Jane pushed.

"That depends on you," he responded.

"On me? Why is that?"

"I would like to know what really happened to you there."

Jane hesitated, apprehensive and distant. At her side, Lester seemed out of place, somewhat useless, feeling stupid.

"Nothing happened," Jane said. "I simply found a good story for the magazine. That's all."

Sir Delamare lost his understanding air. The two strong personalities prepared for a confrontation.

"Look here, Miss Challenger. I believe that Duarte is in some kind of danger. I owe my life to him; it's an old debt, but unpaid nevertheless. I feel an obligation to go to his rescue. He would be incapable of asking for help, but if you know something, I think it would be a good idea to speak up now."

"I don't believe he is in danger, sir," Lester interjected. "He apparently was ruined by a partner."

"Apparently," said Sir Delamare. "But is that all there is to it?"

"His partner is a violent man, unscrupulous," Lester added.

THE END OF THE THIRD WORLD

"Do you agree, Miss Challenger?" Sir Delamare queried Jane.

"The description is accurate."

"Violent enough to invade a woman's room?" Sir Delamare probed, causing a frightened reaction in Jane.

"How did you know about that?" she demanded, looking at Lester angrily.

"Don't rush to accuse your friend. He is innocent. Duarte mentioned it in his letter; it seems that his so-called partner went around bragging about it. Do you still think that nothing out of the ordinary is happening there?"

"I don't know," Jane responded impatiently. "All I want to do is expose that creep."

"We all do," Sir Delamare said. "And we are going to expose him." He took a white envelope from out of a folder and passed it to Jane.

"This is the official invitation from the Brazilian government."

Jane opened it and read the invitation, then passed it to Lester. The invitation, bearing the seal of Brazil, said that for four days aboard the transatlantic *Leviathan*, a Panamanian-flagged vessel, investors and entrepreneurs from various countries would come together to listen to the Brazilian authorities' new plans for the opening of the Amazon region to international capital investment. The trip would take place between the cities of Manaus and Belém.

"Strange, isn't it?" Sir Delamare commented. "It gives the impression of being a tourist trip."

"Are you going to participate in the trip?" Jane asked.

"Perhaps. Duarte was always a curious man. He had a genuine vocation for eccentricity."

The old man paused, noting that Jane was beginning to feel restless.

"I am speaking of these things merely so you will have a better understanding of my Latin friend," he said, resuming the conversation. "I don't intend to burden you with the memories of an old man, if that is what you're fearing."

"I beg your pardon, but I am still very nervous about all that went on there," Jane said, quickly changing her attitude and prompting him to continue.

"I understand. The shock must have been enormous."

"He wanted to talk to me, and he wasn't able to," Jane said. "I am almost certain that he was prevented from doing so."

Sir Delamare became expressionless; not a muscle moved in his face, as if the suspicion wasn't going to superimpose itself over what he still had to tell.

"Duarte had a British university education, but he never completely severed his ties to that savage land," Sir Delamare said. "He was a cultured man, a rare entrepreneurial type for that region of the world. His family had been in the Amazon since 1790. A Portuguese family, of Visigoth origins, which accounts for my friend's white skin, gray eyes, and blond hair. They were bureaucrats when they arrived, but right away they got into commerce which made them famous in the Indies. In two generations they amassed a fortune, because they knew how to take advantage of the appreciation of latex on the world market. They imported things from Europe and sold them to the rubber producers. By 1890 they were an extremely powerful merchant clan, able to ride out all of the financial ups and downs that followed in the twentieth century. Am I too long-winded?"

"No, please go on!" Jane urged.

For the first time, Sir Delamare cracked a smile.

"During the sixties, certain political events affected

Duarte's life. By that time, he commanded the clan, he had created an enormous real estate network, he owned land and a chain of department stores in Manaus. In 1966 the military officers, who held all the political power at the time, appointed Duarte as the governor of the state of Amazonas. What initially seemed to be the coronation of a successful life was, in fact, the beginning of his downfall. His term as governor, which lasted four years, was austere and irreproachable, but the military commanders managed to completely change the profile of the region.

"Upon leaving the governorship, he tried to keep up with the changes, associating himself with a Japanese group. I had almost no contact with him during this time, just once when he passed through here coming from Tokyo, where he had been to close a deal. That was in 1972; more than ten years passed until I ran into him last year at a reception in Lisbon. We paid a visit to Espirito Santo for old times' sake; he was always very spiritual. But I later found out that he had been wiped out; I was told complicated stories about Duarte being pursued by some terrorist organization."

"He was threatened?" Jane asked.

"To tell the truth, I didn't pay much mind to the story. The source wasn't very trustworthy. One of Duarte's eccentricities was to tell fables, to converse by means of parables, which sometimes created terrible misunderstandings, not to speak of how tiring they could be after a while."

"Did you hear the name of the organization that was pursuing him?" Lester asked.

"If I'm not mistaken, they mentioned Jihad Jívaros, or some such thing. Does that make any sense to you? I haven't found any mention of it in my files."

"I have never heard of them," Lester said.

"It is the first time I heard the name," Jane added.

"The only thing I have managed to deduce was by analyzing the two words. Jihad comes from Arabic, and it means holy war; Jívaro is the name of a tribe of Indians from the Peruvian rain forest that was famous for shrinking the heads of their captured enemies. They are the famous headhunters of South America. The juxtaposition of the two words gives a very suggestive connotation regarding the designs of such a terrorist group."

"Interesting," Jane said. "You have said that he was a very eccentric person. I chatted with him in Manaus, and he behaved in a strange manner. He told me some kind of fable, quite enigmatic to be sure."

"That is Duarte, no more, no less. I used to say that he was logic's terror, because he spread ambiguity in a world driven by certainties."

"And now he leaves us in the middle of a most complicated fable," Jane replied.

"Yes, in the middle of one of those fables that carries on even after death," Sir Delamare agreed, fixing his eyes on some indefinite point above the horizon, as if he were recalling significant events. "I hope I can still help him . . ."

"I know what you are feeling," Jane said, empathizing with Sir Delamare. "That's the way it is with terrorism, the stupidity of it. One feels like saying: 'Wait a minute, haven't you learned anything yet?'"

Sir Delamare sighed and lit a cigarette, one of his cheap rat-killing black smokes that gave off a dense, bluish cloud when he exhaled.

"I took the liberty of including the two of you in my entourage," he said, engulfed in smoke.

"Your entourage?" Jane said, finding the whole idea strange.

THE END OF THE THIRD WORLD

"Therefore, we are going to take part in the so-called trip of the transatlantic. They are paying for everything, exceedingly generous. After all, you've been wanting to return there, haven't you?"

A red flush spread across Jane's face. It wasn't out of timidity or surprise; it was irritation at finding herself committed to something without first having been consulted.

"Calm down, Miss Challenger," Sir Delamare said, pacifying her. "I was forced to make the decision, a matter of deadlines, you know. The Brazilian Embassy asked for a reply today at three P.M. I beg your pardon if my precipitation has upset you, but there was no time to lose, and I preferred to take a chance. I think you can understand that."

"When do we leave?" Jane asked, controlling her irritation.

"Tonight," Sir Delamare said. "I am having my plane readied. We will fly to the Azores, and from there on to Manaus."

"The Azores?" Jane was surprised. "But why the Azores?"

"A friend of mine is going to join us there," he replied.

"Can you tell us who he is?" Jane insisted.

"You are going to like him," he responded, enjoying himself as much for the mysteriousness as for Jane's petulance.

Jane's temperature again began to reach the boiling point, and this time it wasn't possible to control it.

"I want to make something perfectly clear, Lord Delamare. I no longer work for you. And don't forget it!"

Sir Delamare raised his right eyebrow in surprise.

"You can organize your safari with the best little group of idle idiots that you can get together, but don't confuse things. I'm going home now to prepare for the trip. I will be at Heathrow; we are leaving from there, right?"

Sir Delamare confirmed with a nod, his mouth slightly ajar as Jane turned on her heel and left the room. Lester stayed behind, not reacting.

"And you, my young man," Sir Delamare asked, recovering from Jane's impact, "aren't you going to pack as well?"

Lester left the Tudor palace with ominous feelings. He got off the subway in Hampstead under a fine rain that left the streets deserted and the sidewalks muddy. A few hours from then, he would be embarking for the Amazon jungle, and it was all Jane's fault. But he didn't feel exactly unhappy about traveling so far; traveling didn't frighten him. What irked him was the sensation that his participation was superfluous; he was nothing more than a decorative figure invented by Jane Challenger's caprices. When he considered this, he felt like joining the Jihad Jívaros.

To avoid letting his anger get the best of him, he threw himself into getting organized for the trip, packing everything he would need in a carry-on bag. He unplugged the electrical appliances, turned off the gas, and headed for the subway station. Heathrow was the most paranoiac airport in the world; people acted nervously, and the ostensive presence of the police force, armed with automatic machine guns, only served to increase the sensation of imminent attack. In that insane climate, Lester made contact with his travel companions, something that didn't give him even minimal comfort.

Right at the entrance to the terminal, he found a dejected Spender grasping an old leather suitcase and sporting an expression of martyrdom that broke into a weak smile upon seeing someone he knew. Further on, they found Sir Delamare, holding a crystal wineglass and eating bits of smoked salmon served to him by a waiter; he

THE END OF THE THIRD WORLD

was chatting excitedly with two gentlemen. The one with a mustache and monocle was Lord William Claredon, the legendary wild-game hunter of the 1930s, explorer of Madagascar and the first white man to interview the Great Elephant Woman of Rhodesia; the other, wearing long white sideburns, was Lord Robert Burton, somewhat weakened by his self-proclaimed 102 years of age, but nevertheless immortalized in history by having survived a trek on foot across the jungles of the Congo in 1928.

"They've come to wish us good luck," said Sir Delamare, upon seeing Lester nearly in a state of shock. "And our dear Miss Challenger?"

"She should be arriving soon, sir."

"I only hope she doesn't change her mind at the last minute. The Challengers always loved surprises."

"We don't change our minds!"

It was Jane, arriving in a lovely jeans outfit and carrying a beautiful Hermes traveling case.

As they took off, Sir Delamare arranged to have Lester at his side. But it wasn't out of consideration; Lester had already realized that. As soon as the jet took off, Sir Delamare lit up one of his stinky cigarettes and leaned over to speak to him. "Keep an eye on your friend. When we arrive in Manaus, don't leave her alone for an instant."

Lester agreed, because he couldn't back out at that point. He confined himself to swallowing a potent sleeping pill to make sure he would be out of the battle the rest of the night. But he unfortunately chose a bad position to do it in, because for days following the flight, he felt acute pain in his back and could hardly look down at his own feet.

Jane Challenger didn't sleep; she was too excited and preoccupied with the identity of the individual who would be joining them in the Azores. But of one thing

LOST WORLD II

she was convinced: No story would be written, not a line would be published. She was certain that Sir Delamare's interest in the whole affair was far from journalistic. But she no longer cared; it was enough that she would have a chance to settle accounts with Pietro Pietra, Jr. She had imagined a whole series of punishments for him, but none seemed sufficiently insulting in order to compensate for the affront that she had suffered.

Jane was still plotting punishments and vengeance when she noticed that it was growing light. From the window, she could see the Atlantic, illuminated by a subtle crimson hue, and the lights of Ponta Delgada shining. When the plane had landed, Sir Delamare went to the door to welcome his guest.

It was Juan Sender, a Chilean writer.

"Sender will be our translator," Sir Delamare informed them.

"In Manaus only Portuguese is spoken," Jane said.

"It doesn't matter; he plays cricket quite well," said Sir Delamare. "And, by the way, never ask him what he is currently writing."

What followed could be called anything but monotonous. The Brazilian government decided to get all the guests together in the Hotel Tropical, the very same one where Jane had stayed. The hotel had been transformed into a veritable confusion of white collars, nervous executives, and hysterical native servers. Teletypes spewed forth messages nearly everywhere, and video terminals were displaying the stock market prices from various parts of the world. It wasn't possible to drink a simple drink without some gadget sitting on the bar counter noisily delivering the futures market in Barcelona or the price of commodities in Singapore.

Lester, indifferent to all the confusion, could hardly move his body; he was weary, sporting deep, dark circles

THE END OF THE THIRD WORLD

under his eyes. He went right to his room, dragged himself into the shower, and let the cold water run over his aching body. The noise of the shower almost prevented him from hearing the doorbell ring. He wrapped up in a towel and went to open the door.

It was Jane, with her clothes changed and radiating freshness, as if the flight across the ocean had been a simple outing in a car.

"What's the matter with you, Lester? You seem ill."

"No, it's nothing. I just slept in a bad position. Now I'm feeling better."

She shut the door and went to the window. All the hotel rooms were located above the lobby floor, and Jane carefully observed the delicate forest that could be seen from the window.

"I managed to talk with Sr. Duarte. It was the first thing I did as soon as I entered the hotel. He is waiting for us at his house."

Lester always thought that certain events of life, as revolting as they often seem, are like proofs of a perverse irony that governs the world. That was what he immediately thought when they arrived at Sr. Duarte's mansion and they were informed by the police that he was dead.

"But he spoke with me on the phone just an hour ago," said Jane, almost shouting.

"He was found by the housekeeper," clarified an older police officer; a polite tone in his voice hid the sadness that he felt giving them the news.

"How did it happen?" Lester asked.

"What we know is that the housekeeper entered the room to do some routine cleaning, and she saw Sr. Duarte in the bed, seemingly sleeping. She said she was sorry, and she was on her way out when she had the intuition that he might be dead."

LOST WORLD II

While they listened to the policeman and attempted to absorb the shock, a fellow wearing an unbelievable checkered sport coat entered the conversation.

"We hope to have a conclusive answer regarding the cause of death as early as this afternoon," the man said. He was one of those bulky men, a veritable giant, which accentuated even more the absurdity of his checkered jacket.

"This is Deputy Officer Rubens of the Federal Police." The older policeman made the introduction somewhat begrudgingly.

Speaking in a sharp voice, rather incongruous with his size, the federal officer continued. "But everything leads us to believe that it was a natural death."

"Of course it was a natural death," the policeman said rather brusquely. "Sr. Duarte had a sudden attack. There are no signs of violence; everything is in order. It's all been checked out."

"That is what is presumed," responded the federal officer.

Jane, who was clutching her purse tightly, gave a sigh of impatience.

"Are you relatives? Friends?" the federal officer asked.

"Neither one nor the other," Lester answered, too vaguely for the policeman's taste.

He shook his head like a hungry ogre and hissed, "I don't understand."

"We didn't know him well," explained Jane. "We had just arrived in the city, and he called us for a meeting."

"Business?" The inquisitive mind of the policeman was racing.

"Not exactly," Lester said, regretting it immediately.

"He was a friend of my father's," Jane said dryly. "I don't know exactly what he intended by inviting us over."

THE END OF THE THIRD WORLD

The federal deputy pulled out a handkerchief and dried his sweaty forehead, observing Jane with great interest. The older policeman, feeling he was dismissed, withdrew and resumed his routine, but he remained attentive to the conversation.

"He was old," the deputy said, "but he seemed to be in good shape. My hypothesis is that he suffered a cardiac arrest. These things happen."

"Is there something we can do?" Jane asked, distressed.

"Leave your addresses. Perhaps I will want to speak with you later."

"We are at the Hotel Tropical," Lester said.

"What do you intend to do?" Jane asked.

"Well, you know—" the lieutenant hesitated, once more drying the sweat from him brow "—Sr. Duarte had been governor of Amazonas. He was greatly respected in the city. I am here to do the preliminary reports. His death was sudden, which can cause suspicions. And we don't want that to happen, but the final word rests with the medical examiner from the Department of Security."

Still under the effects of the surprise, they remained in the spacious living room of the eclectic mansion. They were numbed by the natural perplexity in the face of death, because death is the only fact without ambiguity. Deputy Rubens withdrew, his head down reverently, stepping on the marble floor. Jane watched the immense man as he disappeared in the brightness of the day and the placidity of the beautiful garden; her eyes filled with tears as she faced the difficult task of overcoming the impact of that death. Lester understood her feelings and knew as well that with Sr. Duarte's unexpected death, all the doors had abruptly slammed shut.

"Jane, are you all right?" he asked, concerned.

"Yes," she responded firmly, the tears behind her, struggling against the terrible frustration of that unexpected death.

"What do you plan to do?"

Jane was silent; she reached out and held Lester's arm tightly.

"Are you really okay?" he asked again.

She only shook her head affirmatively and released her grip on his arm.

"I'm worried about you, Jane."

"Don't worry about me. Worry about yourself."

"What do you mean by that?"

"Nothing."

"Nothing?"

"Do you want to know something, Lester? I believe that Sr. Duarte didn't die a natural death."

"No?" he said, but he didn't feel any surprise. The same suspicion had been running through his head since the first moment.

"But the police are going to consider it death from natural causes. And it was murder."

They had no proof, no evidence whatsoever, only the idea that Sr. Duarte had been murdered; in spite of all the police's explanations to the contrary, the possibility didn't seem so absurd.

"Something tells me that he was murdered," Jane reaffirmed. "Someone didn't want him to meet with us."

Lester agreed with her. Perhaps it was due to their long-standing friendship, or Jane's well-developed objectivity, which never was undermined by emotionalism, but they were willing to test their suspicions, even though it might be like throwing a stone at a frozen lake. The possibility that it had been murder left Lester frightened. He hated violence, and he almost preferred to imagine

THE END OF THE THIRD WORLD

Sr. Duarte—whom Jane had met only once or twice—slipping toward death alone in his widower's bed.

"How do you think he was killed?" he asked, thinking about poisons brewed by savage witch doctors in the equatorial jungles.

"I have no idea," she replied.

"If it was murder, the coroners will discover it," he said without much conviction.

"Perhaps," she responded. "What we need to find out is if they managed to silence him forever."

"They?"

"Yes, they, the people who came in here, and killed him, a man who had been governor of Amazonas."

"But why?" Lester asked, somewhat rhetorically.

"Larger interests, money, all of those things."

"Don't you think we ought to inform Sir Delamare?" Lester suggested.

She laughed wryly and bitterly. "Let's go talk to the old mummy," she replied.

Who Could Have Known?

Sir Delamare showed little surprise at the news of his friend's death. Perhaps because he was in his nineties, which must have given him a certain intimacy with death; silence met the news, a reverent hush for the disappearance of someone he esteemed. But also there was frustration in his moderated attitude. It was as if he had failed, reacted too slowly to help an old friend in need. And Sir Delamare, a man of action, a reliable friend, didn't like to fail. In some way, he needed to make amends for the grave mistake that he believed he had committed.

"Spender. Where is Spender?" he called, lighting one of his stinky cigarettes and releasing a whiff of gray smoke.

"He's probably in his room," Sender informed him. The Chilean had been playing chess with the aging magnate when the sad news was given. "He excused himself to rest for a while; he was rather confused."

"Spender is always confused," Sir Delamare said.

Jane, seated near the window, was drinking tea. Her legs were crossed and drawn under the chair; she was barefoot, her feet resting on the soft, velvety rug. She sipped the tea drop by drop, partaking of the silence. Beside her, Lester seemed a sleepwalker. His eyes, wide open, were vacant; his breathing was slow, and his hands, which were resting on his thighs, seemed to be made of wax.

THE END OF THE THIRD WORLD

"Is his son here in the city?" Sir Delamare wanted to know, turning to the two reporters.

"We didn't see any family members," Lester informed him. "The house seemed almost abandoned. So he has a son?"

"Yes, but I don't know him. Duarte spoke sparingly of him. You say the house seemed abandoned?"

"It was a little dirty, with that closed-up smell," Lester said. "It is a huge house, a mansion. But we didn't enter the main room; it was full of policemen."

"I think that the two of you are hiding something," Sir Delamare said from out of a cloud of smoke. "What is it, Lester?"

Lester wasn't able to respond to this. Technically they didn't know anything more than that the death had been natural, according to the initial observations of the police. But Sir Delamare's suspicions were to be taken seriously, and Lester was concentrating on them. He feared appearing ridiculous if he revealed that from the first minute he—and simultaneously Jane—had a gut reaction that the man had been murdered. He nervously tapped his pale fingers on his legs, contemplating how remote his previous existence seemed at that moment. He looked at Jane, then at Sir Delamare. He felt a strange sensation, as if all of that was not really happening; rather, it was just a scene in a play. A bad play.

"I was thinking, Lester, about the last conversation that I had with Duarte," Sir Delamare went on, as if he wanted to draw that strange sensation to its final consequences. "He told me one of his fables, saying that it was quite illustrative of this country."

"Do you agree with him?"

"Well, like all fables are wont to be, it is excessively ambivalent. It occurs to me that my friend might have died because he was too ambiguous, and I try to imagine

LOST WORLD II

what his last moments were like; what he was thinking about when death began to grip his mind. He loved his country; he lived tortured by its problems."

"From what I know, the problems are sufficiently serious to damage even the strongest hearts," Lester commented.

"Who knows? Perhaps he told fables just to soothe his own heart," suggested Sir Delamare.

"Who knows?" replied Lester.

"Perhaps he believed that only a fable would be capable of rendering Brazil understandable," Juan Sender intervened. "As a Latin American, the universe of fables doesn't frighten me."

"It is a hallucinatory place," Sir Delamare agreed.

"Brazil is hallucinatory," the Chilean said, "but the Brazilians seem not to realize it."

"I'll tell you what is hallucinatory: the heat of this place," Lester said.

Juan Sender ignored the commentary and proceeded, "Brazilians still haven't come to the realization that their country is a part of the family of great nations. We, their neighbors, have known it for centuries, and we're afraid because Brazil is important not only territorially—practically half the continent—but also due to its population density, its cultural unity, its technological know-how, and its economic infrastructure."

"So this country has the capacity to frighten the poor as well as the rich," said Sir Delamare. "For the rich, this place is just a horde of Negroes, stirred up and ready to explode. I couldn't have imagined that the poor also were afraid."

"Perhaps afraid is not exactly the correct word; excuse me for using it," Sender clarified. "This country will never be an empire, at least as we have known empires up to now."

THE END OF THE THIRD WORLD

"How can you be so sure that this won't happen?" Sir Delamare asked with a certain doubt.

"Well, we know," Sender responded enigmatically.

"Perhaps it is some determinism? Or atavism? Could it be something that we Nordics can't feel?" asked Sir Delamare.

"Simply stated, Brazil is Latin," the Chilean explained, "and there will never again be a Latin empire. Napoleon was our last attempt."

"And why is that, pray tell?" Sir Delamare said, provoking him.

"Because this business of empires has become a matter for the barbarians," Sender said with contempt. A bluish color tinted his thin face, his voice rising in an impassioned tone. "We are where we are because for the first time the barbarians, the Saxons, the Visigoths, have become lords of the world. The tragedy began with the destruction of the Invincible Armada."

"We aren't to blame if Philip the Second had a mediocre meteorologist," Lester said, angrily.

Sir Delamare lit another cigarette and made a couple of those hacking coughs, loud and thick, as only a longtime smoker can. Since he smoked about five packs of cigarettes a day, it was thought that his lungs had become solid tar.

"I would like to tell one of old Duarte's fables," Sir Delamare said, after clearing his throat, sending smoke throughout the room. "It's a shame that I won't be able to replicate all of the flavor that Duarte knew how to give his stories. He was a very talented storyteller, aside from knowing quite well how to use that Latin exuberance."

He stopped momentarily to observe Sender, who had curled up in a chair to watch the television that was turned on but with the volume off.

LOST WORLD II

Sir Delamare shrugged his shoulders and began: "Once upon a time, there was an incompetent shepherd who mistreated his sheep. He never worried about the quality of the fields, the poor little sheep were always very thin and dirty, but the shepherd could be found at the end of every month at the paymaster's window to receive his wages. The boy was such a negligent shepherd that even the sheep could detect his incompetence, but they believed that there was nothing that could be done about it. After all, the shepherd had been named to the position without the usual interview process, and rumor had it that he knew someone of influence. The shepherd wasn't exactly a bad character. He was, as a matter of fact, a young man with progressive ideas; he spent a lot of time reading political magazines and didn't miss a single protest march, especially those that were made to impede the dismissal of incompetent and unnecessary bureaucrats in the civil service.

"The sheep managed as best they could, struggling peaceably for their daily grass, leaving the shepherd alone. But there was one thing that the sheep just detested. Once in a while, in order to enhance his own worth and contribution and to justify the fact that his flock was so poorly treated, the shepherd would cry out in desperation, saying that the sheep were being attacked by imperialism. The flock would jump out of its woolly skin with fright, already imagining itself in the belly of the monster, and other shepherds would rush to help the threatened little shepherd. As the majority of the other shepherds used the very same tactic, they all rushed over, pretended to be really worried and prepared to repel the threat. They would run from one side to the other, examining the stony field and the little bit of grass and lamenting the bad luck of the skinny sheep, condemned to live out their lives under such conditions of poverty, all due to the cunning and menace of imperialism.

"But the irritating part for the sheep, aside from the fright, was to have to listen to the shepherd make belligerent and challenging speeches against the monster for weeks afterwards, always boasting about his conscientious attitude, his alert spirit, and his unshakable position in defense of the flock. After one of these supposed attacks, even the grass seemed more bitter and sparse than what it actually was, because the shepherd would keep on talking, and talking, and talking, always describing in the most somber tones the threat of the terrible monster. Their vexation was so great that many times the sheep would pray that the so-called imperialism would appear once and for all and do away with that torture.

"But the shepherd, like so many others, knowing that this was the best way to count on the help of his peers, didn't hesitate to use the same strategy, especially when the sheep appeared ready to demand a better shearing technique or better fields of grass. And of course, the repeated use of alarms could only serve to engender frustration and anger amongst those shepherds who really were competent; so much so that after a time, they began to ignore the calls for help and considered committing their colleague to a military hospital for a foolishness test. It was too bad that the shepherd was out of their reach. You see, he enjoyed good corporate protection.

"One day, nevertheless, everyone heard desperate screams for help. It just happened to be our shepherd shouting for help, but no one moved a muscle. Ah, they thought, he must be meeting with some group of black sheep union members concerning the upcoming shearing; they are always negotiating demands at this time of the year. And they left him to shout in vain.

LOST WORLD II

Some days later, almost by chance, someone discovered that the calls for help had been real. A pack of ferocious imperialist wolves had practically decimated the sheep at a ridiculously low price, paying the shepherd a ludicrous kickback for them, which forced the Ministry of Flocks to institute a Commission of Inquiry to investigate the tragedy. The shepherd's name was brought up in the newspapers and TV broadcasts; he was transferred to another position and eventually forgotten. Of course, nothing came of the inquiry, and everything went back to how it was before.

"Do you know what the moral of the story is?" Sir Delamare asked.

Lester was the only one to show signs of life, moving about in his chair nervously. Jane didn't even appear to have heard the long story, and Sender seemed hypnotized in front of the television.

"Never fail to take advantage of a dangerous situation which you yourself created," Sir Delamare said, pointing his yellow, nicotine-stained fingers at Lester. "You, with your leftist sympathies, ought to know that."

There was a knock at the door. Two discreet, dry knocks, typical of Spender, who didn't trust doorbells. Sender extended his arm, in a mechanical gesture, and opened the door. The smoke, which had become dense in the room, was sucked outside as Spender entered, accompanied by Deputy Rubens. The motion of the two of them produced waves in the atmosphere of bluish nicotine that vanished down the hall.

"Lord Delamare, this is Deputy Rubens." Spender introduced the corpulent figure in the loud checkered sport coat.

"I hope you are comfortable, Your Majesty," the federal deputy said with a bow. His ideas regarding monarchies were derived primarily from the way royalty was portrayed by the samba organizations that performed at Carnival.

"It isn't necessary to address him as 'Your Majesty,' " Spender volunteered.

Rubens was undecided what to do next.

"And how am I to call him? He is a lord, isn't he?"

"He is a knight of the British Empire," Spender explained.

"So he is royalty, isn't he?"

Juan Sender shook his head.

"Your Excellency?"

Sender again shook his head.

"Your Magnificence?"

The Chilean shrugged his shoulders.

"What's going on," Sir Delamare asked, having understood not a single thing because the two of them were speaking some hodgepodge of Portuguese and Spanish.

"He is experiencing a problem of protocol," the Chilean explained.

"Well, hell with it," the deputy growled, grabbing the Chilean by the arm. "Translate to him what I say."

Sender, about the same height as Deputy Rubens but much slimmer, looked at the officer from head to toe and declared indignantly, "You ought to know how to address a lord; after all, you had a monarchy here in Brazil."

The deputy released the Chilean's arm, respectfully but not without a certain rancor.

"My English is very bad," he said.

"And I don't speak Portuguese," the Chilean said harshly.

"What is going on?" Spender asked, concerned.

"He wants me to act as the interpreter," the Chilean said.

"But you are the interpreter," Spender replied.

LOST WORLD II

"Very well!" the federal officer exclaimed, shaking invisible grains of dust from his fabulous jacket. "I'll try to make myself understood as much as possible."

"You're here to tell us that it was murder," Jane blurted out.

Deputy Rubens seemed to shrink in size; he lost his composure, and stared at Jane in frustration.

"Yes, yes, yes! It was murder," he repeated, half out of control.

"And how did it happen?" Sir Delamare asked.

"Sr. Duarte was killed by a poisonous dart."

"Indians!" Spender exclaimed. "But I thought that . . ."

"That they were extinct?" the deputy said sardonically. "But it wasn't done by Indians; you can rest easy. In fact, the dart used to kill the victim belonged to an extinct tribe. An anthropologist from the University of Amazonas recognized the weapon used in the crime. According to him, it is a rare artifact. Only three exist in the world. One in Turin, another in Moscow, and we have already verified by telephone that those darts are there; it was confirmed by the curators.

"And the third dart?" Sir Delamare asked.

"The third one ought to be in London," the deputy said, pulling from his coat pocket a very thick, transparent plastic envelope. In the bag they saw a long, pointed dart, quite fragile and innocent-looking. "It belongs to the Challenger collection."

All eyes turned toward Jane. She got up and, still barefooted, walked up to the deputy.

"I am the owner of the Challenger collection," she said.

The deputy was there, showing the dart, precisely because he knew who she was.

"I believe you owe us some explanations," the federal officer said.

There was almost total agreement amongst those present in the room.

"Come on, she didn't kill Sr. Duarte," Lester protested.

"No one is accusing Miss Challenger," the federal deputy said.

"But this poisonous dart belongs to her," Spender said.

"Do we have a consul here?" Sir Delamare asked.

Spender consulted a small notebook and, a little disappointed, informed Sir Delamare, "There is an honorary consul, an orchid exporter. His name is Varney."

"I am not familiar with all of the Amazonian pieces that I have in the house," Jane said, sure of herself. "There are approximately two thousand ethnographic objects collected by my grandfather and my father. As such, I cannot affirm that this dart is the same one that ought to be in the collection." She picked up the envelope, handed over with a certain reluctance by the deputy, and inspected the dangerous object. "As far as I am concerned, they all look the same. What kind of poison do they inject?"

"Curare," the deputy said.

"You must have other very dangerous things in your house, and you don't even know it," Spender said, worriedly.

Sir Delamare extended his hand, and Jane passed him the envelope. He spent some time looking at the delicate lethal weapon, made by a people who no longer existed.

"Interesting!" he declared. "I've always had a fascination for the ability of these primitive peoples to use poisons. On one occasion, in West Africa, I saw a man die, finished off right in front of our faces. He was one of our bearers; he spoke quite intelligible English and appeared to be in good health. He was dead before he hit the ground. We learned later that he had been poisoned by his lover. The native women feed a type of beetle certain plants and use their feces as poison."

"Oh my God!" Spender exclaimed, as pale as could be.

"You have no idea of what women are capable of doing," Sir Delamare said, gravely. "In India they are every bit as treacherous as in Africa. Once, in Jaipur, I was visiting a local potentate, a minor maharaja, quite strict with his harem. Well, right after supper, I noticed that he was very quiet, reclining on his pillows with his eyes wide open while the women of the harem were sexually assaulting me. I was understandably intrigued with the unexpected promiscuity, and I came to find out much later from the colonel who commanded the local garrison that the women of the harem adored white men, especially Englishmen. In order to get back at his severe vigilance over them, and to satisfy their tormented desires, they didn't hesitate to drug the venerable maharaja.

"With curare," exclaimed the deputy, very surprised by the revelation.

"Not exactly; they used a substance retrieved from the Calabar bean," Sir Delamare stated.

"Thank God we live in England!" sighed Spender.

"Unfortunately Sr. Duarte wasn't simply drugged by lascivious odalisques," Jane said.

"You are quite right," agreed the deputy. "And I don't have much time."

"What is it you want to know?" Jane asked.

"If you know a man named Henry Amazon."

"Henry! But of course; he is my childhood companion," she responded with surprise. "What has happened, Officer?"

"Your childhood companion! Well, we have been informed that he was your butler."

THE END OF THE THIRD WORLD

"Has something happened with Henry?" Lester asked.

"We asked the British authorities to verify if any piece of the Challenger collection was missing. We were informed that, in fact, some pieces had disappeared. And the butler, Henry Amazon, was the principal suspect. The problem is that the suspect has since disappeared. Scotland Yard agreed to give us follow-up information."

"Henry was always rather eccentric," Jane muttered. "But I don't understand why he would have taken only a few pieces of the collection. If it had been up to him, the collection would have been sold or donated to some institute. He detested anything having to do with Indians; he said it was bad luck to keep them around. He didn't even go near the showcases."

"Your companion is in hot water," Sir Delamare stated. "The pieces are missing, he is missing. And he is the butler. Scotland Yard must be jubilant."

"I myself," confessed the deputy, blushing, "was relieved upon hearing that the suspect is the butler."

"That fellow never fooled me," Spender inserted. "He looks like a Malayan. A really sinister type."

"No more sinister than the suit that you're wearing!" Jane attacked Spender, forcing him to retreat.

"What's wrong with my suit?" he asked defensively.

"It is wool, idiot. Wool in the middle of the tropics!" Sir Delamare intervened. "Why didn't you listen to my advice?"

"Sir, Bermuda shorts! I haven't worn short pants since I was thirteen."

"What is this business about a Malayan? Isn't the suspect English?" the deputy asked.

"The guy is . . . he is dark," Spender tried to explain. "I don't know him very well; I only saw him once."

"Formerly the best butlers were from Barbados," Sir Delamare said. "But of course, many don't like the idea of having a Negro prepare their bath. I never had this type of bias. I presently have an Irish housekeeper, very efficient but somewhat talkative. Sometimes I miss my old Swinburne; he was from Uganda. I named him myself in honor of the great poet."

"What happened to him?" Spender asked, ingenuously impressed.

"He died, poor chap," Sir Delamare said pensively. "I always said that to pension a man off was the same as signing his death sentence. He had been with me for more than thirty years, very healthy. Against my will, I gave him his retirement, an excellent nest egg. He returned to Kampala just when President Obote was being deposed, and he disappeared. I contracted a group of mercenaries in order to ransom him, but it was useless. He had already been shot and eaten by members of a rival tribe."

"He was . . . eaten!" Spender exclaimed. "Are you just having fun at my expense?"

"And why would I be? By chance are you insinuating that my butler was unpalatable?"

"Well, sir. I don't know what to say . . ."

"What's more, in some parts of Africa, members of opposing ideological groups quite literally swallow each other up. And it is even more decent, believe me. At least they demonstrate to the people what a tough nut to crack the defeated party was."

Deputy Rubens, bewildered, looked at his watch.

"Well, is the fellow Malayan or not?"

"No, he is not Malayan," Jane said ruefully. "Henry actually is an Indian. An Indian from the Amazon. The last member of his tribe."

The Most Marvelous Things Happened

A silver ray of a bright, full moon found the bed where Jane lay sleeping. The pale light made her skin glimmer as she slept uncovered. Her hair, still damp from the shower, spread out on the pillow like dark and mysterious grass. Her white neck turned to the right, her sleep a gentle sigh, she had finally given in to an overpowering fatigue. On the nightstand near the bed, the light of the moon caught a picture in a silver frame. Softened by the light of the moon, the face registered in that old, yellowed photo took on new depth of expression. Lester knew the face that inspired such illusory trust; it was the face of a kind man, a gentle man, an anachronism, prematurely dead at the age of fifty. Jane's father. From death's distant door, those moonlit eyes seemed to understand everything: Jane's impetuosity, Henry's disappearance, Lester's variance, and even the warm Amazonian night that seemed so endless.

The air conditioner, set to run at the most economic level, allowed the heat to fill the room. Lester sat on the bed, unable to sleep, his mind filled with thoughts of the previous day. He did not wish to be any other place, not even his own apartment, filled with empty pizza containers. That night all he wanted was to watch over Jane as she slept, to hear her breathing, to smell the fragrance of her body, to soak in completely the minutes of a rare opportunity. Jane seldom permitted this to happen; you are like a brother, she always said just to torment him. In the beginning, when he discovered how he felt about her, it hadn't been easy to control himself. She had continued to treat him with a foolish benevolence, a generosity full of complicity that rejected any sentiment other than friendship. As they left adolescence, and she continued to pretend she was oblivious to what he was experiencing, Lester gave up. He didn't want it to become an obsession. They stopped seeing each other for some years, each one following a different path. Lester almost believed he was cured when they began working together in the office of the *New Economist*.

Lester knew what was responsible for the almost immediate animosity that was established between them; with all of the talk that their colleagues on the magazine delighted in engaging in, they became rivals, a rivalry without foundation which at heart neither of them took very seriously. It often revolved around politics, because Lester, throughout the years that he had maintained a distance, traveled his own route, while Jane remained faithful to the position of her family: the virtues of old English liberalism, so dear to the Challengers, that he now found to be backward and full of social prejudice.

The constant skirmishes worked for some time, permitting Lester to keep his pride intact, and Jane her independence, without either of them irrevocably shutting the other out. Sometimes they treated each other as they had years before, although this was a strain for Lester. They met for lunch, attended the theater together, a movie now and then; and he felt he was magnanimous to be able to close his eyes to her political insensitivity, even though he had stopped bringing up political issues in their conversations out of fear of being shut out of her life once and for all. The good humor, the quick smile that Jane occasionally radiated in one or another of those

THE END OF THE THIRD WORLD

dates, almost panicked him, and he would take refuge in provoking her. If she liked a play, he would inevitably argue against it, purposely using the most extreme and pejorative jargon, to which Jane's biting irony could not resist responding.

This tiresome repartee would go on just as long as Jane would tolerate it. Lester only came to realize it now. Perhaps this was the purpose of his presence there in her room. Only then, sitting at her side in that hotel, did he discover that their meeting was something that was impossible to improvise.

In the late afternoon, as soon as the federal deputy had departed, leaving behind a mountain of questions, Jane had excused herself, on the pretext of exhaustion, saying she was retiring to her room. Lester instinctively knew to accompany her, in spite of her objections and insistence that she wanted to be alone to think about what had happened.

"I'll walk you to the door," he had insisted as they left Sir Delamare's suite.

Jane sighed, walking at a normal pace, but she didn't stop when they reached her room; rather, she continued on to the elevator.

"Hey," Lester said, "you've passed—"

Before he could get the sentence out, the elevator arrived and Jane motioned for him to follow her. The elevator door closed, brushing his heels.

"I'm going to look for Pietro," she said.

"But aren't you tired?"

"I am tired of those fools," she replied, searching in her pocket and finding an address book. "His work address should be in here."

They took a taxi, leaving the hotel behind. It was five o'clock; the afternoon was still light, with an intensity that indicated nightfall was a long way off. The taxi

LOST WORLD II

traveled at a high speed along a paved road, passing occasional army barracks, modest residential areas, and thatched huts with fruit for sale. Finally they reached the city limits, and they began to pass run-down dwellings, potholed streets filled with garbage heaps, and open sewers flowing past it all. The houses seemed to be still under construction, but they were by no means new, nor would they ever be; rather they would permanently be in a state of decay and deformity.

"This is it," the taxi driver said, parking the taxi.

A dark building made of glass and steel rose above an aging, formerly art nouveau row of houses; the delicate facades rent impiously by shop doors. Upon alighting from the taxi, they were forced to jump over puddles of fetid mud that dotted the sidewalk.

"If I'm not mistaken," Lester commented, "your grandfather used to say that here in Manaus the sidewalks were made of marble."

Jane shrugged and entered the building. From behind a counter, two young women smiled at them in amazement.

"I'm looking for Sr. Pietra, Jr.," Jane said.

"What is your name?" one of them asked.

"Is he here?" Jane insisted.

"What is your name?"

"It is a personal matter. I need to speak with him."

"One moment please," the girl responded, continuing to smile. She dialed a telephone.

Jane didn't wait.

"Hey, you can't—"

But Jane was already disappearing into one of the elevators, dragging Lester along.

The two women looked at each other, and the one holding the phone dialed another number.

"Security? A woman and man, both foreigners, have

THE END OF THE THIRD WORLD

entered the building. They are in elevator number two, going up."

The elevator stopped on the top floor. When the doors opened, the two exited quickly, almost running. They went down an empty hall and entered a room where a secretary looked at them inquisitively. They were breathing heavily, Lester somewhat more because he was the more sedentary of the two.

"Can I help you?" the secretary asked, rising.

"I want to speak with Pietro; I know he is here."

"I don't believe he can see you; he is in a meeting with suppliers; it could go on indefinitely."

"I don't believe the meeting will last long," she said.

The secretary placed herself in Jane's way; she was ready to prevent whatever the foreigner attempted to do. Her boss's office would not be invaded without some resistance on her part. She was very elegant; as skinny as a mannequin, however, and of small stature. She was nearly in a panic and conscious of her disadvantage in size. All she had was the authority that her position as secretary conferred upon her.

A sigh of relief escaped her lips when she saw four muscular and armed uniformed men enter the room.

Jane and Lester were escorted out of the building with a minimum of force. To Lester's relief, Jane did not try to resist. It would have been a massacre. Night was beginning to fall as the two of them stood on the sidewalk in front of the building.

"Are we going to be stuck here?" Lester protested.

"Let's go sit there," Jane said, pointing to the corner where there was a filthy bar, reminiscent of certain Portuguese taverns, that offered a few tables and chairs.

"Don't tell me we are going to hang around here until this guy comes out!"

"Exactly," Jane said, crossing the street.

"And what do you intend to do when he does come out?"

Jane didn't answer; instead she sat down and motioned to the fat man standing behind the counter.

"Cerveja," she ordered.

The fat man lumbered over to them, bringing the beer. The bar had seen better days. The counter and shelves were made of dark mahogany and marble; the grease and dust didn't hide its elegant art nouveau lines. A metal and glass chandelier with floral motifs hung from the ceiling, darkened and sad, with only one small bulb lit. Those furnishings would bring a lot of money in a London antique shop, but the fat proprietor knew nothing of this.

"The beer is good," Jane commented.

Slowly night approached. Traffic jammed the street, and the drivers honked hysterically. Employees of the Pietro Pietra, Jr., firm were beginning to leave the building, adding to the mass of people who hurriedly walked along the sidewalk or ran between the cars stalled by the jam. Jane and Lester remained alert; at any moment the entrepreneur would show his face. They were watching the building's main door so intently that they didn't notice four people, a woman and three men, approach them.

"Excuse me," one of the men said.

Lester was the first one to notice their presence.

"What is it?" he asked, guardedly.

"We work there," the man said, pointing to the building, speaking fluent English. "We are cleaners; we were working on the top floor and overheard everything. You wanted to talk with Pietra, Jr., didn't you?"

"Are you Miss Challenger, by chance?" the woman asked.

THE END OF THE THIRD WORLD

"Yes I am!" Jane exclaimed, intrigued. "Where did you hear my name?"

"Oh, it isn't important where I heard it." The woman hesitated. "That is to say, I don't want to seem impolite, but the fact is, I need to speak with you."

"You need to speak with me? Why?"

"Tomorrow the trip organized by the federal government begins," one of the men said. "And you are going to participate in the trip, aren't you?"

"That is one of the reasons I am here," Jane responded, even more intrigued. "The CEOs of the major economic conglomerates of the world are going to meet aboard that transatlantic ship to discuss the future of investments in this region."

"We are journalists," Lester clarified. "The meeting is of interest to us."

"We know that," one of the men replied.

"And we don't want you and your friend to embark on the ship," the woman said in a soft, respectful tone.

"You don't want us to? Why is that?" Jane said, astounded.

"Things are going to happen," one of the men said. "We can't tell you much. We are here only because a friend of yours, Miss Challenger, has asked us to come."

"A friend? What friend?" Jane's face was serious and doubtful.

"We can't reveal his name," the woman said earnestly.

"He is like your brother," one of the men added.

"And this trip can become dangerous, very dangerous," another reiterated.

"The name of this friend is Henry, isn't it?" Jane said, excitedly. "The rascal is behind this, and he doesn't want to show his face."

"Perhaps," the woman said.

LOST WORLD II

"Why don't you see for yourselves?" one of the men said.

"Just come with us," said another.

"It is far, but we would be happy to take you," the woman said.

"You know why we are sitting here waiting?" Jane asked.

"You want to get even with Pietra, Jr.," the woman said. "Your friend has told us. But it isn't the first time he does this; he is a very bad man."

"If we were to go with you, Pietra, Jr., will get away," Jane argued.

"Don't worry about that," one of the two men assured her. "You won't lose him by waiting a bit longer. Do you know his chauffeur? He is one of us."

"He's one of you?" Lester asked. "Who are you?"

"We are Indians," the woman said.

"Where did you learn English?" Jane asked.

"In the mission," one of the men clarified. "My sister and I studied in the New Tribes Mission school. They studied at the Worldwide Evangelization Crusade."

Jane and Lester were silent, indecisive and tense. They began to scrutinize the group more closely. They were definitely Indians. The men were dressed modestly, but they seemed well nourished; they had good physical conformation and were around thirty years old. Like the men, the woman had brown skin, slanted eyes, and straight black hair, but her facial features were fine and harmonious. Candor and calmness radiated from them.

"Where do you want to take us?" Jane asked.

"There is a discotheque where we get together," one of the two men said.

"It's located in the Compensa neighborhood right now," said the other man.

THE END OF THE THIRD WORLD

"We never stay in one neighborhood for long," the woman explained.

"We are nomads; we aren't able to stay in any one place for long," said the other man.

They left the bar and boarded a bus crammed with people. The two Brits grabbed on to a metal bar that ran the length of the bus as a precaution against the erratic speed and abrupt stops that the driver inflicted upon the rattling bus. The other passengers traveled virtually holding on to each other, chatting happily. It seemed they traveled together like this daily; they would greet the arrival of new riders at each stop and noisily take leave of those lucky ones who got off first. It occurred to Jane that the mass of people, most of whom bore predominantly indigenous features, gave off no more than a neutral body odor; this was surprising considering the long trip on such inadequate public conveyance and the full day's work they had put in. The only smell was that of diesel exhaust.

The woman, who kept close to Jane, smiled sweetly and apologized with her eyes for the inconvenience of the trip. Lester, grabbing firmly to the bar, leaned down to try and make out the road as the bus rambled on. But it was useless; aside from not knowing the city, the crush of people, with their black hair and smiling faces, created a barrier.

After what seemed like an eternity, the bus stopped. Everyone got off, talking all the while, and dispersed in what seemed to be a plaza surrounded by wooden houses; the asphalt was broken by puddles of reddish mud and long, thin tufts of grass.

They left behind them the open plaza area and walked along a labyrinth of wooden and straw houses raised on piles. The full moon, hanging on the horizon, gave little light. The group of Indians made their way with the ease of one who has traveled the road many times, but they stayed close to the Brits, sometimes helping and leading them over the narrow, single-plank bridges that extended across water-soaked lots. The sounds of crickets and frogs and a sulfurous smell emanating from the mud seemed perfectly natural for such a swampy terrain. From the dimly lit dwellings high on their piles came the omnipresent noise of television broadcasts.

"There it is," the woman said.

They were at the bottom of a hill; on the top, at the end of a path opened through low undergrowth, there was a large tin building on piles. The building and its circular veranda stood out in the dim moonlight.

"Today it's not open," one of the men pointed out.

As they were led up the wooden ladder, Jane and Lester noticed the sign that was over the main entrance. The word "Savages" was written in crudely formed letters against a blue background and across the body of a naked Indian woman whom the ingenuous painter must have imagined to be exuberant and erotic.

"Where is Henry?" Jane asked. "Wasn't it here that we were to meet him?"

"He'll be here soon," the woman said, opening a plank in the door through which they all passed.

Someone lit a lamp, and the two Brits were astounded at the dimensions of the room. The entire building, excluding the veranda, was one big, long hall decorated with rows and rows of colorful paper flags and a battery of spotlights. At the end, a stage was set with the musical instruments and the control panels for the lights and sound. The equipment was all very sophisticated, the best to be found anywhere in the world.

They sat down around a circular table, and glasses and bottles of beer were brought to them right away.

"We have several houses like this," one of the men

THE END OF THE THIRD WORLD

explained. "Nearly every city in Amazonas has a similar discotheque, frequented by Indians like us. We all like to dance, and the young people eventually show up."

"In the beginning it was just a place to dance, to let off steam, to forget. Later we realized that it was the only place where our kind could relax and have a good time."

"It is very difficult to be an Indian here."

Jane and Lester listened in silence, almost intimidated, as if they were sticking their noses in something that was none of their business.

"When we go to look for a job," one of them explained, "we try to hide that we're Indian. Because if they find out, they hire anyone else instead."

"That's why we say we're Peruvian or Colombian. We can't lie and say we're Brazilian, because we speak Portuguese with an accent."

"When we go somewhere frequented by Brazilians, they do everything they can to pick a fight with us."

"A lot of Brazilians don't like Indians here because they've all heard bad stories about us. Things that they heard when they were children, or things that happened to someone they know, or to a family member, incidents that happened before they ever moved to Manaus."

"Can we tape what you are saying?" Lester asked, pulling a small tape recorder out of his pocket.

"You can tape whatever you like," someone said.

"Are you all from the same tribe?" Jane asked.

"Not exactly," the woman answered. "Perhaps you could say we are from the largest tribe that exists around here, the tribe of those who no longer have any tribe left."

"But we have come from many different places."

"But why? Did you have problems where you were?" Jane asked.

"For all kinds of reasons. Some of us had land problems, squatters moving in, prospectors. Others needed food, or they were sick and wanted to get help from the Brazilians. Even some who wanted to know more about the world, to know other places."

"Marta, for example," one of the men said, pointing to the woman, "is Tukano. She was born in Pari Cachoeira, quite a ways up the Negro River, in the northwestern corner, almost on the Colombian border. I am from the Solimões River; I am Tikuna. And the other two, one is Parakanã, from southern Pará; and the other is Mawé from the lower Amazon. As you can see, we are almost a confederation."

"My tribe was finished off," the Parakanã said. "I don't have anyone left. Our lands are under the Tucuruí Reservoir."

"When he arrived here," the Tikuna explained, being the most articulate of the men, "he could hardly talk. Marta found him in the street, drunk, tubercular."

"I didn't have anything left to say," the Parakanã said. "It all happened so fast. When I think about it, it seems impossible. Our village had little contact with Brazilians, until some people from the National Indian Foundation showed up around 1972. They said that our land was going to be flooded, and that the river was going to rise and swallow up everything. Six months later, half of our people were dead. Pneumonia, fever, tuberculosis. They were dying like poisoned fish. And the men had taken a liking to our women; they took the youngest off to their camps. There was one who liked young boys, and he would spend the night with them. After that, the young girls and boys starting getting sick; it was gonorrhea. One of the girls was pregnant, but the baby was born deformed and blind, and we had to do away with it. One day an airplane landed and they put all of us in it; there wasn't a single old person remaining alive. I found

THE END OF THE THIRD WORLD

out later that they had transported us to the Xingu. I was very sick with tuberculosis, and they put me in the hospital in Belém. When I was better, I fled the hospital and went to work on a boat that was coming up the river to Manaus. I got sick again. I thought I was a goner, but then Marta found me."

"Are you working now?" Lester asked.

"I take care of the sound equipment here," he explained timidly.

"He is an excellent electronics technician. He can fix any kind of equipment," Marta said, showing the pride she felt for her friend.

"Do you know what he does?" the Tikuna said, pointing to the Mawé. "He is an airplane mechanic, trained by Air France to work on jets."

The Mawé lowered his eyes and shook his head.

"It's true; he lived in Paris for two years," the Tikuna went on, "but now he's unemployed."

"There aren't many jobs for jet mechanics here in Manaus," the Mawé said. "I worked up until last year for Varig."

"But he was unjustly let go," the Tikuna said. "They discovered a package on a plane that arrived from Miami. It was contraband, electronic components. They couldn't find who was responsible for it. He had the bad luck of having been working that day in the terminal. He was brought before an inquiry; it was obvious that he was innocent, but then they found out he was an Indian."

"That's all in the past. It does no good to brood about it," the jet mechanic protested.

"All right," the Tikuna gave in. "He doesn't like to talk about it."

"And you, Marta," Jane asked, "how did you come here?"

"The nuns sold me to an aviator in the Brazilian air force."

"What?"

"They do it all the time. Many people want young girls for domestic work. The nuns think that this is a way for us to become civilized more quickly. I was thirteen years old and very foolish; I was sent to work in the pilot's house in Brasília. Some girls were luckier, but I got a violent boss. When he was off duty, he would go around hitting everyone, his wife, his children, his mother-in-law, his dog. I caught it once in a while. I wasn't allowed out of the house. I spent three years shut up in that house; I couldn't even look out the window.

"One night he started getting really mean, and his wife locked herself and the kids in one of the bedrooms. I was in the kitchen, and I heard him yelling, banging on the door. Before I knew it, he was on top of me, grabbing at me. I thought that it was going to go beyond a few cuffs. I reached for the teapot and threw hot water on him. Thank God only a few drops hit him, but he backed off, shocked, and I managed to escape out the door. I made it to the street with only the clothes on my back. I walked and walked; I spent the night walking. All I wanted was to go home, back to Pari Cachoeira. The next night the police picked me up, and I wound up at the National Indian Foundation office. I was promised that I'd be sent home, but the nuns were furious. They called me a delinquent for having thrown hot water on my benefactor. The Foundation brought me to Manaus and let me go."

"Marta worked in a factory," the Tikuna said. "She was the one who had the idea of transforming the discotheques into meeting places."

"It wasn't exactly like that," she protested. "Everyone was getting together in the discotheque. I only organized them a little bit."

THE END OF THE THIRD WORLD

"What kind of things do you do here?" Lester wanted to know.

"The Brazilians think that we are imbeciles; they believe that Indians have some kind of mental deficiency." Marta said. "We simply do what is necessary to prove them right."

"We want them to think we are retarded."

"What do you mean?" Jane asked.

"Well, they like our manual dexterity. We are unsurpassable in the assembly of solid-state electronic components. The factories here love to give us work. We organize a group of workers, get them all employed in some factory, and after a while, we all walk out. They only find out that we're gone when they see the empty assembly line. It is worse than just a strike because they are forced to close down for some days until they are able to fill the jobs again."

"We heard that Banzai Electronics has on file more than two thousand abandoned work cards," the Mawé said proudly.

"Two executives who worked as personnel directors, a Dutchman and a Swiss, committed suicide after the third walkout," the Parakanã informed them with a touch of vengeance in his voice.

"That is only a part of our many activities," Marta said.

Lester picked up the tape recorder to see if it was recording. He didn't want to lose anything in that revealing conversation. He glanced at Jane; she was pensive, mulling over some thought. He was hoping that she didn't do anything to upset them, to give them any reason to become angry.

"You aren't, by any chance, the Jihad Jívaros?" Jane asked abruptly.

Lester was taken by surprise and dropped the tape

recorder. The noise of the recorder hitting the floor was covered by the sound of laughter coming from Marta and her friends.

"Why are you laughing?" Jane asked, offended.

Marta and the men immediately stopped laughing.

"I am sorry," she said, regretting their reaction.

"Did I say something wrong?" Jane asked again.

"No, you didn't say anything wrong," Marta responded seriously, "but we are not members of the Jihad Jívaros."

"However, there are two or three Jívaros who frequent the discotheque," the Tikuna added.

"The Jihad Jívaros is a Brazilian movement, not an Indian movement," the Parakanã explained.

"And don't forget that we Indians are mental deficients," Marta reminded them. "Our movement doesn't even have a name. It really isn't a movement."

"What were you doing in Pietra, Jr.'s, company?" Jane asked distrustfully.

"We already told you. We do the cleaning."

"Only that?"

The four of them looked at one another and almost broke into laughter again, but they controlled themselves.

"Well," Marta said, "we are giving a hand with the computers."

"We are giving its components a good cleaning with Brillo pads," Tikuna revealed.

"Sometimes we pour sodium bicarbonate on the solid-state components," the Mawé confessed.

"The other day, we left a virus in a disk that finished off all of the files of his second set of books," the Parakanã said.

"When they tried to pull up the file, all that appeared

THE END OF THE THIRD WORLD

was the figure of an Indian," Marta said, holding back a giggle.

Jane got up, stretched, and checked her watch. It was almost nine o'clock. "All right. You must be Henry's friends," Jane said. And turning around to look at the back of the room, she raised her voice. "All that is lacking here is the triumphal entrance. Okay, Henry, you can come in; I know that you are here."

A window opened and the moonlight drew a luminous square on the floor. A bulky figure, known to them all, leaned in through the windowsill.

Jane ran up to him and threw her arms around his neck.

"Are you crazy?" she said to him. "What in the hell are you doing? Why did you take the dart?"

Henry hugged her back. She was his sister, the Challenger girl, and he didn't want any danger to come to her. But the hug was quick, and they pulled apart.

"What is going on here, Henry? Why all of this nonsense?" Jane said, assuming an imperial tone.

With a catlike movement, Henry jumped through the window into the room. He was dressed modestly, like the other Indians, which was unusual for him. Normally vain about his appearance, Henry would spend nearly all of his salary on expensive clothing, especially Italian articles, fine leather shoes, sophisticated watches. Jane often became irritated with his excessive interest in these things. And for that reason, what he was wearing—an ordinary, faded blue shirt, frayed at the collar and out of style, polyester, permanent-press pants—intrigued Jane as much as the fact that he was there, amongst the Indians.

"They need me," Henry said.

"They? But you never had anything to do with them before!" Jane exclaimed.

"Well, actually, I need them," Henry responded.

Jane stepped back a few steps and observed Henry. She could hardly recognize her childhood companion in that gruff, well-nourished, and reserved figure. She looked to Lester for help, but he seemed distant, a taciturn, pathetic, and fragile figure, intently checking the tape recorder for any damage. He seemed as overwhelmed by the silence as she was.

"Listen, Jane," Henry said, "perhaps you don't understand. It is even difficult for me."

"What is going to happen tomorrow morning?" Jane asked.

"The Jihad Jívaros are going to take over the ship," he responded.

"How did you find that out?"

"They contacted the group here at the discotheque to see if the Indians wanted to join them, and of course, they refused. These aren't the tactics used by the group. The Jihad Jívaros have only a few members, but we know that they won't give up. Tomorrow they will board the *Leviathan*."

"What do they intend to do?" Jane asked.

"What do you think?" Henry retorted, indifferently.

"They are going to assume the command of the transatlantic ship," Marta intervened. "They will ask for something that we know is impossible, something that we really don't want."

The Tikuna got up; he seemed angry.

"They will threaten to blow up the ship if all the whites in Amazonia don't withdraw within a certain period of time."

"And since they are also whites," Henry explained, "they will also withdraw, presumably to an Islamic country."

"I think that they sought us out because they think

THE END OF THE THIRD WORLD

that we would be happy with the idea of Amazonia being completely for the Indians, like in the past," Marta explained.

"But we don't want that," the Tikuna said.

"We don't know how to make anything, not even a matchstick," the Mawé said, somewhat disconsolate. "We would have to go back to making fire by friction. Have you ever tried to make a bonfire by rubbing a stick against dry moss?"

"What is it you want then?" Jane asked, irritated.

"Almost nothing," Marta responded.

"We want to enjoy ourselves a little," the Parakanã said.

Lester, who until then had been half-dumb, woke up.

"I can't believe what I am hearing," he said. "If you don't agree with the plans of that organization, you ought to discuss it with them, offer alternatives, find political solutions. You can't just cross your arms and do nothing."

"What can we do?" Marta asked.

"Well, something," Lester insisted. "You could even prevent them from committing this insanity. The repercussions will be terrible."

"The only thing that we can do is ask you not to embark," Henry said.

"You can't ask that of us," Jane said, resolutely. "It's out of the question, idiotic."

"We are idiots," the Tikuna said, without a trace of irony.

"Unless, of course, you intend on stopping us by force," Lester said as a test, watching for some reaction.

They began to laugh, which made Jane furious.

"You must be idiots, without a doubt," she shouted. "Whatever has happened to you, it left you with a screw loose. Or who knows, it could be a genetic defect. Henry, you had to know that we would not stand for such a thing. We would not simply keep quiet about it; we would have to do something. Well, I want you to know, Mr. Henry Amazon, that we are going to be on board the *Leviathan*, regardless of how many primitive Indians you send to plead with us."

"We know that," Henry retorted, ceasing his laughter.

"We asked you because we thought we should," Marta said.

"And what's more," Jane went on, still angry, "we will inform the authorities. Those Jihad Jívaros will be hunted down like mad dogs."

"Well, I don't know about that," countered Lester, for whom the idea of bringing in the police was repulsive.

"What do you mean, you don't know?" Jane insisted.

"We can wait and see what happens," he said, without much conviction. "The ship is probably well protected. With so many of the Fortune Five Hundred aboard, it will be a veritable floating fortress."

"Then stay out of this," Jane exploded at him. "I am not going to allow a bunch of louts to make fish food out of me."

Jane grabbed her purse and started out the door. Henry made a move toward her, but desisted; he knew she would listen to no one.

"Are you staying, Lester?" she asked, the sharpness of her voice making it clear her intention was to take him with her.

Lester nodded to Henry and his companions, harboring an unjustified feeling of guilt. He would have liked to stay a bit longer, learn more about those people, to solve the mystery, if there really was a mystery. But Jane was calling him, and he couldn't do anything about it, which

THE END OF THE THIRD WORLD

only increased his feeling of guilt, and a sensation that he was overlooking something.

"Jane, wait a second!" he said, turning to Henry and asking, "Why was Duarte killed?"

"It is a long story," Henry said.

"Which I don't intend on hearing," Jane shouted, going down the steps.

Leaving the discotheque behind in the dark, they were soon lost in the maze of alleys, wandering through puddles of mud, and jumping at each furtive creature scurrying through the darkness. Two hours later they managed to reach the hotel, thanks to a night-owl taxi driver who also found himself lost in the neighborhood.

"I want you to stay here with me tonight," Jane said at the door to her room.

Without saying a word, Lester accepted the invitation. The mystery thickened for him, but the guilt was gone; it had been completely defeated, obliterated, and extinct in the instant that she invited him to stay.

The two of them were in a hurry; they knew that touching each other, they would discover just how much they had become strangers. Jane admired his discreet musculature, the gentle movement of his hands, the nearly invisible hairs of his firm thighs. Lester, meanwhile, seemed blind; he probed all of the curves and hollows of her body, a Braille reading of the feminine softness, as if he wanted to verify that what he had imagined for so long really existed. In the moon's pale light, an intense heat overwhelmed their bodies, growing stronger with each caress.

A Sometime Hero

Pietro Pietra, Jr., didn't even find out about the fracas between the Englishwoman and the security guards at his office door. Since everything had been taken care of without any major complications, the secretary had decided to leave well enough alone and not tell her boss. After all, this type of disturbance was common. Pietra, Jr., was becoming famous; the *Manchete* magazine had published a long story on him, with color pictures of her boss doing a variety of things: showing his purebred horse stable, relaxing on his luxury yacht in the company of several young women, losing a fortune at a Las Vegas roulette wheel, and stretched out on a white hammock on the veranda of his ten-room mansion. She had no way of knowing that the story had been paid for by Pietra himself, but if she had, she would have forgiven him.

But lately she was having to send away reporters from all kinds of magazines and newspapers, deal with politicians who called simulating an intimacy with her boss that they didn't enjoy, and the saddest of all, handle those people who had no pride and only wanted to pick up the crumbs that he dropped. But she was there to protect him, to keep these rumormongers away, those people who only wanted to publish horrible things about him. Pietra, Jr., lived alone, but his secretary harbored no illusions. She knew her place; she felt good enough just being able to consider herself his guardian angel. The man had a very explosive temperament; his employees

THE END OF THE THIRD WORLD

tiptoed around, and she had witnessed many good and powerful people get a dressing down from him. With her, however, he was different. That is why she would do anything so as not to anger him.

Sometime in the middle of the afternoon, Pietra, Jr., left the office. He said he wouldn't return until the following day. He was depressed, he confessed, over the death of his old partner; he had dark circles under his eyes and he seemed quite dejected as he moved toward the private elevator.

The secretary was full of pity.

However, Pietra, Jr., was not depressed. Actually, he was jubilant. He simply didn't want anyone to know. Duarte's demise came at the right moment. His enemies would disperse; some, he thought, would try to gang up against him. But the few stocks his rival owned before his death were now in his heir's hands, and he could easily be controlled. Pietra, Jr.'s, rise to the top of the company had not been at all peaceful. But by the time old man Duarte had recognized what was happening, it was already too late to effectively oust him. Nevertheless, Duarte had made an attempt by bringing together the most trusted board members and the older employees. In order to show his power, Duarte had refused to hand over the president's office, and he tried to have a general audit done. The struggle didn't last but two months; the stockholders didn't authorize an investigation, and the government agencies involved remained neutral in the dispute. Of course, Pietra, Jr., realized that Duarte would never be able to accept his defeat, and only the most drastic arguments prevented further confrontation.

Pietra, Jr., sent his chauffeur away and got behind the wheel of the Mercedes himself. He drove home, but it really wasn't to his own house that he wanted to go. As he walked in the house, the telephone was ringing.

LOST WORLD II

He hesitated answering; he had hoped to spend the rest of the day free, without any problems to deal with or decisions to make. But the telephone continued ringing; it would stop and begin again. He picked it up in a fit of anger and went to the door to throw it outside. He stopped at the last moment, remembering that he had paid three hundred dollars for that telephone. Three hundred dollars handed over in a New York department store still meant something to him.

He answered and heard a feminine voice. At first he didn't recognize the sweet voice that came through the receiver. She was inviting him to come for ice cream, right then, at that instant. The mention of ice cream brought to his mind the face that went with the voice. It was one of two twins that he had met downtown one afternoon while eating ice cream in the street. They had been delightful, even insisting on paying for his ice cream. Two charming and discreet young women, with brown skin and slanted eyes.

He gave them his card, and they didn't change their demeanor at all when they found out who he was. But he hadn't seen them again. He thought they must have come from somewhere else, from one of the cities farther up the river, perhaps members of one of those well-to-do families that cling to the rural life.

He made a mental note of the address she gave him. It wasn't too far away, a place in the outskirts of the city. If the traffic wasn't too bad, he would be there in less than an hour. The afternoon sun gleamed on the tin roofs, the heat evaporated into humidity, and the pavement out ahead of him looked as if it might be cut off at any moment by a wavy, transparent barrier, a barrier that seemed to move away into the distance.

The address surprised him, and he immediately recognized the place. Whenever he passed by there, he noticed

THE END OF THE THIRD WORLD

the huge wall with barbed wire strung along the top, the strict security, and the elegant wooden plaque which read PONTIAC PLACE. He had looked into the property, trying to find out who owned it, but he hadn't been able to come up with anything. It was all very vague; no one could be found who had ever been on the property or even knew exactly to whom it belonged. That was why he felt so excited as he pulled up and stopped at the gate; he was finally going to be able to satisfy an old curiosity.

Yet he was also uneasy. A sullen-looking guard stepped out of the gatehouse and swaggered toward him over the gravel driveway; he leaned down to the level of the car window. He wasn't armed; all he carried was a clipboard. He heard the name, and after consulting the papers clipped to the board, returned to the gatehouse and operated some device that opened the gate. The wheels of the car bumped along over the stones on the driveway. He looked at the myrtle trees that lined the path, thinking how pleasant they were with their straight trunks, dark green leaves, and graceful, abundant crown. The lane curved right, and finally he saw the house. He wasn't disappointed, but he couldn't exactly say that he liked that type of architecture of varnished wood, tile roof, and glass that were said to be so suitable for the region. But everything there was well tended; the lawn grew luxuriant and the house shone as if the last coat of varnish had been applied minutes before he arrived.

Two servants dressed in white appeared. One of them took his keys and drove the car to a garage, and the other led him inside. As much as he tried not to be, he was intimidated. It was always thus. Every time he was in a luxurious place, he would remember his days as a salesman of contraband cameras. The servant showed him to some wicker chairs around a table, and retired. But

LOST WORLD II

Pietra, Jr., didn't feel like sitting; he remained standing, scrutinizing all of the details of the large living room, calculating the value of each piece. Knowing that he could afford to have all of those things brought him a sense of security.

"I'm so glad you came," he heard one of the twins say.

He hadn't seen them enter the room; they appeared so quietly behind him that they seemed to have simply materialized.

"You certainly have some treasure here," he said frankly, without hiding his admiration. Before they entered, he had been trying to decide on the value of a magnificent urn from the island of Marajo; it stood more than fifty inches tall.

"They are family heirlooms," one of them said.

It must be a family that loved pre-Columbian art, he thought. The room's contents were comparable to any ethnographic museum collection in the world. Just at a glance, one would make an appraisal of a couple million dollars. Any university in the United States or Europe would pay that without batting an eye.

"My name is Iaci." The one in faded jeans and a green T-shirt introduced herself.

"I am Ceuci," said the other twin, who was dressed in a man's shirt a couple of sizes too large.

"You already know me," he said.

"Pietro Pietra, Jr." they said, almost humming.

The two of them laughed mischievously, but Pietra, Jr., didn't find it funny. Hearing his name hummed like that seemed sinister to him.

"You are very famous," Iaci said.

"You're in the paper all the time," Ceuci said.

"So you are interested in these things," he retorted. "I thought you didn't pay any attention to them."

THE END OF THE THIRD WORLD

"But we do pay attention," Iaci explained. "We know they are important."

"We follow everything that comes out about you."

"Even before we met you."

"Before you met me?"

"Right, isn't it curious?" Ceuci said. "We knew that one day you would come here."

A shiver ran through his body, but he couldn't explain where the sensation came from. Apparently everything was normal: The sun was disappearing behind the trees, the crickets were singing outside, the house was tranquil, and the girls were attractive and educated. Even so, he felt uneasy, his senses on edge. He tried to find the source of his discomfort. He had accepted the invitation imagining that it didn't exactly have that much to do with ice cream, but now he wasn't so sure anymore.

"Do you live here?" he asked.

"It is one of our houses," Iaci responded.

"We spend some time here," Ceuci said.

"But you are from Manaus?" he went on.

"We are Amazonians, but not from Manaus," Ceuci said.

"We were born in Nhamundá. Are you familiar with it?" Iaci asked.

"Nhamundá? It is in the lower Amazon, isn't it?" Pietra, Jr., thought for a moment; the place was special for some reason that he couldn't remember. "Unfortunately I still don't know the lower Amazon much. I've only been in Parintins."

"Don't worry," Ceuci said, "we never find anyone who really knows the lower Amazon region."

"Nor the Solimões region," Iaci said.

"Or even the Negro River," Ceuci added.

"People don't live long enough to know anything well," Iaci said.

LOST WORLD II

"I'd say you two have traveled a lot," Pietra, Jr., said.

"Not so much," Iaci explained.

"Just from one home to another," her sister added.

"At the appropriate time," Iaci said.

"And we can't say we are well acquainted with the places where we live."

"Things change."

"When we become familiar with one place, the other has changed."

"And we are always beginning over."

A wave of uneasiness passed over Pietra, Jr. Perhaps it was the way the girls spoke, their two voices identical in timbre, the intonation lazy, but at the same time incisive, pronounced with an almost artificial perfection. In addition, the physical resemblance and the predictability of their gestures, since one nearly repeated what the other was doing, defied reason. To look at them was like suffering from double vision.

"Your lives must not be too hectic," he said.

"It is very hectic," Iaci said.

"We have learned how to avoid boredom," the other said.

"We are not afraid of solitude," Iaci explained.

"How could you be? Eating ice cream," he teased them.

"We like ice cream," Ceuci responded.

"It is a great invention. Don't you think so?" Iaci said. "A machine that makes different flavors of snow."

"Very appropriate for our climate."

"The ancient ones didn't believe in it."

The twins' composure was beginning to get on his nerves.

"I can't stay long," Pietra, Jr., said.

"Are we boring you?" Iaci asked.

"It's not that." He tried to be affable. "Today was a

very difficult day for me, a lot of problems. I feel tired; a few hours of sleep is what I need. In fact, I was arriving home when you called me."

"I'm so sorry," Iaci said, tilting her head to one side.

Pietra, Jr., noticed that Ceuci tilted her head as well; like her sister, she showed an expression that he interpreted as pity.

"We could make a date for another day," Ceuci said. "We didn't know that it had been such a difficult day for you."

"You should have told us," Iaci said.

"It's my fault," Pietra, Jr., admitted. "I wanted to see you again, and when I discovered that you lived here, I was even more eager. This property has always attracted my attention."

"And what do you think?" Ceuci asked. "Do you like our house?"

"It is magnificent, and I had not expected to find the treasures that you keep in this room. It's a shame that my knowledge of pre-Columbian art isn't the best. And to think that my grandfather used to deal in this stuff. Isn't it an incredible coincidence? When I was a child, I used to visit my grandfather in Sao Paulo; he lived in a big house in Higienópolis, surrounded by the latest pieces of his collection. Poor man, he preferred to live in misery rather than sell a single piece of the marvels that he owned. When he wasn't near, I would look at his collection, and I couldn't understand why he was so attached to those pots. Nor could I believe that they were worth anything. As far as I was concerned, Grandpa was lying. I thought it was his way of deceiving me, and of deceiving my father with false hopes."

"Did your grandfather own a muiraquitã like this?" Ceuci asked, showing him a jade pendant, an almost transparent, green-colored stone shaped like a pair of copulating toads, which hung from her neck on a gold chain.

Pietra, Jr., shivered. He was almost sure that he knew that stone, or something closely resembling it. The polished surface gave off small, greenish refractions, and the toads seemed to pulsate, exuding some kind of corporal fluidity. At the same time, it was a finely cut stone, carved by most skilled hands, utilizing a technique that has been lost forever. His grandfather had claimed that all these jade amulets from the lower Amazon were powerful amulets.

"This muiraquitã is exquisite!" he exclaimed.

"It is one of a kind," Ceuci said.

"The only one? Are you sure?" he asked.

"Absolutely; there is only one muiraquitã like this on the face of the earth."

"How did you come by it?" he queried.

"It has been in the family," she responded. "My mother gave it to me."

"Are you sure?" he insisted.

"Of course. I was given it when I had my first menstruation. Why do you ask?"

"Because my grandfather had one exactly like it," he said tensely. "We never found it. My grandfather had an unusual death; he was found with his head in a pot of beans. He used to insist on doing his own cooking, and he must have suffered a heart attack."

"I'm so sorry," Ceuci said, exchanging glances with her sister.

"By the time my father arrived at his big old house, the Indian artifacts had all disappeared. They took everything, including the muiraquitã that he kept in a safe. The police never turned up a suspect, and my father finally lost interest."

"If you say that it was the same as this one," Ceuci

THE END OF THE THIRD WORLD

said, caressing the muiraquitã that hung on her white shirt, "then this is the muiraquitã that your grandfather had."

"Because there is only one of these," Iaci intervened.

They stared at Pietra, Jr., with those almond-shaped eyes. The living room was growing dim in the penumbra of night, but their eyes seemed to radiate light of their own. There is something going on here, he thought. The sensation that something was spying on him was real. It wasn't exactly in the room or even outside; it came from inside the two girls. Their small pupils seemed to harbor the presence of another entity; something that was neither civilized nor refined, rather that was ferocious and implacable.

"Why don't you take a look at the pieces one more time?" Iaci suggested.

"It is dark," he replied.

"Come on, you can see them," Ceuci urged.

Carefully he looked around the dark room. To his astonishment, the pieces stood out clearly in the dimness. But he didn't recall much; he had always thought pre-Columbian art was much the same.

"Do you see those two ceramic vessels?" Iaci pointed out. "They are samples of Tapajo art. Don't you recognize them?"

"No, I don't recall," he stammered.

"A man's memory is only as long as his dick," Ceuci said.

Her sister began to laugh and pointed to a series of paddles hanging on the wall.

"Do you recognize those Porantins oars?"

"I don't know; how can I recognize them?" he rejoined.

"A man forgets as quickly as he ejaculates," Iaci said.

"What in the hell do you want from me?" he shouted, closing his fists.

LOST WORLD II

"Your grandfather robbed us. And now you are robbing us," Ceuci said.

"I am robbing you?" he said with a guffaw. "I hate this Indian junk, if that's what you mean."

"We already know that," Iaci retorted.

"What did I steal from you? What?" he demanded. "I don't even know who you are."

"I am Iaci."

"And I'm Ceuci."

"Well, go to hell," he yelled, making a move to leave. "I don't have time for idle chatter."

"Who was behind those prospectors who landed in the Surumu Mountains?" Iaci asked her sister.

"Yeah, who could it have been?" Ceuci said.

"He must be filthy rich in order to have chartered five planes and sent more than a hundred men there."

"I don't know what you're talking about," Pietra, Jr., snarled.

"He doesn't know what we're talking about," Ceuci said.

"Could you be one of those men whose dick is so short that he suffers from amnesia?" Iaci said, taunting him.

"Watch out or he'll have a premature ejaculation, and he'll forget before he remembers," the other sister said.

Pietra, Jr., had never felt so offended, but he hesitated. He didn't know if he should leave or teach the two upstarts a lesson.

"Are you afraid?" Iaci hissed at him, pulling off her T-shirt in an insolent gesture and flinging it at him.

"Me, afraid? Look here . . ." Pietra, Jr., said, nearly stumbling as he tried to grab the T-shirt and almost lost it.

Iaci smiled, a halo of white teeth taunting him. She approached slowly, arrogantly, facing him down.

THE END OF THE THIRD WORLD

"It won't hurt at all," Ceuci said.

Pietra, Jr., was a large, corpulent man. His body projected itself like a giant across their fragile figures, but somehow they were the ones who dominated the situation.

"What are you waiting for?" Iaci dared.

Nothing, he thought, I am not waiting for a thing, and he trembled. He felt every fiber of his body shake uncontrollably, overtaken by the most primitive form of panic. He tried to control his fear, but it was useless because there was no apparent reason to be afraid. They kept their distance, they weren't armed, and not by a long shot did they appear dangerous. Nevertheless, fear overcame him; and it grew as Ceuci pulled off her loose shirt and then the rest of her clothes, and her sister followed suit, until the full moon, rising over the crown of the myrtle trees, illuminated the nakedness of their brown bodies.

"I am tired," he murmured.

"What is wrong with you?" Iaci said.

"I am tired, I just said it. Don't you understand?"

"I am tired," Ceuci repeated in a perfect imitation of his voice.

"Who are you?" Pietra, Jr., asked, stalling.

"What does it matter?" Iaci said.

"We know who we are," Ceuci said.

"We know who you are," Iaci said.

The two of them approached him. It appeared they didn't move, but they drew closer and closer.

"Do you know, Iaci, when I close my eyes, I can't remember his face."

The other one closed her eyes.

"You're right. With my eyes closed, I can't see him either," Iaci said.

They were very close to Pietra, Jr., almost touching

him, and they kept their eyes closed. It was distressing, and Pietra, Jr., only thought of fleeing, escaping through the door. But he was afraid of losing his equilibrium because he was overcome by fear.

"He is not at all what he seems to be," Ceuci said, with her eyes still closed.

"He is a puny weakling, and he's terrified."

"He is going to piss his pants."

"Why is it that they all piss their pants?"

"Do you hear his breathing?"

"He's going to have a heart attack."

"His arteries are clogged with cholesterol."

"He needs to go on a diet."

"To stop being such a glutton."

"Anyone else who ate so much would be dead by now."

"He's so fat. He's breathing through his mouth. Look, Iaci. His breathing is getting worse; he must suffer from asthma."

"He's huffing and puffing like a horse."

"He's horny," Iaci said, giggling.

"Do you think so?"

"Yeah, he's horny," Iaci insisted. "Just feel his dick. He's got a hard-on."

"Jeez, it's really hard."

"But he can't make up his mind."

"He's afraid of failure; it's the same old story."

"But the thing is really hard."

"Stop it," Pietra, Jr., shouted.

They opened their eyes and began to laugh.

"You don't have to shout," Iaci said, giggling.

"We just wanted to compliment you," Ceuci said.

"After all, men like to know that their dick is big."

"Or is that not important to you?"

"What would you like to hear us say?"

THE END OF THE THIRD WORLD

"Maybe he doesn't like women," Ceuci said.

"Do you like boys?"

"Or did you screw your old partner's son only out of professional obligation?"

"The young man fell in love with you."

"You did a good job on him."

"Quite competent."

"We've heard that the poor fellow is going around heartbroken."

"We could call our gardener."

"No, the gardener won't do."

"You're right, he's too passive."

"You don't change positions once in a while, do you?"

"If you want, we'll call the gardener."

"We can guarantee you he's good. The best."

Pietra, Jr., no longer shook from fear; it was hatred. He wanted to smash the two women; they just keep rattling on.

"That's enough, you bitches," he roared.

"Bitches! He's so predictable," Ceuci said with a shriek of laughter.

"You've gone too far," Pietra, Jr., said.

He tensed his muscles and attempted to reach them both with one blow. His fist shot through empty space, but he didn't give in. He shouted insults and kicked and hit out in all directions, jumping and grunting like a mad dog. But he didn't land anything; the two young women were always out of his reach. Finally the excessive exertion left his arms aching and his legs so weak that they barely held him up.

He staggered, exhausted. He would have fallen down if they hadn't held him up.

"Leave me alone," he begged.

"You're the one who ought to leave us alone."

"We didn't go after you."

"Why? Why are you doing this to me?" he said, sobbing.

"You still don't know?"

"No, I swear I don't know," he whimpered.

"All right, we understand."

"Sit down for a while," Iaci ordered, taking him to a wicker chair. She became maternal, caressing his hair.

Pietra, Jr., sobbed; he couldn't remember the last time that he had cried. The tears rolled down his cheeks, and his nose was running. What could he have done to deserve so much humiliation? he wondered. Many times he had been accused of exploitation, of questionable tactics, of opportunism and even betrayal. But what he did was no different from what so many others were doing; he hadn't come up with anything new. That's why he wasn't as demanding as some were, nor did he pose as a saint. And if everything they said about him was true, his justification was in the fact that he had to conduct his matters in this manner in order to win, to tame the wilderness, to extract the riches from a difficult and dangerous land where those who had preceded him were resigned to their own limitations.

"Is he still crying?" Ceuci asked.

"He is, and he's not going to stop soon," the other twin responded.

"If only men learned that it is useless to cry after the fact," Ceuci said.

"I need to go," Pietra, Jr., moaned, attempting to get out of the chair. "You can't hold me here."

"We can take you home," Ceuci suggested.

Pietra, Jr., got agitated and dispensed with all courtesy. Once he was out of that house, he had no intention of ever seeing the twins again.

"No, no!" He raised his voice. "I can make it without any help from you."

THE END OF THE THIRD WORLD

He made an effort and stood up. His head was light; he felt faint and his vision was blurred. He tried to take a step and discovered that he could walk without too much difficulty. They did nothing to stop him from leaving, and Pietra, half staggering, left the house. The car was parked at the entrance, and the same servant was holding the keys.

When he sat down in the driver's seat, the smell of leather and perfumed disinfectant calmed him. He turned the headlights on and slowly drove along the paved road. He knew that past the curve he would see the gate at the end of the driveway, and beyond it, the avenue. But that didn't happen. Coming around the curve, all he saw was more paved driveway shining in the moonlight and another curve, and after that, another curve, until he realized that he was going in circles without arriving anywhere, as if it were an unending labyrinth lined with myrtle trees.

His heart began to beat faster when, at the next curve, he saw the house outlined in the moonlight. He anxiously felt the car slow down on its own account and die. He made a desperate attempt to get out, without any success. Frustrated and sweating from every pore, he was pounding the door panel when he heard voices.

"Do you want some help?"

"Did you check to see if the motor is flooded?"

"Is the battery dead?"

Pietra, Jr., didn't need to look to see whose voices they were.

"I can't find the way out."

"What way out?"

"I was going in circles. I must have taken the wrong road."

"He couldn't find the way out."

"He was going in circles, poor thing."

LOST WORLD II

"Will you stop that?" Pietra, Jr., ordered.

The twins hadn't even bothered to get dressed. Pietra, Jr., looked at them and began to get exasperated. How could something like this happen to him? And what was going on, anyway? Two naked women in the moonlight could only be a hallucination, some sign of insanity. He didn't like the idea of going crazy.

"This isn't happening," he said.

"Happening?"

Frantically he tried to start the car, turning the key in the ignition with such force that it finally broke.

"Shit!" he bellowed. "All I needed was for this piece of crap to break."

He got out of the car and slammed the door in fury. The car shook slightly, and to his surprise, it fell apart like a jalopy in a circus clown's act. The wheels slipped off the axle, the doors collapsed, and all of the moving parts fell off. A cloud of dust and smoke rose over the rubble.

"I believe you are our guest for the night," Iaci said.

"I want a taxi," Pietra, Jr., demanded in a loud voice. "I'm not going to stay here!"

"I wonder if you still aren't convinced," Ceuci said.

"Convinced of what?" he shouted. "Of what, of what?"

"Of our hospitality," Iaci added.

"I'll kill you," he threatened.

"We know," Iaci said.

"But we don't pay any attention. We're used to it," Ceuci said.

"You'll sleep here tonight; tomorrow we're going to take a trip," Iaci said.

Totally perplexed, Pietra, Jr., gave in without further resistance. The twins, one on each side, took him by the hand and led him into the house like a decrepit

THE END OF THE THIRD WORLD

giant guided by two mischievous little girls. But this time, they led him to one of the bedrooms, the two of them lightly humming a strange song in a language completely unknown to him. The melody, crooned in a high timbre and in the thin female voices, evoked sadness and at the same time a sensation of impossible peacefulness. In some way, Pietra, Jr., knew that the song was a lie, a sonorous ambush, a type of melodious anesthesia.

The bedroom was decorated with complete austerity. Just a solitary hammock made of palm fiber, strung above a clean floor, tracing a curved line in the empty space. The screen window was closed, and a lit candle was placed on the windowsill. Pietra, Jr., found himself standing beside the hammock, being undressed with indifferent diligence by the twins. Their touch was warm and their small hands moved skillfully, but there was no caress or emotion in what they were doing. Pietra, Jr., doubted the twins had the capacity to feel emotions as other women do. The small flame of the candle gave off an uncertain, yellow glow, flickering between darkness and light. When he had finally been undressed, they settled him in the delicately braided hammock.

Pietra, Jr., sighed as he felt the soft palm fibers touch his body. The hammock must have been soaked in aromatic herbs; it gave off a scent of perfumed moss and pitch. The twins continued humming the song, gently lulling him to sleep, invading the last stronghold of his will with the sad music.

"Are you here?" he asked after some time.

They didn't answer, but it was unnecessary as the song continued, along with the flickering candle and the swinging motion of the hammock. Pietra, Jr., opened his eyes; he felt cold, his throat tightened in distress.

"Sleep."

"Rest."

"Why are you after me?" he asked. "I'm no different from the others. I didn't do anything the others haven't already done, and much worse."

"We know."

"Well, why then? Why?"

They stopped singing and in the silence of the night, only the light sound of the wall hook could be heard.

"It is nothing personal," Ceuci explained.

"You don't need to be afraid," Iaci assured him.

"What do you want?" he went on. "That we had never come here?"

"No, it is not that!"

"But you continue to treat us like outsiders, like unscrupulous intruders. I'm not an intruder; don't you understand?"

"We are all intruders," Ceuci said.

"We are also intruders," Iaci reiterated.

"Perhaps things were not yet completed here."

"That is what the ancient ones realized."

"It has been a great struggle."

"But we never forget that we weren't invited."

"And we try to live like simple temporary guests."

Pietra, Jr., shut his eyes and sighed again. The conversation didn't make much sense to him. What in the devil did they mean that Amazonia was still not ready?

"Maybe it wasn't ready when you arrived," he said. "But it is ready now for us."

"No, it isn't," Ceuci said.

"But if it isn't ready for us," he went on, "who is it getting ready for? Who will get all of this when it is ready?"

"We know," Iaci responded.

"Perhaps it is not for any of us," Ceuci added.

"That is why we wanted this meeting."

THE END OF THE THIRD WORLD

"To say that it isn't your presence that makes us uncomfortable."

"Nor the exploitation."

"Because that's just how you are."

"You'll never change."

"All that we ask is that you use restraint."

"That's not asking so much."

"Do what you must, but with a certain propriety."

"Avoid excess so as not to create a scandal."

"Because in the wake of scandal comes pity."

"And pity usually attracts more intruders."

"The most inconvenient kinds of intruders."

"Extremely irritating intruders."

"Because they believe they are the bearers of truth."

"And they want to align themselves with us all the way."

"Which makes us prefer exploitation to certain kinds of solidarity."

Pietra, Jr., slept soundly, unaware of what the twins had just said. They remained still a few minutes observing the giant stretched out in the hammock; then they blew out the candle and left the room. The next day, when he awoke, he would feel for the first time in his life the full weight of his fifty-five years. They, on the other hand, were only a few thousand years old.

It Was Horrible in the Forest

It wasn't the first time that audacious men took advantage of a trip up the Amazon River to discover good opportunities for investment. The person who inaugurated the route and the mania was Francisco Orellana, a Spaniard, half-adrift like all Iberians who took charge of a ship. After him, so many trips were organized that it is surprising that some enterprising tourist company didn't spring up to meet the need.

The Brazilian Minister of Planning was at that very moment welcoming the guests for the upcoming trip. Surrounded by microphones, tape recorders, and TV cameras, he kept his hands resting on the rostrum as he related what had happened on the last great excursion of CEOs there. The audience seated in the convention hall of the Hotel Tropical listened in silence.

Almost twenty-five years had passed, as he recalled, and the results, although controversial, were in many ways surprising. The year was 1966; a clear ecological conscience still hadn't emerged, and little was known about the Amazon. Nevertheless, the government hadn't hesitated. A handful of pioneers, the cream of the great international and national companies, had gotten together on board the transatlantic *Rosa da Fonseca* and had accepted the challenge of opening up the region to the modern world. The government and private companies had invested $150 billion and retrieved profits that amounted to triple what they had put

THE END OF THE THIRD WORLD

up. Of course, many mistakes had been made; part of the virgin forest had been razed, and many people, especially the poor and the Indians, had lost their land, and in many cases, their lives. But that was all in the past; the trip that was waiting to begin would be a new page in history. The past mistakes would be avoided, the ecology would be respected, the future was waiting as they descended on that great river, a road to riches, a sweet sea of fantastic profits.

The minister spoke in an almost colloquial tone, even though he didn't disregard completely a certain rhetorical language. Thinking of the repercussions his speech would have the next day in the media, he addressed the journalists present to a greater degree than those seated there in the room. He knew that his guests were attentive and quiet more out of courtesy than anything else. They were powerful people, with many worries. Before beginning his speech, he observed their faces and tried to calculate the approximate worth of the audience. He didn't reach any precise amount, but all of his estimates surpassed by far Brazil's gross national product. It was with this sense of heightened vanity that he took the podium.

As Sir Delamare sat in the audience, he hardly concealed his worry. Jane Challenger and Billy Lester had not appeared for the ceremony. And what was even more serious, the space reserved at the head table for the president of the Amazonian Federation of Industry was empty. Sir Delamare was concerned about the empty space at the table because it ought to have been occupied by Pietro Pietra, Jr.

"It is a mere coincidence," Spender had said, trying to calm him.

"Only idiots believe in coincidences," he had responded furiously.

The truth was that there was little he could do at that moment. The ceremony was a simple formality, but he wanted to be present until the end to meet the participants, greet his acquaintances, and to check out the kind of company he would have aboard the *Leviathan*.

Happily, the speech part of the evening ended much sooner than he anticipated, and the silence was broken by cordial greetings amongst the guests and a battalion of waiters serving drinks and food. He gave orders to Spender to try to find out where the two journalists were, and he began to circulate through the room, holding on amicably to Juan Sender's arm.

The minister rushed up to greet Sir Delamare, bringing with him an entourage of assistants and hangers-on, each as indistinguishable as the other.

"It is a great honor," the minister said, shaking hands with him. "We hope that the trip will prove that we no longer have any bias against foreign capital."

Sir Delamare smiled and shook his head in disagreement.

"I don't believe that you ever had any bias," Sir Delamare replied.

The minister laughed and tried to get away from him. Sir Delamare's impertinence filled the fact sheets of nearly all of the Third World authorities.

"What craziness!" Sir Delamare exclaimed, still hanging on Juan Sender's arm. "Why don't they change the subject?"

"You must be a little understanding," the Chilean said ironically. "It's a part of the local culture."

"I can't help it. It's unbearable how they use this story as if it were a scapegoat."

"You ought to be happy that now we Latins prefer the Americans," the Chilean said. "They have broad

THE END OF THE THIRD WORLD

shoulders and are able to cast a long enough shadow to cover the worst cases of incompetence and abuse of power."

Sir Delamare chuckled and lit a cigarette, spreading smoke and leaving an opening around him.

"It's incredible how they love scapegoats down here," Sir Delamare continued. "This is one thing that always intrigued me about Latin America. When it isn't the damned imperialists, it's the damned Communists."

"But you don't intend to deny that imperialism is alive and well in Latin America, do you?" Juan Sender asked.

"Of course not, my good man. Just like I'm sure that communism is alive and well."

"If they don't exist, our rich imagination would have come up with some equivalent," the Chilean said. "One thing is certain; there would be a bogeyman to frighten us."

"You don't say, my dear Sender."

"But it's quite evident. Without these scapegoats, to use your terminology, how could we explain so much misery in the midst of so much wealth? We would have to admit to our stupidity or reveal our complicity."

"Wouldn't that be dangerous? After all, it is part of the farce that exists in the agreement between the two opposing forces."

"Yes, it is dangerous, but not because of the opposing forces. The danger exists in the self-indulgence. The profits are a little less, but they are constant and don't require the imagination necessary in the richer centers of the world. Aside from that, poverty has its own charm, its folklore, the exotic appeal of misery. Our literature wouldn't exist without the poetry of pity. And our writers, who more often than not become diplomats, would find life infinitely more boring. Just think of it!"

Sir Delamare took a long drag on his cigarette, and the Chilean novelist stared with apprehension at the large tip of ash that was ready to fall.

"Hum! Hum!" Sir Delamare grumbled. "I don't like literature."

Juan Sender acquiesced, understanding that due to the lack of interest that Sir Delamare had in literature, their friendship had flourished.

"Excuse me!" Sir Delamare said. "I didn't mean to be rude."

The ash from his cigarette finally landed on the chair, but before anyone could notice, Juan Sender brushed it off.

"Don't worry," Sender said, reassuring Sir Delamare. "I wouldn't be interested in literature either if I weren't a writer."

Sir Delamare lit another cigarette and started to stroll through the room. But it wasn't very easy to move about at that point; the room seemed fuller as they circulated or socialized in small, animated groups, and Sir Delamare was forced to stop every few feet to receive embraces and greetings which were accentuated by the flashes of the photographers' cameras.

"We can't talk here," Sir Delamare complained. "I think that we ought to go to the bar by the swimming pool; it is probably less crowded."

The two of them made their way through the people; the puff of smoke coming from Sir Delamare gave him a look of Moses parting the Red Sea. And the sheer force of the nicotine made the process somewhat easier.

They found a table at the edge of the pool and sat down. The bar wasn't empty as Sir Delamare had hoped, but the customers were younger and the night was pleasant. A radiant moon seemed to linger lazily over the crown of the trees.

THE END OF THE THIRD WORLD

"We were speaking of very interesting things," Sir Delamare said.

Juan Sender was listening, his body leaning over the table like a giraffe over a cluster of edible leaves.

"Latin America has always intrigued me," Sir Delamare proceeded. "I mean, I never agreed with the explanations that were given regarding the misery and backwardness of the Latin Americans. That the black Africans have serious development problems, or even some of the Asian countries, is understandable; after all, they are very different from us Europeans. As far as the Latin Americans go, well, they are a little more like us. You, for example, my dear Sender, you have always dressed like us, you were given a Christian education, and you know how to use silverware without even thinking about what you're doing. As far as I am concerned, the great difference between Europe and America, my friend, are the place-names. You Latins chose to baptize certain geographic accidents with exotic names."

"We had no way of knowing that in doing so, we would later have identity problems," Sender said.

"Tsk, tsk, tsk." Sir Delamare reacted with an expression of dismay.

"A child that comes in contact with a word like Aconcagua will never recover from the trauma," Sender added.

"I understand," Sir Delamare said reverently.

"But look here, sir," Sender continued. "Your suspicions with regard to our continent are not groundless. And I am not denying that imperialism is a reality—quite to the contrary—but I think that the persistence and growth with which it has operated here is poorly understood."

"I find it totally incomprehensible that Brazil is an underdeveloped country," Sir Delamare said. "Even New

LOST WORLD II

Zealand, whose economy depends upon sheep, has managed to reach living standards equal to England's in just a few generations."

Sender smiled, because the comparison put the Brazilians in a tight spot. In four centuries they had failed to catch up with Portugal, let alone England.

"Brazil is the eighth largest capitalist economy in the world," Sender said.

Sir Delamare coughed and shook his head. "I've heard that nonsense before," he said with a hoarse voice. "It resembles those bombastic declarations made by the Tories. But in 1860."

"I lived in Brazil," Sender said. "I began my exile in Rio de Janeiro, and it is a country which I admire. I left some good friends here. But one thing that has intrigued me since the first day is that the Brazilians aren't able to conceive of their own country in its actual dimensions. It was so strange for me, how they purposely diminished it, shrank it in their minds. I don't know how to explain it."

"A rather absurd mania, I would dare to say," Sir Delamare exclaimed.

"It was as if they were trying to reduce their responsibilities."

Getting to know Brazilians up close had been surprising for Sender. In many ways, they seemed like Chileans; they were always using superlatives: They had the best soccer players in the world, their television was the best in the world, Sao Paulo was the largest city in South America. But when Sender would bring up the subject of national problems, Brazil suddenly deflated like a punctured balloon. Then it seemed more like a Uganda or a Guatemala.

"Do you know something?" Sender said. "Certain countries are underdeveloped because they want it that way. Brazil is one of those. That is how the ruling class wants it."

"That's a harsh indictment," Sir Delamare commented, weighing what Sender had just said.

"I would say the same about Chile," Sender added. "Or Argentina, or Venezuela, or Colombia, or Mexico. They are all countries with a large population, natural resources, and linguistic unity. I can no longer believe that our countries are defenseless victims of foreign appetites. Do you believe that ITT and the CIA brought down Chilean democracy all by themselves?"

Sir Delamare confined himself to lighting another cigarette.

"In that regard," Sender continued, "we prefer to spread very different ideas; we adore writing entire books showing that the history of Latin America is some kind of Calvary spiced with pepper. A half-hearted martyrdom."

"Some terrible things have happened here," Sir Delamare said.

"It was to be expected, don't you think? From the colonial era until the present, we have done nothing but suffer; we are poor, unfortunate, and exploited. You're lucky not to have read those books, because they are collections of horrors that are reiterated ad nauseam. They go to such great lengths to show our many centuries of unbearable suffering that I wonder if masochism has not become our real national identity. What kind of people are we anyway? Ingenuous? Excessively prudent? Prisoners of a perverted manifest destiny? Or is it that this business of blaming foreigners is no more than idle chat?"

"If Billy Lester were here now," Sir Delamare said, "he would accuse the Latin American oligarchy of having sold out to the foreigners. I don't know if you know it, but he is a laborite."

"That's what the Latin American leftists say as well," Sender explained. "What is most annoying is that our left is only leftist when it is out of power. It has always been so."

"It is really an unusual continent," Sir Delamare said. "But that is probably due to the fact that it is Catholic."

"You're right to a certain extent, but Catholicism hasn't been an obstacle for France, for Italy. Nor even for Spain."

"Without meaning to offend you, I'll say that I find papists to be a peculiar breed," Sir Delamare observed.

"Have you considered the fact that England's best writers are all papists? Joyce, Greene, Waugh, Burgess."

"Writers in general are peculiar," Sir Delamare responded.

Sender acknowledged the observation with a smile. He had the impression that at this point Sir Delamare was listening to him merely out of courtesy; it was a pleasant way of killing time, of little consequence as long as it wasn't overly boring. And therein lies the great virtue of Latin America: It is a subject that isn't too tedious as long as no one transforms it into a messianic obsession. It is an area of the world that has a certain fascination for Europeans, similar to the fascination that children have for dinosaurs.

"My God!" Sir Delamare exclaimed, glancing at his watch. "It is almost ten o'clock and Spender still hasn't returned."

"Mr. Spender ought to be in bed by now, sir. He was complaining about the heat, and feeling weak from dehydration."

"I sent him to look for Miss Challenger and Billy Lester. I hope he hasn't tried to carry out my order down to the last letter and decided to ransack the whole city."

"Would you like me to call his room?" Sender asked.

"Don't bother," Sir Delamare said, getting up from his chair. "I'll look into it myself."

Accompanied by his cloud of smoke, the old gentleman walked stiffly toward the telephone booths.

"I'll be right back," he said with a wave before leaving the bar.

Juan Sender watched his friend's firm step, admiring his physical vitality, the studied nonchalance of his clothing. A few months before, that friendship would have been utterly unthinkable, especially if one considered the circumstances that preceded their first meeting. At the onset of winter, Sender had received a proposal from an English publisher to print the translation of his most recent novel. The letter left him surprised and happy, because the manuscript was still in his desk drawer, gathering dust after two long years waiting for a publisher. Any career as a published writer seemed to be behind him, as his three previous novels had been out of print for some years in Chile as well as in Spain.

He lived off the salary he received as a clerk in the Barcelona branch of the Bank of Brazil. It was strictly a desk job, with no contact with the public; his work was to translate contracts into Portuguese, even though his ear continued to be resistant to the language, which was so similar to Spanish in written form, and so guttural and Slavic when spoken. Nevertheless, the job enabled him to pay the rent, and Sender had few other expenses. Since he didn't belong to any political movement, his exile was solitary, and his only ambition was to have time to write. In this sense, the four-hour shift at the Bank of Brazil was perfect, not counting the great luck that his bank coworkers were very discreet and never asked what he was writing in his spare time.

The letter from the English publisher offered an advance of twenty-five hundred dollars for the novel *Kassov*, which is how the novel was titled, and enclosed the opinion of a team of readers exalting the literary qualities of the work. The two thousand dollars might not be much, but it had arrived at an opportune time. He had just received a bill from a plastic surgeon in Madrid for eighteen hundred dollars for treating an Italian woman, a professor of Latin American literature, who had lost the tip of her nose by inadvertently asking him what he was currently writing.

At the time the professor lost the tip of her nose, he was finishing the final revision of the manuscript of the novel. He still hadn't found a title for the work, but he had decided to send a copy to Colchie Dany-Rose, an agency that specialized in managing dancers with motor coordination problems, magicians with Parkinson's disease, and Latin American writers. By sending the manuscript, he was making a desperate attempt to see that his books could be found in bookstores once again. But more than two years would pass without any results until he received the letter from the English publisher.

First he tried to contact his literary agency; he didn't want to negotiate with the publisher directly, but later he realized that he had no alternative. The international literary market was going through a dangerous test of wills. Sender had found out that Colchie Dany-Rose was temporarily deactivated and its owner had fled to an uncle's house in Palermo. From what was being said, it appeared that the fellow had received death threats for representing a Colombian poet, an act that had been taken as an invasion of territory since Colombia was traditionally controlled by the Medellin cartel.

THE END OF THE THIRD WORLD

Not willing to let the opportunity pass him by, Sender asked for a week's leave at the bank and went to London. Everything went smoothly; he received the advance upon signing the contract, and he was preparing his departure when an invitation to a party arrived. The publishing house was celebrating the sale of two million copies of its recent best-seller, a novel that told of the vicissitudes of a British diplomat in the tropics. The author, the Duchess of Penbroken, was ninety years old and had decided to try her hand at literature when her arthritis no longer allowed her to knit. Her protagonist, an irascible fellow, resentful of the British diplomatic hierarchy, was sent against his will to the Amazon jungle to investigate allegations that Indians were being enslaved on a plantation financed by the United Kingdom. Before it had sold the first one thousand copies, the novel could boast of a collection of the most injurious reviews in the past fifty years. One critic went so far as to recommend a clinic that had miraculous results in the treatment of arthritis, but apparently the twelve rapes, eighty pages of flagellation, the graphic scenes of homosexuality, and a variety of methods of torture prevailed.

The publishing house was part of Sir Delamare's empire. The author herself was a longtime friend. Naturally the gardens of the Tudor mansion in Kensington were chosen to receive the guests at the party.

Sender didn't want to go, knowing the great risk that he would be running, but he finally succumbed to his editors' pleas. He tried to pass unnoticed, and he was nearly home safe when, towards the end of the party, he found himself face-to-face with the feted duchess herself. Introduced as a Latin American writer, he was taken aside by Lady Penbroken as if he were one of the unfortunate natives of the plantation that she had so vividly described in her novel.

"What are you working on at the moment?" she asked after exchanging a few social amenities with the exotic man of letters.

The first attack was against the hand that the duchess had extended to give emphasis to her question. The rest could easily have come from one of the pages of her novel if the author had not failed to include in the story a scene of cannibalism. When they were able to rescue the victim, Sender had in his mouth pieces of lace and a few pearls, and she had teeth marks with which to remember his irrepressible impulses.

"I'm sorry! I'm sorry! I couldn't help it!" he shouted under the weight of six security guards who held him flat on the grass.

Hurriedly taken to a hospital, the duchess survived. But Juan Sender's future was uncertain. The more understanding guests thought he ought to be in an insane asylum; others simply preferred to hand him over to the police and charge him with assault and destruction of property. The members of the publisher's sales department demanded an immediate sentencing.

That was when a man came out of the mansion, and to everyone's surprise, he shouted: "Release him!"

It was Lord Delamare in person.

Although they greatly respected him, they were incredulous. Some of the more outraged guests argued against the arbitrary order, but they were disregarded. The six hefty security guards got up, and Sender tried to see if he was still in one piece. He slowly rose to his feet, bearing such a forlorn expression and sorrowful eyes that he evoked pity.

"Tell me," Sir Delamare asked, "what should we administer, an antidote for poison or a rabies vaccine?"

THE END OF THE THIRD WORLD

Mortified, Sender shook his hands in an impotent gesture.

"Sir, I am perfectly healthy. I assure you that she contracted no disease from me."

"No, I'm not referring to her state of health. I'm worried about your health, young man."

Juan Sender collapsed and woke up forty-two hours later in a hospital room. When he opened his eyes, he was told that Sir Delamare had a job offer for him. That was the beginning of their friendship; because any man capable of biting the Duchess of Penbroken and surviving couldn't go on as a simple clerk in a Barcelona bank.

Sir Delamare's proposal was to rewrite the novel full time, for which he was prepared to pay Sender one hundred pounds a week. Sender accepted, because he was desperate just thinking about the lawsuit and the hospital bills that the aristocratic victim would demand to be paid. But the duchess proved to be magnanimous and preferred to forget the incident, shutting herself up in her Dundee property to begin a new novel.

Sender was beginning to suspect that Sir Delamare's offer was a means of indefinitely extending the publication of his work. No editor in his right mind will tell a writer that he has unlimited time to finish the work if he really wants to see the book in print someday. Worse still is to pay the writer to write without giving him a deadline. That is what they had done with him: a contract that gave him all the time in the world. But he wasn't bitter about it; he liked to write, he worked meticulously, and like all writers, as slow as he was, one day the moment would come to put down the words "The End."

For the first two months of the contract, he worked in a room in Sir Delamare's mansion. The old lord didn't like literature, but he adored listening to and telling stories, especially telling them. He believed in the myth that writers are capable of turning into a story any idea that enters their heads, and not a day passed that he didn't tell Juan one or another of his adventures. Sender had no problem listening to stories; his problem was in trying to tell them. However, Sir Delamare was not so foolish as to repeat the mistake his friend the duchess had made. Nevertheless, the Chilean had begun to think that the old man wasn't the least bit interested in his novel about the life of Leopold Kassov, a tragic figure and a genius of literary criticism who leaves Russia to meet an obscure death in Manaus after wandering through Paris and the Azore Islands.

The happy rhythm of the samba and the movements of the young people who had gotten up to dance at the edge of the pool brought Sender back from his reverie. He checked his watch and realized that he had been waiting for Sir Delamare for two hours. He began to think that he was waiting in vain; the old man at this time of night was probably in bed asleep, gathering strength for the trip the following day. The best thing for him to do was to go to sleep as well.

He entered an empty and unattended elevator, pushed the button, and leaned against the back wall carelessly, wondering if he could fall asleep five hours ahead of his usual bedtime. It should have been a quick trip up, because all of the rooms were on the first floor, but the elevator continued rising. The digital indicator registered an improbable number. When he was just about to push the emergency button, the elevator stopped and the doors opened. Cautiously he leaned out, without leaving the elevator, to see where he was. But everything seemed normal, the same blue hallway, the same rustic tiles, and the same white doors with navy blue molding. He shook

THE END OF THE THIRD WORLD

his head and looked again at the floor indicator, keeping his finger on the button to hold the door open. The indicator said he was on the tenth floor. It was mistaken, he thought, a defect. He left the elevator and headed for his room, which was down the hall. He was totally absorbed in thought, even as he passed a man in a tight, flesh-colored leotard, with his head in a thin transparent plastic bubble.

He opened the door and entered his room; he turned automatically to switch on the light when he realized it wasn't necessary. The room was lit and two men were leaning over some kind of electronic console that was sitting on the bed. They were dressed in leotards, like the man he had passed in the hall, but their heads were uncovered. They seemed engrossed in what they were doing, because they didn't stop their work when Sender entered.

"I beg your pardon!" Sender said, beating a retreat.

One of them, the younger of the two, noticed Sender's presence.

"One moment!" the man asked. "Is this Infopsi?"

"What?" Sender responded, disconcerted.

"Manaus!" exclaimed the other man. He was older, with a sunburned face, a sparse beard, and watery blue eyes that were fixed on some indefinite point.

"Yes, this is Manaus," Sender said.

"Are you an Infopsian?" the younger man insisted, with a sudden alarmed expression and pointing to Sender. "How can you walk around without a vitapoio? It's very imprudent. Who are you, anyway?"

"Well—" Sender hesitated "I—am a guest here, I think. I must be in the wrong room."

"A guest?" the man queried as if the word had as much meaning for him as Infopsi and vitapoio had for Sender.

"And you, who are you?" Sender asked.

The young man rubbed his eyes and sighed.

"Something is wrong here," he said. "We're going to have to start all over again."

"Manaus! Manaus!" the other one repeated with growing excitement.

"Please, Dr. Kxalendjer, remain calm. Do you want some more tea?"

A steaming porcelain teapot was in the young man's hand, and he served the older gentleman. Sender was even more intrigued, because he didn't have the slightest idea how the teapot had appeared in the young man's hand.

"Maaanaaaus!" the older man exclaimed when he had finished his tea.

The young man made a face of disappointment and gestured Sender to approach. "I am not a specialist," the young man said. "But this ought to be the twenty-first century."

"No, it's not the twenty-first century. I am from the twentieth century, the end of the twentieth century."

"Excuse me. You see, they are very similar. I always get confused."

"What is going on here? Is this some kind of joke?"

"Unfortunately not," the young man responded. "Come a little closer."

Cautiously Sender drew near the bed. He could see the console better; it was a thin metallic plate with an iridescent glassy surface that reminded him of a compact disc. But as he entered the room, he had seen bright, minuscule dots of light on the plate.

"You're not going to understand what we're doing," the young man said.

Juan Sender was offended; yet, strangely enough, he wasn't frightened, only intrigued. He reacted in the same way to the unusual nightmare that assailed him nearly every night.

"If you tell me what is going on," he responded, "perhaps I can understand."

The young man acquiesced and passed his hand over the plate. A series of graphics began to emerge in the center of a bright green box that opened up on the shimmering surface.

"These are his nanosomatic diagnostics," the young man said, pointing at the older man. "He is Dr. Kxalendjer, my mentor; we are from the Amazonian Protectorate team. He has been in a state of shock since last year when he returned from an expedition to this state. My colleagues and I don't know how he managed to program his own floatoboat. The problem is that the whole Infopsian team is lost, but he won't admit that he failed. They are very proud; ah, that they are."

"This is really difficult to understand." Sender confessed.

"I told you," the young man replied, and perhaps out of a need to speak with someone, he went on. "It just so happens that such cases of irreversible alienation are extremely rare now, uh, I mean in our time. Almost always the nanopavlovs can detect the most subtle changes in the metabolism provoked by traumatic situations, and very quickly they indicate the exact chemical compensations needed. But Dr. Kxalendjer's case is a mystery."

"He must have seen something that shocked him," Sender said.

"He is not a man who is easily shocked," the young man said, pointing to a specific spot on the plate. "Put your finger on that light; perhaps it will help you to understand what we are doing here. Go on; don't be afraid."

LOST WORLD II

Sender didn't hesitate; he sat down on the bed and placed his index finger on the spot indicated by the young man. When he touched the iridescent surface, he was surprised by its soft texture, warm and almost alive.

Sir Wallace Kxalendjer is the last descendant of a notable line of trailblazers, energetic people, willful almost to the point of audacity; he is very proud of having family roots reaching back to the industrial age and of belonging to a family that became legendary at the end of the last millennium. A brilliant ethno-archaeologist, he was given the commission of director of the Center of Research of the University of the Amazonian Protectorate when he became ill.

"Manaus! Manaus! Manaus!" was all that he would say when he was found. The word, pronounced with disquieting precision, meant absolutely nothing to anyone. Only later was the word "Manaus" identified as the name of an indigenous tribe extinct since the eighteenth century of the last millennium and the denomination of a city that existed in some region of the Protectorate. The word had fallen into disuse more than two hundred years ago, and only a handful of specialists knew it; for that reason, the pronunciation of those lugubrious sounds was initially assumed to be one of the scientist's eccentricities. After all, he was the only one capable of finding beauty in that region and of contemplating for hours on end the clouds of army ants in their December maiden flight, or to declare himself enraptured by the migration of millions of centipedes during the hot season. At that time the insects and the arthropods were almost the absolute masters there, each season of the year being dominated by one of the many species of insects that seemed to burst forth from every corner and darkened the diaphanous dome that protected them

THE END OF THE THIRD WORLD

not only from the periodic plagues, but from a crazed ecosystem.

The Protectorate was one of the most inhospitable and feared regions of the planet; it must have been some kind of atavistic interest that eventually attracted Dr. Kxalendjer's attention to it. Although the rigors of the region were sufficient to drive a more sensitive individual crazy, this could not explain what had happened to a hardened and experienced man like the doctor. He was at the height of his career when he sought out the chancellor of the Council of States in London and asked for an entry visa to the Protectorate. Any public information terminal had records of his latest work, a magnificent report on his excavations in South Africa and a surprising study on an exotic culture of the twentieth century known as "apartheid," including the bitter polemic that it generated.

The council ambassador for the Protectorate received the visitor with apprehension and curiosity. It was to be expected since he represented a regime that caused snickers and symbolized the last traces of backwardness and primitivism on the face of the planet. For this reason, setting aside the long-standing rule of denying every and all entry visas no matter who the applicant happened to be, the ambassador consulted the officials in the home office in Pasárgada,* and to his surprise, he received orders to inform the scientist that he would be conferred the honor of receiving an official government invitation.

Two months later, the scientist disembarked in Pasárgada, the fetid and miserable capital of the council regime. The reception at the airport was quick; he was

---
*Pasárgada: name of a utopian kingdom in a well-known poem by Manuel Bandeira, a northeastern poet of the mid twentieth century.

immediately transported to the hotel, where two thin and nervous men in outdated clothing awaited him. They were local scientists, providentially released from prison because they were the only ethno-archaeologists available. These poor creatures, who had spent the past five years in jail, would become his assistants. The young man at Sender's side happened to be one of the released prisoners. On the following day, the Minister of Science received Kxalendjer with great fanfare and, to everyone's surprise, offered him the position of director of the Department of General Research of the University of the Amazonian Protectorate. The job had been vacant since the death of the former director, an entomologist, who had been devoured alive by army ants. Dr. Kxalendjer's enthusiastic reaction to the offer was in complete contrast to the fear that overcame his assistants. The two scientists pleaded to be returned to their prison cells, but they were thwarted in their attempts to refuse the jobs by the minister, a man with strong convictions, similar to an army sergeant who doesn't allow cowardice or faltering in the face of the enemy.

Some days later, a small caravan, led by a patrol of sanitroops, set out in the direction of the Protectorate. Nothing more is known regarding the expedition nor what transpired there, and the council authorities insist on maintaining secrecy in spite of the protests reiterated by the government in London along with the World Parliament. The only thing that is known for sure is that Dr. Kxalendjer suffered some kind of shock; perhaps he witnessed some frightening event, some dreaded horror capable of rocking his strong constitution. And that part of the planet, blanketed in mystery and kept apart by the authoritarian system of the Protectorate, could well contain something truly monstrous.

Little was known about the Amazonian Protectorate,

THE END OF THE THIRD WORLD

and what was known was enough to cause goose pimples. The final destruction of the rain forest, which took place between 2012 and 2017, prompted by the post ecologists and the large urban demographic explosion coming at the end of the twentieth century, resulted in the appearance of new environmental factors. The temperature of the planet continued rising at the rate of one degree per year, and in the months of August, it easily reached 150 degrees Fahrenheit. Violent storms occurred all year long, causing rivers to pour over their banks, hindering air navigation even for the few sub-orbital lines that serviced the two urban centers in the area that were still reasonably inhabited, both of which had been designated as research centers and were under military command.

Around 2020 there were outbreaks of deadly epidemics known as the green plague, which were caused by mutant arboreal viruses. Those were times of anguish and horror for all of the human inhabitants of the region. The victims of this highly contagious disease would become crazed, lose all muscle control, and die hours after the onset of the initial symptoms. When the first carriers of the disease were discovered in other parts of the world, the military council regime took a drastic step and, in spite of a great uproar in the scientific community, declared a quarantine throughout the Protectorate. The indiscriminate extermination of all the inhabitants of the region followed, until 90 percent of the population had disappeared, a total of twenty-five million victims, which left the area practically unoccupied and isolated.

Even after a vaccine had been discovered in 2050, the act of living there was a kind of technological challenge. In the ancient capital of the Amazonian Protectorate, for example, only the western sector, where the University of the Protectorate was located, was regularly inhabited.

LOST WORLD II

There was a geodesic dome twelve kilometers across and the height of a thirty-story building that covered the university, but aside from that, the rest of the city was a pile of rubble of no particular interest except for those courageous entomologists who occasionally ventured out on a local expedition.

There was a legend that a few tribes of the extreme northern mountain region had survived the outbreaks of plague, the attacks by the council sanitroops, and the heat and voracious insects. But there was no way of proving it. The observation satellites weren't able to penetrate the perennial blanket of clouds that had covered the region for more than two centuries, and sound waves or thermal registers were too imprecise to be conclusive.

"Manaus? Manaus! Maaanaaauuusssh!" Dr. Kxalendjer shouted.

Juan Sender withdrew his finger from the plate and looked at the old scientist who insisted on repeating the word with the happiness and euphoria of a demented person. It wasn't a very nice thing to see. As a matter of fact, nothing about that situation pleased him. His mouth was dry and he urgently needed to urinate. That is why he felt the need to wake up, to free himself of that strange dream, but apparently it wasn't possible. He got up from the bed and began walking around the room, afraid of wetting himself.

The young man tried without any success to calm the sick man, but the medication had no effect. Dr. Kxalendjer jumped up, repeating the name that obsessed him so. Sender, fearing violence, kept his distance. But the scientist didn't seem to be conscious of the other two men in the room.

"Come on, Doctor." The young man tried to motivate him. "Where did you leave the file? You can remember. Please!"

THE END OF THE THIRD WORLD

"Manaus!" Sender said, and repeated, "Manaus! Manaus? Manaus!"

The scientist suddenly became calm, as if the incantatory quality of the word focused him. He faced Sender.

"Manaus?" Sender asked.

"Manaus," the scientist responded, smiling like a child, and pointing to the bathroom.

"Manaus?" Sender asked in confirmation, also pointing to the bathroom.

"Manaus," the scientist confirmed, jumping up and down.

Sender entered the bathroom with the scientist. The old man looked around the room, recognizing it; finally he went up to the sink and happily pointed to the mirror.

The young man entered the bathroom with some kind of flashlight and pointed it at the mirror. No light was emitted from it, but from behind the mirror, between the glass and the plywood, a violet light was shining.

"I can hardly believe it!" the young man exclaimed. "I've been looking for this for six months."

"What is it?" Sender asked curiously.

"It is an organic film of a reading of parallel reasoning. We use it to record field research. It is quite simple and practical; it can be read at any terminal."

The young man retrieved the film and showed it to Sender. Aside from the ray of light emitted by the flashlightlike apparatus, the film was brown and translucent, like a sheet of gelatin.

"The file record indicated a film was missing," the young man continued, taking the scientist by the arm and leading him back to the room. "I always thought for some reason that before losing his mind, Dr. Kxalendjer would have hidden it. And since the floatoboat registered a temporal immersion, my intuition told me that

LOST WORLD II

the film was somewhere in the past." The young man paused and looked at Sender. "You can imagine that a temporal immersion is not easy. What's more, it is forbidden in the territory of the Council of States. The military rulers know that any sort of interaction provokes unforeseen reactions."

Sender remained silent, struggling against the growing desire to empty his bladder. But he didn't want to wake up yet. He needed to hold off just a little bit more.

"Let's see what we have here," the young man said, placing the film on the plate. Immediately the fine brown gelatin dissolved and a triangle appeared on the plate.

"It is a visual record," the young man explained.

The triangle spun around and was substituted by the image of a transatlantic ship traveling down the Amazon River. To Sender's shock, it was the *Leviathan*.

Dr. Kxalendjer, speaking very precisely, began to narrate:

"This is a ship, an ancient means of transportation no longer in use. According to my canonic projections based on alternative historic models, I have reached the conclusion that on this ship, known as the *Leviathan*, the fulcrum point of the tragedy occurred that has subsequently damaged our planet. The events that transpired are the following: In 2045, when the civilian government was newly deposed by the Council of States, the Protectorate's fate was sealed and the catastrophe occurred. However, it could have been avoided if one woman, Maria Pietra by name, had been alive. In the canon of events, Maria Pietra was born in 2025, and she became the greatest leader of the Council of States. In 2045 she consolidated the civil government's power and began a movement to have a fifty-year moratorium on all projects within the Amazonian Protectorate. The Problem: The possibility of Maria Pietra's birth ceased to exist

THE END OF THE THIRD WORLD

with the death of her grandfather, Pietro Pietra, Jr., who dies in the sinking of the *Leviathan*. End of File."

On the plate several explosions began to tear apart the *Leviathan*. The enormous ocean liner slowly turns over and its stern disappears in the churning yellow waters of the Amazon River. Helicopters fly over the tragic scene, and small boats draw near, but the explosions impede any rescue action.

"My God, my God," Sender shouted.

"Do you know about the event?" the young man asked him in an anguished voice. "Has it already happened?"

"No, not yet. But it will happen."

"When?"

"I don't know. I mean, the ship leaves tomorrow morning."

"Can you stop it from leaving?"

"I don't think so! I can't even believe what's going on here myself. I am one of the passengers, and I will probably die in the shipwreck along with the others. I don't know how to swim."

"Manaus! Manaus!" Dr. Kxalendjer shouted, at the same time that a series of sparks escaped from the console sitting on the bed.

"Our immersion is coming to an end," the young man said, unhappily. "We can't stay any longer."

And everything disappeared, leaving Juan Sender in such total darkness that he was afraid to inhale. But he opened his eyes and saw the open window, the full moon, and moonbeams passing through the window to the sheets. He was completely dressed, his shoes on, just as if he had simply fainted on the bed. But inside his head was the image of the burning and sinking ship; it seemed to want to jump out.

Juan Sender got up off the bed and went into the bathroom to pee.

An Unforgettable Vision

Henry Amazon was only three years old when he lost his father, but his family history was quite original. It couldn't be otherwise since it had been invented by Professor Challenger. As there were no photographs of his father, the only thing that Henry knew was that he had inherited nearly all of the deceased's physical traits. Aside from that, he also came to know much of what his father thought and the things that he said simply because his mother's favorite topic of conversation was the life of that young man, who was so sensitive that at the age of twenty-three, he was unable to resist the rigors of a European winter.

Henry remembered now that his father, when he was a child, believed that the city of Manaus was some kind of end of the line, last outpost, final destination. In his childish perception, the city stood out; it had been made to proclaim the last stop of all trips, an avarice trap bursting forth in the middle of the equatorial forest. Those who reached the city knew right away that the trip was over. But this impression wasn't drawn solely from the fact that the city was in the middle of the Amazon jungle. He would come to understand the vastness of his land and the total geographic isolation in which Manaus existed only later in his life. On the contrary, this impression he had gathered as a child wandering the city streets and, most especially, from observing the fate that befell so many of the circuses that had arrived there.

THE END OF THE THIRD WORLD

Indeed, even circus people, who never were known to be sedentary, discovered in Manaus the end of the trail. And so it was that many of the circuses would end up falling victim to the place, absorbed into the vortex of a city without electricity, where enormous and incongruous black Buicks would circulate like lazy primeval reptiles in the dark, airless nights.

It was natural that of all those who made Manaus the end of the line, those who attracted his attention most were the circus people. It seemed that there, in the clearing surrounded by the mysterious jungle, those adventuresome nomads lost their wanderlust. And they began to mix in and become just mere city dwellers. That the trapeze artist became a fisherman and the animal tamer went to work in a butcher shop were mutations that were of small consequence. It was the fate that befell the animals that impressed him. Unable to change their skins, abandoned by their caretakers, the tamer ones were seen wandering through the outskirts, adopted by the children. For some years two elephants bathed in the evenings in the Sao Raimundo Channel, in the midst of the clamor and tumult of the neighborhood kids, like some scene out of a Kipling story. But of all of the abandoned circus animals in Manaus, the ones that most captivated the people were a pair of llamas. Haughty and indifferent, they placidly bore their rejection, ruminating for years on end in the flower beds of the city plazas. His father would emphasize that they represented something very repressed within all of the townspeople. The llamas became stoic emblems, patient symbols of the abandonment that all felt living there.

To live in Manaus was to be somewhat like those two llamas. Everyone knew it but didn't speak of it since animals are by nature laconic and discreet.

On the other hand, perhaps because he sensed the

city's isolation, and because he was an Indian without a tribe, Manaus became the center of the universe. Even though it was far from everything, in one way or another the city never ceased to attract people and things.

What was that Manaus of long ago like? Henry couldn't imagine it, but according to his father's stories, it was a good place to live in spite of everything. Professor Challenger never tired of saying that the meaning of civilization in the twentieth century was the art of living in an urban center. Henry's father agreed fully, if one were to evoke his memories of Manaus in the 1950s. Perhaps it was an urban center of ideal proportions for civilized life in Amazonia.

Those who were not Indians felt some important things were missing, like electricity and a broader educational system. Happily, the isolation was finally broken by Lloyds and Booth Line transatlantic steamers, and by the elegant Pan Am constellation of air carriers. And if there still wasn't any electricity, it didn't really matter that much, because they had been without it for years, and they lived quite well. Those who felt the need to listen to their favorite music could do so on gramophones, and many read by the light of a candelabrum, as in a Balzac novel.

It was interesting how the older residents went on insisting that Manaus had been a very rich city, that it had seen its greatest days fifty years before. And Henry's father would comment that these folks were deceiving themselves; the best of times were those that were transpiring right then, and no one noticed. When Henry's father died, in 1968, the city's death throes were just beginning. Memories of the llamas grazing in the plazas were already gone.

Contrary to all of his expectations, Henry had returned to the land of his ancestors. It was his second time there,

THE END OF THE THIRD WORLD

and he felt like a complete stranger. All alone, seated at the bar in the discotheque, he looked at the city lights that spread out toward the south. Manaus rose up over several hills, and the discotheque sat upon one of these privileged spots. The landscape, bathed in moonlight and saturated with humidity, gave off a wet shine. Seeing him there, immobile and sprawled out on the chair, no one would suspect that he was truly worried. His black eyes slowly searched the horizon, and his face remained totally emotionless, but inside he was tense and nervous.

He had more than enough to worry about. He was the prime suspect in the murder of Danilo Ariel Duarte, he was accused of having robbed his own home, and he was regarded by Scotland Yard as a fugitive. Aside from that, Jane Challenger, the person he loved most in the world, was planning on embarking the following day on a trip that quite possibly would be her last. These recent events in his life weren't part of the story created by Professor Challenger, because Henry Amazon's story began many years before his own birth.

Nevertheless, Henry paid little mind to this story; in fact, he detested everything that had to do with family, Indians, and tropical jungles. For all intents and purposes, he felt very much an Englishman, and he managed to ignore the obvious to such a degree that when he looked in the mirror every morning, he never saw the Indian looking back at him. And since the freewheeling Anglo-Saxon imagination happened to regard him as some kind of Oriental or Malay, he had a mysterious image with which to amuse himself once in a while. But only once in a while.

The organized portion of his life began to unravel on the afternoon that Jane left Enmore Park to return to the Amazon. Henry preemptively refused to give any importance to what Jane was saying. He adored Jane, but his contempt for those scalding jungles was even greater. Nothing that went on there could be of any importance, only minor dramas, small tragedies, stories of melancholy llamas abandoned in the streets. And Henry had seen nothing to make him change his mind; being in Manaus was horrible enough, and he wasn't ready to admit that one of life's perverse ironies had transformed him into one of those sad circus performers of whom his father had spoken. The West End, as far as he was concerned, was the center of the universe.

As he didn't want to be at home when Jane left, he remained out until late that night. Upon returning home, he found Enmore Park completely dark, but he didn't pay much attention to the fact because he imagined that Jane had given the servants the night off. He went directly to his room, passing through the dark halls, happy to have the house all to himself in the weeks that Jane would be gone. Since childhood, Henry had occupied a large room on the ground floor; it was very quiet, because it was on an interior garden and quite a distance from the street. Unlike the predominantly Edwardian style of the mansion, his room was an example of Scandinavian objectivity combined with a high-tech home entertainment center. As Henry got undressed, he noticed that the harmony of the pine and acrylic had been subtly spoiled. And as the housekeeper only entered his room once a month and under his close eye, and not even Jane dared to snoop around his things, he surmised that it had to be an intruder; someone from outside had invaded Enmore Park. He quickly turned off the light and remained alert, almost holding his breath, attempting to hear something that might stand out from

THE END OF THE THIRD WORLD

the usual repertoire of creaks, squeaks, and sinister noises that were so much a part of the silence of Enmore Park.

Not hearing any unusual sound, Henry left his room and began to examine the house room by room, turning on lights, observing the arrangement of the furniture, looking in the many places where a person could hide. He felt so much the master of his domain and so certain that there was no one there but himself that he didn't even bother to put on some clothes, and he carried out the inspection without taking any precautions.

After going over the ground floor, he went upstairs to the first floor. Jane's room was there, as well as a part of the house that he didn't like very much: the three large rooms with the Challenger ethnographic collection. He avowed such aversion to those dusty pieces, arranged and cataloged in mahogany and glass cases, that he tried several times to get rid of them by urging Jane to sell or donate them, something she refused to do. He entered the first room and immediately smelled its characteristic odor, an alchemy of smells: dry straw, dead vegetation, pitch, waxes, oily seeds, exotic bird wings, and dust. The unpleasant olfactory memory of a distant jungle.

Nauseated by it all, Henry hesitated. He caught sight of his image reflected in the glass of the large case that stood against the wall opposite the door. A muscular and naked body, slanted eyes and straight black hair, perfectly juxtaposed against the magnificent indigenous ornaments; it seemed to disapprove of his hesitation. Shocked, Henry stepped back. The richly adorned savage disappeared, but he didn't have time to feel relief, because a violent blow on the head knocked him down.

Before falling, he instinctively evaded a second blow. He heard the dry sound of a war club as it hit the floor, and he saw the bare feet of a white man run past him. He then lost consciousness.

When he came to, he tried to open his eyes, but a terrific headache blurred his vision. Colors and lights crowded his vision, even with his eyes closed. And when he managed to open them, the external world was a pulsating haze.

"He is bad off," a female voice murmured. "Why did he let himself get hit like that?"

Henry reacted; he tried to speak, but he wasn't able to articulate a single word, only moans of pain.

"There, there," a voice in his ear said, "everything will be all right."

Henry felt oddly calm; he trusted the voice. All that he wanted was to open his eyes and not feel pain. Without opening them, he tried to raise his hand to his head to see the extent of the damage, but he was stopped by firm hands.

"Stay still, young man," the voice ordered gently.

Little by little, the lights and colors went away, although the pain continued. The stupor hindered further reasoning, and Henry was overcome by the flashes of pain and moments of relief that alternated in his head. He made an effort and opened his eyes; he was in his own room lying on his bed.

A female face, iridescent like a flower splashed with dew, entered in his field of vision. She was serious, curious, and was wiping his lips with a piece of cotton soaked in a sweet liquid.

"Who are you?" Henry asked.

"Be still. You were nearly killed."

Henry tried to move his body; the pain wasn't as bad as he expected. He finally brought his hand to his head and felt the painful and damp lump. The intruder had aimed a little above the right ear.

THE END OF THE THIRD WORLD

"What happened?" Henry moaned, getting restless again.

"Stay still," she said, holding him down. "You are getting better; you're lucky that the blow didn't fracture your skull."

But Henry struggled to free himself from the stupor and escape the drowsiness that had weakened him. He was afraid that the intruder might decide to return to finish the job. Residential robberies were becoming more and more common in London. Every day the newspapers published articles on the rise in crime.

"Shit, he fainted again!" another feminine voice exclaimed.

"I'm not going to let him," the first voice said, shaking his face.

Henry opened his eyes and tried to rise; he was only able to sit on the edge of the bed. His room and the two women were whirling around him.

"What are you doing here?" he asked, alarmed.

"Silence!" one of them said.

"Are you all right?" the other wanted to know.

"I am better, I think," Henry responded, completely dazed.

"Do you suppose we can turn on the light?" one of them said.

"Are you crazy?" the other retorted. "What if the guy comes back?"

"But in the dark . . ." the woman protested.

"In the dark it's better. We'll be able to do everything that we need to do."

"What is it that you need to do?" Henry asked worriedly.

"Nothing, my little one," said the woman whom Henry had seen first.

LOST WORLD II

"Drink this," the other one ordered, raising a gourd cup to his lips.

"What is it?"

"Just drink!"

Henry obeyed; they possessed some kind of authority over him, a type of supremacy. The liquid was bitter; it slid down his throat, leaving it numb. When he finished drinking it, things abruptly stopped spinning around and he was overcome by a feeling of euphoria. He got up and stood on his own two feet.

"What is happening here? Who attacked me?"

A sharp pain made him double over; he lost his poise and once more tumbled on the bed, moaning. As the pain passed, Henry realized that one of the women had grabbed his penis. The pain that he had felt had been deliberately induced by her squeezing his organ.

"No more shouting. Do you understand?" she warned. "If you shout, he will return, and it will be all over."

Henry remained silent, almost motionless except for his rapid breathing.

"We came here to help you," the other woman said with a smile that gave him the shivers. "And you are really in need of a lot of help."

"Please, that hurts a lot. Be careful!"

"Ah, it hurts? . . . At least you're not dead," the woman said, tightening her grip on the defenseless appendage. "Do you want to see how you're not dead?"

She lessened the pressure and began to play with it, moving the wrinkled member from one side to another, sometimes pumping it gently. And with every movement it grew a few centimeters in length and width.

"Stop that," Henry protested, curled up on the bed.

"We won't stop," they responded in unison. "We very much wanted to meet you."

They didn't give him a chance to make another remark;

instead they began to lick and kiss his totally erect organ, covering it with saliva, dividing between them, with an equanimity drawn from years of practice, the time in which they made it disappear in their mouths with torturous suction.

"Please, please," Henry pleaded.

"Aren't you enjoying it?"

"Not now," he was saying. "Later, later."

"It has to be now," he heard.

"We don't have much time," one of them said.

Henry heard the two women, but their words didn't make any sense. A guttural sound escaped from his throat, and the excitement made him totally captive to their caprices. Resigned to the pleasant task, Henry tried to get a better look at the two intruders. They were small with delicious bodies, and they were dressed with an elegant French touch. But their gestures, as well as their manner of speaking, were neutral, devoid of any emotion.

"Ah! He's going to enjoy this," one of them exclaimed, stopping momentarily.

"No, don't stop," Henry protested.

"Look how it swings," one of them said, laughing.

"What do you think it's looking for, going from side to side like that?"

"And the head, look at how red it is."

"I think we squeezed it too much."

"Please," Henry moaned.

One of them put her hand on the restless organ and began to move it up and down vigorously until it produced spurts of opalescent drops. Henry sighed, his torment spent.

"What are you doing here? How did you get in?" he asked them again as soon as he was able to compose himself.

LOST WORLD II

"Weren't you looking for us?"

"I? But I don't even know you."

"Come on, get up, come with us," they ordered, pulling Henry off the bed.

"Wait," he said. "Let me put some clothes on first."

"No, afterwards. Let's go!"

The house was still dark, but the two women walked through it as though they were well acquainted with Enmore Park's meandering hallways. They climbed the stairs and went directly to the rooms that housed the Challenger collection.

"We failed, little one," they said, showing him one of the showcases.

Using a rather sophisticated brutality, someone had cracked open the case door and taken various pieces. Each one of the missing pieces left its shape perfectly outlined on the wine-colored velvet that covered the shelf.

"Shit!" Henry became furious. "If they wanted to steal these damn things, they didn't need to attack me."

"Do you have any idea of what was taken?" one of them asked him.

"How should I know?" he responded, irritated. "These things never interested me at all."

The two of them stood near the broken case and began to inspect the empty spaces, commenting in a professional tone.

"Here there was a blowgun. A precision weapon for targets of medium distance. This particular example was an extraordinary piece, with a sixty-five-pound thrust."

"And here was the dart. There are only three of these in the world."

"And do you know who makes these weapons?"

Henry shrugged his shoulders; he wasn't exactly interested in the stolen pieces. His major concern was the fact

THE END OF THE THIRD WORLD

that Enmore Park had been so easily broken into by the thief, as well as by the two women.

A resounding slap on the face made him recoil.

"Don't slap him so hard," one of them said.

"He deserves it; he still hasn't woken up."

"Do you know who these stolen weapons used to belong to?" they asked again.

"No, I don't," Henry responded.

"To a people who have since disappeared."

"But not completely."

"The blood of these people runs in your veins."

A chill ran through Henry's body, and he stared with sudden interest at the two women. He felt embarrassed, like a negligent child who hadn't learned his lesson right.

"You don't know anything, do you?" they said.

"Are you afraid?"

"I am," Henry mumbled, as if he were feeling pain.

"The people were called the Tapanhuma."

It was the first time he heard the name.

"Are you saying that I am one of them?"

"You'll find out," they said.

"Well, Jane ... You know who she is, right?" They nodded. "Jane always joked with me, saying that I was at the edge of extinction."

"She is very perceptive."

"But you aren't the only one."

"In the long run we will all become extinct."

"It's not really important."

"What is important is that the dart is going to be used, and we can't prevent it."

"But we would like to change the target."

"Just a minute!" Henry said. "I don't understand any of this."

"It's simple," they said.

"There is a flight to Caracas tonight. From there you can catch another one to Manaus."

"You are crazy!" Henry exclaimed.

"That is possible. To begin with, we shouldn't even be here."

Henry frowned at the last remark, but he tried to understand what was happening, going back over the strange sequence of events in order to see if he could find some sense in it all, some connection between the burglary of the pieces, the assault, and the presence of the two pushy women who didn't stop talking for a moment.

"We have to go," one of them said, smiling.

"No," Henry insisted, anxiously. "Answer one thing for me."

"What?"

"Why must I go to Manaus? What should I do there?"

"Look, that's two things that we have to answer."

"Please!"

"Actually, we don't know."

"But we are going along with you."

"The plane leaves in three hours."

"How am I going to pay for the trip?" Henry asked. "I don't own a credit card."

"Here are the plane tickets; look."

"We are leaving right away. Are you game? We have to go to the airport."

"All right," Henry said, surprised to hear his own voice accepting the absurd proposition.

They returned to his room, and Henry put some clothes and toiletries in a carry-on bag. He did everything very slowly, as if he were expecting that as time passed, that novel situation would cease to be.

"He is worried," one of the women said.

"Maybe he doesn't trust us," the other replied.

"Why should he?"

THE END OF THE THIRD WORLD

"That's true; there is no reason for him to believe us."

Henry finished dressing and looked at his watch. In spite of the deliberate delay in getting ready, less than five minutes had passed since he agreed to accompany the women.

"If only you were more out in the open," he complained.

The two women gestured that there was nothing they could do.

"We already told you that you shouldn't be worried."

"Everything will fall into place eventually."

"Or perhaps not," one of them said.

"You're right. Only in myths does everything fall into place."

"And in Chinese checkers."

"But there is no call for apprehension."

"Apprehension is nonsense."

"A whole lot of nonsense, because what is going to happen will happen, and that's that."

Henry picked up his bag, shook his head in disagreement, and said: "What the hell are you talking about?"

"Oh! Sorry."

"We didn't mean to annoy you."

"You're really getting me pissed off, you know?" Henry raved at them.

The two of them remained still, their eyes frozen and their faces expressionless, not human. Standing there, they seemed to be two mechanical dolls, with dead batteries.

From then on, and as long as the trip lasted, they were quiet, like two sulking girls, responding in monosyllables. The airport procedures, the immigration rituals, the unexpected customs routine, and the tedious hours lost during the flight all gave Henry time to better observe the two women. He didn't find out any more about them, but he was finally able to detect certain differences between the two of them. When they arrived in Caracas, not having an entry visa to Venezuela, they had to wait for the connecting flight in a room set aside for passengers in transit. In the four hours that they sat waiting in isolation, Henry was finally able to find out their names.

The two women appeared to be the same age, around twenty years old; they were the same height, and had the same brown skin color and black, almond-shaped eyes. Their bodies were delicately and well proportioned, but Iaci, who was the first one Henry had seen, had larger breasts. She always took the initiative, and when she spoke, she would gesture gracefully with her hands. The other one, who was called Ceuci, was more discreet, not exactly timid, just reserved; her eyes were a darker shade of black and expressed a curiosity and vivacity that contrasted with the modest movements of her body.

To Henry's complete surprise, the two women lived in Manaus on a magnificent property called "Pontiac Place," a name that evoked enormous American cars but paid homage to the great Ottawa chief.

"Chief Pontiac understood many things," Ceuci said. "In all the powwows, he would ask why the Ottawas were tolerating the whites' entry onto their lands."

"Even today Indians are trying to answer this question," Iaci said.

Once in their home, the two women became very pleasant; they told stories of the old times, laughing about love affairs, and crying about various tragedies. They said they belonged to a people who predated the Indians.

"We are Icamiabas," Iaci revealed.

"In our times, estrogen ruled."

"The Indians only appeared when testosterone became fashionable."

"But we aren't resentful."

THE END OF THE THIRD WORLD

"At least we were able to invent the clitoral orgasm."

"As for the Indians," Ceuci laughed, "the only thing they contributed was popcorn."

Henry was beginning to find the Icamiabas' hospitality quite delightful, but he still didn't feel completely at ease. He couldn't believe that he had crossed an ocean and the equator just to hear two witty women tell stories.

As night began to fall, they heard on the television that the ex-governor of Amazonas had been killed in mysterious circumstances, possibly murdered. According to the police investigation, an Indian blowgun had been used, and the victim had been struck with a dart poisoned with curare. The blowgun as well as the dart were in the hands of the authorities, and the television announcer made a point of showing the two pieces to the viewers. This was followed by an interview with an anthropologist who explained that the blowgun was quite common; it had been damaged, which rendered it useless as a weapon. But the dart was exceedingly special, one of only three such samples in existence in the world, all of which were duly cataloged in respected foreign collections; thus it was exceedingly odd that one of these darts should appear in Amazonia, much less in the chambers of the ex-governor.

"It is the poison dart stolen from your house," Iaci said.

"It isn't possible," Henry said doubtingly.

"But of course it is," Ceuci insisted.

"Now we know who hit you on the head."

"And stole the blowgun and the poison dart."

"You are joking!" Henry exclaimed.

"No, we aren't. We have very little sense of humor."

"It was the Jihad Jívaros," Iaci said.

"What?"

"Jihad Jívaros," Ceuci repeated. "It is a revolutionary organization."

"Headed by Commander Muhammad Azancoth."

"They have undertaken a series of operations in Europe and the United States."

"They've raided a number of ethnographic collections."

"They have only taken weapons: arrows, poison darts, et cetera."

"All of them poisoned with curare."

"And belonging to extinct tribes."

"Wait!" Henry shouted. "Slow down. I'm not understanding anything."

The two fell silent, fixing their analytical black eyes on Henry. He rewarded the breathing spell with a bewildered smile, while he attempted to make sense of what he was hearing.

"Excuse me," Henry said with sweet sincerity, "I am a little slow."

"We are the ones who should excuse ourselves," Iaci said.

"You said you didn't know anything. At least that is what you told me in London. Now we see on the television that a man has been killed, and right away you cut loose with all kinds of information about the case. How did you come to such a conclusion? The impression that I have is that you know a lot more than what you are saying and that you just want to use me."

They shook their heads, annoyed.

"Don't be an idiot, little one."

"We really didn't know anything."

"Just a detail here and another there."

"But not enough to complete the puzzle."

"We knew that someone was stealing pieces from ethnographic collections in different parts of the world. Only pieces of extinct tribes."

THE END OF THE THIRD WORLD

"We were watching the Challenger collection just by chance."

"We thought that the robbers would show up there because the collection has many pieces from extinct tribes."

"At the same time, we had a list of the targets of the Jihad Jívaros."

"These individuals were slated to be killed in the next few days."

"Then we saw that the ex-governor was murdered."

"And due to the fact that his name was at the top of the list—"

"We deduced that it was the Jihad Jívaros who had robbed the Challenger collection pieces."

"Elementary, my dear Henry."

"But we don't want to use you. You can rest assured."

"You have very little importance in all of this."

"There is nothing that you can do."

"We decided to bring you along with us because we can't resist such a handsome fellow as yourself."

"And we thought that you would find it amusing to stay with us for a while."

"Having a few good screws."

"Remembering the days when our grandparents screwed your grandparents."

Too tired to be angry, Henry turned to look at the television and experienced a shock: The screen showed different groups of people who were arriving at a local hotel. He wasn't able to understand the newscaster, but he had the impression that he had seen a lovely redhead who looked just like Jane Challenger.

"Who else do these terrorists intend to kill?" Henry asked.

"If we knew," Iaci said, "the Jihad Jívaros would be able to attach a few more names to their list."

"The only thing that we know for sure is that all of these people will be brought together in one place."

"They will be aboard the *Leviathan*."

"And it follows that the Jihad Jívaros will also be aboard."

"What is the name of the ship?" Henry asked, stunned, exhaling a long sigh.

Iaci and Ceuci smiled indulgently.

"Leviathan," Ceuci responded.

That, he thought, is the ship that Jane is going to board.

"Perhaps I'm not worth much," Henry said, "but at least I can help my sister. She is going to be on that ship."

"Her name doesn't appear on the Jihad Jívaros hit list," Iaci said.

Henry wasn't willing to bet on the terrorists' criteria, and much less on the two women's sense of deduction.

"I'm going to stop Jane from embarking," he said.

"At least you can try," Iaci said.

"And you can count on us to help you," Ceuci said.

"It isn't necessary," Henry responded. "I don't need any help to talk to Jane."

But his efforts were useless. He found out right away that he wouldn't be able to go to the hotel where Jane was staying, because he was a suspect in the ex-governor's murder, and the police were looking for him. And in addition, Jane had simply refused to recognize the danger.

Now, sitting in the moonlight, he remembered his father's words; the damn city seemed more and more like a trap, the beginning and the end of a story that Professor Challenger had attempted to write. First he took Henry's grandfather to London, where he died in 1962, four years before Henry's birth. Next, in order to provide him with a companion, or, as some gossip had

THE END OF THE THIRD WORLD

it, so he wouldn't chase the maids, Professor Challenger brought him a wife from the jungle. Henry's mother was the product of that union, born in 1945, in a London beset by bombing raids and rationing. When the professor died, the small tribe at Enmore Park was an integral part of the Challenger family. Great care was given to prevent miscegenation; thus in 1965 they sent the young daughter off to the Amazon to look for a husband. There she met and married Henry's father.

The next year, a baby was born to the young woman, but she had little vocation for motherhood, and the baby was cared for by his grandmother. Henry's father died of pneumonia in 1968, and his mother spent the following decade trying to organize a religious sect that promised the faithful a world without evil, until she disappeared one Sunday morning in 1979, never to be heard of again. From the age of thirteen on, Henry began to live a life completely removed from his ethnic origins. The truth is that he detested anything having to do with them. If it had been possible, he would have changed everything. Since he couldn't change his facial features, he preferred to be considered an Oriental. He consciously tried to be the last stop, the final stage: his own ethnocide.

Henry looked up at the horizon bathed in moonlight; a chill ran through his body. He forced from his mind the frightening thought: the image of an inscrutable Kashmiri imprisoned in a tropical moonlit night, an evocation of a page out of Kipling.

It Was Horrible in the Forest (Repeat)

His eyes were blurred from a lack of sleep, but Sir Delamare wouldn't give in. Seated in a chair, looking out the hotel window, he brooded irritably. He felt he had been passed over like some useless old household article. Spender, sitting beside him, was slightly uneasy about failing to find any explanation for so many disappearances. Jane Challenger and Billy Lester were nowhere to be found. And to make matters worse, the Chilean had also disappeared without a trace from the poolside bar.

The room was filled with smoke, because Sir Delamare lit one cigarette after another. Spender wondered fearfully if the old man might not sit there, smoking like a boiling teapot, until dawn, but he couldn't find the courage to suggest he go to bed.

"This is just like the Challenger woman," he had said. "She is foolhardy, and she's undermining me. Be careful or she'll do the same to you, Spender."

Spender didn't respond, but he struggled to believe in his boss, because it was a relief to know he was being excluded from that point on from having any responsibility for Jane Challenger's actions. Having arrived at that hotel full of eccentric guests and surrounded by exotic native people was more than he could take.

But Spender's relief was short-lived. The doorbell rang, and he went to answer it. At first he thought it must

THE END OF THE THIRD WORLD

be room service bringing something Sir Delamare had requested, because he found three men dressed in the usual hotel uniform. Two were carrying trays, and the other pushed a meal cart. But it is hard to trick Spender's sense of smell, and he hesitated only an instant before grabbing Sir Delamare and pulling the astonished lord to the floor, nearly smothering him beneath his own body.

It was the Jihad Jívaros command. The guerrillas uncovered the trays and the cart with incredible speed, revealing stacks of books, and they proceeded to throw the heavy volumes at the gray wool target curled up on the floor. Each projectile was a book of more than five hundred pages that landed with admirable precision on Spender's butt.

"Imperialism isn't a simple scapegoat," they shouted.

His calm British conservatism offended, Sir Delamare felt the obligation to strike back; coming between Spender's moans, Sir Delamare's voice could be heard.

"Attack, you idiots. Blame imperialism."

"Get your claws out of Amazonia!" the Jihad Jívaros shouted.

Magnificently bound books flew through the room, aimed at Spender's butt, yet Sir Delamare continued his harangue.

"Come on, I want to hear you blame imperialism," he shouted. "What's that? You're not going to blame the Americans? If imperialism did not exist, your incompetence would certainly necessitate its invention."

The Jihad Jívaros snarled at his provocations, but the initial impact had been lost. In some way, Sir Delamare's defiant words had the effect of a cold shower. A few books were still flying through the room haphazardly when Jane Challenger and Billy Lester entered. Before beating a retreat, the command landed a direct hit on

Lester's forehead with a thick volume of the Gundrisses. The journalist, familiar with the Marxist bibliography, wasn't surprised by the weight of the book, but he still couldn't see for the red stars whirling around his head.

"Are you all right?" Jane asked him.

"It was nothing," Lester responded, holding his hand over the painful bump that revolutionary thought had caused to adorn his head. "Where is Sir Delamare?"

"Give me some help over here, you idiots!" Sir Delamare shouted. "This imbecile has fainted on top of me, and I'm going to end up with fractured ribs."

When Sir Delamare was finally on his feet, freed from Spender's efficient protection, he noticed that the two of them were dressed in their nightclothes. Lester was wearing just a pajama bottom, and Jane had on a cotton T-shirt.

"We were nearly asleep," Lester explained, uncomfortably.

"We came running as soon as we heard the shouting," Jane added, haughtily, without acknowledging the bold appraisal that Sir Delamare gave her.

The old lord coughed and discreetly averted his eyes.

"Why were they throwing books?" Jane asked, picking up a beautifully bound first edition of Lukacs's aesthetics.

"It was the Jihad Jívaros," Sir Delamare said.

"Do you really think so?" Lester asked with doubt.

"What did they want?" Jane asked, intrigued by the books bearing the signet of the British Museum Library.

"I presume it was an assassination attempt," Sir Delamare said. "They wanted to kill us, Miss Challenger."

"With books?" Lester was still full of doubt.

"Of course, with books," Sir Delamare said, irritated. "Some of these volumes weigh at least six kilos. Correctly thrown, they are as lethal as a stone or a brick."

"A post-Gutenberg form of stoning," Jane commented.

"Precisely, Miss Challenger. The Jihad Jívaros are ingenious."

"You didn't insist on denying the existence of imperialism, did you?" Lester asked, still a little stunned.

"I think it is better if you go back to bed, my good fellow," Sir Delamare responded with a wink.

The next day, they all boarded the *Leviathan*.

Book Four

Cucarachopitecus Tragicus

On the Unusual Habits of Writers (Repeat)

To everyone's despair, an incalculable number of Central Americans tried to pass through the U.S. immigration without an entry visa and, judging by the bad temper of the immigration officers, without a single valid document. Since I was lucky enough to have arrived on a flight just after that one, which was full of men in starched *guayaberas* and ladies in flowered dresses, I could hardly imagine what was waiting for me. I already knew that an inordinate amount of time was spent dealing with the Kennedy Airport bureaucrats, one of the most neurotic bunch of immigration officers in the world, but that particular morning one couldn't blame the immigration service for the slow lines. The problem was that each time one of the Central Americans stepped up to the counter, he handed the officer a fistful of grimy papers, and a complicated hassle ensued. Judging by the number of *guayaberas* on the premises, things promised to drag on indefinitely because there didn't seem to be a single document in order.

Two hours later, the officers decided to get tough, and they called the police. I breathed a lot easier seeing the ratio of *guayaberas* reduced to zero, but then I discovered that one ought not to depend solely on mere visual impressions, especially if we are in a line at Kennedy Airport. It turned out that behind the Central Americans, and without any evidence of their traditional clothing, was another group equally unaccustomed

LOST WORLD II

to documents, stamps, and visas, and what was most aggravating was that they didn't even speak Spanish, much less English. They were Iranians, most likely supporters of Reza Pahlavi, avidly awaiting the opportunity to dive headlong into their dream of an affluent society. The result was that I spent almost four hours in the immigration line, and when my turn arrived, I could see that the officer picked up my passport with trepidation. However, he immediately breathed a sigh of relief as he saw that the visa was in order, the bearer didn't wear either a turban or a sombrero, he could speak reasonably intelligently, and he intended on staying in the country only two weeks. Leaving the airport behind, I caught a cab, which proceeded to get caught in the middle of a traffic jam on the Triborough Bridge heading for Manhattan.

"Why in the hell do I always return to this city?" I asked myself in Portuguese, venting pent-up anger.

"B'gyapardon," the cab driver said. He was a large, bucktoothed mulatto who then asked if I was Greek.

It had been three years since I set foot in New York, and here I was again, repeating the same mistake, doubly backsliding, in fact, because I had interrupted work on a novel to accept the invitation to attend a conference, one of those things that we do without sufficiently weighing the consequences. The first mistake was having come to take part in a seminar on Latin American literature in the city of Salem's Lot, New Hampshire, organized by the local university. This prompted the second mistake: that of having to stay in New York for a day and a half.

The bucktoothed mulatto veered onto Harlem River Drive with such speed that the taxi did an imitation of one of those stamping flamenco dancers, in some kind of perverse effort to remind me what I was doing there.

THE END OF THE THIRD WORLD

It was inevitable that, for professional reasons, I would return to New York; still it was difficult to resign myself to the fact. But nothing justified having to face another one of those seminars on Latin American literature, especially after the previous vexations in Berlin and Rome. It was always the same: soberly dressed and serious Hispanic literati who switched roles, first ousted from power, then respected members of the government. I was forced to exhaust my lowly "Portuñol," because no one ever thought of providing an interpreter for those of us who spoke the last flower of Lacio in the innocent assumption that all Latin Americans must automatically speak Spanish as fluently as a Honduran general.

I spent nearly the entire day and a half in the hotel room, thinking about the *Leviathan*'s trip down the Amazon River, about its passengers' fate—all of which was on hold, because quite unexpectedly, I was the one who had embarked on a journey. It was partly because I never liked the streets of Manhattan; they were always in a state of permanent change, with chronically boarded-up sidewalks, traffic jams, multitudes of annoyed faces, mounds of trash, and the irreversible atmosphere of the Third World. Whenever I hear someone say he likes New York, I can't hide my surprise. It was definitely the last city in the world that I would voluntarily choose to visit; nevertheless, I had visited it so many times that I lost count. Only my feelings had never changed: New York frightened me.

Why am I afraid of that city? I honestly tried to understand this fear, but I only found a few hypotheses. My first trip was around 1972, when I still harbored no prejudices. After having lived six years in Sao Paulo, and having a reasonably good command of English, going to New York didn't represent any kind of special problem. Anyone who has lived in a complex city, especially such a baroque urban layout as Sao Paulo, has already developed such a keen sense of direction that the urban "rationality" of New York is a breeze. In that city, no one gets lost, geographically speaking; the people lose themselves in other labyrinths. I believe that even this so-called urban rationality is utilized as a kind of spatial sublimation for the violence that showers down on the people.

It is said that New York is the town of bucks and services. The Americans call it the Big Apple, an insipid fruit that the Puritan imagination links with sin and temptation. And the succulent piece of the Big Apple is Manhattan, a rotting and scintillating island, where one finds the financial conglomerates, the department stores, the movie houses, and the theaters. The rest is merely the rest, beyond the tunnel, Brooklyn, suburbia, weekend oblivion.

I think that the city's problems begin with this strong link between money and services. Naturally, in every large metropolis this link exists. Without money one remains marginalized, on the periphery, making do with the scraps. Those who live in Rio or Sao Paulo know exactly what I mean. But New York became a metropolis relatively recently; it achieved international fame only in the last forty years, although it always showed a certain vocation for it. New York rapidly became the most important port in the country, and early on, with the waves of European immigrants, it proved to be sufficiently attractive to transform itself into a cosmopolitan center, by far the most stimulating city of North America, and a catalytic force for the whole American continent.

The city's atmosphere of crudeness, if to a certain extent bothersome, prevents the city from being contaminated by the provincial mediocrity of the rest of the United States. There is no place for commiseration or complacency there. It's all or nothing at all. The rapidity with which the city became a metropolis didn't allow it to develop equality in the distribution of services. In Rio, or in Paris, even if you don't have them in large amounts, you at least have access to reasonable public services. But in New York, the public services border on sordid destitution. Without a doubt, the public transportation is sordid. The subway system is nauseating and anything but punctual. If you have to rely on a public service office, you will come up against a terrible bureaucracy. That's not even mentioning public protection, since everyone knows that it was the New York police that invented the business of not registering small complaints so as to keep the crime statistics from rising.

One thing is sure; I still can't understand why I fear that city, nor why it disgusts me so. And I can't even decry the lack of equality. My stays in the city were always great, even though they were quick and packed with a full schedule. Some friends I have there say that I need to know New York better, but I don't know if I can place such a thing in the category of necessity. My first hypothesis regarding the persistent aversion that I feel toward New York is cultural. My Amazonian upbringing is Francophone and European. Perhaps that is why I feel so good in Paris or Lisbon. I don't even particularly like Parisians, but for me the atmosphere of the city is entirely breathable; it is as if it were my milieu. I walk around Paris and my feet recognize the streets, my body rejoices. I understand why and how Paris sparkles; it was the last great Latin metropolis. The rhythm of Paris is like a piece of music where I can add a few measures of my own, because I know its logic. The rhythm of New York tends to provoke within me a repudiation, even though its logic as a city of the

LOST WORLD II

same hemisphere where I live does not escape me.

A lasting impression of the city invariably is caused by the masses of destitute, miserable people falling through the cracks. These people arrive from all parts of the country and the world. The majority are Third World people. They all come with the idea of biting a big chunk out of the Apple, but the most they manage to do is drag their dream through underemployment, isolated in the squalid tenements. Nothing is more abject than the condition of the migrant, and New York today seems to be the Mecca of immigration. The immigrants are creatures who attempt to confuse hope with what is possible. Between the two they are forced to create monstrous mechanisms of accommodation. They become the real Philistines, trying to break down barriers with the few arms they bear. And they end up being used like doormats, because they are unprepared, because they are originally from cultures that are intractable to capitalism, and especially because they never come to master the language.

I think that my horror of New York derives from this warehouse nature that the city cultivates. I feel disgust when I see an Oriental immigrant, for example, walking about the city in his national dress and begging to be assimilated. I feel disgust of the Central Americans and the false humility with which they throw themselves on the ground to be stepped on by the rich in exchange for a few dollars. I have completely lost the capacity to feel pity for these imbeciles of underdevelopment. New York, to some extent, serves as a trap that holds these unfortunate souls captive. Even the examples of those who are supposedly victorious cause me disgust, like those idiots who wash dishes for years until they finally get together enough money to open a limousine rental business.

THE END OF THE THIRD WORLD

The anger that I felt over finding myself in New York lasted intact during the short flight on the small plane to Salem's Lot; and indeed, it even grew as I found myself in the middle of an academic reception with all those tweed suits, and khaki blouse and skirt combinations. Too few hors d'oeuvres and too much California white wine stimulated the Anglo-Hispanic commotion that tried to reconcile liberal professors with a high degree of hyperopia and writers with low-level authorial rights.

It was just my luck that the Hispanics were the same bunch as always, either because they are the only ones on a continent with few publishers or because they are experts at grabbing all the invitations. Whatever it is, there seems to be a unanimous addiction to a free meal.

The next day, when the first session of the seminar began, I was possessed by Professor Challenger and I asked for the floor.

"Is this seminar really concerning Latin American literature? And if it is, where are the writers from Haiti, Guadeloupe, and Quebec? Because Francophone literature has been forgotten. Where is Rene Depestre? Why was Roch Carrier not invited? And Marie-Claire Blais; couldn't she come? And Anne Hebert, and Rejeane Ducharme, and Antoine Mallet, and Victor-Levy Beaulieu? What happened with them?"

In the front row, observing with a sarcastic air the commotion created by my words, sat Juan Sender, the real, true Juan Sender, not the one who attacks duchesses, rather the reluctant lacerator of careless fools. I nodded discreetly in his direction, and Sender responded, raising his right thumb. The second thing that could cause Sender to lose his senses was to be called Latin American.

"What, Quebec?" one of the seminar organizers stuttered. "Quebec is Latin America?"

LOST WORLD II

The professor's puzzlement was revealing in all senses: Canadians from Quebec don't eat tacos with chili, they don't use sombreros, they don't take siestas, they don't have strong-armed dictators throughout a hundred years of solitude, and they don't rock their children to sleep to the sound of "La Cucaracha." Aside from that, Canada is a creditor nation, not an international debtor. How can it fit into a Latin American mold?

The seeds of discord, however, were already planted. But despite my questions, very little changed. Because the term *Latin American* is not a cultural concept that accurately reflects the unfolding of Latin civilization in America. What is ingrained in the minds of these well-intentioned people is a geopolitical stigma that imagines a well-drawn demarcation between the northern and southern continents. Quebec's good fortune is being on the wrong side of the Rio Grande, and I was aware that only the most gullible person would be capable of considering Quebec as one of those Latin watersheds. In my mind's eye, I saw the image of Maple White's land, Professor Challenger's mythological plateau, a place of such obstinate conservatism that it was bypassed by evolution itself, like some sort of paleontological metaphor of Latin American. An ideal lost world for research of mentalities and idiosyncrasies, fossil fuel for explanations concerning the persistence of backwardness, and a territory quarantined as an example of the neofeudal tenacity and unfortunate ethnic miscegenation.

The worst thing is that this Maple White of sweat and rumba seems to count on internal help in the perpetuation of its isolation. This was evident in the visible displeasure with which the audience reacted upon hearing Quebec mentioned. And notice that I even emphasized Haiti and Guadeloupe. But I shouldn't be surprised, because the label of Latin American not only brings with it prejudices, but it legitimizes the discomfort of being a member of the elite in a lost world that needs to continue in its isolation in order that this same elite doesn't disappear.

"Are you going insane?" Juan Sender asked, having a good time at my expense some time later. "To include Quebec in Latin America is a terribly low blow. I don't think the Quebecois are going to find it amusing. After all, Quebec's richness would exclude it, because well-fed people don't evoke pity from anyone."

"I can't avoid feeling irritated," I tried to explain. "It must be because literature in Portuguese is just as buried in the Castilian alluvion as is literature in French."

"But you are becoming resentful again," he retorted.

"You're right," I said.

"Resentment, always the resentment," Sender said, each time more sarcastically. "But the idea of including Quebec was diabolical. Without the Canadian Francophones, only the legitimate Latin Americans remain, the cockroaches, as they're called in the United States, with their social ills, their vocation for being victims of history, and their denunciations against imperialism. At least for a Chilean like myself, who knows only too well that we are not a sweet-smelling flower, Quebec redeems me."

"And I don't think that the Quebecois will be offended," I explained, "because they are proud of their Latin culture."

"But that's not important," Sender said. "If they were here, we would have to speak of literature and not of politics. Have you had a chance to get a good look at those who are participating in the seminar? Well, there must be a tacit complicity between the organizers and the unfortunate Latin American writers. I know the scenario well: These people like to punish themselves; they would love a tribunal where they could do some bloodletting in the name of the old rhetoric or recrimination. A short time ago, I heard a colleague accuse American imperialism of filling the bookstores in his country with so many best-sellers, which meant that readers weren't reading his books."

"I've heard the same accusation before," I said. "I don't have any more patience with this kind of nationalistic drivel."

"What he prefers not to accept is that imperialistic forces would never be strong enough to squeeze out of our bookstores an authentic national literature if we happened to produce such a thing. Now, don't ask me to give a definition of authentic national literature."

Sender paused and looked at me with the eyes of a disbelieving visionary; his thin, arched eyebrows belied any hint of humility, and his elongated face bore the expression of one for whom literature had little legitimacy.

"Now consider our hosts' good intentions," he continued in a husky voice. "They listen enthralled as we enumerate the violations of freedom in our countries, and they are mortified when we accuse them of complicity."

"I must confess that I always found it so strange that we are invited to discuss literature, and we end up responding to questions about the illiteracy rate, infant mortality, and the stability of the current regime."

"I was present when that professor asked how you felt writing novels in a city where two hundred people are assassinated in a single weekend."

"Damn, that ticked me off," I said indignantly. "What an age we're living in. It's a good thing that Boccaccio isn't alive; if he were, they would want to know how he could go on writing without proper sanitary facilities when the plague was raging throughout Florence."

THE END OF THE THIRD WORLD

"I have the impression that the answer you gave didn't please them at all," Sender said. "They did like our young militant writer, who is more militant than writer. At least he assured them that he writes in order to protest the suffering of the masses. What a shame that in his country, which is essentially agricultural, there aren't any publishers, and the measly little books that he writes are published with government support."

Our chat continued in this tone for the rest of the afternoon, without our even imagining what our hosts had arranged for entertainment that evening. When we entered the university cafeteria, we saw lined up on an improvised stage a group of young people dressed in colorful ponchos, ready to play those shrill and maddening Andean flutes, which, as far as I'm concerned, were responsible for the downfall of the Inca Empire. It was a folkloric concert in our honor. I resolutely sat through it all, without saying a word, because the young musicians were children of Chilean exiles. God only knows what we do in the name of the good-neighbor policy.

But all of that was a lesson for me. Once this business of Latin American is not a recognition of our civilization, becoming instead a geopolitical ghetto, a kind of bag of cats in which they want to tie us all up together, I bail out. Now, when I get invitations, right away I tell them: I don't speak Spanish, my name isn't Pancho, and I don't live at the foot of the Sierra Madre Mountains. Because when a significant part of the continent becomes mere geopolitical folklore, the hyphen disappears, the whole thing smacks of compliance disguised as libertarian rhetoric, feeding a guilty conscience. Conan Doyle's lost world at least leaves open some possibility of evolution.

For those who continue to like the concept of Latin identity, let me just say that I lean more toward Luandino

LOST WORLD II

Vieira, who is Latin African in this sense, than toward my friend Juan Sender, even if it gives him hives when they call him Latin American.

"No one goes around calling the Congolese Latin Africans," Sender often said furiously. "You remember Luandino Vieira, and you do well to do so. He is lucky that this business of Latin African doesn't exist."

"This would also be too much for our First World friends," I responded. "They aren't sufficiently liberal to see the Portuguese-speaking Africans as Latins. Perhaps a high yellow or light mulatto with a good suntan might pass."

"The French did try," Sender retorted. "In the elementary primers that the children studied in school in French African colonies, there were references to the Gallic peoples as 'our ancestors.'"

This caused me to laugh.

"It really is funny," Sender said. "I have a friend, Mongo Beti, a wonderful novelist from the Republic of Cameroon. He speaks an impeccable French, and he doesn't seem at all like the English-speaking African writers, who cause Shakespeare to turn over in his grave every time they open their mouths. Well, since nothing resembling this Latin African thing exists, Mongo Beti failed to pass the French censorship, during the same period of time that the French public was fascinated by the Latin American literary boom. Sometimes I have the feeling that the French only take seriously that literature that enters the country with the consent of the Quai D'Orsay. If a particular country is so unfortunate as not to have writers with a vocation for diplomatic positions, it will never achieve a citation in the Apostrophe."

I remembered at that time a short story that I had tried to write. If course, I abstained from bringing the subject up since Sender could misinterpret my intentions,

THE END OF THE THIRD WORLD

and I was afraid of the consequences. But the short story was about a Brazilian writer who one day meets the greatest living Latin American writer. The Brazilian was traveling through Europe, going from city to city, from one train station to another, but in the intervals, there was always a luncheon with solicitous professors of Portuguese language and the requisite readings of excerpts from his works. The trip coincided with one of the hottest summers that Europe had experienced in many years, and the writer crossed the stifling hot countryside sleepily, wondering if this wasn't the ideal climate for an exotic Third World type like himself.

Once in a while, he would come across people from his own stomping grounds, colorful salsa groups, samba bands, Andean flute players. But rarely did he meet literary luminaries all dressed up and making the routes of development. The writer would marvel at how different the latter were from the former fellow Latins. They nearly always were having conniption fits because they couldn't get accommodations in certain hotels, or stamping their feet because they had been scheduled to do a reading at the same time as some rival writer. Some puffed-up Andean author had returned to the airport when he found out that an adversary from the Pacific coastal region was also scheduled in the program. This same author from the Pacific went into hysteria when he discovered that the speech that was to open the program would be given by a Mexican poet and diplomat. The Brazilian writer almost excused his colleague's hysteria when he heard the Mexican's speech in which the geographic ignorance of the diplomat-poet was so great that in his mind the so-called Latin American region was limited to only those fortunate ones who spoke the language of a great artist of his country, or, if you will, the language of Cantinflas.

But the surprises didn't stop there, because the salsa group, the samba musicians, and the flutists got together in order to block three very popular figures of popular Brazilian music who should have appeared in the city's philharmonic, forcing them instead to perform in a large, decadent discotheque. Another time, he was taken aback by a literary critic from Argentina, known for his penchant for living the easy life of academia in universities in the United States. The critic affirmed that literature in Brazil was provincial and that all of the works of a great Brazilian writer of the 1930s didn't hold a candle to *Don Segundo Sombra*, that much-lauded novel that idealizes the Argentine gaucho. The Brazilian swallowed hard; he doubled his tact when dealing with sensitive ex-torture victims, political exiles, and government bureaucrats; that was, until he found himself face-to-face with an affable old man, a lonely and reserved fellow, discreetly dressed in a gray suit.

This fellow, with a craggy face and an expression of one who is not long for this world, was considered the greatest writer south of the Rio Grande. A European colleague introduced them, and the author shook his hand with an unexpected strength and effusiveness. They didn't talk for long, but at least the works of that legendary writer weren't unknown to him. Actually, his works were limited to two books, a novel and a book of short stories, published more than thirty years ago, and each no more than a hundred pages long. Perhaps because the Brazilian was steeped in the literary tradition of great Portuguese writers of the ilk of Camoes and Fernao Mendes Pinto, the short stories and novel hadn't impressed him much. He liked poisonous potions that corroded the present in search of the future; for this reason he didn't understand the fascination that the author awakened in the academic and official circles throughout the world, since his was literature that was typical of an archaic world. He recognized that the work didn't delight in reflecting the agonies of the archaic and the rustic; it achieved its success through a tragic despair. Nevertheless, it was difficult for him to accept that this work had been transformed into a paradigm of the so-called Latin American literature. Unfortunately, that is what happened; and it was even expected that Latin American writers would limit themselves to making of literature a kind of subproduct of the agrarian economy.

Some time later, when the Brazilian writer was passing through a small city deep in the heartland of the country, he saw the great Latin American author leaving the city, surrounded by professors and students. He stood on the platform watching the legendary figure board the train, without suspecting that some months later, death would visit the man. When he read the news of his death, he thought about how strange it was that the author who hadn't written anything in thirty years had become the symbol of Latin American literature, and that only death dared to bring to an end the incredible sterility of the most incredibly sterile writer he would ever know.

Upon leaving the train station, the writer was taken to a local university, enclosed in a classroom, and obliged to participate in a seminar on Caribbean literature that went on for ten hours. The objectives of the seminar were particularly clear, but this seemed to be of little concern. One by one the presenters spoke, expounding and giving analyses of the topic that were increasingly more complex, always asking the writer to give his views on what was being presented. Of course, the writer couldn't add much, and even after he had insisted several times that he must have been invited by mistake, he didn't seem to get through to them. The strangest thing was that during the debates that followed each presentation, a

LOST WORLD II

young man dressed in a poncho would raise the issue of cultural identity.

The tenth time that the young man got up, adjusted his poncho, and asked about the "question of identity," the writer lost his patience.

"Look here, *amigo*!" the writer said, doing his best to recall Spanish words he had picked up in Mexican films. "There is no identity problem in Brazil. The Ministry of Justice and the Secretariat of Public Security have given all Brazilians an identification card. If one has an identity problem, he can take out his card and look at it. And the identity problem is solved. This is a technology that Brazil can share with its sister states."

I still didn't know how to end the story. Sometimes I imagined a tragic finish. The young fellow in a poncho with identity problems wouldn't exactly suffer from amnesia but rather would be imbued with the political tradition of the continent. As such, he would take out a revolver and finish off the writer, bringing the seminar to a close with a concrete example of the cultural disparities up until then unknown to the Europeans.

In any event, it wasn't necessary to upset my friend Juan Sender with my doubts. Especially since he had once told me that he believed this business of searching for one's roots to be a dangerous undertaking.

"You Brazilians, for example," he explained, "have the Lusitanian tradition as an integral part of your identity. If you were to search for your roots, you would find that deep in the soul of Portugal is antagonism for Spain."

"What in the devil are you talking about?" I asked, surprised.

"Simply that it is dangerous to transport the Iberian peninsula to the other side of the Atlantic."

I began to laugh, and Juan Sender got angry.

"I'm serious," he said.

"I can see you are," I responded.

"Then why are you laughing?"

"I'm not laughing because I find what you're saying to be funny," I assured him. "I'm just remembering a short story that I was planning to write."

"I don't want to know about it," he said preemptively.

I agreed, nodding my head and making signs with my hands for him to calm down. But I couldn't stop thinking about the meeting between the Brazilian writer and the greatest living Latin American writer, and the fact that on this side of the continent there was no desire for the great American novel. Rather there was an anxious search for the greatest writer of this and the greatest poet of that.

Take a Chance on Miss Challenger

Salem's Lot is a city of seventy thousand inhabitants, near the Vermont state line. The city proper isn't much more than a few streets surrounding the mall, which, in turn, surrounds a large supermarket. The majority of the people live in the rural area, working on small potato farms. The potato was responsible for the university being founded there. When someone tells you to go plant a potato in Salem's Lot, it isn't exactly an insult. Just the opposite. The prosperity of the small burg happened during the depression, thanks to the enterprising spirit of an Irish immigrant who made potato growing a noble endeavor. In 1929 he discovered a method of producing potato chips on a large scale, which meant they could be packaged in six-ounce bags and sold so cheaply that anyone could afford them.

When the depression hit hard in the United States, Salem's Chips were practically the only feed accessible to the millions of unemployed. The immigrant became a millionaire overnight and spread prosperity about him. He was the one who in 1939 donated the funds to found the university, in addition to acquiring various works of art in Europe and financing one of the most complete libraries on Ireland that exists. Since he remained a modest man all his life, the only public record of his gesture is a bronze plaque at the entrance to the rectory that bears his name, dates of birth and death, and a proverb in Latin: *Minima de malis*.

THE END OF THE THIRD WORLD

The house that once belonged to Salem's Lot's benefactor belongs today to the university, and it is used to receive guests. Some of the writers were lodged there, under the care of two ladies of indeterminable ages. Once again it was possible to sense the modesty of the old proprietor, because it wasn't a mansion in spite of the fact it was spacious and modern, a project of a local architect, a disciple of Frank Lloyd Wright. Taking advantage of a natural slope in the terrain, the house jutted forth over a forest of pine trees, elms, silver maples, lindens, and junipers, at night conjuring the setting of a Gothic novel.

Since I wasn't the least bit interested in the seminar, I avoided the subsequent sessions and spent my time walking through the forest, admiring the silence, the calm, and the subtle perfume of the decaying leaves. I felt like walking barefoot, stepping on the dark earth and the carpet of moss, but I wasn't quite brave enough, because it was still a little cold, in spite of the approaching summer. I didn't see any birds or field mice, and I noticed that there were few insects; some bees flitted around some white forest anemones, and a solitary butterfly, lazily fanning its copper-colored wings, sat on a thicket of wild raspberry.

But I was restless; the fact that I wasn't participating in the program made me as uncomfortable as participating did. There was no way out; I shouldn't have accepted the invitation in the first place. My concern was to not hurt the feelings of my hosts, who, after all, believed they were somehow helping us; nor did I want to appear haughty to my colleagues who diligently attended the presentations and the debates. As a Brazilian, my position was delicate; I didn't have anything in common with the young Nicaraguan short story writer who felt the need for legitimacy, much less with the anguish of the eternally exiled Guatemalan novelist, or the proud indignation of the old Ecuadorian poet. With all its misery, Brazil could still offer its writers a vast horizon of readers, a literary tradition with continuity, and the possibility of escaping the strict social function reserved for the act of writing when exercised on the periphery of the world. Brazil was interregnum, transitional, one step beyond the others and one step short of the epicenter. That is why our literature—along with all of our culture—never needed to legitimize political options, nor express anguished circumstances or proud wounds. For that reason, the public demonstrations of Brazilian culture overseas have always been spontaneous and independent of governmental interference or private intentions.

But there was something else, more personal, almost unmentionable, that dismayed me in these encounters. It was the confirmation of just how much there is in Brazilians of what I find most detestable in our poverty-stricken neighbors, but poverty itself can't be the only culprit. We are also prisoners of the wretched corporative societies that took control of a part of the culture as if it had sole right to the social capital. There are tremendous inequities and ruined lives, but they make an appraisal of all the crumbs in order to guarantee for themselves the positions, offices, scholarships, and sinecures: a bizarre fraternity of the middle class keeping track of the achievements, assuring for themselves the best rags. The artists become civil service employees. Art itself is supernumerary. In the most capitalist country of the world, the writers, for example, present the least middle-class biographies imaginable. Ex–truck drivers, ex-stevedores, ex–meat handlers, ex-boxers, as opposed to career diplomats, government officials temporarily ostracized, full-time university professors, and civil service government workers.

THE END OF THE THIRD WORLD

Drowning in corporatism, we have serious problems in establishing models of excellence; the lowering of standards is almost an imperative, because the illusion of art being something to do in one's spare time eliminates the commitment to the reader. In the world's most capitalist country, writers ought to write for their readers, and by dedicating themselves entirely to the task of writing, the model of excellence will never be diluted. Here, the act of publishing a book rarely has anything to do with the reader, rather with the illusion of art. The act of publishing a book in itself is enough, because it fulfills all the needs: it fans the author's vanity and it reinforces the social capital. And since no social capital is legible, a publishing industry is fostered that can't be an industry, and a book market that is so small that it can't even be called a market. And what makes it even worse is that we can't possibly supply this farce of a market.

But what about art? And literature? Happily, there are irrepressible forces, and in a country like Brazil, literature bursts forth spontaneously, even in the worst bureaucratic holes. Nevertheless, the meagerness is limiting, narrow-minded, and enslaving. The vicious circle of poverty is its most wretched feature, but it is necessary for the preservation of the corporative structure, which, in turn, exempts itself from any responsibility by pointing once again to poverty in order to explain the inability of the national writers to earn space on the bookstore shelves and attract the interest of the readers, since if the bookstores and the readers prefer foreign books, the guilt lies with the power of foreigners. A perfectly good explanation, but one that turns to dust in a country with a population the size of Brazil's. And what is even more serious is that it hides the cruelest of inequities, which is that of having confined its serious writers to a ghetto of excellence that is not exactly part of high literature, but of a qualitative limbo that forces us to be well above the second-rate stuff that they export, without ever daring to invade the realm of entertainment that appeals to the masses. Luckily, this wouldn't even cross our minds.

A minimum of evil, I thought. This was, after all, the slogan of the benefactor of the university, who was also the person responsible for the preservation of that forest, and, from all indications, a very wise man. Ironically wise. I returned to my room and caught a ride into town in a van that was going to the post office to pick up a pile of magazines for the college library. The driver was a vigorous sixty-year-old man, a native of Salem's Lot, who thought that the rest of the world must be hostile to Americans. We chatted all the way into the little town; he was quite interested in hearing about Brazil, and I in keeping him out of Juan Sender's path.

"My son died down there," he told me.

"In Brazil? In what city?" I asked, imagining one of those careless tourists run down every summer in the streets of Rio de Janeiro.

"In Santiago," he responded. "It was when they had one of them military revolutions."

I overlooked the geographic confusion and responded.

"Just a minute. The military coup did happen in Santiago, but Santiago isn't in Brazil."

"It isn't?" he exclaimed. "I beg your pardon."

"No problem," I responded, curious to know more details but reluctant to appear rude.

"My son was a pilot in the air force; the Communists shot him."

"I'm very sorry. How did something like that happen?"

"On the day of the military overthrow, he was on leave. At least that is what one of his buddies told us. When the whole mess started, they were having some

THE END OF THE THIRD WORLD

fun in a bar, some Communists arrived, separated the two of them from the rest, and chose one to serve as an example. My son's luck ran out; he was shot in cold blood."

I remained silent, pondering what a pilot of the American air force would be doing in Santiago at that time.

"You can't imagine what his loss has meant to me," he went on. "He was our only son, coming after two daughters. My wife was so grieved that she has never been the same since. Jesus Christ, what am I saying?"

"I can imagine how you feel," I said, awkwardly.

"It took me years to accept his death; my wife, too. Our daughters are married now, with kids of their own. One lives in Peterborough, and the other moved with her husband to Seattle. I thought I had put it all behind me, but I guess I was wrong. It all seems to come back again."

Once again I abstained from making a comment.

But the poor man was upset. "I don't know if you believe in these things," he said nervously. "I am a Baptist myself, and I didn't believe in them either. But last week my wife went with a friend to a spiritualist center. She went against my wishes, and she came back all upset, saying she had spoken with our boy. I was furious, but she couldn't talk about anything else. The spiritualist center is right here in Salem's Lot; it's very old. I think it was founded in 1923. Yesterday she dragged me to one of their sessions. My God, my son appeared; he spoke to me. He said things that only he and I knew. What do you think of these things?"

"I don't know what to say," I responded.

"You don't believe in it, do you?"

"To tell you the truth, I am somewhat skeptical . . ."

He shook his head, knowingly. "We're here in Salem's Lot. Where do you want to go?" he asked courteously.

LOST WORLD II

"Anywhere; there's no chance I'll get lost," I replied.

"It's a small town," he said, parking the van on a street with white houses and green lawns. "If you want a ride back, I'll be leaving the post office in forty minutes."

"Thanks," I said jumping out of the van.

"Do you see that house over there?" he said, pointing to a small structure with a Greek frontage and four columns. "That's the spiritualist center."

I just waved and walked on. The street was deserted and the houses didn't seem inhabited, but the lawns and the hedges were well tended, showing the care given to them by the owners. When I walked past the building that housed the spiritualist center, I raised my eyes. On the triangle formed by the frontage, shining in the bright sunlight, were metal letters forming the words THE HOUSE OF NEW REVELATION. Between the columns there was a large, austere wooden door, set between two glass windows. On the door was a bronze plague that I could only read by approaching the door. The plaque read, "Inaugurated on the second of June of 1923, with the Grace of our Lord Jesus Christ, and the contribution of men of goodwill and in the presence of Sir Arthur Conan Doyle."

Two hours later I was on a plane for New York, in time to catch the next flight to Brazil.

Book Five

Megathere Country

Elementary,
My Dear Sir Delamare

When he woke up, the room was quiet. But Sir Delamare was almost certain that he had not been dreaming; someone was outside, at that early hour of dawn, playing the flute. It was a sad, dissonant, and repetitive melody that had infiltrated his sleep and woken him up. He was not a light sleeper; he could sleep through the worst conditions and the most irritating noises, although lately he slept less and less, as if old age, certain that the long sleep was imminent, preferred the waking to the sleeping hours. So as not to wake Spender, who was sleeping on the couch in the sitting room, he quietly slipped out of bed and went over to the window. It was still mostly dark, and the first rays of sun were timidly peeking through threads of gray clouds. The forest was still immersed in darkness, but it was possible to see a dense mist of evaporating humidity rising from the ground, advancing across the lawn, almost reaching the edge of the light that illuminated the stone walkway encircling the hotel.

He concentrated on listening, but only the vague sounds of dawn could be heard: the distant activity in the kitchen as breakfast was being prepared for the hotel guests, and the even more distant awakening of the city beyond the forest drowned in mist. The fact that he couldn't hear any sound of a flute, any hint of melody, made his heart beat faster. He felt suddenly upset, slightly irritated with himself, because in the still tranquility of dawn, the limitations brought on by age seemed to loom over him; he felt increasingly less active, more sluggish and clumsy. His heart was indifferent, passionless, and he found the phony comedy of life to be tedious and useless. Old age, which had stripped him of almost everything, still hadn't killed his curiosity. Yet curiosity alone, deprived of the youthful ingredients that dreams are made of, had changed him into a dry, selfish, and solitary person, more akin to an old scorpion. He knew himself to be close to death, and there was nothing he could do about it. On the other hand, the fact that he had one foot in the grave gave him the realization that life was nothing more than a foolish but adorable struggle.

Drenched in early morning uneasiness, his thoughts went through some dark association of ideas which focused on the events of the previous hours, beginning with the arrival at the hotel and ending with the death of Danilo Ariel Duarte. Why had he remained at the hotel, suffocated by hours of inertia and overcome by jet lag? He had done nothing to protect his friend, not even notified him of his arrival in the city. Finally he asked himself what he was doing there in that unreal land that was almost a forgery of the Orient, some kind of India without the majesty, where a man's life had not the slightest importance. But they were questions left unanswered, mingling with the effects of the long hours of the flight, the different time zones, and his advanced age. Nevertheless, as Sir Delamare allowed himself to relive these events, he felt he was swimming in an intolerable lethargy. It was then that he heard the flute once again. The same melody that had awakened him. It came from the forest, from within the mist that had moved in between the tree trunks like cotton placed in a packing crate around crystal goblets. The sound entered through the window and gently took control of his senses; it was melodious, repetitive, and slightly menacing in its mysteriousness.

Impulsively, Sir Delamare quietly left the room. Spender snored, curled up on the sofa, still under the effects of the tranquilizers taken after the terrorist attack, another of the strange happenings in that land and whose reminder was still visible in the pile of books that the hotel attendants had stacked up in a corner of the room.

He quickly walked down the empty, silent halls, descended the stairway because he was too much in a hurry to wait for the elevator, constantly aware of the melody as it changed to variations of the same chord. A gust of hot air met him as he stepped out of doors into the hint of light that divided the hotel and the misty carpet of the forest. Coming through the shadows of the foliage, dawn was still ambiguous, timidly held by the trees' delicate leaves in the last moments of night. Even as it began to turn warm, the morning air was invigorating and pure. Sir Delamare inhaled a deep breath of air and savored the odorless purity of the oxygen, at the same time he was aware of other subtle perfumes gravitating about him. He entered the blanket of mist, lulled by the melody that now seemed to him to be an old Irish tune that his mother had often hummed. He saw his legs disappear almost to the knee as he walked into the mist, but his body mass did not seem to displace it at all; in fact, it lay with such indolence that it appeared the heat would never be able to consume it.

He soon found himself totally surrounded by the mist. The warm breath of a tropical morning was gone, and in its place a light, autumnal breeze brushed past him, causing goose pimples on the nape of his neck. He tripped over a tree root and fell, but his fall was cushioned by a thick cover of dead leaves that smelled of earth, of rotting and thriving vegetation. He sat there, stunned and groping about him carefully. Visibility was almost nil; he could only see what was very near to him, and even then not in much detail. Touching the leaves, he found they were dead but flexible and humid.

As he fell, something had scratched his face, a branch moist with dew; the scratch now began to sting. He raised his hand to touch his cheek, and he was shocked. Instead of the wrinkled skin, dry and rough, his fingertips touched a firmness that he could only vaguely recall, a firmness that could be found on the face of a young man who disappeared a half century earlier. A youngster who wore a fine, waxed mustache and went about with empty pockets and lived in a glittering world that was at the point of collapse. Sure that he was suffering from an illusion or near death, he sat there running his hands over that improbable face, with its skin in full-blown youth. Then he reached down to other parts of his body, his shoulders and arms, his chest and thighs; and not finding any of the former devastation of age, he rolled over on the carpet of leaves and let go with a few shouts of glee.

The music from the flute continued with its melody that evoked other eras of inexperience, arrogance, and tenderness. Yes, he thought, I am dying; but it didn't really matter. The sensation of dying was strangely comforting. He opened his eyes and waited for the final darkness to approach, but nothing happened. In the same manner that the mist protected itself from the heat with its indolent slowness, perhaps it protected him from death by some other device. He jumped up and stood there, enjoying the pleasure of a straight back and legs capable of marvels that he no longer remembered.

At that point, he heard a rustle, and two feminine silhouettes approached through the mist, each of them playing a panpipe, concentrating on the complicated execution of the melody. They were dressed in sumptuous, dewy garments, like two fairies; and they were pleasant-looking and gentle, with eyes that shone like stars in the mist. Sir Delamare began to cry from emotion, exactly as he would if one day he had found Titania, the Queen of Dragonflies, in the flesh.

The fairies stopped playing and looked at him as if they were able to understand men because they were mistresses of all male secrets.

"Where am I?" he asked, still sobbing.

They didn't respond; they simply took him by the hands and led him through the forest, opening a path in the mist, through which they passed in silence, until they came upon a shining wet, metallic object, which he recognized to be an automobile. It wasn't just an ordinary automobile, but a magnificent Rolls-Royce Silver Shadow, iridescent and as frightening as a silver rhinoceros.

They departed in that dome of metal and leather, the passenger compartment separated from the driver by a window of dark glass. The car began to slide through the mist as if it were on a perfectly smooth paved road, the tires turning firmly. The movement was barely perceptible; Sir Delamare could hardly feel the quiet motor pushing the car ahead, but the mist clung to the windows with an intense motionlessness. Sir Delamare turned his attention to the two young things sitting on either side of him with enchanting carelessness. They seemed to be young adolescents;

their breasts were almost unnoticeable, and the lines of their bodies retained the gracefulness of infancy and a certain ripeness of form. They didn't seem to be older than fifteen, although they seemed to possess some ancestral conquering spirit, an age-old geological sediment with an ostentation tested in successive generations.

"I feel like I'm eighteen years old," Sir Delamare said.

"You are eighteen," one of them said in a hesitant but perfect English.

"No, I'm not," he responded sadly. "I know my age."

"You've lived ninety years, haven't you?"

"One could say so," Sir Delamare said.

"So you are eighteen."

"I don't understand!" he exclaimed.

"It's simple. Life is accumulation; do you understand?"

"Whoever has lived ninety years can be whatever age he wants between zero and the present moment."

"So, my young man," one of them said, smiling, "you are eighteen years old if you want to be."

"Where are we going?" Sir Delamare said, frightened.

"We don't know."

"That's a question that one ought never to ask."

"It doesn't matter at all where we're going."

"Because we will never arrive anywhere."

"We are too short-lived to reach the end of the road."

"That's why it is unimportant where we're going."

"I understand," Sir Delamare said.

"We understand that you don't understand."

"And we understand that you understand that we also don't understand."

The soft hum of the car in motion occupied the silence, but there was something terrible, a primeval threat that was barely hidden behind the dreamy

THE END OF THE THIRD WORLD

and sensual atmosphere that the two girls created. Sir Delamare suspected that if a world existed within that foggy shroud, it was a world where the senses would have the consistency of thick, boiling syrup, where humans would be reduced to a complete lassitude of satiated instincts, a world where the total absence of the tragic would eliminate all ambitions in the perverse quiet of Paradise. In such a world, Sir Delamare would die of boredom, but he couldn't forget that the two girls were daughters of such a Nirvana.

The car finally turned and stopped. The visibility outside was still nil, but the mist now had taken on a milky opalescence. When the door was opened, Sir Delamare felt a gust of the tropical heat, and sweat immediately began to drench his body.

"Have we arrived?" he asked out of the pure instinct to speak.

They didn't respond, but they took his hands in their warm and delicate little hands.

"It's hot here," he commented.

"It does one good to sweat once in a while," one of them responded.

Sir Delamare feared that they would once again start up one of those strange dialogues, but the young women only smiled and led him confidently along the mist-covered road. They didn't walk for long, only a few steps, before they stopped. They were in front of a door.

"Go on in," one of them said, opening the door.

"We will wait for you here."

"You must come out of the same door. Don't forget."

"What is inside?" Sir Delamare asked.

"Things that you want to know."

"And we, too."

"You can go in. Don't be afraid."
"Nothing is going to happen to you."
"You aren't coming?"
"No, we can't."
"But we will be here when you come out."

They spoke with so much innocence that he crossed the threshold and saw a kind of Spanish-style interior garden with a fountain in the middle. He turned around to speak with the girls, but the door was already closed. He shrugged, sweating from every pore, and contemplated with envy the fish that were swimming about in the fresh, clear water of the fountain. And it was sunny, a morning sun that radiated from an intensely blue sky. The oppressive mist was gone; there was a light breeze that battled with the warmth and gently swayed the red poppies and the rare snapdragons that were so purple, they seemed to be spoiled little children holding their breath.

"Well it's so nice you came," someone said with effusive satisfaction.

Stunned, Sir Delamare wiped his sweaty forehead with his handkerchief and tried to make out the person who was half-hidden by a large clump of ferns. It was Deputy Rubens in his checkered sport coat.

"Are you feeling all right?" the deputy asked, seeing that Sir Delamare was as red as a beet.

"Yes, I am fine. It's just the heat . . ."

"Come in, come in," the deputy insisted. "Here inside it is cooler."

Sir Delamare crossed the garden and entered the house, followed by Deputy Rubens. He immediately recognized where he was, because on the wall there was an enormous portrait of his friend Danilo Ariel Duarte in academic garb.

THE END OF THE THIRD WORLD

"I called the hotel and was told that you weren't there," the deputy explained. "I deduced that you were on your way here."

The deputy's hesitant and heavily accented English irritated Sir Delamare, but it wasn't any worse than what was spoken by certain native politicians whom he had known in India.

"A strange method of deduction," Sir Delamare replied. "Since I didn't even know myself where I was going."

The deputy observed the old aristocrat for a few seconds, without being able to discern his meaning.

"Are you saying you didn't get my message?" the deputy asked.

"Message? What message?"

"The damned hotel reception desk didn't give you my message."

"When did you leave the message?"

"Yesterday, around midnight. I didn't want to awaken you."

"Well, it must have coincided with the Jihad Jívaros' assault."

The deputy looked at Sir Delamare with a quizzical expression on his face.

"The Jihad Jívaros? Are you sure?"

"Well, that's what they called themselves. But they didn't harm anyone."

"I didn't hear anything about it at the Department of Security. It's because they don't take this matter of the Jihad Jívaros very seriously."

"I noticed that. When we called the police, they weren't very impressed. Only the hotel security showed up."

"The authorities are underestimating the Jihad Jívaros," the deputy complained. "But they have robbed a number of private libraries and have been shown to have international connections. With the help of various radical organizations, they have stolen ethnographic pieces spread out over two continents."

"Really!" Sir Delamare said, surprised. "They are stealing books and arrows, then? How peculiar."

"That's why the authorities aren't taking them seriously. They think that real terrorists assault banks and plant bombs."

"Don't blame the authorities since books are extremely devaluated nowadays," Sir Delamare said philosophically, as one who himself placed little value on books.

Sir Delamare mopped his face again and looked around the room. It was a large room, furnished with heavy furniture that would be much more appropriate in a villa in Sintra, Portugal. His friend Duarte must have seen in that atmosphere some kind of connection to his Lusitanian past.

"Come with me," the deputy requested. "I have discovered something of interest."

The two of them ascended the wide marble staircase and went to the master bedroom. Everything was in its proper place, but it displayed a lack of use, an abandonment that the cleaning and the care of mere servants could not hide.

"Sr. Duarte continued to use this room and this bed even after his wife's death. Perhaps he wanted to die here as well."

"He was found dead in this bed then, I suppose!" said a surprised Sir Delamare.

"But he didn't die here. He was brought here afterwards. You see, he was in the house, but not in this room. Sr. Duarte was assassinated downstairs in his study and carried up here."

THE END OF THE THIRD WORLD

"I hope you have arrived at this conclusion by some orthodox method of deduction."

Deputy Rubens smiled respectfully and went on. "First, the dart hit him just beneath the right armpit. If it had been blown at him while he was lying in bed, it would have hit some other part of the body. Look here." And he approached the bed, theatrically repeating what he had just said. "If he had been seated, there would have been three options to do this. But he always sat on this side of the bed, the right side, as we can see by the depression in the mattress. Sitting in this position, the dart would have hit him on the left side, because the only spot to shoot from is the door. But at the desk, there are windows all around. He had the custom of sitting at the desk right after breakfast to do some work, catch up on correspondence or write in his book of fables. You know that he adored telling fables."

"Yes, I knew that. Please go on."

Deputy Rubens patted his hair vainly, picking up his narration. "Well, my theory is that he was working, he received a telephone call from Miss Challenger, and then he was killed. The culprit was outside and shot through the window, aiming directly below his right arm. It must have been a tall man, because the angle of the dart indicates that its trajectory was from high to low, shot by someone who is over five foot ten inches. There is no possibility that the murderer was standing on something, a bench or some such thing, because then he would have had to lean down to make the shot."

"Very good. And what else?"

"The curare doesn't take immediate effect. The poison paralyzes the muscles, and the victim dies of a cardiac arrest and a lack of oxygen. It takes two or three minutes to die. That's a lot of time, sir. In three minutes a dying person can do many things, including call the police. My hunch is that the murderer was an acquaintance of the victim who came into the room and convinced Sr. Duarte that he was suffering from a sudden attack of some sort and helped him up to his room, knowing that very soon the poor man would—excuse the expression—kick the bucket."

"But why would he do it? What would be the motive of such a crime?"

"Let's go step by step, Your Excellency."

"Very well; I'm listening."

The deputy opened the bedroom window and called Sir Delamare over. The two of them leaned out the window, and the deputy pointed to the lawn that ran along the side of the house.

"There, at the end, is the study. The murderer placed himself near the window. He was a heavy individual, wearing very large shoes. I examined the spot and found his footprints. What's more, I found very strange residue in the footprints."

"Residue?"

"The plant residue from distilled sugarcane rum. Cane bagasse, which is very common in the distillery owned by Pietro Pietra, Jr., who just happens to be a giant of a man, weighing two hundred and fifty pounds and measuring six feet tall."

"My God. Have you mentioned this to your superiors?"

"I'm no longer on the case. They removed me."

"Which means that . . ."

"My questions concerning the case were beginning to be very inconvenient, because the official explanation is that Sr. Duarte died of natural causes, a cardiac arrest. This matter of curare was completely erased, and a new

THE END OF THE THIRD WORLD

team of medical examiners redid the board of inquiry report."

"But the dart was stolen by the Jihad Jívaros; how did the murderer wind up with it? Unless he is . . . No, it doesn't make sense, does it?"

"I can't prove it, but my theory is that that swindler Pietra, Jr., is setting up some scheme, and Sr. Duarte was going to denounce him."

"From what I could find out, this fellow Pietra, Jr., took control of my friend Duarte's company fraudulently, leaving him completely broke."

"I know; everyone here in Manaus knows the story. The son of a bitch arrived here as the lover of Sr. Duarte's son. But that isn't important. As far as I'm concerned, there is something even more terrible, worse than losing one's fortune."

"What do you mean? Is there by chance something worse than losing one's fortune?"

Deputy Rubens pondered the old aristocrat's words, but he was a man of strong convictions and he wasn't put off. "Worse than destitution is seeing the thief get off scot-free," the deputy said. "Worse than losing one's fortune is not being able to take revenge."

"You're right, young man. You are an excellent police officer."

"Thank you very much, Your Excellency."

"Do you mean to say that my friend Duarte possessed something that not only would stop the thief but even mortally wound him?"

"That is what I believe. It must be a really dirty racket, one of those scandals than can provoke an international clamor."

"He didn't have to kill poor Duarte," Sir Delamare lamented with bitter irony. "My poor friend was never very clear. He most certainly would have tried to make the denunciation through one of his incomprehensible fables."

"But the assassin didn't want to risk it."

"You know, Rubens, my friend Duarte handed over some papers to Miss Challenger." Deputy Rubens nodded. "But only a part of them arrived in London, what remained after a brutal act by this fellow Pietra, Jr."

"Did you see the papers?" the deputy asked.

"Yes, I even had a team from my accounting department do an examination of them. But they revealed little; apparently they were loose sheets from a second set of books."

"Pietra, Jr., is very shrewd," the deputy said. "He must have taken the most important ones. Who knows? We might find amongst the papers what Sr. Duarte intended to do."

"It is possible," Sir Delamare agreed. "But how can it be proven?"

"By finding Sr. Duarte's files. If they haven't already been destroyed." Deputy Rubens looked at his fingernails and sighed. "If you don't mind spending a few more minutes, I would like you to come to Sr. Duarte's study."

"Certainly," Sir Delamare agreed.

They went to the study, not a large room in such a commodious house, with just a small Portuguese colonial desk, a heavy mahogany chair with a blue velvet cushion, a collection of gouache sketches of eighteenth-century Portuguese uniforms in silver frames, arranged symmetrically on the wall, and a locked Dona Maria I glass-enclosed bookcase with large bound books, seemingly a venerable antiquity.

"This is a famous collection of fable books," the deputy said, pointing to the bookcase. "There are rare works, first editions, incunabula, eighteenth-century manuscripts, secret seventeenth-century prints."

THE END OF THE THIRD WORLD

"A delirium for the Jihad Jívaros, wouldn't you say?"

"I believe they prefer heavier editions, sir."

"They certainly do!"

"But it isn't the collection of rare books that interests us," the deputy said, passing his fingers along the solid wood of the bookcase, then turning to the desk and removing the cover of the old Remington typewriter. "Sr. Duarte worked at this table, writing at this same machine that had belonged to his family's rubber plantation."

Sir Delamare approached the desk and examined the typewriter. The machine must have been more than forty years old, but it was well preserved and in perfect working condition. Duarte must have valued this memento of his family's pioneer times.

"Only lately he wasn't using the Remington," the deputy said.

"He wasn't?"

"I discovered by chance that two months ago he returned from the United States with one of those portable personal computers. A Toshiba brand, if I'm not mistaken. He had to register it at customs, because the importation of these contraptions is prohibited, and Sr. Duarte had to pay duty in order to keep the thing. Well, in the customs files, it is clearly recorded that he paid the tax and kept the machine." Deputy Rubens reached out and opened the only drawer in the desk; inside, underneath a few papers, he found an instruction manual. "Look here; it was a Toshiba. My memory is not letting me down."

"Very good, and where is the personal computer?"

"It's not here; it disappeared."

"It disappeared? Then, young man, you can answer thus: 'Elementary, my dear Sir Delamare. The murderer carried off the computer because everything he wanted was in it.' "

"Exactly. It is a shame that no one, not even his maid, not even his son, could confirm that Sr. Duarte had such a personal computer. As far as they were concerned, he only used his old Remington."

Sir Delamare assimilated this last bit of information and glanced over at the grand old Remington with its chrome plating and black enamel.

He pursed his lips in thought, took out a cigarette, and lit it.

"What do you want me to do, my good man?" he asked, engulfed in a cloud of blue smoke.

Deputy Rubens lowered his eyes and tried to hide how frustrated and troubled he felt.

"I don't know, sir. I really don't know. But I would like to settle the score with Pietra, Jr."

He raised his eyes to Sir Delamare, this time without trying to hide his sadness over his impotence.

"You have a strong sense of duty, young man. That is highly laudable."

"I'm sorry to disappoint you, sir. My business with him is personal, and nothing would give me more pleasure than to catch Pietra, Jr., red-handed."

"I understand. He must be quite despised around here."

"Excuse the expression—he has screwed nearly everyone."

Sir Delamare contemplated the deputy's tense face without responding. A new puff of smoke escaped his lips and wafted through the study as the deputy stared at him imploringly.

"Do you think that he will be on that trip?" Sir Delamare finally asked. Then, glancing at his watch, he exclaimed, "My God, it's time to embark! It's eleven

THE END OF THE THIRD WORLD

o'clock. I should have been at the wharf at nine in the morning."

"Do you want a ride? I have a car," the deputy offered.

Sir Delamare declined the offer and rushed outside almost at a run, followed by Deputy Rubens. The old man crossed the garden and opened a gate that the deputy had not noticed.

"Thanks a lot," Sir Delamare said before shutting the gate.

"Just a moment," the deputy shouted.

But the gate shut.

Nervously Deputy Rubens ran to the gate and tried in vain to open it, but it was locked with two rusty bolts as if that path had not been used in years.

"I'm late," Sir Delamare said, puffing, once inside the Rolls-Royce, seated between the two girls. "And I need to be on board that ship."

"You will be," one of the girls said.

"There's no need to worry," the other added.

"Did you find out anything we didn't know?" they asked.

"The deputy believes that Pietra, Jr., killed my friend Duarte," Sir Delamare said, settling back in the comfortable seat, grateful for the car's excellent air conditioner. "He killed him with a poison arrow. That's what I don't understand."

"What is it that you don't understand?"

"The use of the dart. The dart was stolen by the Jihad Jívaros, wasn't it? How did it wind up in Pietra, Jr.'s, hands?"

"Because the Jihad Jívaros are inept."

"They're nothing more than a band of pathetic simpletons."

"They're the shame of international terrorism."

"What do you mean by that?"

"The Jihad Jívaros were obsessed with killing old man Duarte. They considered him the symbol of Amazonian collaboration."

"Just because he was the only rubber exporter who agreed to work with companies that came in after 1967."

"He paid dearly for his boldness."

"There was no preparation here for the modern economic model."

"Being modern is dangerous business around here."

"Yes, and what happened?" Sir Delamare cut them short before the two of them succumbed to mindless chatter.

"They sent one of their militants to shoot him with the dart. Pietra, Jr., arrived at the right moment and surprised the fellow."

"Pietra is no wimp. The hit man was scared out of his wits and ran off."

"He dropped the blowgun and the dart."

"Which Pietra picked up and used."

"It's obvious, isn't it?"

"Then you already knew?"

"We picked up Pietra, Jr., but he's tough. We didn't get much out of him, but we knew he had killed old man Duarte."

"You kidnaped Pietra, Jr.!" Sir Delamare exclaimed.

"Well, not exactly."

"He escaped."

"We can also be simpletons once in a while."

"We left him asleep in a room in our house."

"And this morning he was gone."

"God almighty, what have I gotten mixed up with!" Sir Delamare lamented. "That man is planning something very serious. My friend Duarte paid with his life because he found out what plans were in the making."

"And have you discovered what the plans are?"

THE END OF THE THIRD WORLD

"No, not even Deputy Rubens managed to get a lead. Duarte was working on a personal computer, but it was stolen. The scheme ought to be in the computer's memory."

The two girls looked at each other, disillusioned.

"You need to help me get to the ship," Sir Delamare said. "He will be on board; he is one of the presenters invited by the Brazilian government to speak."

One of them opened the car door and moved her legs so Sir Delamare could get out.

"Good-bye," she said, her eyes sad and teary.

"Good-bye," Sir Delamare said as he left the car.

He felt a burst of hot air and squinted his eyes because the sun was so bright. He instinctively reached into his pocket, pulled out his cigarette case, chose a cigarette, and lit it. Exhaling puffs of smoke like a ship under full steam, he entered the hotel. As he arrived at his room, he checked his watch. Not more than ten minutes had passed since he went out into the mist.

What Was That?

No novel by Juan Sender could be convincingly summarized. To define his first novel, *Atacama*, as the story of a fifty-year-old peg leg who wandered through the desert of the same name, with only a jug of table wine, obsessed by a woman whom he had seen just once in Valparaiso when he was eighteen years old, is to limit the stylistic circumvolutions of the 430 dry and crimped pages. Or to say that *Northeast*, his next novel, is the drama of a young blind girl with poor motor coordination who repeatedly attempts suicide, without ever succeeding, wounding and mutilating herself for 712 pages of tortured prose, is at the very least irresponsible. The novel that he was currently condemned by Sir Delamare's generosity to rewrite was no less complex, and the successive publication postponements only exacerbated the problem.

First, because the novel was already eight hundred pages long, and most likely the final version was not even in sight. Secondly, and no less important, Juan Sender had the habit of reviewing his story each night before falling asleep, which meant that lately he was sleeping less and less. *Kassov* was perhaps his most ambitious novel yet, because he was working with an especially dangerous theme: the genesis of a theory of literary analysis. In the first part, the novel dealt with the posthumous publication of the works of Leopold Kassov, the protagonist, accomplished by his Chilean disciples exiled in Paris. When his texts come out in publication, modern literary criticism takes notice of the revolutionary theories of this postformalist Soviet genius, born in Kiev in 1887, professor of Slavic phonology and specialist of Sikh fairy tales, tenured professor of the University of Saint Petersburg, where he had taught from 1895 to 1912, until he was banished to Siberia for his anticzarist activities. Leopold Kassov founded at that time, in his Siberian log cabin, the "Red Tundra Movement," which preached the blending of Sikh passivism with the Bolshevik activism.

The Bolsheviks, however, never quite got used to the ritual Sikh dagger that the professor insisted on using during the political meetings. This extreme faithfulness would cost him an extended exile until 1919, the year in which the professor suffered frostbite on his hands and the loss of all of his fingers, and obtained a pardon by Lenin himself, who received him solemnly in the Supreme Soviet during the 1920 Hay Harvest Feast. Kassov took advantage of the opportunity to present the revolutionary leader with a few copies of the only work published during his lifetime, the essay "The Orthogenetic and Philogenetic Dimensions of the Leninist Texts." In a clear demonstration of how much the work impressed Lenin, Professor Kassov was named vice president of the Agricultural University of Srednekolymsk in Siberia.

In 1935, while preparing a similar study on the texts of Joseph Stalin, Kassov was removed from his position, and as he was still in Siberia, he was named stockroom clerk of a vodka warehouse in Bulun, where he remained until the end of World War II. The years as a stockroom clerk, or the "Bulun Cycle," as this period of his life came to be known, were most useful. Far from the horrors of war, protected from the cold, Kassov would develop his theory of perpendiculars, inspired by topology and by enology, producing more than twelve hundred essays, which remained unpublished until 1984.

The most extraordinary of the pieces produced during this period is the work entitled "Repressed Heartbeats in Dostoyevski," where his theory of perpendiculars appears for the first time. In this essay, Kassov traces perpendicular lines, or hyperstructural cuts, crossing the mystical outburst of the Dostoyevskian characters with the author's epilepsy and the crises of Russian feudalism and orthodox religion, without omitting the great vodka crisis of 1867, like interpersonal echoes of the repressed heartbeats that would prompt the 1917 Revolution.

In the study "The Monarchical Sacrality," written at the same time, he explains the idealistic terms of Anglo-Saxon alienation as signs of the expansion of Britannic mercantilism in relation to the great excess of whiskey production of 1598, analyzing the Shakespearean tragedies and comedies. The interesting thing about this essay, unique in the annals of Shakespearean studies, is that being in Bulun, a city of two hundred inhabitants and whose library only contained books of political doctrine, Kassov was obliged to resort to a Serbo-Croation translation of the theater production of Shakespeare.

In 1964, during the thaw of the Khrushchev years, Leopold Kassov was rehabilitated and brought to Moscow, where he remained as adjunct secretary to the Commission of the Five-Year Plan of Children's Literature for Peace until 1967. In that year, as a special prize, he was sent to Paris to participate in the Second International Congress of the Post-Formalists, an opportunity he took to ask for asylum in the Indian Embassy, which was denied especially rudely. He remained in Paris, giving classes in the Sorbonne, and making periodic conference trips to the United States and England, but because he was a very unusual dissident, after a while he was ignored, and he managed to remain above complete destitution because he ingratiated himself with a Portuguese entrepreneur, the owner of a hotel in the Azores, who commissioned him to write a work on Camões.

For six months Kassov researched and wrote in the isolation of his room in Ponta Delgada, finally presenting the rough draft of an essay that has been lost, where he proved that the Camõnian epic was a poetic counterpart to the impetus that the production of rum experienced in the sixteenth century, almost like the principal fuel that moved the navigators across the unknown seas, a secret and intoxicating muse of the discoveries. The hotel owner, offended upon seeing the great national bard treated in such an unconventional manner, ceased his career as a patron and turned the astonished and practically penniless Russian genius out into the streets of Lisbon. He was saved by a Brazilian stockbroker who invited him to work in his country. The job was that of teaching Russian in the Slavic department of the University of Amazonia, right in the middle of the tropical jungle, an invitation that he accepted with the same stoicism that had enabled him to face the years in Siberia.

But upon arriving in Amazonia, he finds out that there is no Slavic department in the university, nor is there anything like it. So as not to die of hunger, he takes a job on a televison program of Slavic cuisine, where he prepares dishes and is able to eat them afterwards. Unfortunately, it was only a weekly program, and the professor finally dies in 1978, from successive bouts of cirrhosis, a consequence of his years in Bulun, and from the efforts expended to bring forth his last text of analysis, "Plentiful Wine," in which he traces perpendiculars between the oscillations in the quality of Pablo Neruda's poetry and the highs and lows of the Chilean wine production.

The second part of Juan Sender's novel begins with the

polemic surrounding the French translation of Kassov's texts, published in twelve enormous volumes. This work appears between 1981 and 1984, edited by the critics Jorge Gardel and Amparo Peron of the Department of Advanced Slavic-Latin Studies of the University of Paris VII. The work of editing and translating, accomplished by Argentine critics, right away received a series of restrictions on the part of the Chilean critics, creating a Kassovian dissidence, as they recorded in the annals of the Third International Congress of Kassovian Studies held in Geneva, in February 1986, the occasion in which the Argentine translator, the eloquent Jorge Gardel, is hospitalized with numerous abrasions after a heated debate with five Chilean theorists.

In general terms, the disagreement was based on the rather arbitrary form in which the gerunds and the second declinations of the Russian language had been treated in the French translation, especially because Leopold Kassov, in his 1932 essay "Russian and the Neurosis of the Gerunds," called attention to the question of the gerunds in Slavic languages, particularly in nineteenth-century Russian, and its iconic implications in the morphemes shaped in the poetic syntagmas of Pushkin, an angular stone of the incapacity of the Soviet people to free itself from the bureaucratic structures.

In the third part of the novel, Sender backtracked and attempted to deal with the Red Tundra period, a time when Kassov developed his theory of the Sikh fairy tales, a prodigious union of the irrational and irreflective myth transmuting into a philosophy of the remote nature of the psychological, in a state of preconsciousness that phosphoresces between the ancient and the modern, in order to materialize in the minds of children as a binary hysteria that recalls the logic of submission of the Russian muzhiks after 1667.

THE END OF THE THIRD WORLD

This meaningful cycle brought forth many questions, like the hyperstructural concept and the theory of perpendicular, matrix of the scientific vision which is capable of achieving a connection between the aesthetic/psychological with the historic/economic, and whose basic work is the surprising study entitled "The Theme of Bourgeouis Incest in Trotskyism." The final outpouring will be the parallelism of the essay on Pablo Neruda, where his time spent in the tropics gives him an illuminating vision of the affinity between primitivism and civilization that nourishes the unchanging dichotomy of class consciousness and Freudian repression as the reverse of materiality. Thus refuting the formalist opposition to change and the structuralist solidification, Kassov traces a sign of ineliminability of the modern/archaic nexus present in literature as a reproduction of the evolution/involution dichotomy, a worn-out metaphor of the Nerudian poems that are nothing more than positivist Darwinian formulas.

What devastated Juan Sender the most, aside from the constant postponements of the publication, was the fact that he received complaints in the form of memoranda from the publisher, the format that the latter chose to communicate with him, always referring to what he considered a lack of local color in the work; the problem was that it didn't seem to be a Latin American novel, or so each memo said. Where are the yellow butterflies, the crimes of honor, the peasants in white clothing, and the scenes of vigorous sexual encounters between rustic plantation owners and fragile señoritas in lace dresses?

Sender was terribly frustrated by the English publisher's lack of understanding of what he considered profoundly Latin American in his novel. Because, rather than plantation owners raping young girls, Latin America was a theoretical nightmare comparable to that constructed by the Russian genius. Rather than crimes of honor, of colonels with false frustrations, and of starving peasants, the damned continent resembled the grotesque invention of some perverse destiny, exactly like that of the long-suffering Professor Kassov.

But his editor didn't understand. He insisted on peasants; he wanted mystery, swarms of insects. All that he did was send missives that threatened drastic cuts in the manuscript, in the name of legibility, as if it were possible to write a real Latin American novel with complete legibility.

Sender was very disillusioned, and each time that he thought of his problems with the editor, he felt an enormous repugnance. As if that weren't enough, the strange incident the night before on the nonexistent hotel floor caused some kind of emotional spasm, a subtle pang that indicated that an even more unnerving reality was awaiting him above and beyond his drama as a writer. Nevertheless, he didn't blame anyone, because since he began to be dragged along by Sir Delamare's caprices, his life had lost its prosaic incertitude and began to be blown by some kind of uncomfortable haste, full of reasons to break away. This was lethal for a writer, and Sender was almost certain that Sir Delamare was aware of it.

But if his fate was tied in some way to that of his protagonist, all that was left to do was embark on the next circle of surprises on board a condemned ship, because he decided without hesitation to accompany Sir Delamare.

As lighthearted as a child, Juan Sender left his room. Come what may, he was ready. In the same way that Kassov's life ended in that land, he could as well find death in the middle of the Amazon River. He had no regrets, because at least in his novel, Kassov's death didn't exactly mean the end of the novel.

What Was That Again?

Ah, readers. What kind of a mess did I get myself into, just so I wouldn't look bad in some newspaper article? Yes, I know that it's too late for regrets, and even lies eventually come to an end. And what is a novel, after all, if not a very polished lie? I'm sorry. I swear that from now on, I am going to abstain from saying things like that. It would be better to try to arrive at the end with a minimum of coherence, if that is at all possible.

One thing is for sure; I should have known from the start that to bring Jane Challenger to the equatorial region would result in more than fears concerning the climate and the hardships caused by the environment. Other problems, less climatic, should have deserved my attention. The most worrisome, for example, and one that only now am I aware of, was the extent of the unwholesomeness of these end-of-the-century novels. Ah! If that journalist had only known.

If it were another epoch, Professor Challenger's descendant would have no problem being the protagonist in an old-fashioned, ingenuous adventure novel; one of those that our youthful memory fondly recalls, with their charming about-faces, their doses of action and histamine, narrated with enough simplicity to make the worst foolishness seem real, without losing the irony of it all. Sir Arthur Conan Doyle was the trailblazer in this account, and without the slightest remorse, because he had the good luck to live on the other side of the abyss that split literature after August 1917.

Looking around a bit, one gets the impression that the mass culture took over the adventure stories. All one has to do is turn on the television and there are the serials, the soap operas, all electronically filtered.

And in the bookstores, what was left?

In order to find adventure novels, it is necessary to look in the shelves of trash novels, lost amongst the basest books of horror stories, detective stories, spies, science fiction, fantasies, etc. Professor Challenger, a nineteenth-century protagonist, wouldn't find the company strange, but he would be surprised by the direction that natural selection took in the present century, as far as the novel goes. During Professor Challenger's youth, in the times of Dickens, the novel was not considered an elevated form of literature. The poets were the ones who won all the honors. However, strangely enough, as they were deciding to confer certain distinction on the novel, they were beginning at the same time the attempts to kill it, much in the same way that the machine busters did in the first industrial revolution, only with more refinement. So much primitive sophistication would not be understood by Professor Challenger, but the results nearly banished the art of telling stories in Maple White's home country.

Unfortunately the consequences were perverse, because telling stories nearly became the exclusive domain of the mass culture. Today novels seem more like prefabricated products, utilitarian and highly perishable, necessarily diluted in order to reach the broadest spectrum of the market possible, as is the rule of thumb in the industrial game. The literary novel, meanwhile, needed to stay clear of this dilution; it did so by abdicating its popularity, which wound up in the hands of the industry, which today sells a lot of books, not exactly because they have mass appeal, but because they are a simulacrum of the great popular novel.

All right, let's forget the whole thing. We all are refined and cultured people who would never stoop to opening the cover of one of those thick, bad-taste editions. And I won't be the one to force Miss Challenger to visit such suspicious places. As impulsive and arrogant as she is, without any problems of social ascension, she wouldn't have much to do in one of these novels where Amazonia will most certainly end up being the principal victim.

But there is a positive aspect to all of this digression, because the novel of mass appeal, in spite of everything, will remain a permanent challenge, prompting us to lose our shyness about telling stories and look to the readers on the other side of the page.

If it is pleasure that makes it worthwhile, then Jane Challenger, who very soon will be encountering Pietro Pietra, Jr., will advance the narrative a little bit more. I would like it if the scene were theatrical but devoid of mystery, because the mysterious climate of this story—already filled with accidental mythology—has reached a level of nearly independent importance. I know, ahead of time, that the myth will be stronger and will continue to dominate the story. Myth has the capacity to act as an incentive, consisting, as it does, of poetry and primitive nostalgia, which are so dear to today's sensibilities. So there is nothing much one can do but enjoy this stylistic peculiarity of our time.

The morning sun, strong enough to invade the room through a small hole in the curtain, was responsible for waking Jane. She saw that Lester was still sleeping, snoring happily at her side, and the idea of sharing her bed with him every night didn't appeal to her at all.

She quietly dressed and left the room to have breakfast in the restaurant, feeling slightly irritated about what had transpired between the two of them the night before. She wasn't sorry about it; she simply didn't want Lester to misinterpret what had happened. He was a sentimental fool, capable of blowing way out of proportion a simple moment of weakness.

The hotel restaurant was still empty, and Jane had breakfast calmly, going over her strategy for convincing Lester that he shouldn't have any hopes about them, which, as she knew, would not be easy. Her friend is one of those well-intentioned creatures who secretly believe that everyone is born with the same defect. It's not that he is ingenuous, but usually when he discovers that good intentions are out of style and currently in disuse, he shuts himself up and bellows against the cold, cruel world, against an unfair society that is responsible for the existence of calculating, envious, and self-serving jerks. The worst thing is that when it comes to feelings, he borders on childishness, which transforms his few love affairs, which she always found out about, into actual emotional dead ends, from which he would slide into total indolence, drunken binges, empty looks out the window, and compulsive readings of Marxist texts. The fact is that in spite of the closeness that they had shared for so long, Lester was the last person with whom she should have gone to bed. And even had it been very good, she would still be regretting it.

Jane was wrapped up in her thoughts, glancing occasionally about the nearly empty restaurant, when she saw Sir Delamare enter, cross the room with its tables set and waiting for the guests, and without even seeing her, exit by the side door. In the initial surprise of the moment, she didn't do anything to attract his attention; the old man was exactly the kind of company that she

THE END OF THE THIRD WORLD

didn't want for breakfast. Hardly had Sir Delamare left the restaurant when she began to ponder his strange actions. The old man seemed to be sleepwalking; his clothes were more disheveled than usual, and in addition, she had the impression that he was barefoot. Jane was intrigued; she got up and went to the door. The bright morning sunshine had still not completely dispersed the mist that lay like a white carpet, wrapped around the trunks of the trees, hiding the low bushes and partially submerging the forest.

What she saw was a touching, idyllic scene. Sir Delamare was chatting gaily with two young native girls; they were all three seated in the damp, dewy grass. The two native girls were very pretty, as defenseless as two butterflies and apparently very happy. Sir Delamare didn't behave toward them as a ninety-year-old man; he laughed with the delight of an adolescent, and from time to time he caressed the girls, who responded with caresses of their own. There was nothing really strange about what Jane was seeing, an older man enjoying himself innocently enough with two young girls in the dew. Nevertheless, there was something hypnotically joyful about it, a force that attracted her attention and forced her to continue watching, held captive by the happiness that they were exuding.

Then they got up. The two girls took Sir Delamare by the hands and led him to an incredible Rolls-Royce that sat shining in the mist. They finally drove off, leaving the hotel grounds.

Jane ran out and nearly caught up with the Rolls.

"Sir Delamare," she shouted.

But the car continued on its way without slowing down, the dark windows raised so no one could see what was going on inside.

LOST WORLD II

Terribly worried, Jane stood in the middle of the road, watching the Rolls disappear from sight.

"Those two are idiots," someone said scornfully.

Jane shuddered as she recognized the voice and turned around. It was a shaken Pietra, Jr.

"What did you say?" Jane asked.

"Those two," he repeated, "are idiots."

"Who are they? Do you know them?"

"I'm not sure who they are. Yesterday they tried to make a fool of me. But they failed."

"What do you mean? Is Sir Delamare in any danger?"

"I don't think so. They are inoffensive."

"Who are they?" Jane insisted.

"Excuse the expression, but they are whores," he responded.

Jane shook her head, not understanding. It didn't make the slightest bit of sense that Sir Delamare would leave so early in the morning to go cavorting with two local whores.

"Whores!" she exclaimed, staring at Pietra, Jr. "Do you know something? Since the moment I arrived here, I have been thinking about how I would react the moment that I encountered you, Pietra, Jr."

"I hope that you won't be too tough on me."

Jane shrugged her shoulders. "I really don't care anymore. I am sick to death of this damned place, of its damned entrepreneurs, and its damned people."

Pietra, Jr., sighed and wiped his hand across a ravaged face. He had large, dark circles under his bloodshot eyes, his skin was crusty and dry, and his enormous hands seemed to tremble slightly.

"I love you, Jane," Pietra, Jr., said.

Jane felt as if she had been struck in the pit of the stomach; she doubled over and almost vomited. Her legs became wobbly, and she almost collapsed. Quickly

THE END OF THE THIRD WORLD

she composed herself and responded to the declaration with an expression of disgust, repugnance, and total arrogance, of which she was a consummate master.

Pietra, Jr., opened his mouth, but then decided not to speak.

"If you mention again what you just said," Jane warned him, "there's no telling what I'll do."

"All right," he agreed, dropping his shoulders even lower. "I didn't come here to fight with you. I just wanted to chat. Perhaps to give you a ride to the dock."

"To chat about what? About Sr. Duarte's death? About the papers you took from my room?" she challenged.

"If that's what you want to talk about," he responded.

"You don't intend to talk here and now, do you?" she asked.

"Where do you suggest?" Pietra, Jr., asked. "In your room?"

Furious, Jane turned around and headed for the restaurant.

"Wait," he shouted. "You misunderstood..."

But Jane didn't stop. Before she could disappear into the hotel, Pietra, Jr., reached her and grabbed her by the arm.

"What's up with journalists today?" he said. "They walk away from news just like that."

"I already said that I'm not interested in what you have to say," Jane responded furiously, freeing herself with a push.

Pietra, Jr., began to laugh, which only served to infuriate her more. His laughter sounded like the roar of a crazed buffalo.

"Come with me," he ordered, no longer laughing. "Or do I have to drag you?"

Before Jane had time to think, he took hold of her arm and, as he had threatened, pulled her forcibly. Perplexed,

LOST WORLD II

she allowed herself to be taken to the parking lot without reacting. Once there, Pietra, Jr., opened the car door, literally threw her inside, and went around to the driver's seat with surprising speed for a man his size. Astonished and frightened, Jane watched as the car took off, quickly leaving the hotel behind.

"I've never seen anyone so stubborn," he mumbled.

Jane didn't respond. She was always like this when facing physical violence; she would become nearly catatonic, losing her petulance, her verbal luster, and turning as quiet as a lamb.

"In 1966 a similar trip was organized by the government," Pietra, Jr., said. "Aboard the *Rosa da Fonseca*, sailing from Manaus to Belém. The new role the Amazon region was to play was the topic of discussion. They called it 'Operation Amazonia.' Fifty farm and ranch projects were presented; a select commission of technicians, specialists, politicians, and entrepreneurs came from central and southern Brazil, from Peru, Mexico, the United States, and Europe. Locally produced items like sugar, jute, rice, vegetable oils, lumber, and cellulose were presented for their inspection.

"The result was not long in being felt. Large ranches were built here, motivated by tax incentives. Industrial and agricultural capital from the South was invested in the production of cattle for export. One year later, Manaus was transformed into a tax-free zone. The government allocated two billion dollars in order to develop transportation, communication, and energy infrastructure in this region. Prospecting for natural resources received a big boost as well. The cattle industry, for one, was a major success. Devil International, Ltd., one of the largest private investment banks in the world, bought International Parrot, Inc., through its South American subsidiary, Devil Panamerican. With this transaction, it gained control of the holdings of Parrot in the Goofy-Skimpy Company of Brazil, which was already merging with the Crook Ranch of Texas, in order to establish a ranch of one hundred seventy-six thousand acres in the south of the state. And all of this with money from the Brazilian government.

"At the same time, still thinking of meat, Devil couldn't keep its eyes off of Marajó Island, at the mouth of the Amazon. With all of this, within three years it controlled thirty percent of all of the meat exported from Brazil; it went on to sell its interests in Goofy-Skimpy to Hotrod and Litter, keeping only the division that distributed the product overseas."

Jane listened to Pietra, Jr., with an alarmed expression, partly because he continued driving fast, but also because the torrent of information muddled her brain.

"There was never a business like Amazonia," he went on, excitedly. "Four years after the journey of the *Rosa da Fonseca*, the government launched the 'National Integration Plan.' Brazil was experiencing a period of euphoria, of growth. It was necessary to once and for all rip through the jungle with highways, tear down the obstacles of progress. And the answer was here. In twelve months, three and a half billion dollars were put into the region. Aside from the ranching business, there are the miners who began to attract investors. In 1971 alone, over seven hundred thousand acres of jungle were burned. Five years later, the total was around three hundred million. And by now, one fifth of the jungle has fallen. The empty spaces were being occupied, the regional structures were revitalized.

Pietra, Jr., paused, waiting for some reaction on Jane's part. But she seemed uninterested; her arms crossed over her chest and an expression of panic on her face indicated the fear that gripped her.

"All right, I'll take you back to the hotel," Pietra, Jr., said finally.

He impulsively made a rapid U-turn onto the other lane amid the sounds of the blowing horns and squealing tires of the other drivers.

"What in the devil are you doing?" Jane shouted, scared out of her wits.

"So you haven't lost your tongue," Pietra, Jr., said, stabilizing the car and regaining speed.

"You killed Duarte, didn't you?" Jane said, recovering some of her self-control.

"No, it wasn't me," Pietra, Jr., responded vehemently. "He was shot with a poisonous dart. Duarte wanted to die; he couldn't stand the idea of losing the directorship of the factory. As far as he was concerned, the running of a business was like a title of nobility. He was never a real businessman."

"You're the only one who believes that," Jane rebutted. "Why would he kill himself? That would only make life easier for his greatest enemy."

"Who is I, right? But you are wrong."

"Then why did you take the papers that he had given me?"

"Purely business. The papers had important information. I was the only one who knew about it. I have no idea how he found out. And I couldn't allow a leak before the time was right. It meant the loss of a couple of million dollars."

"And you have the nerve to say that you didn't kill him."

"I surely wanted to. Not only once, but many times in the last few months. The old guy was cunning; he always treated me with contempt. Our battle had to end like this, with one of us dead. But I didn't kill him. And before long, you and everyone else will find out what

THE END OF THE THIRD WORLD

those papers that I took from your room contained."

"Is that what you intend on doing during the trip?"

"Exactly. The Japanese and Korean businessmen are participating in the project. The business amounts to more than one hundred billion dollars. I can make a summary of the deal for you. The details, you will receive in a folder that will be given to all of the reporters that make the trip."

The car crossed the Hotel Tropical property line, and Pietra, Jr., stopped. At the same time, Jane jumped out of the car and rushed from the parking lot.

"Hey, wait! Don't you want to hear the rest?" he shouted.

Jane didn't stop, forcing Pietra, Jr., to leave the car, with the door ajar, and rush after her. Huffing, he managed to catch up with her just as she entered the elevator.

"I am not interested. I already told you," Jane said harshly.

Nevertheless, Pietra, Jr., was not deterred.

"It's like this," he said, taking her by the arm once more and compelling her to sit down in one of the sofas spread out in the hotel lobby. "We are going to build a hydroelectric plant on the Amazon River."

Jane rolled her eyes in a gesture of impatience.

"Can you imagine? On the Amazon River. Just think of it!"

"You're full of shit."

"Shit? That's what the environmentalists are going to do when they find out about it. They think they own the goose that laid the golden eggs, but we're going to kill it."

"You're insane."

"The hydroelectric dam will be built on the Breves Strait, in the state of Pará. The land already belongs to a Japanese consortium. At that point, the river is less than two miles across, but we will have to make a dike three times that wide. It will be the largest on the planet, capable of holding not a lake but an inland sea."

"I have heard these plans before," Jane retorted.

"Of course you have. But they didn't have the balls to go through with it. And do you know why? Because the project will be the definitive end of the Amazon question. At the same time, it will end the culture of misery. When the lake has flooded the region, the world's climate will be modified. There will no longer be a torrid zone; do you understand? The whole planet will be either temperate or glacial. No more tropics, only civilized temperatures. It will be the end of the Third World. The end of all the miserable underdeveloped civilizations that survived thanks to the tropical heat. With the cool climate, the lazy bastards will have to work in order to buy warm clothing and fuel to heat their houses. Good-bye to the slums and the laziness that perpetuates them, good-bye to the vagabonds who go around all year in shorts and sandals."

"What in the hell are you talking about?" she said, frightened by his vehemence.

"Just what you're hearing. The Third World and the historically miserable tropics are not long for this world. Our project will begin in ninety days; the funds will be available within the same amount of time. In one thousand days the liberals, the environmentalists, and those who practice benevolence will no longer have a cause. You can understand why I couldn't let the news get out before its time. Those priests of backwardness are very powerful; they would have tried to exert enormous pressure on the governments and groups involved . . ."

"You are pulling my leg," Jane said, irritated.

"Not at all. Just wait and see."

"A dam across the Amazon River!" she exclaimed, incredulous.

"And an inland sea, with calm waters, navigable, and the mixing of all of the Amazon's tributaries. The formation of this sea, more than the electricity generated by the hydroelectric turbines, will be the most important part of the project. Just think, Jane! A planet with temperate climate."

"In the sixties," Jane said, still skeptical, "when Herman Kahn proposed this, a number of scientists pointed out the grave environmental consequences. The submerged forest, for example, in the decaying process, would release toxic gases into the atmosphere."

"Nonsense!"

"The rotation of the earth would slow down by two seconds, if I remember correctly."

"Which would be good; the evolution of species only became possible because the rotation of the earth was gradually slowed down by the approaching moon."

Jane looked at Pietra, Jr., with increasingly disbelief.

"Do you know how I am going to christen this new ocean?"

She shook her head with an air of little interest. "The Dementia Ocean!" Jane interrupted, nearly shouting.

Pietra, Jr., chortled as he got up to leave the lobby. "The Challenger Ocean; do you hear? The Challenger Ocean!"

Jane felt her hands suddenly begin to perspire.

The Jihad Jívaros Effect

The transatlantic *Leviathan*, sailing under a Panamanian flag, was the largest, most modern, and most luxurious passenger ship ever built. This floating colossus weighed eighty thousand tons, measured 350 meters long, and had four decks, three swimming pools, two tennis courts, eight dance floors, five restaurants, a conference room for five hundred people, and 150 cabins. On its normal cruises in the Caribbean, or on Atlantic crossings, a passage cost more than one hundred thousand dollars. The enormous white hull was moored directly at the floating pier in the port of Manaus. But this time, unlike the usual passengers—South American millionaires, North American retirees, and honeymooners—the ship was receiving a very different clientele. Petulant Saudi Arabian sheiks, dressed up in their costumes, smiling Japanese executives, sunburned Yankees, and European businessmen slowly dehydrating in their cashmere suits all boarded the ship to the sound of a band playing Brazilian music, under a shower of confetti and paper streamers. Sir Delamare's entourage was no less unusual, with its own knight of the British Empire, growling and cursing; not to mention Spender's sinister silence, and Jane Challenger's enigmatic smile.

Lester's state of mind was also not the best. Somehow all of his solidarity in relation to the Third World had disappeared shortly after the attack of the Jihad Jívaros

THE END OF THE THIRD WORLD

command. In addition to that, moved by a perversely odd sense of humor, Sir Delamare had ordered all the members of his entourage to wear what he called special clothing for the tropics. And these tropical clothes, to the general dismay, were nothing more than starched khaki safari suits, topped off by anachronistic cork hats personally ordered by him from a haberdashery that specialized in fashions from different epochs. From Lester's point of view, everything was conspiring to make him feel even more wretched: the Bermuda shorts with sharp creases, the boots and thick cotton knee-high socks, along with the dark glasses that he felt he had to wear since his left eye was black and blue from the impact of the Gundrisse. He felt as grotesque as a Boy Scout ready for his retirement, and the sensation of being ridiculous increased every time his eyes caught Jane Challenger, independence personified, exposing her white legs and a bit more in very short shorts and a brief halter top, round, red-framed dark glasses, and a straw hat. But the worst thing of all was looking at Spender's miserable figure, nearly swallowed up by clothing too large for his frame, giving him the air of a grotesque caricature of a Victorian explorer, a Sir Richard Burton in the process of shrinking.

But all of these sensations that were assailing him were irrelevant in the face of the tumult that was taking charge of the transatlantic. For some mysterious reason, the ship's computer had decided to make some absurd coupling, lodging Israelis with Iranians, Senegalese with Afrikaners, and other such novel and explosive juxtapositions. Spender, for a change, was bunked with an obese Japanese manufacturer of electronic components, and Lester wound up in a cabin with a pontificating, paranoiac Texan, a manufacturer of agricultural preservatives, whose baggage seemed more like a showcase of a company manufacturing war equipment than something in the agricultural line.

The departure was delayed for five hours, which was the length of time that it took the Brazilian government employees to situate the angry passengers. But Lester's luck ran out, and he was lodged in a lower cabin with the taciturn and sober Spender. The cabin door was no sooner shut than Lester, ignoring his editor's stubborn silence, tried to get rid of that ridiculous outfit that had been burning his body. Later, dressed in jeans and a lightweight cotton shirt, he stretched out in the berth, trying to overcome the recent tribulations of the trip. The cabin wasn't very big, but it had a good air conditioner. The pleasant room temperature enabled him to fall asleep. Or at least what transpired next, he supposed, was a dream. The lights suddenly dimmed and a charming and gentle man came into the room. At first he judged him to be a member of the crew, or an employee of the host government. The man shut the door carefully; after contemplating Spender for a few moments as he lay sleeping, he smiled at Lester. He realized by the smile, or perhaps by some other even more mysterious means, that the man was Muhammad Azancoth, the leader of the Jihad Jívaros.

"Have you ever been in Highgate?" the intruder asked.

Lester awoke and jumped out of the berth. There was no one in the cabin except him and Spender, but the question remained hammering away in his brain. What in devil did he mean by Highgate?

"What's the matter?" Spender moaned.

"Sorry," Lester said. "I think I was hallucinating."

"Don't worry," Spender said. "I haven't done anything else but hallucinate since we arrived in this city."

"It was so vivid! It seemed so real!"

THE END OF THE THIRD WORLD

"Everything seems very real here," Spender said, getting up. "I think I'm going to die."

"What's this, Spender? Have a little more courage."

Spender shrugged and rubbed his face several times with his hands. He sighed in a particularly distressing manner and lay back down in the berth.

"What did you see, Lester?" Spender asked.

"I thought that someone had entered the cabin."

"Someone? You saw a person and you are complaining! You should see my hallucinations. Ever since yesterday my prick has been talking to me."

"What's that?"

"That's right. I can't even piss in peace without my damned prick starting a conversation. And it has such a petulant way of saying things."

"I don't want to be indiscreet, but what does it say exactly?"

"The son of a bitch says that I'm a shithead because I never went to Highgate."

"Highgate?"

"Highgate, the frigging cemetery. All I needed was a necrophilic prick."

"It's funny. The fellow who opened the door also asked me about Highgate."

"What fellow?"

"The guy in my hallucination."

"Another necrophiliac, right?"

"Well, I don't know about that. I had never seen the guy before."

"Lester, for the love of God, let's get out of here," Spender begged.

"Highgate . . . what does Highgate have?" Lester asked himself. "That's where Karl Marx is buried," he recalled.

"You're right, Lester. The cemetery is famous due to Marx's tomb."

"It is a Mecca for leftist pilgrimages," Lester said.

"Do you mean to say that my frigging dick is Communist?"

Lester didn't respond; he stood looking at the landscape that slowly and inexorably passed by the hatch: a reddish bank, rent out of the green slope of the jungle, exposed like scarred skin. At the top of the bank, a sawmill swallowed majestic tree trucks and spit out pieces of wood and fine sawdust that ran down the slope like face powder on a wound.

"I didn't see the Chilean come aboard," Spender said.

"He's on board. But I don't know which cabin he's in."

Spender got up from the berth, adjusted the horrible Bermuda shorts, put on the socks and high-top shoes, and opened the cabin door.

"I want to see if they assigned Sir Delamare an adequate cabin," he said.

"I think I'll go with you." Lester joined him, not being willing to face his hallucinations alone. "I'll take the opportunity to see how Jane is."

"Lester, I don't know if we are going to get out of this alive," Spender said. "But if someday I manage to get back to London, I'm going to do what my prick suggested to me earlier today."

"Who suggested it?" Lester asked, surprised.

"My prick, you know. I told you that it talks to me."

"What did it suggest?"

"It said to drop everything, get my savings out of the bank, sell all my property, and go to Monte Carlo."

"Are you serious about this?"

"Of course I am. It guaranteed me that the damned principality is the place where there is the greatest concentration of pussy in the world. I'm going to work the son of a bitch to death."

THE END OF THE THIRD WORLD

The two of them walked down the narrow corridor, continually passing bustling deckhands. They asked about Sir Delamare, Jane Challenger, and Juan Sender, but no one could give them a conclusive answer. Most of them stepped aside, responding evasively and with excuses, returning to their frenetic tasks.

One deck below, following right behind a plump steward who elegantly pushed the baggage cart, strolled Sir Delamare. The deck was quite modest, seemingly third class, if there was such a thing on a luxury liner like the *Leviathan*. But Sir Delamare wasn't complaining; he was tired, being one of the last ones to receive his cabin assignment after hours of conflicts and confusion. No excuse would be sufficient to compensate for the discomfort that he had suffered, but Sir Delamare wanted peace and quiet, a hot bath, and a pot of very hot tea.

The steward parked the cart and opened the door, making a gesture for Sir Delamare to enter. The elder man looked at the size of the room and stopped dead in his tracks.

"My goodness! Just a moment! This can't be my cabin."

"It is, sir. Cabin fifty-eight, sir."

"Fifty-eight! That's a very large number for a cubicle this size."

The steward placed the baggage in the room and left. Sir Delamare could hardly move about, because the suitcase—one of those large and anachronistic steamer trunks from the time when one only traveled by ship—occupied nearly all of the available space in the cabin. Crooning a melody and in an unexpected good humor, Sir Delamare got on the bed and opened the trunk. Much to his surprise, a man came out from between his clothes.

"Hello, boss!" the man said.

"What are you doing there?" Sir Delamare said, losing his good mood. "And I thought this was going to be a perfect trip. This is my trunk, young man."

"It is indeed," the man confirmed, opening the drawer closest to the ground and revealing another man, who was placidly sleeping.

"I don't remember having packed you two," Sir Delamare said.

"Don't wake him; he suffers from insomnia and he just got to sleep."

"This is the most unlikely thing that I've ever seen," Sir Delamare said.

Smiling, the man tried to retrieve his companion from the drawer, but in such a clumsy manner that Sir Delamare's first reaction was to get off the bed and help him. He stopped himself, however, because the fellow came out of the drawer like a soft cloth doll, collapsing over his companion, still sound asleep. Even though he might suffer from insomnia, he apparently slept like a log.

Sir Delamare observed worriedly the man's reckless efforts to help the sleeper.

"Put him there," Sir Delamare ordered, pointing to the bed.

Without waiting to be told again, he threw his companion on the berth, but the sleeper didn't awaken; rather he snored contentedly and snuggled up in the sheets.

"We are here because we came to realize just how complacent we have been," the man said, with a smile of satisfaction.

"Sorry, I don't understand!" Sir Delamare said.

"We were always beaten down, Captain, sir, but our cordiality is an abyss that has swallowed all of our opportunities."

THE END OF THE THIRD WORLD

"You could be more specific," Sir Delamare pleaded.
"This is the captain's cabin, isn't it?"
"No, it isn't."
"You mean you aren't the captain of this ship?"
"No, I am not," Sir Delamare said warily.
"Are you sure?"
"Absolutely."

The man looked at his sleeping companion and shook his head.

"Another mistake. This just isn't possible!" the man said bitterly, losing his smile. "What rank do you have on this ship?" he asked somewhat rudely.

"The rank of passenger," the elder lord responded proudly.

"Passenger? What are you doing in a cabin designated for the crew?"

"Well," Sir Delamare attempted to explain, "this is where they brought me after hours of waiting."

"I understand," the man responded, meditating for some seconds. "But this was supposed to be the captain's cabin. This is number forty-eight, isn't it?"

"Fifty-eight," Sir Delamare corrected.

"Fifty-eight; that's not possible. Can't we do anything right?"

"Can you tell me what is going on?" Sir Delamare said.

The man looked at his wristwatch, sighed, and shook his head, disheartened.

"Do you see that hole there beside the air conditioner?" he said, pointing to a small opening in a chrome plate beside the screen in the air conditioner. "That is the vent for the air purifier. This is a very sophisticated ship, Mr. . . ."

"Delamare."

"Mr. Delamare, the on-board computer controls everything, even the workings of the interior air exhaust units. Periodically the old air is changed, and through this hole a fragrance of wildflowers is sprayed into the cabins and throughout the whole ship."

"Very ingenious," Sir Delamare agreed, somewhat apprehensive.

"In a half hour the dose of perfume will be exchanged for laughing gas."

"My God," Sir Delamare exclaimed, frightened.

"But don't worry. This is the only cabin that will not be sprayed. Our people had orders to obstruct the duct in the cabin where your baggage was placed."

"God willing, this time they got it right," Sir Delamare commented.

The man's reaction was to stare intently at the menacing opening. At that moment the doorbell rang and Sir Delamare calmly went to open the door.

"We finally found you," Juan Sender said happily, standing alongside Jane Challenger. "It took us nearly an hour to find out where you were."

"Come in. We have company," Sir Delamare said, closing the door.

"Company?" Jane asked, observing guardedly the man who was sleeping so placidly in a fetal position on the berth.

New knocks on the door, and Sir Delamare opened it again. Two young men and a woman entered.

"Cleaning service," the woman said. "We came to change the sheets and sweep the floor."

"Is this the cleaning service or the prevention service?" Sir Delamare asked ironically. "We haven't even had time to get anything dirty."

"Wait!" Jane Challenger exclaimed. "I know you!"

Sir Delamare turned around and looked more closely at the cleaners.

THE END OF THE THIRD WORLD

"What is it, Miss Challenger?" he asked.

"We were together just yesterday," Jane responded, uncertain, and turned to the three who claimed to be porters. "You said that you weren't going to make the trip, that you had not agreed to participate . . ."

"But what is going on here?" Sir Delamare insisted.

"They are Indians," Jane said, without further explanation.

"We aren't participating," the Tukano woman said. "We simply want to see firsthand what is going to happen."

"Our people have occupied the five dance floors," the Tikuna informed them.

Sir Delamare was just opening his mouth to speak when the doorbell rang again. Jane turned and opened the door. Two young women, accompanied by a corpulent fellow, entered.

"My name is Iaci," one of them said.

"I am Ceuci," said the other.

"And this is Pietro Pietra, Jr." The first one spoke, passing her hand gently across the man's cheek. He simply made a slight sign of acknowledgment.

"What makes this cabin so special?" Sir Delamare said. "This is the largest ocean liner in the world, and you are all squeezed in here."

"I am seasick," Pietro Pietra, Jr., said. "I hate boat trips."

Someone rang the doorbell, but this time no one moved. He rang again, and the man who was standing in Sir Delamare's trunk, opening a path through the group, went to the door.

"Come on in," he said, pulling Lester and Spender inside the cabin. "Pretty soon this is going to be the only safe spot on the whole ship."

"But, but . . ." Lester stuttered, widening his eyes upon

LOST WORLD II

seeing Jane Challenger and Sir Delamare in the middle of the crowded cabin.

"Is there anyone missing?" Sir Delamare asked, without expecting an answer.

The cabin door opened, pushing Spender on top of the two girls, and Henry Amazon slipped in between Juan Sender's legs, emerging near the berth where the sleeping man lay snoring.

"They don't even ring the bell anymore," Sir Delamare complained, searching for a more comfortable position between the muscular Pietra, Jr., and the trembling Spender.

"This is Muhammad Azancoth," Lester said, trying to point without much success to the sleeping man. "But don't ask me how I know that."

"That's him," Henry confirmed.

Muhammad Azancoth stretched out his legs and then his arms and got up off the bed. His companion quickly placed himself at his leader's side.

"Comrades, will you please sit down," Commander Azancoth said, yawning. "In a few moments, the ship's public address system will be transmitting our message to the world. You are all hostages of the Jihad Jívaros Command. Don't be alarmed. Don't try to react against us, and you won't be harmed. We will respect the integrity of each one of you."

"This is absurd," Sir Delamare roared. "What do you intend to accomplish by this deranged act?"

"Our message is very clear in that regard," Commander Azancoth stated, paying little attention to the commotion in the room. "From the nineteenth century until the present time, the Amazon basin has been a part of the international division of labor, having been integrated into the world market as one of the well-defined group of suppliers of raw materials."

THE END OF THE THIRD WORLD

"Silence!" demanded Commander Azancoth's companion, who had been listening with an expression of profound adoration.

"The historical contingencies prohibited even the development of agriculture in this region," the commander went on, raising his voice to be heard over the mumbling in the cabin. "Our agricultural dreams were swept away by the greed with which the world market consumed our rubber. It established itself in this manner, without missing the chance to take advantage of the comfortable structure of Portuguese colonialism, a social form known by the name of . . . of . . . ?"

"Extractivism," the other man responded hurriedly to show how much he knew of the group's ideas. "A subsystem perfectly compatible with the international role in which Brazil plays a part even today. Thus, a substantial part of the national territory came to serve as an extractivist source, while the entire country lay dozing through an archaic system of monoculture. In an essentially agrarian country, we were emerging from the most primitive way of supplying our production, completely dependent on nature, and at the same time facing the impossibility of dominating, transforming, and domesticating to our advantage this very same nature. The prospects of agricultural policies that would succeed over the course of time, all of which were prematurely aborted, turned into ideological nightmares. We were not only prevented from planting potatoes, but we were incapable of establishing an economic base that was ongoing and free from dependence."

"You are deceiving yourselves," the Tukano woman interrupted. "You have yet to discover that our salvation is not that easy."

"Nor should we depend upon messianic movements," the Tikuna added.

"Pay attention," Iaci intervened, "because there is a basic flaw in the whole system that you have been developing."

Muhammad Azancoth raised his arms, silencing those who had interrupted.

"This is why our job is to face a new way of looking at the alternatives to history. We know that history moves quickly; it can rip into our lacerated hopes as it has done again and again. We must recognize that our paths cross in the suburbs; our face is closer to the faces of the oppressed than they are to the arrogant faces of the oppressors."

"This is one of your mistakes," Ceuci shouted. "To want to achieve solidarity with the oppressed."

"In this way you will always have one foot tactically behind the other," Iaci shouted.

"Why should you condemn yourselves to searching for the future in the anguish of misery?" Ceuci asked, provocatively. "Why bear bitter recriminations and open wounds on your bodies?"

"Because for now," Commander Azancoth defended himself, "we can't change the course of history, forcing it to make restitution for that which was taken from us."

"But what was taken from you?" the Tikuna Indian asked. "If you were the ones who arrived here and cut off our path, how can you hope to understand the nature of the anguish of those who were plundered?"

"And you call that the search for solidarity," the Parakanã Indian intervened. "But there is no solidarity. No one can feel solidarity with the weak. Whoever says he can is lying. Lying! Do you hear me?"

"Because solidarity amongst the wretched," the Tikuna woman added, "winds up being contagion. They all end up hungry, poor, tortured, and revolting."

THE END OF THE THIRD WORLD

"Those people who want to mix with the poor," the Tikuna intervened, "eventually have to wear the mask of poverty themselves. And those poor who hope to find solidarity with the rich end up exiled from themselves."

"What in the hell is going on here?" Sir Delamare raged, without understanding a single word of what had been said. "Is it possible that one can no longer take an honest cruise through the tropics?"

"Why don't you just keep quiet?" Lester said rudely. "Is it possible you can't see what is happening? Are you so insensitive that you don't feel the anguish of these people?"

"Nonsense," Sir Delamare replied. "These people are always grumbling about something because grumbling is very lucrative and makes for less work."

"History," Commander Azancoth said solemnly, "is only one category and a concept to be constructed. The understanding of history, as Marx said, is a process of synthesis of a multiplicity of determinations. In this sense, our characteristics are real, concrete, and singular; our perplexity has real motives."

"There is only one problem," Lester said. "You are mistaken with respect to the revolutionary potential. Because the persistence of backward means of production simply run at cross purposes with the operational means of the capitalist model operative in contemporary Brazil. This doesn't propitiate a revolutionary situation."

"Would you please not rub my thigh," the Tukano woman demanded, moving Spender's hand away.

"Excuse me," Spender responded. "But I wasn't rubbing your thigh; I was just trying to scratch my leg."

"Your elbow is squashing my breast," Ceuci protested, pushing Sender, who was completely engrossed in what was being said.

"What is happening," Lester went on, enthusiastically, "is that your economy can't hold out against large capital, because it always depended on generating economic surpluses for the export of raw materials. Growth should have presented an inflexible course of action, something that is admittedly quite difficult to accomplish since the process of substitution of products on the market is exceedingly rapid. In addition, your economic techniques are obsolete, and the system only survives because it is an agglomerate of many means of production."

"We feel this quite acutely," Commander Azancoth said, "because production is maintained at the cost of social neglect."

"There never was a classic laborer outside of England," Pietra, Jr., proclaimed, breaking his silence. "And in a country like this one, it is necessary to demand that the workers actually work, because they are lazy, backward, and of low intelligence."

Sir Delamare tried to light a cigarette, but Jane Challenger wouldn't allow it.

"There's no room for smoke here, if you don't mind my saying so," Jane said.

"An English worker in 1880," Lester began, caught up in a sudden enthusiasm, "was forced to work a shift of ten, twelve, and fifteen hours; compare that to the fifteen and even twenty hours for an Amazonian worker. It should be clear as well that the English laborer could count on laws that guaranteed his work shift; here they never dealt with the issue, leaving it all up to the criterion of the individual boss and the marketplace."

"The Amazonian boss," Commander Azancoth said, "never needed to use the contrivances of his English counterpart, who, in order to lengthen the work shift,

THE END OF THE THIRD WORLD

regularly robbed the laborers of a few miserable minutes. Here the surplus value was always extracted by extortion because the Amazonian laborer is hardly organized."

"Would you stop touching my buttocks?" Spender protested, doing as much as possible to withdraw from Pietra, Jr.

"I would say that the problem rests with the country's economy," Sir Delamare interjected. "In underdeveloped countries, the economy is like a monster with swollen legs, who gets fat on statistics and profits, but who has the head of a mosquito."

"You ought to know what you're talking about," the Jihad Jívaros leader retorted. "As an Englishman, you know well the schemes of economic piracy."

"Evidently, my young man," Sir Delamare attacked, "it just so happens that you pirated yourselves; you survived by continual stagnation, guaranteeing, for example, a mentality that transforms the rationality of the capitalist system into a spirit of pure extortionism. And do you know why? In order to preserve the concentration of revenue and political power, and the social functions of prestige. And in order to maintain yourselves afloat in the fickle life of the international market. Which is good for us in the First World, as long as there are countries with dominant classes like yours."

"You hit it on the head," Jane Challenger applauded. "The last thing that ought to be offered to one who persists in living in misery is clemency."

"That is absurd," Lester protested.

"Why?" Jane countered. "Perhaps my position denigrates your good intentions? But don't worry, Lester, feeling pity for the poor is a form of sublimation like any other. It helps the soul but not the souls."

"You have a wonderful body," Pietra, Jr., said, complimenting Spender in one corner of the cabin. "But I bet you've heard that a million times!"

Pietra, Jr.'s, preposterous flirtation silenced the debate for a few instants. At that moment a terrible clamor was heard coming from outside, followed by things falling, people running, and strange noises.

"Listen," Commander Azancoth shouted. "The gas has just been released. Right now the *Leviathan*'s communication systems are transmitting the following message." He put his hand into his pants pocket and pulled out a crumpled piece of paper. Unfolding it, he began to read. "To the Brazilian and international authorities. The Revolutionary Movement Jihad Jívaros, vanguard of the Amazonian masses, has just taken control of the *Leviathan* transatlantic liner. All of the passengers are hostages of the Amazonian Revolution, which in this instant has begun. The seizure of the *Leviathan* is a symbol and a concrete act of the popular power of the people of the land. It is a symbol because the helm of the liner, formerly at the service of spurious and foreign interests, passes to the command of the peoples of the forest. It is a concrete act because the seizure of the liner represents the reconquest of the Amazon River by the native peoples of the riverbanks.

"The *Leviathan* and its passengers will remain under our control until all of the white, black, and mulatto residents have withdrawn from the Amazonian region, leaving behind in the great river basin only the indigenous peoples and their half-breeds. The period of time given to complete this withdrawal is ten days; it is nondeferrable and nonnegotiable. The safety of the liner and that of the hostages lies entirely in the hands of the governments of Brazil and the other involved countries. Until the final victory. Long live Amazonia!"

"From the literary point of view, it is a very poor statement," Sender said. "I always believed that Portuguese is not as good as Spanish for political pronouncements."

"Shut up," Commander Azancoth ordered.

"If I had my way," Sir Delamare spoke up, "I would leave this region right now."

"As would I," Spender hurriedly added.

The four Indians who were in the cabin seemed to be in a state of shock.

"And you," Iaci asked. "What are you going to do? From what we know, there isn't a single Indian amongst the Jihad Jívaros."

"We will leave as well," Commander Azancoth said. "We plan to ask for asylum in Iran. We have everything arranged."

"Do you know what happens with them?" Ceuci said, pointing to Commander Azancoth, who was observing everything with a doltish candor. "They go overboard when it comes to theoretical limits."

"They call themselves Jihad Jívaros," Iaci added, "less for the holy war of the Muslims than for the headhunter fame. The difference is that the real Jívaros shrink the heads of their dead adversaries."

"While they decided to shrink their own heads to narrow their ideological positions," Ceuci said.

"They were afraid of giving in to a reformist temptation," Iaci said.

"All dogmatic groups do that," Ceuci said. "But the Jihad Jívaros do it literally."

"In our heads there is only the desire to free our people," Commander Azancoth responded, taking off what everyone had believed was his real face but was nothing more than an ingenious latex mask. Beneath the mask, like a miniature reproduction of the flacid latex skin that now hung from his hand, was his real head. Sharp eyes peered at them from out of a small face covered with sparse strands of beard. "We don't need anything more."

"This is nothing more than idiocy, brothers and sisters," the Tukano woman said.

The cabin door was forcibly opened, and a man with red, weeping eyes, laughing like a lunatic, entered. It was Deputy Rubens.

"The door," someone shouted.

"The gas," Commander Azancoth warned, covering his little, doll-like nose.

But it was too late; the cabin was slowly being filled with gas.

"I have figured it out, I have figured it out," shouted the giggling deputy. "I know what Pietro Pietra, Jr., was planning to do. He wanted to construct a hydroelectric dam at Breves Strait in order to channel the Amazon River into a huge inland sea. Can you believe it? Can you? Isn't that crazy? A lake, which in fact is a sea, with the definitive hydroelectric power plant built with resources capable of generating the definitive advantage and definitively finish off the Amazon region once and for all. To turn the tropics into a temperate zone and even slow down the rotation of the earth by two seconds per year. How about that? Isn't that a big joke?"

It's not known if it was the effects of the gas, but the whole cabin was transformed into sonorous laughter, which joined the larger general guffaw, united and majestic, boisterous like the eddy of that magnificent ship that sailed down the Amazon River, arousing the curiosity of the riverbank dwellers, the fishermen, the young, red-faced boys swimming in the yellow river water, the washwomen, turtle hunters, the jute gatherers, the lowland planters, in short,

THE END OF THE THIRD WORLD

all of those people who are children of the Amazon River.

As he approached the end of his novel, *The Lost World*, Sir Arthur Conan Doyle raised a few conjectures regarding the fate of the pterodactyl taken to London by Professor Challenger. According to certain reports, it had been seen on a certain rooftop in Queen's Hall. Others said that a winged monster had caused a poor soldier to desert his sentry post at the main gate of Marborough House. But one bit of news seemed to indicate that it was actually the city of London that was frightening to the flying reptile. The liner SS *Friesland*, sailing about ten miles northeast of Star Point, out in the middle of the Atlantic, came across something that looked like a billy goat with bat wings. The strange creature was flying at a prodigious speed.
It was flying southeast.
It was returning to the endless lands.

Sailing eastward, practically unencumbered of any control, determined to sweep past all boundaries, lacking the divine mercy—which in our times has ceased to notice such navigators, let alone make gentle winds or peaceful lulls for them—the *Leviathan* continued on without a captain's voice or any such official or pilot at the helm, only the constant laughter to wash the decks, far from the Cape of Good Hope or the currents of the tropics, proceeding under the false happiness of that laughter.
While it navigated the current of the river-sea, a ship where bonhomie reigned in the extreme, the sound of joy aroused the same feeling on the shores, spreading out along the riverbanks, rising to solid soil, reaching the hills, bluffs, and ridges, traversing the channels, the

floodlands, and the backwaters, stuck in the mud in the mining camps and scorched in the burning forests. The laughter.
. . . . . .
    . . . . . .
        . . . . . .

                and all of Amazonia laughed.

Finally for the information of the readers who dared
to get this far facing so many setbacks and excessive
digressions showing patience perseverance and
admirable condescension in this precise and exact
moment the currents of the sea carry amidst
laughter and the storms of their delirium
having crossed without dangers or grazes
the current of the yellow river of the
Amazon or sweet Spanish sea and lost
in some locale of the Atlantic Ocean
without any law or command and the
unfortunate passengers of the
belle transatlantic called
the Liner *Leviathan* oh!
modern brigantine and
being thus
fin